D0949517

SUPER
MOON

SUPER
MOON

H. A. SWAIN

FEIWEL AND FRIENDS
NEW YORK

A Feiwel and Friends Book
An imprint of Macmillan Publishing Group, LLC
175 Fifth Avenue, New York, NY 10010

Our books may be purchased in bulk for promotional, educational, or business use. Please contact
your local bookseller or the Macmillan Corporate and Premium Sales Department at
(800) 221-7945 ext. 5442 or by e-mail at MacmillanSpecialMarkets@macmillan.com.

Library of Congress Cataloging-in-Publication Data is available.
ISBN 978-1-250-11627-7 (hardcover) / ISBN 978-1-250-11628-4 (ebook)

Book design by Heather Palisi-Reyes
Feiwel and Friends logo designed by Filomena Tuosto

First edition, 2018

1 3 5 7 9 10 8 6 4 2

fiercereads.com

In memory of my dog Mahati, who sat at my feet for every book I've written—except this one.

For my mother-in-law, Tanya V. Beck, who would go to the moon and back for the people she loves, including (and especially) for her dogs.

*Any community that gets its laughs by pretending to be idiots
will eventually be flooded by actual idiots who mistakenly believe
that they're in good company.*
—DarkShikari via Y Combinator.com, circa 2010ish
Most likely falsely attributed to René Descartes by a community
of idiots on the Internet

It is not enough to have a good mind. The main thing is to use it well.
—René Descartes, *Discourse on the Method, Part 1,* 1637

TIME STAMP

MOON
DAY 28, MONTH 6, MUSC YEAR 94

EARTH
JUNE 17, 2XXX

UMA JEMISON

MOON UTILITARIAN
SURVIVAL COLONY

HOLOGRAM OR REAL? I think-text to Kepler, who's scrunched in the seat beside me as usual, his limbs folded like telescoping landing legs to fit in the cramped space of the small MUSC auditorium.

Hologram, duh. He shifts, trying to get comfortable. The designers of the Moon survival colony didn't account for humans getting taller as they evolved off Earth. If anything, they thought our species would get smaller. But none of this is a problem for me. I'm a short terrestrial transplant on the Moon, and my legs fit just fine.

"Greetings, Cohort 54! This is the final Moon Utilitarian Survival Colony lab assessment for G3C54!" MUSC president Dr. Valentine Fornax announces from the center stage, where she is surrounded by forty-eight kids I grew up with here. Her voice reverberates through the auditorium, making the event feel strangely hallowed, since it's in real time and not on our Streams.

I squint past Kep's thotz on my Lenz to study Dr. Fornax, who paces the stage, surrounded by our entire cohort in this circular mini arena. As always, she is stunning. Tall and strong with a square jaw and nearly black eyes under her thick shock of steel-colored hair. Although she's at least twelve years older than my mother, she looks younger.

Something in the way she holds herself, shoulders down and back, head high, and a mischievous twinkle in those eyes, as if she perpetually has a great idea she can't wait to unleash. She's my hero for all of those reasons, but also because, like my family, Dr. Fornax was born on Earth and emigrated to the Moon.

As Dr. Fornax moves across the stage, I look for the telltale holo shimmer, but she looks solid from every angle.

Real, I think to Kep.

We're not important enough for the president/CEO to show up IRL.

"You are the best and the brightest of the human race," Dr. Fornax proclaims. "You have worked diligently through the last decade of superior education. You are the future of our colony."

I raise both eyebrows at Kep. *We are the future.*

Gad help us all. He blinks me an image of Gemini Chen-Ning, sitting across the auditorium from us, glassy-eyed and slack-jawed, most likely blasting alien Viking serpent creatures in some Torrent VRPG on his Stream.

I snort a quiet laugh, barely audible, but of course, Micra whips around from her seat in front of me to give us an evil side-eye glare. The kind lizardlike aliens give their next victim in the archived 2-D Earthling sci-fi movies Kep and I watch from our hacked Earth connection.

"Shush," she hisses as if spitting acid that will melt my skin. Then she tucks a silver strand of hair behind her ear and turns away with an expert eye roll, no doubt thotzing something horrible about me to Cassio and Alma, her satellites sitting on either side, forever in her orbit.

When my parents and I moved to MUSC ten years ago, those three made my life a living hell. You would think Third Gen Moonlings who are the children of the greatest living scientists in the universe would master compassion, but Micra and her minions are just as mean as any earthly primate troupe threatened by an interloper.

It doesn't help that on top of my hereditary skin pigmentation, gravity-defying curls, and prominent facial features, my parents couldn't afford to buy me a communication implant, and for some reason—maybe the dry MUSC air—I'm prone to ear and eye infections so I can't use an iEye or HearEar, which means I'm the only person in my cohort with an external communication device strapped to my head. I might as well be sporting a centuries-old plastic prosthetic leg. Needless to say, those girls have been merciless since the moment I showed up on the Moon.

The only saving grace of my cohort placement was having a last name that starts with *J*. Since children are always arranged in alphabetical order, I have been smack-dab in the middle of Kepler Jackson on my right and Fermi Kaku on my left since the day I showed up. Lucky for me, Fermi is intensely introverted and Kepler is the nicest person in our cohort. Even luckier, Kep and I both have the same goofball sense of humor and taste for bad Earth Streams.

Without missing a beat, Kep sends a scribble to my Lenz of Micra standing on Mars, alone. I swallow another laugh and add the Dark Overlord from our favorite Earth sci-fi movie, *Howard the Duck*, sneaking up behind her, its toothy maw open and crab claws ready to attack. Kep puts me in a space pod, ray guns blasting toward Micra as she's being chased by the Overlord. We pass the doodle back and forth from his mind to my Lenz, each adding more stupid details until we're both shaking from trying not to laugh while Dr. Fornax yammers on about how we are standing on the precipice of our futures.

Then Dr. Fornax proclaims, "Childhood is behind you, and a Life's Work Assignment is on the horizon!"

I gulp and stop doodling. *Is space rodeo clown an option for my life's work?* I thotz Kep. *Maybe evil quark hunter?*

A little muscle in his jaw twitches. A happy little dance. The one part of his body that won't obey the no-laughing edict his brain has issued. Kepler knows as well as I do that there are very few job options here that fit my "skill set." Other than creating beautiful bacteria colonies for fun, I haven't exactly excelled at much on MUSC.

How about comet badminton diva? Kep thinks. I snort. Micra glares.

Kep and I exchange a glance. He's also the only person in G3C54 who finds Micra as annoying as I do. When we were twelve, I plucked a hair from her head and convinced him to help me sequence her genome in his mother's immunology lab. I was determined to find out what accounted for her moon-dust-colored hair and bright yellow eyes blinking like two suns, spaghetti arms and itty-bitty bump of a nearly nonexistent nose. I thought if I could scientifically prove she was the anomaly, not me, people would be nicer.

But it didn't matter because genetics are only half the story. Experience and perception are the other half. No matter how many anomalies I could locate on her genome, Micra remains the standard for Moon beauty, and I will always be the freak of nature up here.

"Tomorrow is Leap Day, when each of you will embark on a twenty-eight-day personal journey during the month of Sol," Dr. Fornax says. "This is a time for you to explore new worlds of experience before you settle into your young adult life."

My stomach burbles with excitement. Only three things have made my life at MUSC bearable the past ten years: 1) knowing that as long as I'm here, my mother will be safe, 2) being friends with Kepler, and 3) holding out for Sol of my sixteenth year, when I can go back to Earth for twenty-eight days, which will happen in approximately twelve hours, forty-eight minutes, and nineteen seconds. Not that I'm counting or anything.

"At the end of Sol, you will return to MUSC as young adult members of our colony," Dr. Fornax reminds us, as if we could forget. "At that time, you will receive your Life's Work Assignment, which will support the MUSC corporate mission of interstellar colonization!"

Everyone breaks into wild applause.

Except for me. My stomach turns sour, and I have to swallow down a nasty taste. There is nothing I dread more than receiving my LWA. Everyone else believes that's when life starts, but for me, it will be the end. No more watching banned Earth Streams with Kep. No more time to work on my bacteria botanical garden. No more dreaming of the day when I return to Earth, because that day will have come and gone. From the moment I receive my LWA, my life will be all work, all the time, and there's not a job up here that could make me happy.

"The future of our species depends on each of us. So work hard and make us proud!" Dr. Fornax says.

No pressure there, I thotz Kep. In return, he sends me an image of the moon exploding.

"And remember, Cohort 54 . . ." She waits as we all inhale and sit up straight, ready to proclaim our colony's motto.

"Science will see us through!" we all recite in unison. Then Dr. Fornax's image blips off the stage.

A QUICK WHISTLE and clap is all it takes for the lantana bush to rustle and Quasar to appear on the buckled sidewalk beside me. One perky little ear is turned inside out, so he looks to be wearing a jaunty pink cap on the side of his small furry head.

"Look at you! Sleeping on the job," I say. He yawns and shakes away his dreams, flipping the ear back to brown fur again. "Castor and I are doing all the work here," I tell him as I drop to one knee. Quasar trots over, pointy snout going straight into my hair to snuffle around my ear. I give him a good long scratch between the shoulder blades, then pat him on the side. His belly tumps like the ripe watermelons in my mother's greenhouse garden.

"You have any food for him?" my brother asks.

I search my pockets. "Just some Mango Bango Oink Oink Jerky I found inside an old SelfServ on Santa Monica Avenue." Quasar stands on hind legs and whines as I tear off a piece of the jerky, which he snarffles straight from my palm. "This stuff lasts forever." I try to take a bite, but it's too tough for me, so I give the rest to the dog.

"This place is desolate," Castor says as he surveys the altered coastline below the empty promenade. Sometimes when the tide is out, we catch a glimpse of the sunken Ferris wheel caught on pilings in the shallow ocean water, but no such luck tonight. "We had some of our best finds down here but now . . . nothing."

Castor's right. When we first arrived, the followers on our Stream loved to see what we'd find in Santa Monica Basin. But that was before everything was picked clean. Our best hauls included a seaweed-covered fishing boat with a beer-filled cooler still intact, slatted wooden tables floating like rafts, wicker chairs with waterlogged cushions tied on, a giant mirror that somehow hadn't cracked, an entire leather sofa crusted with salt and bright green barnacles, deck chairs, glass bottle lamps, slabs of cork flooring, slate roof tiles, sink basins, an electric guitar, a swing set and slide, countless car tires, coach cushions, and mattresses. Plus lots of useless stuff like buoys, soccer balls, mismatched shoes, and empty plastic bottles no one needs.

"Remember that day we were on the beach and a bunch of body parts floated up like a dismembered parade and you freaked out?" Castor laughs.

"They looked real washing up on the sand," I insist, and shudder at the memory. "How was I supposed to know they were from mannequins?"

"It was too late for bodies," Castor says, like I'm stupid.

After all the big finds were gone, we still came back to scavenge through the tiny, personal reminders of daily life—a tarnished bracelet engraved with *Happy 50th Wedding Anniversary, Dreama*; a shell-encrusted brass owl with one missing jeweled eye; a weird one-legged metal chicken standing on an arrow; and once, a small diamond ring that had roiled up through the sand—everything ripped away by the Great Tsunami, then washed ashore for illegals like us to find.

I throw a rock over the promenade edge and listen to it thud on the sand below. "Let's leave," I say. "Your Yoobie isn't coming."

"Don't use that word!" Castor snaps.

"Oh, I'm sorry," I say, sarcasm clear. "Let me rephrase. The universal-basic-income-receiving brain-chipped zombie from Alpha-Zonia who wants your mind-melting drug isn't going to show." I pause and stare at him. "Better?"

"They're called citizen shareholders." Castor rolls his eyes at me. "And she'll be here. She pinged me."

"I wish you'd stop," I say. "Hacking the dopamine regulators in TouchyFeelyTech implants is so against the law."

"Our entire existence in AlphaZonia is against the law."

"Yeah, but as long as we stay under the radar . . ."

Castor pulls the straps of his red knapsack tighter and walks away, impatient with my worry. He's carried that bag since the day he found it in the remains of a tsunami relief center at the Emergency Operations building on the west side. The logo on its front—a white circle with a red cross in the center—has almost faded away, but the bag itself is nearly indestructible.

From behind, he and I look just alike. We have the same long legs, broad shoulders, and narrow waist. We move alike, too. We lope rather than walk, more the way wolves move, loose-limbed and easy, as if they could go for miles without a rest.

We even dress alike in slim-fit pants, loose shirts, and comfy sneakers, all lifted from gutted warehouses and abandoned shops. With hoods up, we're dead ringers for each other. When we were little, we went back and forth. Sometimes girls. Sometimes boys. Sometimes I was Castor. Sometimes he was me. But as we got older, that changed. I sprouted small breasts when he got wisps of chin hair and a slightly lower voice. Castor's the boy. I'm the girl. Unless of course, that's inconvenient, and then we switch.

The only obvious way to distinguish me from my twin is our hair. Castor keeps his shaved close to his skull. Mine is long. The color, though, is the same burnt orange of ripe persimmons, which is striking against our brown skin, smattering of dark freckles, and bright green eyes. We look alike and yet unlike anyone else, although in the correct clothing, we can pass for Yoobies who have the credentials to live inside the borders of this privatized city.

Quasar whines as Castor gets farther from us.

"I have a bad feeling about tonight," I call. "You've been pushing things too far lately. Taking more risks than you need to." He continues to ignore me. "Sometimes I think you're an adrenaline junkie, always looking for the next big rush."

He whips around. "Or maybe you're just too cautious, *rywor tar.*"

"I'm not a worry rat!" I huff and stamp my foot because I hate it when he insults me in our twin language. It feels like such a betrayal. We stare at each other across the empty street. This is how it's always been. Him on one side of a line, and me on the other.

"Your dopamine hacks make me more nervous than our thieving. It's one thing to take stuff that used to belong to people. It's another to rearrange the circuitry of a Yoobie's cerebral implant."

"It's fine!" he insists. "They come to me. They ask for it."

"Yeah, but you'll be the one to pay the price if they get caught. Remember what Mom says, 'Whatever a Yoobie asks you for, there's always more in it for them.'"

"We need the money," he barks. "So, if it makes you uncomfortable, go wait for me somewhere else. I'll ping you when I'm done."

"Fine, you *toidi,*" I grouse.

"You're the idiot," he gripes back at me.

"I'll be over there." I point up the block to an abandoned church with a walled-off garden. Quasar stands between us, looking from me to Castor and back to me. He is a herding dog at heart and doesn't like his flock separated. "It's okay, Quasar," I tell him. "We'll stay close by."

Up ahead, lights sweep the sides of the deserted buildings. "There she is," Castor says as an AutoPod crests the hill. "Go!"

Quasar and I jog away as the car makes its way slowly toward Castor. We hop over the caved-in stone fence surrounding the persistent garden of the church—a good place to hide. Quasar sniffs around, peeing on the plants while I trample over pine-needle-covered rubble. My toe catches something solid, and I fall onto all fours, face-to-face with a literal fallen angel made of stone, eyes weeping mildew, wings broken on the ground. Oh, city of lost angels for sure!

I look up to see where it came from and catch sight of an empty alcove on the top of the white bell tower that juts up from tangles of ivy and climbing roses. Broken half-moon windows beneath a crooked cross gaze out like sad eyes. Quasar trots to my side.

"See those flowers?" I whisper to my dog. "They may look pretty and delicate, but someday their vines will bring down that tower, something even the earthquake and tsunami couldn't do."

Above the church, the Moon—a waxing silver lightbulb three quarters full—peers down from between two tall palms. When I was little, six or seven years old, I stood on the tallest trash heap in the Wasteland Dumps and waved to my father on the Moon.

That's dumb, Castor told me when he found out what I was doing.

No it's not, I argued. *Maybe he can see us with his bionic eyes.*

He doesn't have bionic eyes, toidi. *And he's probably been deep-spaced by now. That's what happens to ExploroBots when their work is done, you know. The people on the Moon just cut them loose from their tethers and let them float away.* He kicked a soggy bag of trash that burst into a slurry. *Whatever's left of him is cosmic junk by now.*

Back on the street, we hear voices. Quasar and I crawl closer to the half wall to get a better look. Although it makes me nervous, I want to see what's going on in case Castor gets in trouble. I zoom in with my Glaz to watch the Yoobie girl and my brother standing in a yellow circle of the AutoPod's lights. She's gorgeous, of course. Trying to appear as authentically human as humanly possible. Her hair is long and flowing, dyed in variations of brown and gold to bring out the warmth of her sun-kissed skin. Her clothes are spun from plant material, marking her as über wealthy. Her family must have bought into AlphaZonia long ago, then watched their universal basic income grow with each subsequent generation. And since RayNay DeShoppingCart took over ten years ago, the corporate city is more profitable for its citizens than ever.

From his knapsack, Castor extracts long, thin tweezers and a small black box. The Yoobie girl leans forward eagerly, stretching her neck to watch my brother with bright blue eyes engineered to resemble the sky. With the precision of a surgeon, he plucks a tiny silver ball, the size of a seed, from the box. He holds it up, and her eyes glow brighter. She lifts up her chin so Castor can insert the tweezers deep into her right nostril.

Slowly, delicately, he pushes them higher and higher into her nose, then says, "Now."

She sniffs and steps back to wait, eyes closed, until a few seconds later, she swoons. Her face melts into a sloppy mask of rapturous delight as her whole body relaxes. While she stands, in momentary ecstasy as the dopamine regulator deep in her brain pumps harder, Castor presses a thumb-sized scanner just above her right ear.

"Shit," I say aloud and stand up straight. "Shit, shit, shit." I didn't know he was going to hack her data packet.

She's too deep into her reverie to notice. When he's done, she dances in the moonlight, arms and legs slowly gliding through the air as if she's underwater.

I scramble over the wall to pull Castor out of here, but another set of headlights creeps slowly across the tower of the abandoned church. "Castor, watch out!" I shout, and jump back inside the garden.

He spins, sees the lights, and runs.

MOON UTILITARIAN SURVIVAL COLONY

"TOLD YOU, OOM!" Kep says aloud after Fornax disappears. "Classic Fornax hologram visit."

"And here I thought we were special," I say with a sigh. All around us, everyone stretches and talks about what they're doing for Leap Day tomorrow and where they're going for the month of Sol.

"Guess you'll have to wait to meet her in person at the LWA ceremony," I tell Kep.

Micra spins around and asks, "Did you hear the news? I'm going to be Dr. Fornax's personal intern during Sol. I get to go everywhere with her for twenty-eight days."

"Poor Fornax," I mutter.

But Kepler says, "Congratulations. That's great for your career scaffold."

I send him a mind scribble of me barfing. The guy is way too nice.

"What are you doing for Sol?" Micra asks while angling her body away from me just enough so I know she's only addressing Kepler.

He shrugs. "Nothing special. A few days of SimuSkiing on the surface, hitting TourEsa casinos with some guys, then lying around at a SimuBeach."

"Aiming high, as usual," I joke, but I have to admit, I wish I could be more like Kepler. He has the perpetual calm of a person who assumes everything will work out fine. My mother says that attitude is the province of the privileged and that people like us always have to worry.

"I'm sure Kepler has a perfectly good reason for his request," Micra snaps.

"I do," says Kep.

Micra purses her lips and lifts her eyebrows as if to say, *Told you!*

"A body at rest stays at rest, and I'm the embodiment of inertia," he says.

"Excellent reasoning." I smirk at her.

"Thank you," he says. Then he adds, "Uma's going to Earth."

"For good?" Micra says. Cassio and Alma snicker beside her.

"Maybe," I say, and Kepler's eyes bug out. "Earth is a fascinating place."

"Only if you're an Earthling," Micra says it like an insult, then quickly turns away. Cassio and Alma make no effort to hide their cackles.

Before I can create any kind of evil mind scribble showing Micra, Cassio, and Alma's joint demise, Deimos, our cohort supervisor, takes over the Stream, and we're all cut off from one another.

"Okay, Cohort 54," Deimos says. "I know you're all excited Leap Day is tomorrow, but we still have work to do today."

Like everyone whose grandparents were the first humans here, Deimos has the slightly fetal look of the Third Gen off-planet evolution, with a shrunken nasal cavity and large eyes. I called them Baby People when my family first arrived from Earth and found them freakish to look at. Now my face is the one that surprises me each time I see my reflection.

"This is your last lab assessment," he says. "The one you've all been waiting for. It's ExploroBot time!"

Everyone bursts with excitement. Even Gemini sits up, blinking and wiping spittle from the corner of his mouth. "I'm so pumped for this!" he shouts loud enough for us to hear on the other side of the auditorium.

I look at Kepler and whisper, "Am I the only person in the room who thinks this will suck?"

"I doubt the ExploroBots are too excited about it," he whispers back.

Then we both settle in for the narrated ExploroBot history lesson that fills our Streams.

The ExploroBot project has been the keystone of MUSC expansion for the past two decades, the narrator says over a holo vid of our colony's history that's been drilled into our minds since we were small. *From the first inhabited inflatable pods on the Moon's surface in MUSC Year 1 to the warren of underground lava tube bunkers the colony used for fifteen years, we've been expanding and making life better on the Moon.*

To truly advance our colony, we needed more sophisticated domiciles and labs, yet clearly, inhabitants of MUSC were far too valuable to risk on dangerous exterior construction projects.

I huff. The underlying premise that a MUSC life is more valuable than an Earth life gets under my skin like an antiviral nanobot.

Despite the brilliant minds and advanced technology here at MUSC, no AI robot that we can build is as dexterous and nimble as the masterpiece of the human body. The human hand alone is one of the most complex and amazing feats of engineering in the known universe.

I look down at my hands and wonder what they'll be used for once I get my LWA. Cleaning space toilets? No. CleanerBots do that.

Finally, in MUSC Year 65, a breakthrough in the area of brain-to-brain interface enabled us to combine resources from Earth with the incredible mental talent here at MUSC.

I lean close to Kep and whisper, "Did you know that an Earth girl named Zaniah Nashira invented that BBI? She was a scholarship kid just like me, but then she disappeared when she was fifteen and was never heard from again."

Kep puts his lips so close to my ear that it tickles when he says, "You've told me about her at least ten million times."

"So you were listening," I say.

Kep rolls his eyes.

Images of early ExploroBots fill the Stream. I squirm in my seat and offer Kep an alternate narration. "Here at MUSC, we stick brain-dead Earth soldiers inside a protective exoskeleton, tether them to our station, and control them with our minds!"

He shakes his head, but fights a smile.

"I bet half of these morons are hoping for an LWA placement in the ExploroBot lab," I whisper.

"And this surprises you because . . ." He waggles his head, waiting for me to see the folly of my thinking.

I sigh. "It doesn't," I admit. "Or at least it shouldn't." The truth is, most MUSCies see Zero Gens like me as barely human, so there's no way kids in my cohort will recognize the humanity of a brain-dead soldier shipped up to us from Earth to do our dirty work.

And so the ExploroBot program was born! the narrator proclaims with far too much enthusiasm. *This incredible combination of MUSC minds and Earth bodies has allowed us to construct our state-of-the-art Sky-Labs and domiciles and is the reason we continue to expand today!*

An image of our station anchored to the surface of the Moon comes into view. Six hinged legs, symmetrically arranged around a baseplate, hold us in place. A long elevator shaft from the surface lifts us to the sky, where we continually rotate around a stationary core that gathers sunrays on our multifaceted surface. This image of my spinning adopted home triggers a vague memory from my childhood of brightly colored plastic pinwheels poking up from compacted dirt on Earth under a bright blue sky.

Darshan, where did this occur? I ask my cyber assistant to comb the archives of my memory for the image.

The former town of Hesperia, located in the Wastelands of Earth, he says, but that doesn't mean much to me. I can't contextualize the image except to say it makes me feel happy. Still, I blink on it to save so I can look at it again later.

We are on the cusp of new horizons, expanding our home so all MUSCies can live in comfort on three new stations with state-of-the-art labs that will enable us to launch our species beyond the Moon.

The new stations, in various states of completion, come into view. The legs and shaft of one are done. On another, ExploroBots install the solar panels. The third is nearly complete and will be in rotation soon. Everyone in my cohort hopes they'll be assigned to domiciles in the newest station, but I don't really care. I'd be just as happy to stay in this one, close to my mom.

Now it's your turn to see if dedicating your life to the ExploroBot program could be right for you!

"Who in their right mind would want this for an LWA?" I ask out loud just as the montage ends and our Streams are returned to our control.

People gape at me from every direction. I shrink in my seat.

"For your information," Micra turns to me and huffs, "the ExploroBot program is the preeminent breeding ground for some of best research that's occurred on MUSC in the past two decades. Anyone who doesn't want an ExploroBot LWA is a vacuum brain."

"What can I say?" I tell her. "My heart belongs to microbiology!" I press both hands over my chest in an overly dramatic gesture just to annoy her. Then I flash her a smile. My big horsey teeth make her cringe.

"Gross!" She shakes her head, dumbfounded as usual by how far off from normal I am. "What's there to *love* about bacteria and viruses?"

"For one thing, they're beautiful," I say, which elicits an indignant snort from all three girls in front of me. "And also," I say gravely, narrowing my eyes, "they can be deadly."

"Oh, please," says Micra as she turns away.

I can't let it go. I lean forward, elbows on knees so I can get closer to her ear. "You know, Micra, it's not a meteor that'll wipe out this Moon Utilitarian Survival Colony," I tell her out loud because she would never accept thotz from me. "It'll be an itty-bitty, teeny-weeny, little strand of killer DNA, because at the end of the day, we're all just fragile skin bags of water trying to survive in the hostility of space."

"Just when I think you can't get any weirder . . ." she says.

Why do you let her get to you? Kep thotz me.

I sit back hard. *Who says she gets to me?*

Kep rolls his eyes.

"Okay!" Deimos claps his hands to get our attention. "Just for fun, since it's our last day, let's go in random order. First up . . ." He blinks to retrieve information. "Gemini Chen-Ning."

Gemini literally jumps up from his seat, pumping his fist, shouting, "Yes!"

Deimos blinks again. "Cassiopeia Noether."

She squeals and hugs Micra as if she's won the Miss Universe contest.

One last blink, and he says, "And Uma Jemison."

"Ah, gad!" I slump down and swallow the bile in my throat.

Lucky you, Kep thotz.

"Shut up," I whisper as I climb over him.

As I make my way down to the stage, life-size holos of three ExploroBots tethered to the SkyLab appear so everyone can see. Behind each one, a three-quarter Earth zooms by as our entire colony spins. I might be the only person here who finds this view beautiful . . . and nauseating. I have to look away. Since I wasn't born on MUSC, I'm supersensitive to the gravity-induced rotation when I see the spinning stars and distant planets outside our station.

Cassio and Gemini each place themselves in front of a holo and focus in to establish a connection on their Streams, but mine won't work.

"Um . . . Deimos," I say quietly. "Psst. Deimos." I wave my hand. He looks at me, annoyed. "I need a . . . you know, an external device or something." I point to my headset, which is too primitive to connect to the ExploroBot feed.

"Right, yeah, sorry. I forgot." He forages through an equipment cart at the side of the stage. "You'll have to wear this over your device." He holds out the mesh hood with tiny probes as if it were a contagion. A ripple of twitters and snorts goes through my cohort as I put on the hood that will connect my thoughts to the CPU implanted in an ExploroBot's brain.

I can barely look at the bot's holo in front of me. Knowing that the being beneath the silver and white exoskeleton was once a sentient human makes me physically ill. The darkened faceplate only makes it worse. I want so badly to see this person's eyes.

"In this simulation," Deimos says aloud for everyone to hear, "your job is to repair a radiation shield on the exterior face of our new SkyLab 2. Remember what you learned in your tutorials. First, assess the problem in front of you, then think step-by-step through a solution. If your thought process is detailed and clear enough, the brain-to-brain interface will send your action signals to the CPU embedded in your ExploroBot's brain. The more you can convince your brain that your body is doing the action, the more likely your ExploroBot will react."

I try.

I really, really try.

I focus on my bot, working to block out the spinning sky behind him, her, it? That only makes my stomach churn and my head swim more. *Hand to tool belt. Hand to tool belt,* I think over and over, trying to feel my arm lifting, elbow bending, fingers reaching for the wrench on the ExB's hip without actually moving my own limbs. But my mind is clouded with visions of who this person might have been on Earth.

Had I not won a scholarship to MUSC when I was five, it could have been my mother or my father forced to fight in the never-ending Water Wars. One of them could have been blown apart, then put back together inside these suits and sold off to MUSC so that my family could survive down below. Instead, we had to come all the way up here for my dad to die in the one place we were supposed to be safe.

"Uma, come on," Deimos says. He stands beside me. "You haven't even gotten your wrench out of the tool belt yet."

"I'm trying," I tell him, but I can feel myself getting queasier and queasier as I watch my bot float aimlessly in the rotating blur. I glance at Cassio's ExB. She's at least three steps ahead of me, already removing the damaged radiation shingle. On the other side, Gemini's ExB is turned upside down, but still drilling a new shingle into place with no problem.

"Think about it!" Deimos says. "Reach your hand into the tool belt."

"I . . . I . . . I . . ." My stomach starts to heave. "I think I'm going to barf!"

I rip the hood off my head, rocket up the stairs, and dart out of the auditorium doors.

"DAMN IT, CASTOR! What did you do?" I demand when he jumps the wall to crouch beside Quasar and me in the shadows of the church. Overhead, lights sweep by, illuminating the broken stained-glass windows.

"It'll all be fine," he pants. "But we should get out of here."

"You think!" I say.

"Wolflo em." He grabs my hand, and, as always, I follow him, just like he asks.

We run across the garden, bent-kneed and hunched like the PredatorBots that guard the aqueducts up north. Quasar stays close behind. When we pop out on the sidewalk on the other side of the garden, an automated transportation shuttle pulls up to the curb. We both stop short, crash into each other, then plaster ourselves against the side of the building so we won't be seen.

Ahead of us, the shuttle bus idles beside a long line of tired Re-Construction workers, washed out and gray like ghosts of past inhabitants of this city.

"I didn't know they'd gotten this far," I whisper, and scan the streets, because if ReConstruction workers are here, then SecuriBots are not far behind.

Castor clicks his scanner into his TouchCuff to upload the Yoobie girl's data packet to his device while I watch the workers board the shuttle. Once he has the data, he shoves the scanner back into his bag. I hold my breath until the last worker, a woman about our mother's age, clomps down the aisle and drops into a seat, exhausted. She appears to fall asleep the moment her forehead touches the window.

I shudder. Being on a bus like that is the other way people like us get inside this city. The difference is, they go back to the Wastelands every night, while we stay here, carving out a life in the shadows.

"Jack-a-Pod!" Castor says.

"No, please, Castor! Don't do that—"

But it's too late. The Yoobie girl's AutoPod screeches around the corner at the far end of the block.

"Come on." Castor grabs me again. "Run!"

"I hate when you hijack Pods!" I say as we bolt away from the church and waiting bus.

"Hello, Cristela Wong Holtzmann," the Pod says as we scramble inside. "Where would you like to go?"

"Pink Palace," my brother says.

The AutoPod peels out, and Quasar jumps, paws scratching at the window, barking like a maniac as we pass the ambling shuttle bus full of sleeping workers.

"Get down!" I pull him to my lap, afraid his noise will trigger some kind of alarm. "Castor, come on! We can't go up there!"

"Sure we can! Look," Castor says brightly, and holds up his Touch-Cuff screen for me to see. "The Yoobie girl was invited."

The whole way up Santa Monica Boulevard to Wilshire, I try my best to talk Castor out of his stupid plan, but he won't budge.

"We're not Yoobies!" I insist.

"Beside the point. There's a big party at the Palace tonight. We can stream from there."

"No way," I tell him. My heart is in my throat. "It's too dangerous."

"Stop being such a *rywor tar*," he says. "I've been trying to get us inside for a year."

"Castor, please don't make me do this," I beg, but my brother barely listens.

Instead, he has his face pressed against the window just like the dog. "Look how smooth and straight the roads are up here. Every plant is manicured. All the streetlights shine. It's like the earthquake and tsunami never happened."

"No shit," I say. "This is where D'Cart lives. Of course it's the first priority for repair. Which is why we should turn around. Now!"

Still, Castor doesn't stop. We round a corner, and I glimpse the turrets of the Pink Palace above an expansive fringe of palm fronds.

"This used to be a hotel for rich people and celebrities," Castor says.

"Who cares? Let's get out of here."

"Then D'Cart took it over and knocked down everything around it to make this crazy palace. The grounds alone go on for miles."

My stomach tightens, sending bile into my throat. "I really don't want to do this."

"Why?" asks Castor, finally clueing in to the fact that I'm freaking out.

"Because! It's too risky. There's no place to hide. And clearly we do not belong."

"We will," he says with a grin.

He commands the Pod to pull over a few hundred meters short of the black-and-white-striped awning covering the portico of the

Palace. Ahead of us a steady line of AutoPods inch up the half-moon drive.

"Doors open," Castor commands. "Time to go," he says to me.

"Castor. No. Please don't leave," I whisper-yell, but it's no use. He hops out, and Quasar tumbles after him. They won't come back, so I dart after them across the grass.

UMA JEMISON

MOON UTILITARIAN
SURVIVAL COLONY

AFTER I'VE HURLED what was left of my lunch into a trash tube, I slump on a bench outside the auditorium waiting for the class to end. If I go back in and see the spinning sky, I'll barf again for sure.

"You okay, starshine?" I look up and see Randazza Marmesh in her little food and beverage delivery vehicle idling in front of me. She is pleasingly plump in a way no MUSCies are. Soft folds of skin around her arms and belly make for the best hugs. When I was little, I'd curl into her lap at night when my parents were down in the mines because they didn't trust a NanniBot to take care of me.

"Yes, ma'am," I say. "Just a little queasy."

"Here, try this, it'll settle your stomach." Ms. Marmesh smiles kindly and hands me a foil packet from her stash in the back of the vehicle. As a Zero Gen herself, she still looks out for me, especially when my mom is down on the surface, which is most of the time.

I unwrap the treat and pop it in my mouth. The bite of ginger coats my tongue and immediately soothes my stomach. "Thank you."

"You're welcome, starshine."

Before she can drive away, a woman steps off the AutoWalk on the other side of the hallway and stares from me to Ms. Marmesh and back to me. I glance at the patch on her blue and white tunic indicating her generation, cohort, and domicile number, G2C29D237. Of course, a Second Gen who lives in the tony two hundreds!

"Are you in the right place?" she asks as if concerned for my well-being, but really she's worried that I'm a low-level employee sitting down on the job.

I catch Ms. Marmesh's eye. She looks to the ceiling and sighs.

"I'm part of Cohort 54." I point to my own patch, G0C54D1235, then cross my arms and stare at the woman.

"Oh!" she says, then nods in what she supposes is encouragement. *Good for you, Earth Girl, making it out of the squalor of our ancestral planet!* But really, she's congratulating herself. *Aren't we progressive up here at MUSC, letting Zero Gens like you coexist with our Third Gen children?*

I glare back at her until she flinches and steps back on the moving walkway to hurry down the corridor.

Ms. Marmesh winks at me, then, chuckling under her breath, she drives away.

I sit quietly for another few minutes while the ginger candy melts on my tongue. I'm in no hurry to get anywhere until Darshan, my cyber assistant, shimmers in the peripheral vision of my Lenz and announces, *Urgent message!* I call him forward. His image sharpens, and he says, *You are requested to meet with MUSC president and CEO Valentine Fornax in person. Please proceed to her personal work space.*

"What?" I say out loud. "Must be a mistake."

Darshan repeats the message.

My heart races. I've only been summoned to see Dr. Fornax one time since I've lived here, and that was the worst day of my life.

Why? I ask Darshan, and stay put on the bench.

I have no other information, he says. *Please proceed to Valentine Fornax's personal work space.*

Is my mother okay? I ask before I move.

I have no information to the contrary, Darshan says. *Your heart rate is elevated and yet you are not proceeding at a pace that would indicate physiological exertion. Are you stressed? Would you like a relaxation exercise?*

Shut up, Darshan, I command, then hustle onto the empty Auto-Walk.

I send a series of thotz to my mom on my way to Dr. Fornax's workstation, but she doesn't reply. Which isn't unusual. Everyone's off Stream while they work, except when we're on break, which is when Mom and I usually check in.

Half of me wonders if someone hacked Darshan and sent me a fake message so I'd look like a dorkbot showing up at the MUSC CEO's door while vicious malware publicly Streams every moment of my stupidity, but as soon as I near the vestibule of Dr. Fornax's work space, a VirtuVoice connects to my Stream and says, *Welcome, Uma Jemison. Dr. Fornax is expecting you.* The AutoWalk diverts me, and a door *wheesh*es open.

Too embarrassed to be seen by the MUSC CEO wearing my old clunky device, I remove it from my head and fold it into my pocket before I step inside. I assume I'll be greeted by a hologram (Dr. Fornax could be anywhere), but inside the room, the real Valentine Fornax rises from her workstation and walks toward me with her hand extended. She is even more imposing in person. Taller than I remember. Her cropped silver hair shimmers, and her eyes drill into me.

"So you're Uma Jemison?"

My palm is sweaty in her firm grip. "Yes, ma'am. We've met before."

"We have?" She looks at me, perplexed.

"Is my mother okay?" I brace myself.

"Your mother . . ."

"Persis Sarachik. Chief of DrillBot repair." My voice is tight with worry.

Dr. Fornax blinks quickly, no doubt calling up my life history archive to her Stream, then her mouth falls open slightly. "I'm sorry. I had forgotten. Your father died in the MUSC Year 88 mining explosion."

"Yes." I glance around the room and see that everything is just as I remember it, including a blooming orange zinnia plant under a grow light on the corner of her desk. "You called me here with my mother to tell us in person." My chest is tight, and I can barely breathe.

"I apologize." Dr. Fornax sighs and offers me a place to sit. I settle on the edge of the white sofa, the same place I sat last time I was here, but then my feet didn't touch the floor.

"The system should have warned me to be more attentive to your emotional needs. I'll make a note for improvement," Dr. Fornax says. "Your mother is fine, by the way. Absolutely nothing to worry about."

I let go an enormous sigh.

"Are you okay now?" Dr. Fornax leans forward, her eyes locked with mine. She reaches out to squeeze my shoulder—a gesture so Earthly that I slump back with relief. "Do you need to rehydrate?"

"I . . . uh . . . um . . . I'm fine," I stammer as I sit up, perched like a nervous bird on the edge of the seating unit again. "But why am I here exactly?"

"I remember when you first came to us." Dr. Fornax leans against her workstation, arms crossed, looking down at me. "You were the youngest Zero Gen we had ever accepted on scholarship."

"Yes, ma'am. I know." The story of my family's emigration is well-worn lore. Where I'm from in North America, if you didn't have the means to buy your way into a privatized city like AlphaZonia, you had two choices: live in the libertarian nightmare of Merica or eke out a living in the Wastelands. My parents chose the Wastelands. Until I came along. Then they wanted something better and pinned all their hopes on me. They stuffed me so full of knowledge that the moment I turned five, I tested off the MUSC scholarship charts, which was our ticket to the Moon.

"Not everybody was happy that I let you come," Dr. Fornax says.

"I'm sure they weren't," I say quietly, because I'm well aware of the controversy my family caused.

Before me, Zero Gen scholarship kids had to be at least ten years old and were brought up here without their families. But most of them wilted under the pressure and eventually left the colony. Over the years, I've searched all kinds of data archives for any information on deserters who went back to Earth: Yuriko Blevan left on a business trip then stayed on Earth to start a no-tech colony in the Amazon; Jiyun Watts built her own escape pod that went sideways and burned up on reentry to the Earth's atmosphere; Reza T. Sunshine called it quits when she was assigned her LWA and became a sea vegetable farmer on a garbage patch in the center of the Pacific Ocean; and the most infamous of all, Zaniah Nashira, a young scholarship kid who changed the course of MUSC history with her BBI breakthrough in Dr. Fornax's lab. The formation of the ExploroBot program propelled Fornax to CEO, but Zaniah disappeared when she was fifteen without a trace. I've looked and looked for more info on her, but there's nothing else. Not a single image of her survives. It's as if she's been officially erased from our history. After her debacle, the scholarship program was suspended until my family unit was taken as a whole.

"We saw enormous promise in you," Dr. Fornax says. "So we took a chance. I *personally* took a chance on you. I staked my reputation bringing your family here together. What do you have to say about that?"

"Um . . . thank you, I guess?"

"You guess?" She draws in a sharp breath.

I cringe. "Sorry. It's just that, well, I don't understand why I'm here."

"Given all that I just told you, imagine my shock and utter dismay when I learned that you want to go back to Earth for the month of Sol."

"But . . . what's the problem with that? I thought we could do anything we wanted on the Sol of our sixteenth year."

"In my experience, Earth-born humans like you go back for only two reasons." She pauses, then points her index finger in the air. "One: to attend to family matters. But as far as I know, you have no family there to speak of, do you?"

"No, ma'am," I admit. "My parents were each only children, and my grandparents died long ago."

"Or, two." She holds up a second finger. "They leave and don't intend to come back."

"Oh!" I flinch. "No, not me! I don't want to go for good." A wave of nausea engulfs me as I remember what I said to Micra. "That was a joke!" My temperature rises. Did she rat me out? Again? "Going back is just my Sol request. You know. Twenty-eight days to do anything I want before . . ." I trail off.

"Before what?"

"I get my LWA," I mumble.

"Why not take a few weeks down at TourEsa on the surface of the Moon? Or hit the beach simulators? Or take a rover for a crater run, then head up to the casinos on the dark side? Or apply for a satellite internship to hone your skills in your favorite field of study?"

She walks around to the other side of her desk as she lists all the things everyone else in my cohort will do during our month off. But those people are perfectly happy at MUSC. A few weeks away from the SkyLab is enough for them to recharge before dedicating themselves to a Life's Work Assignment. I can't say this to the president of MUSC, though, so I sit meekly, withering under her stare, as I gather up my courage to whisper, "I don't want to do those things. I want to go to Earth."

She stops, spins on her heel, and looks at me again. "Why?"

I sit, stupidly mute. Do I dare tell her that every night I dream I'm swimming in the ocean, being pulled closer and closer to shore? "It's like the tides on Earth," I finally say. "I feel drawn."

"You feel *drawn*?" Dr. Fornax rolls her eyes, so obviously annoyed with my emotions getting in the way of logic. "That's not a real reason. Unless you can come up with something better, you'll need to put in a different request."

"Are you . . ." I hesitate, afraid to articulate the truth. "Canceling my trip to Earth?"

"That's correct."

"But, but, but . . ." My entire body feels heavy, as if the g-force of rotation has increased and pressed me harder against the seat. "Tomorrow is Leap Day. My flight leaves in less than twelve hours!"

"Not anymore it doesn't," she says. "Do you understand?"

I sit, stunned into silence, ready to burst with anger and frustration, but as I've done a thousand times at MUSC, I push my emotions into the hard pit of my stomach. I swallow down my tears because only Earthlings cry. MUSCies don't. They are taught from the time they are little that expressing emotions marks one as intellectually inferior. And gad forbid anyone be inferior up here on the Moon!

"Well?" says Dr. Fornax. In that moment, the dark eyes of my hero seem more sinister than mischievous, and the hard line of her jaw marks her as stolid instead of strong.

"Yes," I say quietly as I rise on shaking legs. "I understand."

"Good," Dr. Fornax says as I turn to go. "And, Uma," she calls after me, "come up with something quickly. I wouldn't want you to miss out on Sol altogether."

"WE CAN'T DO this. It's crazy!" I argue in harsh whispers as I follow my brother and Quasar across the lush side lawn of the Pink Palace. We flee into the shadow of a giant rhododendron bush. Castor pushes inside a tangle of purple flowers and leads us to a small clearing between the tall security wall and the greenery.

"Look." He holds up his cuff again. "I already snagged the identity data from the Yoobie girl's TFT chip. The party's on her agenda, and she has a plus one. The security system will think we're legit and let us in."

"Hello? Castor! Neither of us looks a thing like Cristela Wong Holtzmann!"

"Really?" he says, completely deadpan. "If only I weren't a complete amateur and had thought of attaching your appearance data into her files. Oh, wait." He smacks his forehead with the flat of his palm. "I already did that."

"Okay, fine, my face will show up in the security file, but what if the girl shows up in person?"

"There's no way that girl is coming to this party. She's zooming like a comet down in the Basin. She'll be there for at least an hour until the stuff wears off."

"But—"

"Talitha!" He waves away my concern. "It'll be okay. Her AutoPod will go back to pick her up. She'll be fine. We'll go inside and stay for ten minutes, fifteen tops. Which will give us just enough time to Stream the party, hack some product links, and get the hell out. Nobody will even notice that we're here."

"Except all of our followers!" I say.

He nods, happily. "And they'll love it!"

"But we don't look like Yoobies."

"First off, if you're going to pass as one, stop calling them Yoobies," Castor says smugly. "And secondly, put this on." He hands me a black bundle he's dug out of his knapsack.

"What is it?" The thing unfolds into thousands of tiny, hard nylon tessellated triangles, each hinged together to form a mosaic of moveable fabric. Murky moonlight filters through the bush, casting a botanical pattern on my arms and legs as if I've got some kind of strange skin disease.

"Kinematic Jumpsuit!" Castor says. "The latest fashion craze for discerning AlphaZonian females."

"Oh, gross!" I hold the suit away from my body as if it might be contaminated. "Did you steal this from the girl?"

"God, no! I'm not that uncivilized. This is the newest RayNay De-ShoppingCart design. I hacked the manufacturer specs and printed it to your exact measurements. You'll look like one of the crowd in there."

"I don't know." My stomach roils with worry as I turn the outfit over and over, trying to make sense of one large hole and four tubes.

"Come on, Tal!" He huffs. "How many opportunities do we get like this? It's perfect! We'll be in and out super quick. It's a no-brainer."

He laughs. "Get it? No-brainer. 'Cause we don't have TouchyFeelyTech in our brains and—"

"I get your stupid joke, but I'm not so sure about your stupider idea."

"It's not stupid," he says seriously. "We haven't had a good haul in months. There's less and less to scavenge, and we have nothing left to sell. Our followers are getting bored and hopping onto other Streams. We have to make some money, or we'll be on that bus of ReConstruction workers."

"Maybe we could go legit," I argue. "Work for D'Cart like Mundie?"

"Indentured servants with chips in our heads, fixing lame robots?" Castor scoffs. "No way. I like my brain the way it is and the freedom to come and go as I please. And if this hack goes well, we'll have enough to live off for months."

I groan. I know he's right. We need the money, and I don't want to work for D'Cart any more than he does. "But if we get caught—"

"We won't." He reaches out and puts both hands on my shoulders. We are still exactly the same height. Eye to eye. Nose to nose. He is the mirror image of me. "It'll be okay. *Meprosi!*"

"You can't promise anything," I grumble, "but fine, I'll do it." I squelch my fears and worries like I've done over and over with my brother. I always give in to his questionable ideas, like creating a D'Cart parody Stream, sneaking into AlphaZonia to live, selling what we scavenge, and now, hacking the biggest CelebriStreamer event there is. "Everything we do is risky, so what's one more ten-minute hack?" I ask.

"Now you're talking!"

I look down at the jumpsuit in my hands. "How do I put this on?"

"Step through the back, duh," he says.

I move behind a screen of branches and strip down to my tank top and undies, then toss Castor my clothes. He wads them up and shoves them inside his knapsack while I slide my legs into the lower tubes of the jumpsuit. I tug and jump to get the thing up over my hips, then I reach into the arm tubes and yank so that the whole outfit snaps into place, precisely conforming to the dimensions of my body.

"I feel like a fish caught in a net!" I say as I walk out to join him in the clearing.

"Do something with your hair."

"You do something with your hair," I snap at him.

He rubs his hand across his scalp. "There," he says. "Done."

"You have it so easy."

"So shave your head."

"I just might."

He plunges his hand into his knapsack and pulls out a small solar-powered razor. "Here you go."

I grab for the razor, but he snatches it away.

"Would you really?" he asks.

"Sure," I say. "It might be nice not to mess with so much hair."

"Not tonight, though." He pushes the razor down inside his bag of tricks. "Tonight you have to fit in to Yoobie culture, and the girls love their long, flowing locks!"

"Blech!" I've never been the kind of girl who defines myself by what other people choose to see. Still, I know he's right. If I want to pass, I have to play the game, so I sweep my hair on top of my head. "Why are you carrying around a razor, anyway?"

"Found it," he says, and hands me two pins to secure my updo. "Thought it might come in handy someday." He reaches out to rearrange my hair, but I duck.

"Stop it," I say.

"No, you stop it," he says back, like we're three again.

We smack at each other, half laughing like toddlers, but all the tussling frees a few strands to hang around my face, and he says, "There! That's better. Now you look just like a Yoobie."

"I thought that was a rude word."

"It is," he insists. "But the real question is whether you can act like one when I Stream you."

"In my sleep," I say, because the truth is, I like the challenge of morphing into someone else. I step back, widen my eyes, and smile big as I run a hand up my arm. "Can you feel the tiny tessellated triangles of extruded microplastics digging into your skin?" I parrot D'Cart's breathy delivery when she launches a new product.

Castor laughs. I've always been a good mimic. From the time I was little, I could perfectly imitate the lilt, the head tilt, and the wide-eyed innocent blink of CelebriStreamers beckoning to their followers. But I was always best at D'Cart, which is why our parody Stream was born.

I draw my arm under my nose from elbow to my wrist, exaggerating a huge sniff. "Aaaaah! Can you smell the newly printed materials off-gassing into the night air?" I lick my arm. "Mmmm, can you taste that? The sweet sweat of complete and total discomfort."

"Brilliant!" Castor laughs. "Our followers are going to love this. Streaming from inside a D'Cart party, live from the Pink Palace! We'll have a deluge. Now, give me your headset. I have Wearables for you."

I sigh and dutifully trade my old beat-up device for a neatly wrapped packet of stolen Wearables.

"Yuck." Castor drops my device in his bag. "I don't know why you hang on to this thing."

"I like it!" I whine. "It's more comfortable than this half robot stuff." I dab the iEye contact lens into my right eye, then insert the HearEar bud into the canal of my ear. Next, I slip the TouchCuff onto my wrist.

Castor hands me one more thing. "Behold, your Personal Ecosystem Streaming Tech device!"

"I hate these PESTs." I pluck the tiny silver insect from his up-turned palm.

"Nest it somewhere safe until you need it."

I snuggle the minuscule flying camera between the ridge on top of my left ear and the side of my head. After a few seconds, the devices all link up with the CPU I've slipped inside my shoe, and everything comes online. The full-color softness of the leaves and grass and flowers surrounding me is marred by an overlay of superimposed information on the iEye. The date. The time. My location. As if I'm a moron who has no sense of my existence without confirmation from the AlphaZonia Cloud. Then the HearEar starts to talk. *Hello, there,* it says in a soothing female voice. *What's your name?*

"Shut up," I say, and the voice goes silent.

"Rude," says Castor.

"It's an algorithm. Not sentient."

"Yet," he says, one eyebrow up. He takes off his hooded jacket to reveal a black and silver jumpsuit with mesh sleeves, just like the Yoobie guys wear. He shoves the jacket into his knapsack, then stashes the whole thing in a slight depression on the ground near the wall. He kicks leaves over it for cover.

"Ready?" he asks as he heads for the Palace.

"No," I say, but he isn't listening.

UMA JEMISON

MOON UTILITARIAN
SURVIVAL COLONY

I'M SO UPSET when I leave Dr. Fornax's office that I nearly bump into a group of Second Gens on the AutoWalk. I fight hard to keep my tears in check. I don't want to be on a transport with those goons staring at my red and watery eyes. And there's no way I'm going to rejoin my cohort today. I don't need Micra and her evil minions watching me fight back my Earthly emotions. I hop off the mover and scurry down a maintenance hall, head down, willing myself not to break.

I slip around a corner out of sight of the others and look over my shoulder to make sure no one's watching. I dig my device out of my pocket. *Entry*, I command. A floor-door slides open, and I disappear into the HabiTrails.

As soon as my feet hit the ground and I know that I'm alone, I burst. My sobs echo down the empty, well-lit tube like neutrons zipping around the exterior of a spinning atom. I ping my mom again, but she still doesn't answer.

Do you wish to leave a message? Darshan asks, but I say no and disconnect. If I try to talk now, I'll just blubber, and she'll have no idea why I'm crying, which will make her worry. Instead, I keep walking through the HabiTrail.

When we first moved here, the idea of popping up from the floor and climbing down from the ceiling was bizarre to me. It took a while to understand that there is no actual up and down because we're in constant rotation around a stationary core and you're moving either closer to the center or farther away. Travelator capsules are on an interior track. HabiTrails on the exterior. And right now, I want to be as far away from the heart of this place as possible. If there were an escape hatch nearby, I'd open it and willingly get sucked into the void of space.

But of course, there's not. The only choice is to trudge on home.

Most MUSCies never use the HabiTrails because the g-force this far from the core makes their legs feel like iron. But for my family, the rate of induced-gravity in these tubes running around the exterior of the station feels more like Earth, which my parents found comforting after a long day in the gravity-less Moon surface mines. When I was little, we came here every night after dinner for a walk, which is why I'm like a rat in a maze. I don't have to see through my blur of tears to know exactly which tube to take from the work area to our domicile.

I don't bother to hide my blathering when I pop up the ladder into the empty hall. Since everyone is at work or at school, this is the one place on MUSC where no one will bother me.

The door to Domicile 1235 automatically opens when I reach it. I enter our home and plod past everything: the hyper-efficient kitchen with our monthly allotment of prepackaged food and two backless stools attached to a small round table. Past the well-worn seating surfaces of the common room, where I pause in front of our family photo stream on the wall. I stop and watch the familiar pix of my parents. They made a funny pair. For every ounce of my mother's lithe and sinewy muscle, my father was short, squat, and compact. She was the giraffe to his rhino, and she towered over him by nearly a foot. Her skin is darker than his was, but her hair is lighter. I inherited my curls from him. My big smile from her. Despite their differences, they were gorgeous together. Only no MUSCies can see that.

Although my mother is one of the most beautiful and smartest women I've ever met, she feels perpetually ugly and stupid here. The other cohort mothers have little to do with her. Only Kepler's mom is friendly, and even that feels more like mercy than actual esteem.

"I miss you," I whisper when my father's pix comes up. He stands on Earth with our dog next to a Joshua tree beneath the blazing sun, his smiling face in the shadow of a floppy hat. Next is the two of us standing hand in hand at an ocean pier where he taught me to swim. There is one of the three of us in front of the MUSC Shuttle, me, tiny on my father's shoulders as he grips my legs and grins next to my mom. And last us on the Moon, both my parents in their protective mining gear, helmets in hand, looking serious and proud of the life they were making for me here at MUSC.

There are no pix of where he is now. His body is forever wrapped in a shining silver sheath and tethered to the surface of the Moon. The dead are arranged like rows of strange metallic flowers sprouting in the darkness of the far side.

When the slide show begins again, I walk to my room, where I slump at my desk and stare at my collection of petri dishes. These beautiful bacteria colonies sampled from Earth shuttles are my solace. I feed them, starve them, warm them, freeze them, add dyes to make them pretty as they organize themselves past obstacles I put in their paths and search for new avenues of exploration.

I've watched them grow from a few lonely individuals into intricate societies. Once the dye is set, some look like vibrant magenta blooms with chartreuse fronds. Others twist and turn like bright green tendrils ending with lavender blossoms and deep red berries. Some are fancy dancing girls with giant purple fans.

My favorite is *Paenibacillus vortex*, a gram-positive swarming bacteria that loves oxygen, hates the cold, and uses tiny flagella to colonize the dish in the shape of brilliant blue peacock feathers. But even my mini botanical garden can't cheer me up today. Now it's just a reminder of where I'm not going.

I leave my desk and climb into my sleeping berth (affixed to the wall a requisite two meters above the floor) and slip beneath my blankets—one MUSC-issued ultra-thin, energy-efficient coverlet (white); the other pieced together from scraps of blue and green and brown fabrics my family brought to the Moon when we emigrated. (A piece of my father's hand-knit woolen sweater. A strip from my mother's soft flannel shirt. Patches from a baby blanket I hugged down to holes.) I snuggle into those fabrics searching for a smell lost in the olfactory synapses of my brain. Is it rain on rocks, or fresh-cut coconut, or ferns unfurling in the morning sun? Or an ocean breeze? I can't remember anymore because every scent has been superseded by the strange MUSC smell of soap and metal.

I was so homesick for Earth when we arrived here that Mom programmed my ceiling blue with fluffy white clouds. My wall screen projects images of Earth flora and fauna. Flamboyant pink hibiscus flowers. Purple and yellow hummingbirds. Whorls of green leaves on trees. An image of our dog, Mahati—his kind eyes asking why we left him behind. These are the last images I've seen every night when I go to sleep and the first ones I've seen every morning when I wake. For the past ten years, I've assumed I would see it all again someday in person. And now . . . there's no chance. Never again. For the rest of my life, I'll only catch fleeting glimpses of the Earth whizzing past our station 384,000 kilometers away. And that will make me nauseous.

The only other images projected in my room are two calendars on the wall directly beside me. One from Earth that my mother prefers because she still likes knowing the date down there. The months each have names and distinct personalities according to her. January was barren. February dour. March had hope. April was volatile. May optimistic. June was sunny. July hot. August unbearable. The other is the thirteen-month fixed calendar we use on MUSC. The months proceed in numerical order. Each month has twenty-eight days divided into four seven-day weeks. Like the weather here, the days are perpetually the same. The only anomalies are the month of Sol, which falls between months six and seven, and the two extra Leap Days scheduled in to make up for lost time. Methodically, I've color-blocked in the days as they've passed. A countdown until I would leave. Leap Day of MUSC Year 94. June 18 on Earth. Less than ten hours away.

When I see those dates, so anticipated for so long, I'm overwhelmed with a wave of sadness. It sucks at me and carries me away. I take my device off and stash it beneath my pillow as I close my eyes and drift toward an abyss of sorrow. At least if I'm asleep, I can't cry anymore.

I FOLLOW CASTOR up to the edge of the bush and peek through the branches at the line of AlphaZonian CelebriStreamers snaking from their AutoPods to the Palace portico, PESTs swarming around their heads. As with all of these events, a high-intensity viewing ensemble of Wastelanders hired for the day to act like fans adds frenzy to the air. The Yoobies strut through the HIVE, waving and blowing kisses, live-streaming every minute of their lives.

"I can't believe any of these dumdums have followers on their Streams," I say.

"Why wouldn't they?" says Castor. "One Yoobie's reality is everybody else's entertainment."

"This is all so stupid. Why does D'Cart even have these parties? I thought the whole point of having a TouchyFeelyTech brain implant is that you didn't have to go anywhere to have an experience. Can't they all just stay home and feel everything their beloved D'Cart feels?"

"They might be tech enabled, but they're still human enough to be social creatures," says Castor. "They want to be together. But also," he says in his explainy voice, "Yoobies like to flaunt that only they can afford the TFT chips. *I buy, therefore I am.*"

"As if consuming confirms their existence," I say with a sneer.

"Yep," says Castor. "And everybody else in the world who wants to live the Yoobie life but can't afford it watches their favorite Streamers endorse their favorite D'Cart products."

"Why live your own life, when you can live vicariously through someone else?"

"Do you know what the real beauty and brilliance of this system is?" Castor asks me.

"The real question is, do I care?" I say, but my brother ignores me and keeps talking.

"D'Cart makes a product. Yoobies endorse that product. Streamers buy that product, and the money goes into the bank of D'Cart then gets redistributed as a universal basic income to the Yoobies. It's a closed circle of profit with D'Cart at the center and the Yoobies orbiting around the edges."

"While the rest of us rot in the void beyond," I add.

"Except for me," he says. "I intend to get a cut one way or another."

"Hmph" is all I can say. "No one in that line deserves to be here. Their only achievement is being born into families that bought into this city a long time ago and still have the money to live here."

"No shit, Talitha," says Castor, looking me in the eye. "And nobody's going to open the door for us, which is why we have to find a way through. So . . . are you coming or not?"

"I'm coming," I grumble. But, just as we're about to step out of the bushes, I grab Castor's arm and yank him back. "Oh, no! It's Mundie."

I point across the lawn to the lanky guy slouched by a side entrance of the Palace. Mundie is unmistakable. He's all legs, like a large wading bird, with spiky dark hair tinted silver on the ends. His face is so chiseled you could sharpen a blade against his cheekbones or open a bottle with his beaky nose. But he's one of us. An urchin from the

Wastelands originally. Though, unlike us, he's legit. He came in as a ReConstruction worker and got in good with D'Cart when he repaired her broken ConstructiBots on the fly. Since then, he's risen up the ranks to chief robot repairer at the Palace.

"We can't go in." I back away. "If Mundie sees us, he'll know we don't belong."

"No, no, wait a sec." Castor holds up a finger. "This could work in our favor. He'd never rat you out."

My cheeks flare up bright red. The last time I saw Mundie, Castor and I had just come home from scavenging at a Yoobie beach barbecue. Mundie was waiting in our driveway. When I stepped out of our hijacked AutoPod in a gauzy cover-up over a black bikini, he grabbed my arm and said, *I almost didn't recognize you, Tal.* He looked me up and down. His leer felt like a small assault. *You should dress like that more often. You look good.*

I yanked my arm away. *It's none of your business how I look.*

It was a compliment, he called after me. *Most girls like compliments.*

I'm not most girls, I told him, and went inside to change my clothes.

"I don't want him thinking there's a chance of something between us," I tell Castor.

"Who cares what he thinks?" Castor shoots back.

"I care," I say. "You don't have to put up with him ogling you." I shudder. More than once I've had to duck away from Mundie's face looming up next to mine, as if he thinks I'm going to let him kiss me. I've told him flat out more than once that I don't like guys, but each time he says, *Yet.* Even now the memories make my stomach churn and my face burn with anger.

"Anyway, there's nothing to worry about," says Castor as Mundie goes inside the Palace. "He mostly works behind the scenes. I doubt they let him mingle with the guests. He probably won't even see us. But if he does—"

"I'm not asking him for any favors," I say.

"You won't have to. That's the beauty of him having a crush on you. All you have to do is flirt a little. Make him think you're into him."

"But I'm not," I say. "I can't pretend I am. You know I'm a terrible liar."

Castor looks at me and laughs. "No you're not, Talitha. You're an excellent liar. Always have been. Now, let's go."

I huff, frustrated by the position Castor has put me in, yet again. But I know what I have to do if we're going to make some money. I step through the bushes after my brother. As always, Quasar scampers after us.

"No, no." I stop and pat his head. "No dogs allowed. You have to stay here."

Quasar sighs, clearly irked, but turns away, looking over his shoulder as if hurt, then he ambles off to curl up next to Castor's red knapsack beneath the bushes as we head for the Palace.

UMA JEMISON

MOON UTILITARIAN SURVIVAL COLONY

"OOM. UMA. PSST. Wake up!" Something small pelts my face. I swat the thing away. "Come on." Another pellet tags my cheek.

"What in the name of Jupiter!" I sit up, tossing away the covers, and peer angrily over the side of my sleeping berth.

Kepler stands in my doorway, grinning. His head nearly touches the top, and his shoulders fill the frame.

"What are you doing?" I demand, and look around confused. "What time is it?"

"A) Throwing Earth candy at you." He lobs a small blue disk at me. Then a red one. "These are called M&M's. Gemini's dad snuck them back from Earth that last time he went down for business. You should try one. They're delicious. And B) It's almost Leap Day! You slept through dinner. Get up. Let's celebrate. Your Shuttle leaves in an hour." He walks into the common area saying, "I sent you, like, a thousand thotz, but you didn't answer."

I slide my hand under my pillow and pull out my device. His messages flash on my Lenz. "Sorry," I call after him, then I drag myself down my sleeping berth ladder, pulling my Earth blanket along behind me like a tail.

"Were you even going to say good-bye?" Kep asks when I trudge after him. He plops down on the sofa and commands our hacked satellite connection to appear on the wall screen. "And why didn't you come back to the lab? Deimos was pissed." He chomps handfuls of the contraband candy as he scans muted Streams from Earth.

Part of me wants to collapse onto the floor and sob, but I don't. Kep is sweeter than most MUSCies, but tears still freak him out. So instead, I stand in the center of the room, wrapped in my blanket like a cocooned caterpillar, with a single fat tear trailing down my cheek.

He looks up at me and frowns. "Are you . . . ?" He leans forward, elbows on knees, to peer more closely at my face. Then he sits back, mortified. "Crying?"

"No." I swat at the tear.

"Yes, you are," he says. I can hear the near panic in his voice. "Are those tears of joy? I thought you'd be excited! You're going back to Earth. This is all you've talked about since I met you."

I suck in a ragged breath, then blurt it out. "Dr. Fornax canceled my trip!"

Kep's jaw drops. "She did? When?"

"Today." I sniff and manage to keep myself together.

"The day before Leap Day? The day you're supposed to leave?"

I nod again, but my stomach knots up and my chest tightens at the thought of spending the entire month of Sol up here and never seeing the Earth in person again.

"Because you ran out of the lab today?" he asks.

"No," I say, and drop down next to him on the sofa. "That had nothing to do with it. She thinks if I go to Earth, I won't come back."

"Ohhhh," he says with a grimace. Then his eyes widen. "Did Micra rat you out for saying you might stay there?"

I shrug.

"Did you mean it?"

"I don't know," I admit. We sit quietly side by side as the muted Streams go by.

"I can't believe she did this to you," he says. "That's harsh. Even for Fornax. It's, like, no-atmosphere harsh. That's, like, sucked-into-a-black-hole-and-spaghettized harsh."

"Yeah, it blows meteorite chunks." I curl up in a ball with my head by his knee. "Now I'm stuck here."

"Cheer up," he says. "If you were going to AlphaZonia, you'd have to contend with people like them." He points to a barrage of Celebri-Streamer on the wall.

"Turn on sound," I command, because if nothing else, at least I can get lost in the absurdity of Earth.

"Elysium Phantastic's Hair Today Give Away!" says a perky Earthling with a ponytail so long and thick it looks like a tree branch growing from her head. "Check out my DIY vid *Transforming Tresses: From Forgettable to Fabulous in 4 Easy Steps* with RayNay DeShoppingCart's Stressless Tresses product line of shampoo, root cream, gel, finishing crème, and nourishmante!"

"Next," I say.

"Hoity Toity Cherry Pie Smackerooni Lip Glaze by RayNay De-ShoppingCart!" giant lips yell at us. The camera zooms out so we see a face, purple eyes, green-tinged skin, and those big pink lips. "Lips so luscious, you'll want to eat them!"

"Next," says Kep.

"Prunella McAllister-Gopti here. PruGop for short! Check out my vids! RayNay DeShoppingCart products galore! Pranks, yanks, and skanks are my specialty." PruGop strikes a sexy baby pose, one hip out, boobs pressed forward, knees turned in.

"No thank you! Next," I say.

"It's a MegaHaul of RayNay DeShoppingCart's finest pet products hand-picked for the pooch of your dreams," yells a short guy in a furry shirt surrounded by yapping dogs. "How about a BakonTastic-BubbleBlower? Or SweetSpot Anal Covers for your furry friends!"

"These people are the single most convincing argument against the existence of intelligent life-forms on Earth," Kepler says as we skate past more Streams, each AlphaZonian citizen hawking RayNay DeShoppingCart products more useless than the next.

"Go to the main Stream," I beg. "I want to see RayNay DeShoppingCart."

"The high priestess of product placement?" Kep asks.

"CelebriStreamer ExtraOrdinaire."

"CEO of AlphaZonia!" we both say together when he lands on the queen herself.

RayNay DeShoppingCart stands on an Earth beach, enhanced no doubt to make the sands whiter, the sky bluer, and the ocean behind her clean and jewel-toned. Just like the place I swim in my dreams, which is no more real than her augmented reality on our wall screen. She is oddly ageless in that way AlphaZonians are. Smooth, bronzed skin polished with a strange luminescent glow—not the way skin should really look but weirdly attractive. Her eyes are bright blue today, although they change every time we see her. Her hair falls in soft burnished ringlets over her shoulders. Though sometimes it's short, other times long and wavy, and changes colors as quick as a chameleon.

"Hello, my LUVs. My shining stars," she says, and reaches up to pluck a virtual star from the fake pink sky. She holds the star on her palm, then blows it into glittery holo dust. Kep and I instinctively duck as the nonexistent sparkles rain down inside the room, then disappear.

"Every one of you is a perfect individual in the infinity of this vast universe," she tells us. "And to each of you, I say hello!"

I'm so drawn in by her that I raise my hand and say, "Hello!" as if I'm waving to someone I'll see soon, then my world folds in on itself again when I remember—I'm not going anywhere.

"If I know you, and I do," D'Cart tells us, and all her millions of followers tuned in around the Earth, "then I know that you need the newest DeShoppingCart HoverTread & Foot Spa!"

"That's exactly what I need," Kep says.

"I consume, therefore I am!" I say, and we both crack up at the silly AlphaZonia motto.

"It's a revolution in exercise and beauty," she tells us. "Step into our luxurious XeroGrav slippers to glide your way toward a healthy body and pretty toes." We watch her swan around an airy white room while balanced in glowing blue booties. "My patented technology sloughs off dead skin, trims corns and nails, removes unwanted toe hair, and leaves you with ten gorgeous digits." She sits beside a pool now, oohing and ahhhing over her own feet. "Now TouchyFeelyTech enabled!" She dips her toes into the water. "Aaaaah! Can you feel that?" she asks. "Order yours today."

Kep mutes the sounds. "How on Earth is it possible," he asks, "that someone as vapid as this woman can own an entire city where everyone who lives there single-mindedly tries to sell her products to other people in the world?"

"She's not as dumb as you think," I point out. "She invented TouchyFeelyTech."

"Which is super creepy." Kepler gets up and walks into the kitchen area to rummage through our food storage. He pulls out a bag of dehydra fries and shoves handfuls into his mouth. "Is life on Earth so terrible that most people want to live vicariously through one person's visceral experiences instead of having their own?"

"Um, duh," I say.

"Then why," he asks, bag paused halfway to his mouth, "were you so intent on going back?" He lifts the bag and tilts the rest of the crispy fries straight into his gullet.

"It wasn't because of her!" I glance at the screen again. Now D'Cart runs through a green grassy meadow with butterflies and birds darting around her head. Although I know what I'm seeing on the screen is not the reality on Earth, there is part of my brain that still believes it might be possible.

"Then what is it?" he asks.

"I think . . ." I struggle to find the right way to say it. "I just want to know for sure that MUSC is where I want to be for the rest of my life before I accept my LWA."

"But what if you went to Earth and you loved it and you didn't want to come back?" He brushes crumbs from his shirt, then stuffs the bag into our compactor. "Wouldn't that be worse? Then you'd have to stay down there, which would force your mom to go back. Or you'd have to return to MUSC and know for sure you didn't want to be here."

"But that wouldn't happen, right?"

Before he answers, Darshan blinks on my Lenz and says, *You have received a time-delayed holo message from your mother.*

"What? How did I miss her?" I grouse.

"Sun flares," Kepler says. "They're bad today."

"Project and play," I tell Darshan.

A shimmery image of my mother stands in the center of the room. She's in her mining gear, and, as usual, she looks exhausted. Trouble-shooting and repairing the helium-mining robots down on the Moon's surface for twelve hours a day is a brutal job. Most mine workers live down there, too, in the original Moon Utilitarian Survival Colony tunnels, but we're lucky. My parents got to live in the Sky Domicile with me.

"Oh, Uma!" Mom says. "I'm so sorry I missed you earlier. I'm deep in the mines all day with an emergency repair. Now there are solar flares, and my pings won't go through. And worst of all, I have to work overnight!" I hear anguish in her voice. "Myra El Saud is sick and had to be evacuated to triage, so I won't be there to say good-bye before your trip."

Her voice catches, and I see her eyes go moist. Like mother, like daughter. Our Earthly emotions always writ large on our expressive faces.

"Listen to me," she says and composes herself. "Don't do anything reckless on Earth. Stay safe. And come back to me. I will miss you so much, my love. So very much." She leans forward and presses her lips to her Cam before her image blinks off.

"Guess she doesn't know your trip is canceled," Kep says.

"Guess not," I say with a sigh. "But she won't be disappointed. She didn't want me to go in the first place."

"So . . . maybe it's good you're not going."

"No!" I whine. "I wanted to see everything one last time. Flowers and trees and the ocean and . . . and . . . and dogs!" I point up at a photo of my father with Mahati.

Kepler stands over me, shaking his head, hands on hips. "We're going to have to cheer you up. Get your mind off this whole not-going-to-Earth thing."

"I don't want to cheer up." I hunker down in my blanket even more. "I want to mope right here on this sofa for the next twenty-eight days."

"That's literally the worst plan I've ever heard." He reaches down and grabs my hands. I keep my arms loose and floppy. "Let's go." He pulls.

I refuse to get up.

"Come on." He yanks a bit harder, which forces me to a sit.

"Where?" I whine.

"You'll see!" he says, and gives one last heroic tug that pulls me to my feet.

"Fine," I grumble, and drop the blanket. "But this better be good!"

CASTOR NEVA

ALPHAZONIA, EARTH

TALITHA AND I slide into the back of the line of Yoobies snaking through the cheering HIVE toward the Pink Palace entrance. I can feel my sister's perpetual nervousness radiating from her like beta waves. She sees this kind of thing as a threat to our safety, while I take it as a challenge.

I keep my chin up and eyes forward, mimicking the haughty confidence of a CelebriStreamer while Talitha minces along beside me, probably worried we'll be spotted by someone from the Wastelands who's in the hired cheering crowd, but no one seems to notice us. That doesn't surprise me. We look the part in our Yoobie clothes with Talitha's PEST flittering around our faces.

One by one, each invitee steps up to the door. I'm buzzing with excitement. I know the data packet is going to work, thanks to Cristela Wong Holtzmann dancing under the stars down at the Basin. I've been following her Stream for months, waiting for the perfect intersection of a Pink Palace party on a night she wanted a DopaHack. Tonight, the planets aligned.

As we get closer, Talitha's anxiety rises. "What if—" she whispers in my ear.

"No *what if*s," I say through a big fake smile.

The people directly in front of us step up and wait for their TFT chips to connect to the security system. To ensure Talitha doesn't bolt, I wrap my fingers around her upper arm and squeeze. The extruded black plastic of her jumpsuit is warm from the heat rising off her body. The couple in front of us is recognized by the system, and the door slides open, granting them entry into the Palace.

"We're up!" I announce, and steer my sister forward. "Don't freak out."

As always, Talitha comes through. She's brilliant at this kind of thing, but needs a little push. Now she turns on her best Yoobie impersonation—shoulders back, head up as we surge ahead through the gauntlet of the HIVE. They hoot and holler, whistle and clap while we wave and blow kisses, pretending to narrate our own existence even though we're not yet Streaming. And then, in less than two seconds, it's all over. The data I hijacked from the Yoobie girl's TFT chip connects exactly as I knew it would. We hear the ding, the doors *wheesh* open, and we strut through to the rhythm of the D'Cart anthem playing in our HearEars.

"Don't gawk," I hiss at Talitha as we follow the others through the plush lobby. My sister's eyes are wide with wonder, and who can blame her. The interior of the palace is unbelievably decadent, with its pillars and columns. We pass deep, soft settees and elegant armchairs with polished end tables nearly toppling over from the enormous bouquets of roses balanced on them. Everything, from the coral-colored marble floor under our feet to the glimmering rose glass chandeliers over our heads is a shade of pink, from the softest interior of a swirling shell to the deepest red of Mars. Once through the lobby, we pass through another set of doors to a courtyard where the elite of TFT CelebriStreamers circulate among the grassy hills and leveled terraces of the Pink Palace grounds.

We stay on the outskirts of the crowd, hidden in the shadow of the towering pink building. "Come on," I tell Talitha, and pull her along the banks of a small precisely crafted stream that meanders past flowing fountains and full-blossoming bushes so I can get the lay of the land. We pass a small waterfall that burbles into a lily pond where gold, orange, and white koi fish swim. The stream goes on for another few hundred yards and flows out through a grate in the security wall.

"Remember all the times we hauled stolen water from the reservoir so Mom could wash clothes or cook?" Talitha asks.

"That's why I built her an irrigation system, duh," I say as I scan the area for Streaming opportunities. Across the lawn, I spot an enormous swimming pool. "There!" I say. "Let's go."

"Doesn't it kind of burn your ass that these people have enough to spare for all these stupid ponds full of flowers and fish or that ridiculous swimming pool, when we worked so hard for every drop we got in the Wastelands?"

"Wait!" I stop and jerk my head to look at her. "Are you telling me that life isn't fair? That people in this privatized city have more than their share of resources and don't give two shits about the rest us except to use us to fight their wars with Merica over fresh water?" I smack my forehead. "This is a complete and total shock to me." I press my hand over my chest and pretend to keel over. "I might have a heart attack."

"Shut up," she says. "You're a *shalose*."

"Yes, I am. But think about it. By being here, we're evening things out a little bit. Taking something for ourselves because, as you so eloquently pointed out, Life Ain't Fair, and we got the raw end of the deal. The question is, what are we going to do about it?"

Talitha rolls her eyes at me, but as usual, she gives in. "Fine, but let's get this over with and get the hell out of here. I'm jumping out of my skin."

I lead the way to the pool's edge. "Your PEST is going live in ten seconds," I tell her, then step away as I blink to switch my iEye to Streaming mode. She takes a deep breath and shifts her body from a slouching, insecure Wastelander into her bubbly party-girl parody persona. I don't know how she does it. It's almost as if she shifts her center of gravity upward and unhinges her shoulders and hips. She's looser, more graceful, and infinitely more fun when she becomes her alter ego, NayRay DeDumpingCart.

I give her a slight nod. She launches her PEST. My left iEye dilates to black so I can watch her Stream. On my TouchCuff, I open up my hacking page.

"Hey, guys! It's me," she squees in her best CelebriStream imitation. "Tonight we're at an exclusive event in the fabled Pink Palace! How much do you love this new Kinematic Jumpsuit I've got on?" She spins, strikes a pose, does a little dance to the tune on our HearEars that I've diverted to our Stream so our followers can feel like they're here, too. "Looks like every lovely lady is wearing one tonight!"

She flicks the PEST several inches back to widen the shot so our followers can see her standing in a sea of tessellated-triangle-clad Yoobies mingling by the pool. Then I start my real job of the night—hijacking product links for the jumpsuits from D'Cart's virtual warehouse while Talitha talks up the sales. It's not hard, but I have to work fast. I've already created a backdoor in D'Cart's site so I can slip in and divert our followers' click-thrus to a mirror landing page.

"This jumpsuit is super comfy!" Talitha lies. "It moves with you as you move because it's printed to your exact measurements. Click the link to order now!"

On my cuff screen, I watch as orders roll in and payments are processed. Talitha knows the game—she has to keep talking until the program I created can make the money trail disappear but keep the orders in the D'Cart queue so they're filled. Everything seems to be going smoothly, so I scan the area for other D'Cart products we can hijack.

I spot the perfect setup on the pool deck. *FlipChairs, behind you,* I text to Talitha's iEye lens. She sees the message and nods.

She turns and gasps. "Oh, look at this!" She rushes over to a row of empty deck chairs. "D'Cart's Foldable FlipChair Deluxe Model 6 with built-in sunbrellas, moonbeam collectors, cup holders, water vapor fan, and decorative solar lights." She plops down, crosses her legs, and sighs as if she's in heaven. The PEST zooms in close. "Don't you just love it? Foldable FlipChair, a chair other chairs want to sit in!"

I embed a link, and orders for the chairs pour in. Our followers might love it when Talitha makes fun of D'Cart, but they want the products just the same as everybody else who streams.

Then Talitha's up again. "Hey, look! Here's something fun!" She points to a couple of CelebriStreamers at the far end of the deck, and I know she's hit a jackpot. "It's everybody's fave TFTers—Lil Cutie Wootie and her pal Squeegee Bop!"

The PEST pans over to this week's "It" girl of the D'Cart Touchy-FeelyTech world. She's a few years older than we are, with skin the color of a goldfish and hair dyed two-tone pink. Her enormously long false eyelashes graze her cheeks when she blinks. At the mention of Lil Cutie Wootie, more followers jump into our Stream to get a look. I use my TouchCuff to augment Cutie Wootie with a pink tutu, piggy nose, and pointy ears, then I add little piglet angels circling her head. I augment Squeegee Bop with rainbows farting from his butt in rhythm to the music on the Stream. In a stroke of luck, Lil Cutie Wootie calls out her massively popular catchphrase of the week, "Well, slap my ass and call me Jimmy, I'm happy as poop on a stick!"

Within seconds, the rivulet I created has caught on. An InstaMeme is born. Our NayRay parody Stream is inundated with followers farting rainbows and dancing like little pigs while clicking on our stolen product links. I'm so caught up in keeping everything moving smoothly that I don't notice what's happening until Talitha grabs my arm.

Over the piercing noise of a siren, she shouts, "Run! We're busted!"

UMA JEMISON

MOON UTILITARIAN
SURVIVAL COLONY

INSIDE A TRAVELATOR capsule with Kepler, I brace myself against the wall. As soon as we start to move inward on the station, I'm woozy. The Coriolis effect is exponentially worse for me since my Earthling inner ears aren't finely tuned to the changes of induced gravity on MUSC.

When we stop, my feet begin to lift. "Whoa, whoa, whoa!" I grapple for something to hang on to, swallowing down the sick feeling in the pit of my stomach.

"Ready?" Kepler says. Then the airlock hisses open and the capsule doors slide apart. My whole body rises, but I grip the side of the capsule to keep myself from floating into the large open space in front of us.

"We're in the core!" I yell.

"I know!" Kepler shouts, and tumbles past me into the gravity-less space of the stationary center on our ever-rotating station.

"How do you have the code to get in here?" I ask, still clinging to the wall like a bug because I'm too scared to let go.

"I'm very tricky," he says, and zooms by me in midair.

"You stole it from your mom, didn't you?"

"Yep! Watch this!" He runs up a wall, over my head, and turns slow somersaults in midair. "Come on! Give it a try." He tugs on my legs.

"Noooooo!" I yell, but my grip loosens, and I float into the center of the room. Underneath the floor far below us, the core continues down to the base of the station. Most of that space is taken up with storage and machinery, but here in the emptiness, MUSCie kids can come to play. Once I'm airborne, I start to relax. "I haven't been here for years."

"Didn't every kid in our cohort have a birthday party here when we turned ten?"

"Not me!"

"Where was yours?"

I turn over and stare up at Kep. "I didn't have a party that year," I remind him.

He thinks back and then visibly reddens. "Sorry," he says. "That's the year your father died."

I nod.

"I'm sorry I forgot, Oom."

"That's all right," I tell him, shutting down the conversation, because it's not one I want to have. "It was a long time ago to remember."

"Come up here, to the top!" he calls.

"Why?"

"Just come on!" he insists. "You're going to like this."

I swim after him, kicking my legs and paddling my arms as if I'm in water. When I reach him, I see we are hovering beneath one big round window at the very top of the MUSC core—the only place here that looks out into the universe but doesn't spin.

"No way," I say as I press my hands against the window to shade my eyes so I can see outside better. Kepler does the same. From this vantage point, the sky is still, and I feel at ease. Pinpricks of stars populate the perpetual night instead of speeding past in a blur. In the distance a blue and white hump hangs in space—the Earth in half shadow rising over the lunar horizon.

I push off the window and float aimlessly, not wanting to look at the place where I'm not going.

Kep swims toward me. "Why don't you come down to the surface with me? There's a bunch of people going. Gemini and Fermi and Cassio. We leave tomorrow night."

"No thanks," I say.

"We can ditch the others and have fun," he offers. "Or just hang out with Gemini. He's not so bad. Kind of fun, once you get to know him."

I shake my head.

"You have to do something during Sol."

"Why?" I ask, feeling hopeless as I float. "No matter what, in twenty-eight days, I'm going to get my LWA and then life is over."

We start to drift apart, so Kep reaches for my hand. "Maybe we'll end up in the same lab." He squeezes my fingers. "We're both really good at immunology, so—"

"Yeah, maybe." I squeeze back.

My feelings for Kepler have always been difficult to grasp or explain. Most of the time, he's my best friend, plain and simple. More of a brother. But then there are moments like this when I think he might want more than friendship. When his emotions seem to morph into something stronger than I feel. I try to imagine whether my usual urge to punch him playfully or say something stupid to make him laugh could shift to wanting to hug him tight or press my mouth against his, but that thought makes my stomach churn with uncertainty. I'm not sure why. Maybe because we're so close.

We kissed once. Two years ago. It was unexpected and strange. It was late at night. We were both punchy from studying but too revved up to go to bed, so we turned on an old 2-D Earth movie about a boy and girl. She had a lung disease. He had cancer. One of them was going to die. I got caught up in the emotion of that story, and it must have affected Kepler the same way, because even though people here consider it a weakness to be swayed by art (no tears for beautiful sonatas, no swooning over the strokes of a master's brush), before we knew it, our mouths were pressed together, our tongues doing some kind of strange tango, as if we needed to experience for ourselves what we were seeing on the screen.

Only, for me, it wasn't what I had imagined when I watched the boy and dying girl in the movie because, as usual, the person I wanted most to kiss was the girl, not Kepler. I've tried to be more like the others here. To them, gender is no issue. You like who you like, plain and simple. But I'm different. I've only ever had crushes on girls. That night with Kep, I pulled away from our kiss and wiped my mouth, laughing nervously, barely able to look at him. We never talked about it again.

My palm begins to sweat in his, and my heart gets fluttery. We've drifted farther apart, our arms outstretched between our floating bodies, fingers still loosely entwined. As close as I feel to Kepler, sometimes I wonder if we'll always be tidally locked, like the Earth and Moon, at a safe distance and only able to see one side of each other.

Slowly, I turn my head to face him. I want to say something. Something meaningful and kind. I want him to know how important his friendship has been to me. How I could have never survived my childhood on MUSC without him. How although I'm so sad that I'm not going back to Earth, it'll be okay because he'll be here. But, before I can find a way to say any of this, Kep's cyber assistant, Mazie, projects and says, "Happy Leap Day, Kepler! You have five parties to attend."

We both startle and move apart.

"Woohoo! Must be midnight. Let the parties begin!" Kep turns a somersault. "Want to come with me?"

"No," I say way too quickly.

"Come on, Oom. Everybody is going. It's what you do right before you leave for Sol."

"No, it's what *you* and all the other Third Gens do. I was supposed to be on a flight about now, remember? I scheduled it that way on purpose."

A harsh buzzer sounds outside the core and startles both of us.

"What was that?" I ask.

"I don't know." Kepler grabs my hand, but this time his grip is tense and tight. "But I don't want to find out. Let's get the hell out of here!"

CASTOR NEVA

ALPHAZONIA, EARTH

TALITHA AND I clutch each other as the siren blares. I take off toward the wall. She runs for the Palace. We pull apart, then collide like two protons. The rhythmic thrum of tiny 'copter blades drowns out the music in our ears. We both know it's too late to run, so my sister and I cower as a fleet of drones darkens the sky.

"I told you!" she yells.

"I'm sorry!" I yell back, still looking for a way to escape.

Then I notice that all around us the Yoobies jump in time to the music and reach up to the sky. They aren't concerned that something's wrong. They're excited for what's coming.

"Now, hear this!" a voice booms over a driving beat of music. *Un-chh, un-chh, un-chh, un-chh.* I look up, trying to understand what's going on.

The cyber voice answers my question. *It's a VirtuProduct Drop!* the voice announces.

The Yoobies scream with delight and begin to chant, "Things make us happy! Things make us happy! Things make us happy!"

"Oh, my god!" I double over, laughing. "I thought we were goners!"

"That scared me half to death," Talitha yells, and bangs on my back with her fists.

From the sky, glittering, glowing D'Cart product holos rain down on the crowd. Individually wrapped Strawberry ScrumCrumpets. Pappy's Pineapple Papaya Elixir. Lightening Smile Teeth Whitening Wands. Diamond-Tipped ExfoliLasers. Torso Toner Compression T-shirts. Dragonfly Drones. Neat Meat Multi-Use Eating Tools.

All around us, a scrum of bodies swipe at the air with their cuffs. They throw elbows, flail wildly, and stomp on one another's toes to fill their VirtuCarts with as many falling hologram products as they can.

"Go! Go! Go!" I shout.

Talitha understands. She catches her breath, relaunches her PEST, and starts grabbing at the holos with her TouchCuff, while I work like crazy to embed links and sell the loot as quick as she can grab it.

When the last of the VirtuProds are gone, the crowd disperses, chattering away to their followers, and the voice announces, *And now . . . It's the moment you've been waiting for! The highlight of the night! The stuff dreams are made of!*

An eerie hush falls over the grounds as all the Yoobies stop in their tracks.

Please welcome, live and in person, the High Priestess of Product Placement, CelebriStreamer ExtraOrdinairre, Inventor of TouchyFeelyTech, and AlphaZonia CEO, the Queen herself . . .

Two spotlights from the drones sweep across the great lawn. As if in slow motion, every person and their PEST on the lawn turns to face a twenty-foot hologram of bikini-clad D'Cart stepping out onto a second-floor balcony of the Palace overlooking the far end of the glimmering swimming pool.

Then the voice shouts, *RayNay DeShoppingCart!* and her name reverberates through the air.

Yoobies rush past us to get closer to their leader, but Talitha and I stay put. My sister shakes her head wearily. I can see exhaustion settle over her as she slouches back into her fretful self. She stows her PEST and says, "Now can we get out of here?"

"No way," I tell her. "D'Cart is here IRL. We have to give this to our followers!"

"Castor, no," she hisses.

"If you won't do it, I will!" I slip away and run up a small hill to get a better shot with my iEye. In my HearEar, the music swells—all strings and woodwinds building up. The pool lights fade to pink as the spotlights from the drones swirl to the rhythm of the drums. The subtle aroma of jasmine fills the air.

D'Cart works the moment like a pro. Her giant holo blinks—eyes as wide as windows. Lashes long as arms. She looks left, then makes an O with her mouth as if she's really seeing all of her followers down below.

"Hello, my LUVs. My shining stars. Each and every one of you is as perfect an individual as a star up in the sky." I switch my iEye to the D'Cart stream and watch her reach up to pluck a virtual star from her augmented reality. She blows it into glittery holo dust over everyone's heads. Then she licks her unnaturally plump lips covered in trademark pink candy gloss as she smiles to reveal white teeth straight as a wall.

D'Cart laughs, bubbly. Tosses back her hair—smooth as paper, colored caramel with streaks of blond and strands of red today. "Are you ready?" she asks her followers. They scream for more. "Then let's go! Dive in, everyone. Dive in!"

I look past my iEye and see the real D'Cart in the flesh standing on the balcony. She runs on tiptoes toward the edge, then lifts off in a perfect swan. Her twenty-foot hologram image soars over the Yoobie crowd. They reach up as if to touch their CEO hero, then *SPLASH!* The crowd gasps as the real D'Cart hits the crystalline water below. All the TFT-chippers reflexively wipe their hands across their dry faces, pushing nonexistent water droplets away because they feel every sensation that D'Cart feels.

When she emerges, mermaid-like, out of the water to settle on folded arms at the pool's edge, she asks her TFT followers, "Aaaah! Can you feel the cool water against your skin? Smell the freshness of this glorious night?"

"Yes we can!" her followers shout in unison.

In one easy movement, she pushes out of the pool and walks over to a single crystalline bottle of D'Cart VitaJuv Lapis Lazuli Gem Water perfectly positioned on a poolside table close to where Talitha stands. My sister shrinks back, looking for a place to hide. At that exact moment, on D'Cart Streams all over the world, the image of that bottle fills people's minds. Shining beads of water, blue as the pool, roll down the frosty glass. I watch in real time as D'Cart lifts it to her lips, tosses her head so her hair drips down her back, and takes a long, sultry draft.

"Aaaaah! Can you taste that cool, refreshing water?" she asks her followers. "Feel the vitamins and minerals coursing through your veins, revitalizing your internal organs? Mmmmmm. Delicious, right?" She pauses for her followers to swallow as their TFT chips process the taste she tastes and feel the sensation of the water down their dry throats. She raises the bottle as if in a toast. "Get yours today!"

All around us, DomestiBots fill the courtyard with trays of the VitaJuv Lapis Lazuli Gem Waters. The Yoobies converge. Each grabs a bottle, pops it open, and yammers away to their followers, hoping to get more product click-thrus to supplement their incomes. Just as I'm about to go, I see D'Cart hesitate on the pool deck. I could swear she catches sight of my sister half cowering in the shadows. A chill goes through my body, but then D'Cart turns away. There's no way she saw. Or if she did, she'd think Talitha was just another TFTer from the city.

I turn away and head toward a knot of people to claim a bottle of the Gem Water, then I hear my name. I spin in a circle. Out of the corner of my eye, I see a tussle. The crowd behind me parts, and two red SecuriBots roll up the grassy hill. Without thinking, I dodge one and shoulder slam the other, knocking it off balance. Before it rights itself, I take off in the opposite direction toward Talitha by the pool.

"Castor!" she shouts, and like an idiot, she runs toward me, rather than away.

"No!" I scream, and motion at the small river running toward the wall. "Go! Go!" But Talitha's too caught up in saving me to turn around and run for the only exit. The SecuriBot I knocked down is up again and cuts on the diagonal toward Talitha. The other shoots out a thin steel cable that hooks onto my wrist. Pain shoots up my arm as it spins me, reeling me in until I'm wrapped tightly with my arms pinned against my torso, like a fly caught in spider silk. I struggle, but I know I'm not going anywhere.

"Watch out!" I scream at my sister. "Go back!" Before she can turn around, the other SecuriBot shoots out a metal tentacle that attaches to her ankle. Talitha falls face-first into the soft grass.

"Help!" she squeaks as she's dragged backward, fingers clawing at the perfect lawn. The SecuriBot picks her up. Every Yoobie has stopped to gawk at our capture. I wrench around, trying to hide my face, then I catch sight of Mundie, standing stricken in the pale light of the pool deck. He starts to run toward my sister, but then stops short, chest heaving and hands in fists at his sides. He remains there, motionless, face slack, as if he doesn't care that red SecuriBots are carrying us away.

"Coward," I hiss at him, but he doesn't hear.

Talitha calls out for me, her voice high-pitched, desperate, and alone.

"I'm here!" I shout as the robots wheel us through a large door into the Pink Palace.

UMA JEMISON

MOON UTILITARIAN
SURVIVAL COLONY

KEP AND I swim back toward the airlock on the wall. My heart races—I'm certain we'll be busted for breaking and entering the core. If Fornax didn't already think I was a miscreant, this will surely seal the deal. When the door whooshes open, we pull ourselves inside and hover over the floor, shoulders bumping, while the airlock reengages. Our feet hit the floor, and to our surprise, the small room we're inside zips forward, carrying us away from the center. I startle and grab for something to keep me steady.

"This isn't the direction we came from," says Kep.

The ride is quick, and the gravity comes back fast. I'm nauseated when the doors on the opposite side of the capsule open, but I swallow it down as I peer into a small room that's vaguely familiar.

"We must have gotten turned around and come out the other side," says Kep. "Let's go back." He shrinks inside and commands the door to close, but I put my foot over the threshold to stop it.

"Wait," I say. "I think I know where we are."

"Wherever it is, we shouldn't be here."

"This is in the main Shuttle loading bay. But it's not how I remember it."

"Remember what?" Kepler says, one foot in the airlock and the other in the room.

"This is where the Shuttle docks," I whisper.

"Whoa," says Kepler. "I've never been in here."

"My family came through when I was little." I marvel at how small everything feels all these years later. "I don't remember much. I was half asleep when my dad carried me off the Shuttle. It seemed so much bigger and scarier then."

I leave the airlock and walk to a large rectangular window on the exterior wall. "There it is," I whisper as I gaze out at the Shuttle's nose, sleek and silver as a seal, docked on the port beside us. SCIENCE WILL SEE US THROUGH is written in bold script below the MUSC logo across the rear flank. I have to look away because the blur of stars and the Earth passing by makes my stomach lurch.

"I would have been boarding soon," I say with a sigh.

Kep stays at the window. "Look at that! He points to a robotic arm taking cargo from the Shuttle's belly into another open bay on our station. "A delivery! Wonder if there's anything good."

"Like a DeShoppingCart HoverTread & Foot Spa?" I joke.

"As if Dr. Fornax would ever let that on board!"

"I would have brought you one as a souvenir."

"Now I'm really sad your trip got canceled," Kepler says.

Once the cargo is removed, a buzzer sounds and the door on the other side of the bay *wheesh*es open. Kepler and I scramble back against the far wall as a group of people file into the room.

Passengers, please prepare for boarding, a cyber voice announces.

I brace myself for a First or Second Gen in the group to ask what we're doing here, but they're all so caught up in the Streams playing in their minds that they barely notice us.

Kepler grips my arm. *We have to get out of here* appears on my

Lenz. But I can't move. This was supposed to be my flight. I was supposed to board with these people. I watch each of them step through a scanner beam that confirms their identity, then they each remove one of the personalized blue and white flight suits hanging on hooks by the window.

Look. I point to a suit with my name and number embroidered across the front. Last month I was measured for the suit, which was made to fit me exactly.

You should take it, Kep thotz to me.

A souvenir of the trip I never took?

He nods.

As I move toward the suits, the cyber voice comes onto my Stream. *Welcome, Uma Jemison. Please step into the body scan and prepare for departure.*

I freeze.

What's wrong? Kep thotz.

I open my Stream to him. The message repeats. On my Lenz, I see that Darshan has connected to the system. *The system still thinks I'm on this Shuttle,* I thotz to Kep.

He snorts. *Hello, irony!*

I scan the flight info on my Lenz and my heart pounds.

Dr. Fornax didn't cancel my trip!

It takes a moment for my message to sink in. Kep looks at me. *But she told you not to go.*

But she didn't cancel it, I repeat, and a shiver crawls over my entire body as I realize what's happening.

His eyes cut toward the one remaining flight suit hanging on the peg.

Boarding will begin in thirty seconds, the cyber voice announces out loud. The others congregate next to the airlock where the Shuttle is docked.

I swallow hard. *What should I do?*

I don't know. I see the excitement and fear in Kepler's eyes and wonder if I look the same.

I think I should go.

Back to your domicile?

No, to Earth.

I take another step toward the suit. He bites his bottom lip.

The boarding door *wheesh*es open. The others make their way through the door one at a time.

Should I do it? I ask him. I bounce from foot to foot. Another passenger disappears into the belly of the Shuttle.

"Go!" Kep says out loud. The two remaining people glance at us but quickly lose interest.

I jump and grab the suit. Kep watches me, mouth hanging open as I whip off my blue and white tunic and step out of my blue pants, then shimmy the flight suit up over the silver antimicrobial long underwear we all wear. I wriggle my arms in, tucking down my undershirt, and zip up. My whole body shivers with anticipation.

What should I tell your mom? Or Deimos? Or Dr. Fornax?

I don't know! Any moment the doors will close and my chance to go will be over. *Don't tell them anything. Tell them you didn't know I left! Or tell them the truth. Tell them I went to Earth, but I'll be back.*

Promise?

He stands beside me then. The top of my head comes to the top of his shoulder—the perfect ratio for the best hugs. The last passenger marches through the door, which means if I want to go, I have just enough time to throw my arms around Kepler's shoulders. He slips his hands around my waist. I sink my cheek into the tender spot between his collarbone and chin. He lifts me up so my toes sweep the ground as if I'm floating again. The airlock door starts to *wheesh*. I wriggle free.

"I have to go!" I say out loud. I leap like a bug to kiss him on the cheek before I run for the closing door.

Once I'm through, for a few seconds, I am the only one between the station that has been my home for ten years and the Shuttle that will carry me back to my birthplace. I take a breath, debating whether I should turn back. But then the doors behind me close and the airlock ahead of me opens. I see inside the Shuttle where the other passengers are strapping into place. This is it. My only chance. Quickly, I step inside.

Please take your seat and engage restraint system, the cyber voice instructs me.

I do as I'm told with shaking hands. Surely some camera or human-recognition bot has caught my movements. Surely I'll be busted any moment. But I don't stop. Because maybe, just maybe, nobody will notice until it's too late. I sit, quaking in my harness, looking out the small circular window to my left. Kepler presses one hand against a docking bay window a few meters away. I place my hand against my Shuttle window as if reaching for him again. The countdown to launch begins, and my device pings.

I'm almost afraid to look at who it is. My mother? Deimos? Dr. Fornax calling me back? Darshan shimmers into view and says, *Kepler has sent you an audio message.*

Play, I command.

Over the whir of the robotic loading arms gently pushing us away from the dock, I hear a faint melody. From the window, the strip of darkness widens between our tiny ship and the MUSC station where Kepler watches me leave.

I hear the rockets rev and the loading arm engage, cocking back to fling us headlong into space when the station's rotation reaches the farthest point from the surface of the Moon. Any moment we'll be catapulted into a trajectory toward the Earth.

Just then, the melody of Kepler's audio message becomes clear. It's an old song, one that he loves because it appears in lots of the Earth movies we watch. Something about an astronaut named Major Tom. I can't remember the name of the song or who sang it first. The man who fell to Earth with a lightning bolt across his face is all that sticks in my mind. Is that me now? Am I some kind of space oddity?

I look out my window, toward the stations jutting up from the surface of the Moon like the spinning pinwheels of my Earth memories. Somewhere down there, my mother's working in a helium mine, and on the other side, my father's silver-wrapped body is tethered in the field of the dead. *Wish me luck!* I think to my parents, but I don't send the message.

I grip the armrests, preparing for the thrust as the rocket boosters rev and we're catapulted away. The singer tells me that the stars look very different today, and he's right. Everything is strange. Right then, I know it's true—planet Earth is blue and there's nothing I can do but hold on tight because finally, after ten years of living on the Moon, I'm on my way back home.

CASTOR NEVA

ALPHAZONIA, EARTH

THE SECURIBOTS DUMP Talitha and me in a small narrow room with one tiny window somewhere high up in the palace. The room is bare except for two white chairs, a small table, and a wall screen playing the D'Cart Stream.

As soon as the bots leave and lock the door, I pick myself up off the floor and straighten my clothes. "At least they didn't take our devices." I walk around the tiny space looking for a signal, but no luck. "Damn," I say. "Blocked."

Talitha is shaking so hard she can't stand up, so she stays put on the floor, where she hugs her knees close to her chest. "I can't believe this happened. I told you we'd get caught, but you wouldn't listen!" she keeps repeating.

"Don't get upset."

"How can I not!" she shouts. "This is terrible. My worst nightmare! I told you it would go wrong."

"It's going to be okay."

"You don't know that," she snarls at me.

Half of me wants to shake her and tell her to pull herself together, but I know that doesn't work. What she needs now is reassurance. Not my strong suit, but I gather up my patience to comfort her.

"Talitha," I say calmly, and squat in front of her. I reach out and put both hands on her shoulders so we're looking at each other eye to eye. She is my mirror image. "Breathe," I say, and squeeze. "We've been in tighter spots before. Remember when we stole all those rare orchids from the flower district and that weird guy with a wheel for a foot chased us into an alley?"

"And we had to climb a wall to get away."

"Yep. And the first time I ever tried to Jack-a-Pod?"

"Only there were already people inside of it?" she remembers, and almost grins.

"Yeah, they looked like this when their car pulled up and opened its doors to us rat-faced urchins in dirty pants." I twist my face into shock, fear, and disgust, the same as the Yoobies.

Talitha nods, trying not to laugh.

"We got out of those tight spots and a lot of other ones, too, so we'll get out of this one." I massage her shoulders to reassure her.

"No, this is worse." She pushes my hands away. "You got greedy."

"Yeah, well . . ." I stand up. "You're right. I did. But I'm not going to apologize for trying to get what I deserve."

"No one deserves any of this!" She tosses her arms out wide.

"I can't talk to you when you're like this," I mumble, then I turn away and stare at the wall screen. On the Stream, D'Cart winks and sips the Gem Water. "Hey, look at that," I say. "There's a time delay. That was at least five minutes ago. I bet they'll edit out what just happened."

"If we'd only gotten out earlier—" says Talitha.

"Shush," I tell my sister. "I want to hear what she's saying." I command the sound louder.

Sure enough, the scene by the pool switches. Now D'Cart is super-imposed on a beach at sunrise with her arms outstretched. Behind her, the morning moon is faint in the salmon-colored sky. Our tussle with the SecuriBots is nowhere to be seen.

"Yep," I say, and laugh. "Edited."

"So our followers didn't see us get carted off?" Talitha asks.

"No," I say. "That's a bit of luck at least."

"No it's not!" Talitha whines. "It means nobody knows we're here." She sniffles.

I don't mention that Mundie knows exactly where we are. That's not what Talitha needs to hear right now.

On-screen, D'Cart says, "I'd like to take a moment to pay homage to some fallen heroes."

"This oughtta be good," I say, and drop into a chair.

"Let us remember the brave individuals . . . mothers, fathers, sisters, and brothers who fight for us in the Central Valley Water War to protect our way of life . . ." A low, mournful oboe accompanies a scroll of smiling soldiers parading across the screen.

"What the . . ." I say, then trail off to watch the weirdness unfolding in front of me.

"Through their hard work and sacrifice, these fine people help secure our water rights . . ."

A proud, lantern-jawed, gun-wielding soldier who could have been our father winks and nods from his perch atop a tower at Silverwood Lake in the San Gabriel Mountains. I know that lake, of course. I diverted water from it to irrigate my mother's land in the foothills down below.

"They protect our power sources," D'Cart says over images of wind turbines and solar farms patrolled by armored tanks. "And help us rebuild our city."

A ReConstruction worker with pretty eyes and corkscrew curls takes a break from clearing rubble to wave at the camera. She looks nothing like the tired woman we watched board the bus earlier tonight.

"Some of these brave people have lost their lives in an attempt to secure a better future for all of us."

Talitha snorts. "Not all of us."

A crying woman and two waifs stand over a coffin draped with an AlphaZonian flag.

"Hey, look," I say. "It's us!" I laugh.

"Not funny," she says, still pissed at me.

"These fine people served us bravely," D'Cart says. "Shouldn't they be allowed to die with dignity instead of being sold off like chattel to the Moon once their usefulness on Earth has expired?"

"Like our mother had a choice?" Talitha mutters. "She needed money to raise us, not a postconscious husband."

"It's a travesty when the Moon Utilitarian Survival Colony buys the ravaged bodies of these once-proud soldiers." D'Cart's voice is full of emotion.

Talitha and I look at each other. "Am I hearing this right?" she asks, and I shrug.

"Did you know that MUSC merges the bodies of these soldiers with machines," D'Cart asks her followers, "then connects CPU boards to their limbs in order create a cadre of technoslaves they call Exploro-Bots?"

Your father is a kind of astronaut now, Mom told us when she sold off Dad's damaged body. *He'll fly up to the moon,* she said. *Will it hurt?* we asked, and Mom said, *No, he can't feel anything anymore.*

"The MUSC ExploroBot program is a calamity!" D'Cart proclaims.

I lean forward, captivated. "Is RayNay DeShoppingCart, the queen

of insipid product placement, taking a political stand against MUSC?"
I ask.

"Maybe she's going to launch her own Space Bot program and doesn't want the competition," Talitha mumbles.

"You could be right," I say.

But D'Cart is on another trajectory right then. "Don't those brilliant *scientists* on MUSC know that the mind and body exist on different planes?" She pauses for effect. "The earthly body, the astral mind." A silvery holo outline of herself is projected behind her on the screen. "Think about it," she implores her followers. "If you replaced each part of a person's body, one by one, over time . . . a leg . . ."

Her right leg disappears. It's replaced by another leg.

"An arm . . ."

Then her left arm is replaced. Her right ear, her nose. She continues naming body parts until her entire form is another human being, but her voice remains the same.

"Who do I become when my body no longer exists but I am still here?" She waits, as if allowing everyone to ponder this deep thought before she supplies them with her answer. "When the body dies, the soul lives on." The silver holo of her original form floats up to hover above the stranger's body with her voice.

It's the same question we had for our mother. *Is he alive?* we wanted to know, but she didn't have an answer except to say our father would never come home again. I understood that much, but I wanted to know what had happened to his mind. Where did it go when his body was usurped by MUSC?

"Where have these people gone?" D'Cart asks, and of course, no one answers. The crowd is deathly quiet, likely as confused as we are by this departure from pure consumerism.

"They are out there," D'Cart whispers. Other silvery holos float above her head. "Soulless bodies and bodiless souls floating in the ether, waiting to be reunited."

"Reunited?" Talitha says incredulous. "Has she lost her mind?"

"They are gathering," says D'Cart. Outlines of ExploroBots hovering in the vast emptiness of space fill the screen. D'Cart's silvery holo floats up to join them.

"Maybe she has, but," I whisper to my sister, "don't you ever wonder where Dad is?"

"Of course I do," she says, and climbs into the chair beside me. "But since when did D'Cart give two craps about people from the Wastelands or ExploroBots?"

I shake my head, as bewildered as my sister, though something in what D'Cart says resonates with me. Sometimes I dream I'm floating— weightlessly, aimlessly in space, aware that I'll stay in that suspended state forever. Then I wake up in a panic, worried that was my father's fate. Did he know what was happening to him? Or was his mind replaced when they took over his body? Are the mind and body different things?

I open my mouth to tell this to Talitha, but I don't because that's when D'Cart says, "We are coming. We are coming for them soon!"

My sister and I look at each other, then the screen goes blank.

TIME STAMP

MOON
LEAP DAY, MUSC YEAR 94

EARTH
JUNE 18, 2XXX

UMA JEMISON

MUSC SHUTTLE TO EARTH

GENTLE SHAKING WAKES me. Groggy and confused, I squint one eye, expecting to see my mother standing beside my sleeping berth, rousing me for another day at school, but then I remember that I'm hurtling through space at eight kilometers per second toward Earth, and I bolt upright from my slouch. The harness straps jerk me back against my seat.

"Ouch," I mutter, and rub a spot above my collarbone as I sit up to take a look around.

The others on the Shuttle sleep or have the glassy-eyed stare of people deeply engrossed in their Streams. I immediately glance at where my Lenz should be, then remember that I muted Darshan and took off my device to avoid the wrath of my mother and Dr. Fornax once they realize that I'm gone. But that means I have no idea what time it is, how long I slept, or how much farther we have to go before we land.

To my left, a slice of bright white light bisects the circular window, cutting it into two distinct halves—one side glows greenish purple, and the other is dark, with a shrinking silver ball.

Is that the Moon? I ask Darshan out of habit. It's so strange not to have an immediate answer. I sit for a moment listening to the silence. At first I find it eerie. No Stream, no Darshan, no thotz. I feel completely cut off and isolated, as if I'm floating on my own in space, untethered. But then I realize what I'm hearing isn't silence at all, but a different set of noises—the *shu-shu-shu* of the Shuttle engine; the *bzzt* of some loose bolt. The click of someone picking at her nails.

I look out the window again at the quickly receding silver dot, and I feel excitement building in my belly. The truth is, I don't know what it is, and that's okay with me. Sometimes I don't want empirical truth. Sometimes I want conjecture. Maybe it's the moon, or a satellite, or the body of an ExploroBot that's been deep-spaced, or a sky wolf, or a white hare, or just a chunk of ice rebounding after a celestial collision.

Slowly, the bright white line in the center of the window spins like the point of a compass, and I realize the Shuttle must be changing directions. I try to get my bearings and puzzle through what I see. The light cuts the window horizontally now, with the top half black and the bottom shifting from purple toward blue. Then the center line goes from pure white light to fuzzy orange and bends as if frowning, and suddenly the image clicks. I understand that I'm looking at the curved horizon of a planet and that planet must be Earth.

The dot of silver light in the darkness winks, then disappears. *Good night, Moon!* I think, and remember an artifact from my early childhood. An ancient book on a tablet that my mother read to me before bed when I was small. I expect to feel the tug of some emotion now that my home for the past decade is no longer in my sight, but what I feel instead is the buzzing of anticipation in my belly.

"Earth," I whisper, and press my hand against the window as if I could feel the warmth of the glowing horizon, but the window is as cold as empty space.

A narrow arc appears over the growing blue and purple planet. We seem to slow suddenly. The warp galumphs in my belly and pops my ears as the Shuttle tilts and shudders. I expect to feel sick, but mostly I feel giddy. Then I gasp at an eerie green glow swirling over the top of the Earth's surface. Thin rays of white, pink, and purple light flicker like lost souls beaming into the darkness—no spaceships and travel suits needed. They are free now. Unencumbered by arms and legs and bully brains. But that's not true. What I'm seeing is the aurora borealis.

We learned about this phenomenon in my third-year Atmospheres class. When I told my mother the northern lights occur when charged particles from the sun cause atoms to release particles of light called photons across the Earth's magnetic field, she quoted a long-dead Earth poet named Thoreau: "What sort of science is that which enriches the understanding but robs the imagination?" At the time, I thought she was being so Earthy and closed-minded about truth, but now I see her point. The beauty of the aurora borealis isn't captured by its explanation. I want to paint, sing, and dance what I see outside the window. Along with understanding *why* it happens, I want to celebrate *that* it happens at all. Something we never do on MUSC.

The glowing lights fade as we cruise around the top of the Earth. In its place, the thin lip of black space has faded to striations of blue, from the darkest ink to what I remember as the color of the sky, and my heart speeds up. When I was little, my father told me that the Earth is like a beautiful marble floating inside a protective bubble. *But why is the inside of the bubble blue?* I asked, looking up at the sky. *Because blue light waves are the shortest and scatter more easily so that's mostly what you see even though all of the other colors are still there,* he said. Soon we'll pierce the blue bubble, which contains the happiest memories of my youngest years. Will it be anything like I remember? Or are my memories like a child's drawing that captures only best parts of life?

I grip the arms of my seat. Out the window, strings of tiny white and orange dots appear. The pattern reminds me of bacteria colonies, but surely they are cities. Then they're gone beneath a thick blanket of gray clouds, where flashes of lightning ricochet around like ideas inside a brain.

As we cross the planet, the sky grows less dark. On the horizon I see a faint pinkish-orange line. The sun setting to the west. I look again for the moon and find it faint and ghostly in the window across the aisle. I gasp at its beauty. I haven't seen the Moon like this since I was small.

Gears whirl, and the Shuttle tilts, sending me forward in my harness as the body of the ship comes into alignment with the tail fins and we flatten out to glide. This should be the easy part, when we descend smoothly and effortlessly toward the ground, only I feel jittery and uncertain. As we get closer and closer to the ground, my heart swells up with fear. What was I thinking? I purposely disobeyed the MUSC CEO! I left without permission! I abandoned my mom and implicated my best friend in my misbehavior! And for what? This dying planet down below populated by the worst of what's left of humanity caught in endless wars. What in the name of Jupiter was I thinking?

I can barely breathe, then two loud *BOOM*s rattle the windows. My heart jumps into my throat.

"No!" I wail, and shoot my arm out to grip the man beside me. "I don't want to die!" I say as the Shuttle shakes violently and plummets toward the Earth.

BOOM! BOOM! TWO louds bangs wake me. I jump up from where I'm slumped in a chair, then hit the ground, arms overhead, expecting dust and debris to fall from the ceiling. But it doesn't. Everything stays intact. Only the window and the glasses on the table rattle.

"What the hell was that?" I ask as I pick up myself up off the floor.

At the window, Castor points to a silver streak trailing twin exhaust streams across the early evening sky. "Shuttle," he says.

"I thought it was another quake."

"Remember when we were little and stood up like meerkats looking for eagles whenever the MUSC Shuttles came down?"

"I always waved," I admit, and join my brother at the window. "I imagined there was a pilot waving back at us from the cockpit."

"Shuttles are automated, duh."

"I know that now," I say. Then I turn away. "Oh, poor Quasar!" I cry, and pace across the room. "He hates the booms! You don't think he'll bolt, do you?"

Castor goes back to a chair and sits, legs crossed, elbows on his knees. "He'll wait for us."

"For how long?" My stomach knots up as I try to estimate how long we've been inside. "We were probably nabbed around ten or eleven last night, and it's evening now of the next day . . ."

"At least they're feeding us." Castor picks at what's left of the fresh fruit, bean paste, and hard crackers a DomestiBot left for us in the afternoon.

"But . . . what if . . ."

"What if . . . what if! You worry so much, Talitha. Always have."

"Maybe you should worry a little more," I grouse.

Castor stares at me, face hardened, arms crossed. "Mundie will come for you, you know that, right?"

Sweat pools under the tessellated triangles of the stupid jumpsuit pressing into my skin. My whole body feels itchy.

"I saw him," Castor admits. "He watched the whole thing when we got nabbed."

"Ugh! That's even worse." My stomach churns. "If he bails us out, I'll feel indebted to him."

"You don't owe Mundie anything!" Castor says. "Life is just a series of transactions."

"Yeah, well, some emotions cost more than others," I tell him.

He shakes his head. "You've got to have thicker skin if you're going to survive here."

"Maybe I don't want to stay anymore," I tell him, and stomp around the perimeter of the cramped space. "Maybe I'm tired of always skulking around, pretending I don't exist, living off everybody else's scraps!" I fling my arm at the leftovers on the tables. "Always worrying that we'll get caught!"

"So stop worrying."

"How can I when you do such stupid stuff?" I yell.

"So you're going back to the Wastelands? Is that what you're saying? Gonna live with Mom?"

I rest against the wall. "Might be better than eking out a living here where we're barely considered human!"

"It's no better there, and you know it," says Castor. "Mom lives inside a bubble of her own creation."

I sigh. "At least in her bubble, I wouldn't be afraid all the time."

"That's called complacency, Talitha." Castor stretches his arms overhead and yawns.

"Or maybe it's just called life," I argue.

"Yeah, well, if living in the Wastelands is life, then I'll pass."

"You always wanted more," I say quietly, and turn away. "Even when we were little. More food. More water. More stuff." I wish I could go someplace else, away from my brother, but the room is barely big enough to hold both of us and the furniture.

"Of course I want more," he says. "And so should you. We're just as good as any Yoobie. Probably better."

I gaze out the window again. Somewhere in the desert, not far from the Dumps, where we grew up, another Shuttle will soon land. Moonlings will disembark and head our way.

"Mom should have tested you for a MUSC scholarship. You would have gotten in, I bet."

"I wouldn't have gone," he says. "Not after what they did to Dad. D'Cart may be a little loopy, but she's right. What MUSC does to soldiers is despicable."

Every once in a while, we catch sight of Moon visitors walking around the tourist spots in AlphaZonia. They are tall and thin, neither male nor female as far as I can tell. They remind me of the pale worms Castor and I used to dig up in the Dumps that would recoil from sunlight and fresh air as soon as we exposed them.

"MUSCies are so strange-looking, all walking around in their matching blue and white travel suits," I say.

"But their faces are weirdly cute," says Castor. He's sprawled across both chairs, his long legs hanging over the edge of one and his arms akimbo off the other. "Almost cartoonish with their long bodies and big heads with giant round eyes blinking out from their protective hoods."

"Yeah, what's with the hoods?" I ask.

"Chronic neutropenia."

"English, please."

"Low white blood cell counts. Comes from being born off-planet and growing up in induced gravity. Plus, their environment is so sterile, they haven't built up antibodies to pathogens down here. One breath of fresh air, and they could all die!"

"Why do they even come here, then?" I ask, but don't expect an answer. "What do they want?"

"Earth products. Food. Minerals and other resources they can't get up there," Castor says. "They're not as self-sufficient as they like to pretend."

"Nobody is," I say, and slide down the wall to sit with my head on my knees, half hoping Mundie will come and half dreading what will happen if he does.

UMA JEMISON

MUSC SHUTTLE TO EARTH

"HEY," THE SECOND Gen guy beside me looks down at the arm that I'm clutching.

"Sorry!" I retract my hand, mortified that I screamed and grabbed a stranger, thinking I was about to die.

I look around. No one else seems to have noticed what I've done. Most people are asleep. The few who are awake are so engrossed that the sights and sounds of real life are blocked out by what's playing inside their minds.

"You okay?" the man asks in a rare show of MUSC compassion.

"What was that noise?" I ask.

"Sonic booms. It happens when we drop below the speed of sound," he explains.

"Do people on the ground hear them, too?"

"They're used to them by now," he says with a shrug. "Probably barely notice."

I look out the window and try to imagine what it's like to be down there. On the ground. What do people do? Is anyone like me? Or will I be as different on Earth as I am on the Moon? Will I ever fit in anywhere?

The man looks out his window, then says, "We'll be on the ground soon. We're at about thirteen thousand meters up. Two minutes from touchdown, I'd say. I'm Burnell Chen-Ning, by the way."

I whip around to face him and see the resemblance around his eyes to Gemini, his son.

"You're Uma, right?" he says, and points to the name and number embroidered on my flight suit.

"Uh, yeah." I cringe, waiting for him to nail me for running away.

"Nice to meet you," he says, and offers me his hand. "Aren't you in my son's cohort?"

"Yes," I say, still half holding my breath.

"I wish he'd come to Earth for his Sol trip," Mr. Chen-Ning says.

"You do?"

"Absolutely! I wish more kids your age would come." He looks out the window again. "It's a fascinating place."

We're close enough to the ground that I can see the patterns on the surface of the Earth. I trace the fractal arms of a river winding its way across the land, then the ridges of some mountain chain, like the spine of a sleeping creature.

"There's the landing strip," Mr. Chen-Ning says.

I see a straight, dark path outlined on either side by small dots of light. I tense up again when I hear the whirl of gears.

"Those are the wheels coming down," he tells me with a smile. "Just a minute or so, and we'll be on the ground."

Suddenly I can't breathe. That means in a few moments, I'll set foot on Earth for the first time in ten years. I have no plan. No place to go. No way to get around. I figured I'd let Darshan take care of everything once I arrived, but now I can't turn Darshan on, and I have no idea what I'm going to do. I hold on to the armrest and brace myself as the concrete of the runway looms up and up. I expect a jolt, but the landing is smooth as the wheels touch down and the gravity of my situation takes hold.

When we come to a stop, everyone around me moves. Unbuckles harnesses, gathers belongings, stands to stretch their legs, but I stay put. I haven't yet let go of the armrests. Not because the landing was scary but because I'm not sure what comes next.

Mr. Chen-Ning leans over. "Don't be nervous," he tells me. "People say Earth is a hellhole, but there are nice things about AlphaZonia. Automated food marts in Lost Feelies, where you can get anything you want to eat. GladiatorBot Smackdowns, where you can watch robots fight to the finish. The virtushops on Rodeo Drive, where you can try on different versions of yourself. And Soggywood has tons of entertainment options." He unrolls the protective hood from the back of his jumpsuit and zips it over his head to stave off Earth infections his immune system can't handle. "Just stay away from the Wastelands," he tells me through the tiny speaker built into the face mask, "and you'll be fine."

"Thank you." I wave good-bye.

I wait until everyone else has exited before I pick up my device. I leave Darshan off, but I attach it to my head in case I need him, then I cloak myself in the protective hood. As I leave the Shuttle, I breathe so hard with anticipation and fear that my mask fogs up. The autotemp controls kick in and pump cool air so that my mask clears just as the doors to the terminal *wheesh* open. I stand, stunned, blinking into the sunlight bursting through clear ceiling panels overhead. Swirls of white on darkening blue trail across the sky like thick splays of cake icing that I haven't eaten since I was five.

"Clouds!" I say aloud like a giddy toddler. Then I draw in a deep breath of filtered air. Already it is moister, more fragrant than what we breathe on MUSC. I taste the greenness in the back of my throat as it fills my nostrils, and I think, *Home.*

Gingerly, I step onto an escalator that descends between two waterfalls that crisscross beneath a small bridge then flow along either side of the moving walkway that takes passengers through an oasis of palm trees, zebra grass, and flower beds on the floor. Red benches jut up among banks of blooming white flowers. At the far end of the terminal, in the center of a living wall, covered with delicate green vines climbing a metal trellis, a blue and green glowing sign proclaims, WELCOME TO PLANET EARTH.

Wheeled HelperBots that look like human-size shopping carts with rotating heads carry the other passengers toward the exit. A lone robot idles at the end of the moving walkway. I step backward, trying to retreat, sure that the moment I'm recognized, a siren will go off, lights will flash, and SecuriBots will wheel out and arrest me, but as I inch forward, the waiting robot announces, "Welcome to Earth! I hope you enjoyed your flight!" Then it spins around and lowers its platform for me to board.

I'm stunned. Is it possible that no one's figured out yet that I'm gone? Of course, I haven't turned on Darshan yet, so it's equally possible I'm in deep trouble. But for now I feel giddy, like a little kid getting away with something. At some point I know someone will figure out that I'm not where I'm supposed to be. But as long as the system keeps inviting me to move forward, I'm going to have some fun.

"Thanks!" I tell the HelperBot, and I step aboard. "Let's go!"

It whisks me out the front doors of the terminal. Although it's early evening, god-awful heat still rises from the concrete in waves. I begin to melt inside my suit. The air pump works harder, but it can't keep up. My hair droops against my neck inside my hood, and a bead of sweat rolls down my spine. There is nothing but hard, compacted dirt and sand surrounding the Shuttle terminal building—more like Mars than the Earth that I remember. Other than the people from my flight who have boarded AutoPods that carry them away, there seem to be no humans anywhere nearby.

A little red and blue car zips up in front of me. The door swishes open, and the car greets me. "Hello. Would you like transport?"

"Okay," I tell the car, and climb in.

"Where would you like to go?" it asks.

"AlphaZonia?" I say, like there's any other choice out here.

"Great choice!" says the car. "Any place in particular?"

I rack my brain for something I know, then blurt out the first thing that pops into my mind. "The Pink Palace?"

"Excellent! I'll take you there now," the Pod says. I crack up and wish I could ping Kep. He would die if he knew I'm heading to the Pink Palace. What do I think I'm going to do there? Meet RayNay DeShoppingCart in person?

The car zips away. Up ahead I see a mountain range that looks like the spine of that giant sleeping creature napping on the desert floor that I traced from up in the sky.

"What's that?" I ask the AutoNav system.

"The San Gabriel Mountains," the car informs me, and then blathers on about the range's flora and fauna, but I don't listen.

I'm too busy taking in what I haven't seen since I was five. I try to remember the names of plants, but the words are long buried under the information stuffed into my brain at MUSC. When I was little, I could name every plant and animal. Catalog them into species groups. That was so long ago. Back when I thought my family (Mom, Dad, the dog, and I) would always be together and I could be anything I wanted to be when I grew up. Now, seeing the terraforms and plant life that I've missed all these years, I realize that I've returned looking for something that I can't go back to. My family had nothing when we lived here except one another. Now I'm here again, but this time I'm on my own.

Just as we're about to be swallowed by a tunnel cutting into the side of the mountain up ahead, a loud roar rattles the windows of the Pod. I look up and see a low-flying, large red drone with the MUSC security logo emblazoned in silver on its belly. I scream and duck, but it doesn't swoop down on the Pod. It keeps going. I turn, heart in my throat, palms wet with sweat, and watch out the back window as the drone screams across the sky, heading straight for the Shuttle landing site, no doubt looking for me.

My Pod enters the tunnel, and everything goes black. "Turn on the light!" I gasp.

To my relief, the windshield lights up. A perky Earth woman with silky blue hair and violet eyes appears. "Hello, there," she says. "I hope you're enjoying your trip. Is this your first time in AlphaZonia?"

"No, not exactly, I mean . . ." I search for words to explain that I am from this place but I don't belong.

"Great!" she says without waiting for me to finish, because the car doesn't really care. "Whether it's your first time here or you're a repeat visitor, you'll need a few things to get by."

"Okay," I say, and let it go. Maybe the trick is to pretend that I fit in. As we zoom through the darkness of the tunnel, I try to leave MUSC Uma behind. Slough off the worrier, the fretter, the girl who assumes the worst. Can I be an Earth girl full of optimism and promise? At least for a few days before I'm summoned back to the Moon?

The blue-haired female is replaced on-screen by a burly-armed man in canvas pants with an urgent voice. "Hey, you guys," he grumbles. "I'm Hank the Tank McGrank, and I'm here to tell you that every traveler to Earth needs the DeShoppingCart Armageddon-Ready Multipurpose Urban Survival Tool!" He whips out a small handheld doohickey from a holster on his hip. "An entire toolbox in your palm for every eventuality." He unfolds it one way, then drills a hole in a wall. Another few twists, and he burns through metal with a blow torch. Next, he's stripping the wires of a gutted robot. "Because you never know what might happen!" he says, and points straight at me.

"No, thank you," I say. "Pass?"

He's replaced by the back of a willowy woman in a flowing white dress and enormous circular hat. She spins slowly until I see a strange gauzy white layer covering her face. A voice-over says, "The best De-ShoppingCart solar-powered wrinkle-reducing UV reflection unit with a lipid distribution mask. Keeps your skin smooth and moist even in the harshest conditions—"

"I already have a mask. Next?"

"The DeShoppingCart Bristleless Brush with Sonic Stimulation Hair-Gro Technology—"

"Next."

"Thinstinctual Thigh Slimmers—"

"No!"

"Shoe Tubes—"

"Nope!"

"Armpit Perspiration Pads with built-in LED Flab-Be-Gone lipo action—"

"Oh, my gad, no no no!" I'm cracking up as the Streamers try to sell me so much DeShoppingCart crap that I don't need—a Mind Spa that looks like two giant spiders trying to eat my eyeballs; a portable warm gel toilet seat cover and air purifying device, "now with woodland sounds"; a machine that imprints my face on meat. I wish Kep were here. He'd find all of this hilarious.

Just then, the AutoPod pops out of the tunnel into the light. I plaster myself against the side window as we zip past tall metal and glass buildings. Out of the corner of my eye, I catch a glimpse of a stone wall with the letters *JPL* under a blue circle with a red swish and white dots.

WELCOME TO OUR UNIVERSE, the wall proclaims in faded letters. A few moments later, we pass a large oval structure, almost like a crater but human made, with a giant red rose hanging precariously above white columns.

Is that where they grow flowers? I ask Darshan, forgetting that he's off.

The AutoPod climbs a ramp toward an elevated roadway surrounded by a long glass tube with the number 101 painted along the sides. Once we're inside, the car speed doubles. I'm pushed against the back of my seat. We round a curve, and the centripetal force shifts my body to the opposite window. To the west, I see the sun, a fiery ball about to set above the blue line of the ocean. We continue past an expanse of green on one side and a wide, murky gray river on the other. Everything is moving so fast, I can only make out a blur of green and brown plant life on the jagged hills. On the windshield, Streamers keep trying to sell me personal oxygen bars and germ removal wands, but I ignore them because what's outside is far more interesting.

"Now entering AlphaZonia," the car tells me.

"Whoa," I say. "Slow down! I want to see everything."

"Would you like to travel via surface road?" the car asks, and I say yes because I want to drink in everything that I see while memories flood my mind. Our house was yellow. There was a flagstone path. The pinwheels were stuck in hard dirt, lined up perfectly on either side of the walkway. My father dropped to one knee when he came home each night after trying to find work, and I ran out the front door into his arms. Sometimes he took me to the ocean to teach me how to swim. He'd stand in the water at the end of the rickety pier, beckoning me to get up the nerve to jump.

I know I can never have that again, but maybe if I'm away from MUSC and back on this Earth, I can create some memories that are all my own. And maybe I'll make more sense to myself. Like why I have so much trouble making friends and love Earth Streams but never wanted to kiss Kepler and whether there's an LWA that won't make me miserable when I go back.

The car switches to the far right lane and takes a circular ramp among a knot of twisting and turning roads, some heading north-south, others east-west. The car slows as it goes down and around until we're on a surface street with buildings, mostly abandoned, from the looks of their dark windows. But there are also trees and vines and other plant life that have encroached on the remnants of this city. I can't make out where one plant stops and another begins because my brain is a blur with all the things I haven't seen in so long and memories that won't stop flooding my mind.

"Slow down!" I beg. "Go really, really slow." Am I talking to the car or to my brain?

"You've got it," says the car. "Is this okay?" It rolls along the street at such a reduced pace that I can read the signs for Sunset Boulevard and La Cienega. But I don't see a single human being.

"Is this all there is?" I ask aloud. "Abandoned buildings and street signs? Where is everyone?"

The car has no answer, but as we round a gentle curve and cross an intersection called North Beverly, out of the corner of my eye, I see a little flash of movement in the road up ahead.

"Wait!" I say. "What's that?" I squint and see the shadow move again.

"Would you like a closer look?" the car asks, and the windscreen zooms in. I gasp when I see a small furry creature trotting toward us. From a distance, it could be a fox or coyote.

"What is that?" I ask.

"It appears to be a dog."

"A dog!" I leap toward the door. "Stop! Stop the car. I want to get out."

"For your safety, please stay inside the AutoPod."

"No!" I insist. "Stop. I want out."

"Are you sure?" the car asks. "We haven't made it to our destination yet."

"Yes! I'm sure." The car screeches to a stop. "Open the doors!" I bang on the window until the door pops open, and I scramble onto the pavement. "Wait there!" I tell the Pod.

The little animal stops when it sees me approaching in the road. I want to run toward it, but I move slowly, like my mother taught me when we lived here, holding out my hand in a fist. The dog stays put, head cocked to the side, watching me cautiously. It has a sweet, curious face with a long, slender snout and perky ears. Not big, nor small. It has a regal brown-and-white mane and slender hips plus a bushy tail and pointy ears folded over like page corners of a well-worn book. It almost could be my dog, Mahati, from when I was small! But that's impossible. My dog would be long gone by now.

"Here, pup," I call, but it stays put. I desperately want a holo of this animal. A record of its existence. *Darshan, on,* I command. *Record.* I blink to capture the images.

Recording, Darshan says.

"It's okay," I say as I creep closer, but the dog backs up, tail down, and looks at me askance. I wish I had some food to entice it my way. I must look menacing in my strange flight suit and protective hood.

"I won't hurt you," I say, and take another step forward. "I just want to say hi!" I hear the desperation in my voice, and clearly so does the dog, because it will have nothing to do with me. I take one more step, which sends it scurrying to the other side of the street.

"Don't go!" I call after it. "Come back!"

It takes off up the hill and disappears.

"Damn!" I say, and debate whether I should follow. But I don't know where I am. I should have been more careful. Moved more slowly. Maybe crouched down so I didn't look so big.

As I stand there alone, among the abandoned buildings with no people around, a funny feeling creeps across my skin. Suddenly it occurs to me that I shouldn't have broken orders and come to Earth on a whim. What I remembered as a happy place now seems menacing with its eerily empty streets and no one here to help me. Maybe my mother has been right all these years. Maybe Earth is not a place I want to be.

As I turn to head back toward the car, I hear a voice call my name. I startle at the sound, then realize Darshan is still connected.

"Oh, no. No, no, no! What did I do?" I run toward the car, searching the sky for the red security drone while shouting, "Off! Off! Darshan, turn off!" But it's too late.

Darshan's image blinks furiously from the periphery of my Lenz as he says, *Emergency incoming call.*

TALITHA NEVA

ALPHAZONIA, EARTH

CASTOR AND I jump when the door to our small locked room swings open and Mundie rushes inside.

"You came!" I say, and scramble to my feet.

Castor stays put and mutters, "Finally." I glare at him, but he only shrugs.

"Can we go now?" I ask Mundie.

"Sorry. Not yet."

Castor and I both moan.

"But I do have news." Mundie strides toward me. I keep my back against the wall. "D'Cart wants to see the two of you."

Castor and I look at each other, then at Mundie.

"Is that a good thing?" I ask.

"Or a bad thing?" asks Castor.

Mundie doesn't answer. Instead, he holds out his hands to me and says, "Come on. You don't want to keep her waiting."

I cross my arms tightly so I don't have to hold Mundie's hand, but I fold my mouth into a smile so I don't seem too standoffish.

Castor grabs me by the elbow and hisses, "Be nicer to him," in my ear.

"You be nicer," I hiss back, and yank my arm away.

We follow Mundie to an elevator that takes us up several floors to a hallway with thick velvet roses embossed on the walls and plush magenta carpet that absorbs every sound. As I'm taking in the beauty of the Palace, I see Castor trying to blink onto a connection, but our iEyes remain transparent.

Mundie notices, too. "Nice try." He smirks. "All signals are locked down inside the Palace. Not even hackers can get in."

"Wanna bet?" says Castor.

I punch him and mouth, *Stop it*.

Mundie takes us to a large, sunny room where D'Cart stands with her back to us, watching a floor-to-ceiling holo of red MUSC security drones zigzagging above the desert.

"What's going on?" Mundie asks, marching forward.

"Something's up at the MUSC landing site," D'Cart says, still facing away.

"A crash?" Mundie joins her to study the scene.

D'Cart shakes her head. "No, the Shuttle landed fine about fifteen minutes ago, but they seem to be looking for someone. Probably an escapee." She looks at Mundie and wiggles her eyebrows. Then she notices us over her shoulder.

"Oh, lookie here!" She spins, sending the silk of her rose-colored kimono swirling around her legs. "The amazing Neva twins have arrived!" She glides across the room toward us, her robe swishing with every step.

I know I should feel afraid, but actually I'm giddy. RayNay De-ShoppingCart is more gorgeous up close and in person without all her makeup and a crazy hairdo. Her skin glows. Her eyes are bright. And she looks almost, well, friendly.

"Have Mundie and the DomestiBots been treating you well during your stay?" she asks us warmly.

I nod, uncertain and guarded. There's no reason for her to be so nice, but Castor, as usual, has to be combative.

"Our stay?" He snorts. "We're here against our will—you know that, right?"

I try to stomp on his foot to shut him up, but he's too quick and hops away so I look like I'm stamping my foot in frustration. Castor and I glare at one another for a quick second until D'Cart says, "Yes, well, that's what happens when you get caught stealing from me."

I reach for Castor's hand as a wave of dizziness rolls over me. This is when things will get bad. This is when she will tell us we're being sold to some ReConstruction project to pay off our debt to her. We wrap our fingers together and hold tight. But, instead of staying mad, D'Cart tosses her head back and laughs, melting all the tension in the room like ice cream on a hot day.

"Watermelon juice?" She points to a pitcher and four glasses that appear to hover above the pink marble floor.

"Yes, please!" I jump at the chance for a drink because my mouth has gone as dry as the Salton Sea.

"It's real," says D'Cart as I step toward the levitating beverage. "We grow actual fruits and veggies in our climate-controlled greenhouses."

"We've had watermelon before," Castor says. "Our mother grows it."

"In the desert?" asks D'Cart. "How?"

"It's called irrigation. I diverted water," Castor says, and it comes out snotty, like he thinks she's stupid. "And I don't like watermelon juice. It's too cloying and sweet."

"How come it's floating?" I ask, hoping to distract D'Cart from Castor's surliness.

"Good question," she says, then turns to my brother. "Sounds like you're quite the engineer. Can you explain my floating pitcher?" A smug little smile works at the corners of her mouth.

I can't tell if she dislikes my brother or finds this back-and-forth with him entertaining. Whichever it is, the whole thing makes my stomach clench.

Castor studies the pitcher and glasses for a moment, then says, "Invisibility cloaking, I'd guess. Some kind of thin reflective film over a structure so it bends the light and appears to blend into the room."

He reaches out to gingerly poke what must be beneath the pitcher. Lights outlining a table and six chairs slowly begin to blink.

"And sensors," he says, nodding. "Smart. They blink when you get close, so you don't bump into it."

"Very good," says D'Cart. "I'm impressed." She pours two glasses, hands one to me, and raises hers to my brother as if in a toast. "You're as smart as I suspected."

"Not that smart, obviously," says Castor. "Your SecuriBots saw right through us at the party so—"

"No they didn't," D'Cart says, and Castor frowns. "I saw you at the party." She points at me. "You were by the pool deck watching."

My stomach bottoms out, and I think I might barf up the juice I just drank.

"Awww, man," says Castor, hands on hips and head tossed back. "I saw you look at Talitha, but I didn't think you'd know she wasn't one of your followers. She looked just like a Yoobie, er um, citizen shareholder. How did you know we didn't belong?"

"Ah, well, you see, your reputation preceded you," says D'Cart. "I know who you are from your Stream, NayRay DeDumpingCart."

Castor and I lock eyes. I grab the table to steady myself.

"I've been watching you for a long time." She slips into one of the blinking chairs and leans back, one elbow propped on the top. "Longer than you might think. You, my dear"—she points at me again—"doing a parody of me—"

"I'm so sorry," I pant. My breath is shallow. My eyes burn. I can't believe D'Cart knows we've been making fun of her all these years.

"Oh, don't be!" she says. "Come sit." She pats the seat beside her.

I walk on wobbly legs and take the chair as she instructs. She nods to Castor, and he does the same on the other side of the table from me.

"Your stream is very . . ." She pauses, then says, "Entertaining! And you've amassed quite a following."

"So you like it?" Castor asks.

"Oh, yes!" she says brightly. "Imitation is the sincerest form of flattery, after all. Especially when that imitation makes some commentary on society. I love how you've captured the inanity of our rabid consumer culture."

"Wow," says Castor. "I did not see that coming."

"I think you have a lot of potential," she adds. "Which is why I'm ready to make you a deal."

Castor and I glance at each other. He sits up taller, ready to say yes to anything, but I shrink in my seat. Whatever deal she offers, I remind myself, there will be more in it for her than there is for us.

D'Cart turns in her seat and points to the holo of the red MUSC SecuriDrones sweeping across the sky. "See that?"

We nod.

"I believe MUSC lost someone. A runaway, probably. It happens from time to time. If one of you can find the Moonling these drones are looking for and bring that person to me, I'll trade you for the other twin, who stays behind."

"How do you know there's a runaway?" Castor asks.

"Oh, I know," she assures us with a smirk. "Because that"—she pokes her finger toward the holo again—"is exactly what the MUSCies do when a citizen goes rogue on Earth."

"Why not send Mundie to find them?" Castor asks.

"Him?" D'Cart jerks her thumb toward Mundie, who's slouched against the wall, picking at his nails. "He has the charm of a rattle-snake."

"So send a bot or your own drone," says Castor.

I kick him under the table and whisper, "What are you doing?"

"Look," he says, shoulders up in a shrug, "I want to know why you need one of us to do your dirty work before we accept."

"It's not dirty," D'Cart says. "You'll be doing this poor person a favor. But Moonlings can be . . ." She stops and searches for the word, then settles on "Skittish. Especially if this person isn't supposed to be here. They'll have their location software blocked, but MUSC will be looking for them, so they'll need to hide. It'll take a human touch, finesse, and charm to gain their trust and bring them in before MUSC finds them."

"You should send Talitha, then," says Mundie. "Castor couldn't sweet-talk a honeybeebot."

Castor ignores the jab, then asks, "Why do you want the Moonling, anyway?"

"None of your business," says D'Cart. For once, Castor shuts up and doesn't push for an answer. "So, who's it going to be? Which one of you wants to stay with me? And which one wants to go?"

"I'll go," I say. Castor glances at me, surprised, but I nod at him and say, "It's okay. I can do it," because I know Mundie's right. I'll have a better chance at befriending and gaining the trust of a person than Castor would.

"Perfect!" says D'Cart, with her sunniest smile.

"Just one question," I say. "How am I supposed to find someone if

I have no idea who it is? Am I looking for a male or female? Old or young?"

"It can't be that hard," says Castor. "There's only a handful of MUSCies in the city at any given time. And they all look the same. Creepy big eyes, protective hood. You won't be able to miss them."

"Plus, all the MUSCies go to the same places. The automated food marts, Soggywood for entertainment, Rodeo Drive to virtushop, the hologram zoo," D'Cart adds. "Go poke around. Get to know who's here. See who's acting funny. At some point, when MUSC security is desperate, they'll release pix and holos of the runaway. Then you can make your move before our target gets swept up by those drones."

"Okay," I say with as much confidence as I can muster, but the truth is, I have no idea how I'm going to pull this off. I might be the more charming one, but Castor is definitely the better planner. I turn to him. "Are you going to be okay?"

"Of course," he says. "Mundie will take excellent care of me." He shoots Mundie a look, which makes D'Cart laugh.

"You wish," says Mundie.

"Ah, now, boys!" She waggles her finger at them. "We're all on the same team here."

Both Castor and Mundie blanch.

I look at my brother, fighting back the urge to throw myself at him and yell, *I hate to be on my own!* Castor senses my panic. He walks around the table and hugs me, which is odd. I know he cares about me, but he rarely shows this much affection. As he pulls me in, he whispers, "Here's what you do: Get the knapsack and Quasar, then look for the Moonling. Try Lost Feelies, then Soggywood. That's where they always go. And remember, keep Mundie on your side. I'll work on D'Cart."

I take a deep breath, hug him tight, and say, "Okay."

Mundie pushes off the wall. "Let's go," he says, and takes my hand.

I swallow hard, wishing I could pull away from his grip, but Castor lets go of me while keeping his eyes trained on mine. I know what he's telling me. I have to work every angle. Keep all our options open. Especially when it comes to Mundie.

"Take her to a back exit," D'Cart says. "I don't want any of my followers to see her leaving."

"Got it," says Mundie.

He keeps me close to his side with my hand trapped in his sweaty palm the whole way down to the first floor in the elevator. I grit my teeth and let him.

"You know I'll help you, right?" he says. "Anything you need, just ask."

"I need you to keep Castor safe," I say.

Mundie's face hardens. "He never wanted my help before—"

"Please," I ask more softly, and give his hand a squeeze, which makes me feel like I'm covered in dirt. "For me?"

"Fine," he says. "I'll do what I can."

The elevator doors open, and we walk through a huge room filled with all kinds of dead-eyed robots. I stare at the floor-to-ceiling shelves lined with overflowing bins of metal appendages, faceplates, wiring, and circuitry.

When we reach the back door, Mundie grabs me by the shoulders. He breathes hard, and his face is flushed. "This whole thing has all been so strange! Seeing you get nabbed. Not knowing what D'Cart would do with you, and now this!"

"Yeah, well, strange is right." I try to squirm away, but Mundie tugs hard on me. Before I can stop him, he pulls me in and kisses me on the lips. That kiss stings and I want to get away, but I know Castor's safety rests with Mundie, so I stand there, stiff and sick to my stomach for a few seconds before I wriggle free, wiping the back of my hand across my mouth and trying not to spit.

"Okay, so," he says, eye blazing and a stupid smile plastered across his face. "I'll be in touch soon!" He swings open the back door and pushes me into the waning light of evening.

TRANSMISSION FROM KEPLER, Darshan says, and I nearly fall down in the middle of the empty road with relief. "Kep! Kepler! I'm so glad it's you! I thought I was busted!" I shout as I hustle toward the waiting Pod.

Only, Kepler doesn't show up on my Lenz. Instead, a raw feed opens.

I command the car to go, then sit back and squint at the unsteady and grainy feed being transmitted. It takes me a few seconds to realize that Kep has opened his personal Stream to me so that I can see and hear what he sees and hears, but we can't communicate directly. It's strangely unsettling not to see his face or read his thotz. I feel so far away and disconnected. I squint at the room I'm seeing on my Lenz, trying to figure out where he is. Down on the surface? At TourEsa? Then I see a blurry orange zinnia plant and realize that he's inside Dr. Fornax's office, where I sat less than twenty-four hours ago. And Kepler's not alone.

He looks to his left, and I see a holo of my mother, pinched and rumpled in her mining gear, like she's been woken up too early or, more likely, never went to sleep. My mother yells and paces, throwing her arms around, while Dr. Fornax sits, ramrod straight at her desk, hands folded in front of her.

Volume up, I command Darshan.

My mom's voice comes through loud and clear. "I don't believe this! With all the technology you have—cameras, body scans, retinal recognition, ThoughtStream chips that record our every experience— she got on board and went to Earth. Without anybody knowing! How is that possible?"

"Uh-oh," I murmur.

"He knew," Dr. Fornax says, pointing at Kepler.

My mother shouts, "Why didn't you tell someone, Kepler?"

Since I can't see him, I can only imagine how he looks, shamefaced, head hanging, shoulders hunched. "The system let her on so she thought maybe Dr. Fornax changed her mind," he mutters, covering for me.

"She ran away," Dr. Fornax snaps.

"No!" My mother spins around and jabs her finger toward Fornax, making her flinch. "You messed up. You didn't tell me that you canceled her trip and then your system failed by allowing her on the flight!"

"My orders were clear," Dr. Fornax says, her face stony. "I told her not to go, but she deliberately and knowingly disobeyed me."

My stomach churns as I shrink in my seat. I knew this would be bad, but maybe not this bad.

"How are you going to get her back?" Mom asks.

"First, we have to find her," Dr. Fornax says. "Which won't be a problem. Our SecuriDrones are already looking. Her implant will work on Earth, so we'll override her privacy settings and—"

"She doesn't have an implant," my mother says.

"Why not?" Dr. Fornax asks, as if offended.

"Because," my mother says, standing tall as she levels her gaze straight at the MUSC CEO. "I didn't want her under your thumb."

"What?" I say aloud, then press my hands over my mouth, afraid that they'll hear me. All these years, my mother told me we didn't have enough money for an implant, but the truth was, she didn't want me to have one!

Dr. Fornax shifts uncomfortably. "Well . . . that's not a problem. We can initiate contact with whatever kind of device she uses."

"Oh, no!" I sit up tall, wondering if I should rip the device off my head or get out of the car and run into the tangle of vine-covered palm trees and dilapidated houses lining the road.

Then Kepler asks a question that I don't hear, but both my mom and Dr. Fornax whip around to face him.

"What did you say?" Dr. Fornax asks.

"I said, what if she takes off her communication device?" His words are slow and clear and deliberate.

"Why would she do that?" Dr. Fornax asks. "Without a device, she won't have any currency or a way to communicate. She'd have no Stream and won't be able to get around."

"In fact," Kep says, "she could take off her protective hood and her flight suit, too. Since she was born down there, she has plenty of white blood cells, plus natural immunity to Earth viruses and bacteria." Then very slowly and carefully, he says, "If she wanted to, she could blend right in on Earth, couldn't she?"

I gasp. Is he right? Could I pass for an Earthling after all these years away?

"She won't do that," Dr. Fornax insists.

My mother fixes her jaw tight and shakes her head. "She will if she doesn't want to be found."

Dr. Fornax draws in a tight breath and says to my mother, "I need your permission to override all privacy settings and break into her Stream right now."

My mother sighs, but then she nods and says, "Go ahead, you have my permission."

"Thumbprint," Fornax says.

My mother holds up her thumb to be scanned, and instantly Kep's feed on my Lenz is overtaken by Valentine Fornax.

"Uma?" she says. "Uma Jemison?"

My mother's holo crowds the view. The deep lines etched from the edges of her nose to her chin make her look as if she's cut from wood. "Uma, are you there?" I can hear the desperation in her voice. "Can you hear us?"

For a moment, I sit, paralyzed. I've never broken this many rules before. I know what Kepler is telling me—that I could command the car to stop right now in this hilly area dotted with ruined houses. I could get out, ditch my device, go down to where the people are, and blend in with the Earthlings. But if I do that, my mom will worry herself sick.

I take a deep breath and say, "I'm here."

"Oh thank god!" Mom lets go an enormous sigh.

"You are in a world of trouble!" Dr. Fornax rages at me. "You had direct orders not to board that Shuttle."

"The system welcomed me aboard. I thought maybe you changed your mind," I say, even though it's a lie.

Fornax looks at me, one eyebrow up, silently calling my bluff.

"Okay, fine," I say, voice shaky. "I left, but you had no right to cancel my trip when I did nothing wrong."

Fornax guffaws. "I have every right to do whatever I think is best for people in my employ."

"You don't know what's best for me," I snap at her, then sit back, surprised by my outburst.

"Where are you?" Dr. Fornax commands.

The car slows to wind around a gentle curve beneath a line of evenly spaced palm trees swaying under the darkening blue sky.

"I think you know," I say, because I'm not an idiot. "Surely you're tracking me by now."

The car pulls into a half-moon driveway and stops in front of a gigantic pink building with a black-and-white-striped awning. "You have arrived," the car announces.

"Initiate contact with transportation device," Dr. Fornax commands some bot in her system.

"Contact initiating," the system announces. "AutoPod detected. Commandeer vehicle in thirty, twenty-nine, twenty-eight . . ."

Dr. Fornax looks at me and says, "This AutoPod will immediately return you to the Shuttle launch site, where you will wait for the next return Shuttle to MUSC."

"Fifteen, fourteen, thirteen . . ."

"No!" I say, with my heart in my throat.

"Ten, nine, eight . . ."

"Doors open!" I command, and it works! I beat the bot. I jump out, looking for any place to run and hide. In front of me is a giant bush overflowing with purple blossoms.

"Get back in that AutoPod!" Dr. Fornax yells at me from my Lenz.

The good girl in me almost does as I am told, but something inside me snaps. "No! I won't," I say. "I've waited for this for too long. I've made it this far, and I'm not going back. Not yet." I run across the soft and springy grass.

"What do you think you're doing?" Dr. Fornax shouts. "You already disobeyed a direct order from me. You've lost the privilege to be there."

I stop and shout, "I've done everything right. Followed every rule. Never been a problem. Now I want a break! I need to get away from my life on MUSC for a little bit. That's what's best for me, and you can't take that away!"

Dr. Fornax stiffens. I can tell I hit a nerve. I don't know what it is, maybe being so far from home, maybe the Earth air filling my lungs, but I feel bold, and I start to rant. "Just once, I want to know what it feels like to belong. For people not to stare at me and ask stupid questions because I'm a Zero Gen on the Moon!"

"You think you're going to fit in down there?" my mother says incredulously. "Uma, you're not a Yoobie. We're from the Wastelands, which is why we left in the first place. We needed a ticket out for you, or you would have withered away, wasting all that intellect either as a conscripted soldier in a senseless war with Merica or picking up trash in the Wastelands. I might disagree with how Dr. Fornax is handling this situation—" She cuts her eyes to Fornax, and I wonder whose side she's on. "But the truth is, MUSC saved us a lifetime of heartache, and we owe Dr. Fornax our lives."

"Your mother's right," Fornax says. "Your family gave up literally everything on Earth to make a safe life for you on MUSC."

"Safe?" I scoff. "My father died working for you!"

My mother winces and looks away.

"Your father's death was deeply unfortunate," Dr. Fornax says. "A freak accident. We rarely have such fatalities. He was given a proper MUSC tethering in the field of the dead to honor him for his work."

In my mind, I see the silver pinwheel that is my father stuck on the far side of the moon, and I think that he wouldn't want me to give in so easily. *Swim, Uma, swim,* he yelled at me when I jumped into the ocean and the undertow dragged me away from the pier. I kicked and fought to make it back to the safety of his arms. *You're a fighter,* he told me. *Never give up on anything.*

"That's not enough," I say.

"You're not thinking clearly!" Dr. Fornax tells me. "If something happens to you, your mother will be forced to return to Earth. You wouldn't want that on your shoulders, would you?"

My mother's eyes flash. "Don't you put that on her. I'm not Uma's responsibility."

"No, but she is my responsibility," Dr. Fornax says. "I took a chance on your family. I spent a lot of money on your education, and I expect obedience in return."

I see my mother grit her teeth at the word *obedience.*

"You only say that because we're Zero Gens," I shout, knowing she would never say such a thing to a Second or Third Gen Moonling.

"You're right," Mom says. "But, Uma, life is a series of trade-offs. Yes, you are a Zero Gen on the Moon, and that means you have to work twice as hard and be twice as good to get half as much." She pauses, no doubt to let her statement resonate with Dr. Fornax. "But that's just the way it is. The truth is, we're the lucky ones, and we should be grateful—"

"No!" I shout. "I will not be grateful. I've waited so long to get here!" I spin, taking in all the vibrant colors of the Earth. The greenness of the grass. A bank of purple and red and yellow flowers. Bumblebees and butterflies. A dragonfly or two. Ants and flies and a shimmering spiderweb caught in the filter of the sun. Although part of me thinks I should obey Dr. Fornax and my mother, another bigger part takes over, and I say, "I'm not going to leave. Not yet. I'm going to take my trip for twenty-eight days like I was promised, like I deserve, then I'll return to MUSC and dedicate myself to my LWA like the good, obedient Zero

Gen girl I've always been." I root my feet on the ground. "I've come too far. I've waited too long. I'm not letting you take this away from me."

Suddenly, Kepler's face looms into Dr. Fornax's frame. "Go, Uma!" he yells. "Don't let them stop you! Take off your suit. Ditch your device. Go! Go! Go!"

Dr. Fornax elbows him out of the way, but I know he's right. It's what I've got to do. Without waiting, I run toward the giant bush, unzipping my hood. My hair springs out in all directions. Unfiltered Earth air overtakes me, and it is glorious. Warm and moist! It fills my lungs with brown and green and yellow, smells so deep and earthy that I can taste them. I whoop with delight and run into the bush while unzipping my flight suit. I duck beneath thick, waxy leaves and pull my arms out of the sleeves. One catches on a branch. I keep going, letting the whole suit strip down off my hips and past my knees. I step out and go deeper, looking for a place to stash my device until I want it again. My brain is scrambling to process the jumble of images, colors, and scents. I can barely make out what's in front of me, but I think I see a wall.

"I will find you!" Dr. Fornax threatens. "And when you return to MUSC, there will be consequences. Don't expect a Life's Work Assignment that you hoped for or a step up in your domicile . . ." She continues, but I ignore her.

"I love you, Mom! Please don't be mad!" I shout. "Thank you, Kepler! I'll see you all in twenty-eight days! Darshan, off!" I say, then I rip the device from my head and hurl it away.

I STUMBLE ONTO a cracked concrete ramp behind the Pink Palace cluttered with robot scraps and broken furniture. Scurrying like a rat, I slip between rows of dumpsters full of stinking trash from last night's party. Food waste, disposable cutlery, Gem Water bottles that have lost their sparkle, biodegradable tablecloths that will never see the sun, all waiting to be hauled out to the Wastelands and picked through by another version of me.

In the distance, I hear the familiar rumble and beep of automated trash trucks making their rounds. That sound defines my childhood. Endless trucks, like a line of ants, carrying detritus from AlphaZonia to the Dumps. Castor and I reversed the flow when we came into the Palace yesterday.

As I skirt inside the brick security wall to the front of the building, I hear some kind of commotion on the lawn. A person yelling. Ranting, really, but I can't make out the words. Probably some Yoobie reality drama—a breakup or product-placement war. When I get to the far edge of the big bush where we hid last night, I push through the thicket, moving branches out of the way with my shoulders.

"Quasar! Quasar!" I whisper-yell. "Come here, boy!"

The leaves are cool and waxy against my cheeks, but Quasar is nowhere to be found. Obviously the dog took off. Probably spooked by the sonic booms earlier this evening, or maybe he just got hungry and went to find some food. Now I'll have to find him.

I drop down to my hands and knees to search the ground for Castor's red knapsack, half buried under leaves. I find it quickly, then strip off the stupid Kinematic Jumpsuit and shove it into the bag. My skin tingles with relief as I put on my soft pants and shirt. Next, I remove the PEST and the other Wearables Castor gave me last night and reattach my old, beat-up device to my head, then wait for it to boot up. Years ago, Castor injected a crude RFID chip under Quasar's skin that connects to my device. Half the time it doesn't work, but it's my best chance to find him. Then I won't be alone. Like Quasar, I want my pack together before I go off in search of this Moonling. I strap the bag across my shoulders, then just as I'm about to leave, I hear more shouting.

I press myself against the wall, trying not to make a sound as I creep away. The bushes rustle, and I stop. Then something flies past and smacks the wall behind me.

"What the hell?" I yell as I duck.

Ahead of me, someone crashes through the brush. I cower, half expecting SecuriBot tentacles to wrap around my arms and legs and drag me back inside. What if D'Cart just changed her mind? What if Castor pissed her off? But it's not a bot. A person skids to a stop and crashes sideways into a tangle of branches. When she sees me, she screams. I scream back. We both stand stock-still, eyes locked, screaming like a couple of idiots.

Then I stop. There's no reason for me to be afraid. This girl is not a SecuriBot. Or even a Yoobie. In fact, she's about my age, with warm brown skin and springy dark curls. She's obviously not from around here, though. She's wearing some kind of strange silver fitted pants made of close-knit mesh with a short-sleeved silver shirt the likes of which I've never seen.

"Oh, my gad! Oh, my gad!" The girl sucks in giant gulps of air. One hand is pressed against her chest; the other clings to the branches so she won't fall over. "I didn't expect to see anyone. What are you doing in here?"

"What are *you* doing in here?" I shoot back.

"I . . . I . . . I . . ." She looks around wildly. "I got lost."

"Oh," I say, caught off guard. "Did you lose your group? Are you with a tour?"

She looks up to scan the darkening sky. A few early evening stars have appeared. "Sort of," she says. "Not really. I'm not with a group." She switches her gaze to me. "Can you help me?"

"No, I'm sorry," I say, and turn away. "I have to find my dog."

"A dog?" She jumps after me and clamps her hand on my arm. Her touch startles me, and I whip around to face her.

"Let go!" I say.

"No, wait! Was he about this big?" She holds up her hand to her knee. "Brown and white. Little pointy ears with a white star between his eyes and a fluffy white tail?"

"Yes!" I say, blinking back my surprise. "You saw him?"

"I did!"

I feel electricity pass between us. Goose bumps rise on my skin when a smile breaks across her face like sunlight through a morning haze. I realize then that she's beautiful. Beneath her curls, she has large, deep-set eyes the color of moss with flecks of gold.

"He was up the hill. By some buildings? Or houses? I don't know, but I could show you! Come on! I'll take you there."

She takes off, and I follow, because if this girl can lead me straight to Quasar, then I can start looking for the Moonling sooner.

We pop out of the bush, and she points at the winding road leading up into the hills. "This way! Come on!"

We both charge uphill, but neither of us lasts long at that pace. The steep incline kills my thighs, and soon I'm doubled over, panting. She trudges behind me, even more out of breath than I am.

"Where is he? Come on!" I beg the tracking device. "I need one thing to go right today!"

"You and me both!" the girl says.

I walk up the hill with the strange girl beside me, betting that Quasar is headed toward Aurelia in the Wildlands of 'Fith.

"Wow, wow, wow!" The girl turns in a circle, arms wide. "I can't get over how beautiful this place is! Everything here is glorious and amazing and . . . and . . ."

I look at her, spinning like a little kid. "Did you have your dopamine regulator hacked or something? Because I don't want any trouble."

She stops spinning. "My what?"

"No offense, but you seem far too excited over everything, and I can't afford to be an accomplice right now." I start to walk away.

But the girl laughs. "Oh, gad. Sorry. I didn't hack anything." She jogs to catch up with me again. "And I don't have a dopamine pump or whatever you said. It's just that I'm not from here, and I'm sort of overwhelmed, and—"

"Yeah, that's obvious. Where did you come from? One World?"

She shakes her head.

"The Distract?"

She shakes it again.

"Democratic Republic of New Yorkistan?"

"No, no, none of those," she assures me.

"Oh," I say, and understand. "So, you're from Merica?"

"Uh . . . um . . ." She hesitates. Probably embarrassed to admit it.

"Listen, I don't care where you're from. The Water Wars are stupid, if you ask me," I say, and she looks relieved.

"I'm just a tourist," she says. "I wanted to go to the Pink Palace, where RayNay DeShoppingCart lives."

Now I laugh.

"Why's that funny?"

"First off, you need an invite to go there. Even the Yoobies can't just show up. And secondly, nobody calls her by her full name. We just say D'Cart." We crest the hill and walk more easily.

"Like the philosopher?"

"The who?"

"René Descartes. Mr. I-Think-Therefore-I-Am? Father of Dualism?"

I wrinkle my nose and shake my head. "Never heard of him. The only D'Cart I know literally owns this town." I motion to the city spread out below us.

"Right. I consume, therefore I am." The girl chuckles.

"Yes, that's their motto."

"Don't you think that's ridiculous?" she asks.

"Oh, yeah. Definitely!" I say. "But, you know, in Yoobie minds, buying stuff is what distinguishes them from the robots and the people in the Wastelands, who have no income. Being a consumer makes them feel human."

"Sounds like an empty life to me," she says, and shakes her head, and I like her a little more.

We come to a streak of garbage strewn in front of a house. "Look at that." I crouch down, searching for paw prints in the muck. "Obviously, something has been by here recently."

"Your dog?" she asks.

"Maybe," I say. "Or cats or coyotes?" I shudder at the thought. Little Quasar believes that he's mightier than his size. He'd pick a fight with a mountain lion, but of course he'd never win.

"But I was miles from here when I saw him," she says, standing up to look around. "Closer to some kind of park or something."

Just then, a tiny blip quivers on my map. "There he is!" I shout.

"Where?" the girl shouts back. She spins and ducks and looks all around.

"On my map!" I tell her as I poke at the Glaz over my right eye. I move around, dancing from foot to foot to find a better signal. The blip is faint and cuts out for several seconds, then comes back. "Map! Zoom in!" I command before I lose his signal again.

The map enlarges fifty percent, and I see that he's in the Wildlands of 'Fith. "Yep. Just what I thought." I take off up the road but stop when a yellow AutoPod cruises around the curve ahead of us.

"Look out!" the girl yells, and tries to grab me, but I step into its path with my arms out.

"Jack-a-Pod!" I say, and Castor's hijacking app installed on my device works like a charm. Some rando's data he's uploaded tells the Pod to screech to a stop and the door to open.

"Hello, Braga Tralluri," it says. "Where would you like to go?"

"Share location," I tell my device as I climb in.

The girl stays at my heels, blocking the door so it won't close. "Please, can I come with you?" she asks. "I want to make sure your dog is okay."

The late-evening sun hits her from behind, sending golden rays of light through her corkscrew curls so that she radiates a sense of warmth that I rarely see in AlphaZonia. I should say no. I don't know her at all, but she looks so sincere. So worried about Quasar. And honestly, she seems so lost that I feel bad leaving her on her own. Plus, the truth is, I don't want to be alone, so I say, "Come on. Get in."

"Thank you! Thank you so much." She climbs aboard.

The blip from my map transfers to the Pod's AutoNav system, and we make a U-turn, then head northeast.

"So, your name is Braga?" she asks.

"No . . . um . . ." I stutter, not wanting to explain how my brother hijacks data packets. "That's someone else. I'm Talitha."

"Talitha?" She laughs with disbelief.

"Why's that funny?"

"Because my name is Uma."

"And . . . ?" I lean away, regretting that I let her come with me. Do I hate to be alone so much that I'd let a stranger come with me? Or am I just a sucker for a cute girl?

"I'm named for Ursa Major—the greater bear constellation. There's a star called Talitha on my constellation's front paw."

"Did you just make that up?"

"No, not at all—it's true! Look it up on your device! You are a star in my constellation."

A little ripple travels down my spine. "Uma and Talitha, hmmm?"

"Yes." She laughs, delighted. "Our meeting was written in the stars!"

"Oh, I don't know about that," I say, but I have to look away because I'm probably blushing.

"Well, however it happened, I'm really lucky I met you, because my plans got all screwed up and I'm kind of lost, but I don't care because this place is miraculous! Look at all of the plant life! And the colors! And the smells!" She jabs her finger against the window, pointing at everything outside. "You're so lucky to live here!"

I snort. "Lucky if you're a Yoobie, which I'm not."

"What are you, then?"

"Well . . ." I try to find the right word. "I guess I'm just a girl."

"Oh, I like that!" Uma smiles, and I'm struck by her beauty again. "That's what I am, too. Just a girl. On a trip. Trying to find my way."

I nod at her but think to myself, *Oh, dear, she's so much more than just a girl.* Then I shake myself to refocus on what Castor told me: First the knapsack—check! Now Quasar. Then to Lost Feelies and Soggywood to look for the Moonling. This girl has no place in my plan.

From the surface street, we cross beneath the 101 transportation tube. AutoPods zip by overhead, flashing like phosphorescent animals in the sea.

"I think I was up there earlier," Uma says.

"If you came from outside the city, you were," I tell her. "That's the only way in." Then I add, "Legally, that is."

"Oh, look!" she says, giddy like a little kid. "It's me! A she bear!" She points out the window at a bear statue, standing upright on hind legs with paws out as if forever guarding the old entrance of what was once a park. "FITH P K?" she reads what's left of the letters on an old sign we pass.

"That's the Wildlands of 'Fith." I point at the hills separating AlphaZonia from the Wastelands. "My dog's up there." I take over the nav system and steer the Pod up a winding path lined with ruins of old houses to get as close as possible to the city-Wildlands boundary, then I pull over and idle on the side of the road.

"Why are we stopping?" Uma asks.

"The AutoPods won't go inside the Wildlands." I grab the knapsack and climb out of the car.

Uma follows. We stand side by side, facing the steep hill. "Whoa," she says, her mouth open.

"Yeah, it's a bit of a hike," I tell her. "You can have the AutoPod if you want." I feel a twinge of disappointment at the thought of saying good-bye to her, even though we just met and she's a bit strange and she'll slow me down if she stays with me.

"But I want to come with you!" she says. "I want to make sure you find your dog."

Despite my wariness, I have to smile at this Uma girl. "Most people don't care about dogs that much."

"Oh, I love dogs!" she says. "It's one of the reasons I'm here! We don't have them where I'm from."

"Wow," I say. "Merica sounds truly awful."

"Let's go," she says. "Before he gets too far away!" Then she runs straight ahead.

"Stop!" I yell and grab her. "There's an invisible barrier!" I yank her back just before she steps into the electrified shield. "It'll shock you." I pick up a stick and throw it. It pops and sizzles in the air.

"Oh!" She shivers at my side. I see goose bumps rise up on her skin.

I pat her arm to calm her. "You okay?"

"Yeah," she says, and laughs nervously. "But how do we get in, then?"

"Over here." I point to a large rock on the other side of a creosote bush. "My brother and I dug a hole."

AS SOON AS Mundie and Talitha are gone, I look directly at D'Cart and say, "I liked what you said about the ExploroBots last night on your Stream. I agree with you. What MUSC does to human soldiers is unconscionable."

"I meant every word," she says. "That topic is especially important to me."

"Really?" I ask. "Why do you care?"

A look passes over her face that I can't quite read. A flash of anger maybe? Sadness? Some kind of regret? It resolves quickly into her placid stare. "Because somebody has to."

Although I should probably keep my mouth shut, as usual, I don't. "Yeah, but . . ." I lean back and watch her carefully. "What's in it for you?"

"There has to be something in it for me?"

"Of course. You're a capitalist. First and foremost. You own an entire city."

"Ha!" Her laugh is bitter. "Just as I suspected. You're too smart for your own good. Or mine, probably." She looks at me carefully and shakes her head. "Believe it or not, I started out a lot like you, Castor Neva."

"I sincerely doubt that."

"It's true." She gets up and commands the holo screen to show a map of the western landmass.

I've seen old maps of North America when it was a single nation from sea to shining sea, when education was free and humans drove cars and the government dictated who could marry whom and what women could do with their bodies. Back before the Moon colony even existed. How quaint! Now, Merica, a sickly yellow swath, takes up most of the area between the privatized cities like One World, the Distract, and New Yorkistan on the east coast and the Rocky Mountains in the west. AlphaZonia is a tiny red dot sandwiched between the Pacific Ocean and the San Gabriels. And in between is a gray area—the Wastelands.

"I'm from there, too," she says almost wistfully.

I study her while she gazes at the map. Although her skin is smooth and dewy in the waning light coming through the windows, I can see tiny lines etched around her eyes and the smallest sag beneath her chin. I have no idea how old she is or where she's really from. When Talitha first started parodying her Stream, I tried to trace D'Cart's background, but all the references to her only go back twenty years. Before that, it's as if she didn't exist. So maybe she's telling the truth. Maybe she did come from the Wastelands after all.

"If you're from the Wastelands, then how'd you get out?" I ask.

She hesitates then says, "MUSC scholarship."

I smack my leg. "I knew there had to be a catch. You were one of the lucky ones."

"Lucky?" She whips her head around to me. "That's what you think?"

I nod. "Look what you have! Your own privatized city with thousands of citizen shareholders selling the stuff you make to millions of followers all over the world."

"I'm not sure luck had much to do with it," she says. "I worked hard. Most people in the Wastelands are happy to exist off the scraps from the rich. Some are even grateful for the waste. One person's trash is another person's treasure and all that nonsense. But not me. When I was growing up, I knew I deserved more."

"I know the feeling."

"Is that the reason you stole from me?" D'Cart walks back to the table to sit. She laces her fingers together and leans in closer, waiting for my answer.

I sigh and rub my hands down my face. "I'm sorry. That was wrong. I shouldn't have hacked your product stream. I'll return all of the money and remove the product links and—"

"I already took care of that," she says, dismissively. "Any half-rate hacker can do that. Honestly, I expected more out of you."

That ticks me off, and I take it as a challenge. "You mean, like, being able to hack your followers' TFT chips?"

Her eyebrows shoot up, and she stares at me for a moment. Then she surprises me by chuckling when I thought that she'd get mad. "Well, Castor Neva, you've got me there. That is pretty impressive. So why don't you explain to me exactly how you scanned the data from inside Cristela Wong Holtzmann's brain."

I squirm. "I know it's illegal to mess with their implants." My palms sweat, and my heart speeds up. "But she came to me, you know! They all do. I don't seek them out."

D'Cart narrows her eyes. "What do they want?"

I pause, not sure if I should admit the truth, but then I realize I don't have much choice. "DopaHacks," I say quickly, without looking at her. "They want more dopamine."

"Dopamine?" D'Cart seems genuinely surprised. "Why dopamine?"

"Because the old drugs don't work on them anymore. The neural web you install regulates exactly how much dopamine and serotonin their brains produce, no matter what they drink or smoke or snort. But I found a way around that by going straight to the implants to temporarily rev up the dopamine and—"

"Stop," she says.

I shut up immediately.

Her eyes look a little wild. "Tell me exactly how you access their implants."

"Through the transnasal corridor your EndoscoBots make when they install the neural webs, duh," I say.

"Not possible." With eyebrows flexed, she thinks out loud, puzzling through the process. "When I install TouchyFeelyTech, my EndoscoBots go in through the nostril, create a corridor through the sphenoid sinus and the sella in the skull behind the nose to insert our TFT between the pituitary gland and VTA. The neural web implants into the brain and connects my followers to me so they can experience my visceral sensations, which is why we control dopamine and serotonin, among other neurotransmitters. Then the EndoscoBot exits the same way, leaving a teeny lipid-covered graphene gate to protect the corridor."

"Yes, but I found something that can get through to the neural web."

Her mouth opens, just slightly, enough for me to know she's intrigued. "What is it?"

"If I tell you, will you let me go?" I ask.

She rears back. "No."

So I cross my arms and look away. "Then I won't tell you."

"Then I'll kill your sister."

My breath leaves me like I've been punched. "What?"

The warmth in her eyes has been extinguished. She looks at me, cold and calculating. "You and your sister are just two more Wasteland urchins that nobody's looking for. I can make you or her disappear anytime I want. You're both lucky I let you stay this long."

I swallow hard, but my mouth's gone dry. "What about the Moonling?" I ask in a raspy voice.

D'Cart thinks this over for about two seconds before she says, "Oh, yeah. I almost forgot. I could probably find another way to pick up that Moonling, but since your sister's already working on it, we can stick to the plan." She pauses, then says, "If . . ."

I nod. I get it. "If I tell you how I access the implants?"

She reaches over and pats my hand. "So smart, Castor Neva. So very, very smart."

I squirm away from her touch. "Okay, fine. But if I tell you, I want to know why you want the Moonling."

She shrugs. "Fair enough. You go first."

I lean forward and talk quietly. "I found something. At the MUSC dump behind the ExploroBot Creation Center near the Shuttle landing site. I think they might use the same transnasal endoscopy procedure as you to insert their brain-to-brain interface webs into the soldiers—"

"Of course they do!" She smacks the table with both hands. "But what's that got to do with it?"

"Well, see, I was looking for fuel at the MUSC dump, but I found this other stuff. This goo. At first I ignored it, but—"

"What is it?" she demands, impatient with my hemming and hawing.

"I think it might be a bacteria or a virus. Whatever it is, it can cross the blood-brain barrier—"

"Like meningitis?"

"Yep, but it doesn't kill anybody. Just makes them a little sick. Like with a cold or something, but the really cool part is, you can piggyback other stuff on it that will go straight to the implant. I use *Banisteriopsis caapi*," I tell her.

"Ayahuasca?"

"Well, sort of. I isolate one compound from the caapi plant called harmaline that I piggyback on the goo. Then I put the goo up their noses so it goes into the neural web to temporarily increase the amount of dopamine being manufactured. And sometimes, while a Yoobie is flying high, I can get close enough to scan a little extra data from a TFT implant with this little device I made . . ." I reach for my cuff.

"I'm not interested in that." She swats my arm away, then sits back, eyes narrow, mouth pursed. "I want to know more about the goo you found. Is it still there? At the MUSC dump?"

"Oh, yeah. There's a vat of it half buried behind the facility. You don't need much. I could get it for you," I offer. "If you let me go."

"Nice try," she says, and rolls her eyes. "We'll send your sister."

"Aw, man," I say, and slump. "Talitha's going to kill me."

"Better than me killing her." D'Cart cracks herself up, but I feel sick.

Once she stops laughing, I say, "Okay, now it's your turn. I told you how I get into the TFT implants. Now you tell me what you want with the Moonling."

D'Cart chuckles as if she finds my curiosity amusing. She gets up from the chair and walks back to the holo map once again. This time, she commands it to zoom out farther and farther. To the south of

AlphaZonia, I see remnants of the half-built wall that used to separate the old United States from what was Mexico. To the north, over the San Gabriels, there's a blue circle drawn around the designated MUSC Shuttle landing site. Not far from that are the ExploroBot Creation Site and the Dumps in the Wastelands near where we grew up. She keeps going, zooming out until we've left the Earth and are peering down at the planet from space.

Without looking at me she says, "Let's just say I'm looking to expand."

UMA JEMISON

WILDLANDS OF 'FITH, EARTH

TALITHA SHOVES THE rock aside, which isn't really a rock but a decoy made of hard plastic that's half covering a hole. "We found this washed up on the shore one day," she says. "For a while there were lots of old movie props that floated in. We figured some of them would come in handy. And they did."

A cool wind rises from the shallow opening in the ground. "Look, paw prints," she says, and points to the ground with her toe. She smiles. "Quasar definitely came through here," she says, and slides into the hole feetfirst and disappears. A few seconds later, she pops out from behind a bush on the other side of the invisible barrier. "Your turn!"

I slide in, pulling the rock behind me to hide the hole. I inch my way forward through the musky, earthy smell until I see light on the other side. There's just enough room for me to curl up and flip over so I can climb out headfirst.

Talitha offers me her hand and pulls me up.

"Wow," I say, grinning and brushing dirt from my clothes. "That was fun!"

Talitha snickers, then says, "You have a strange sense of fun. But I like it!"

I feel strangely validated when she says this. Not to mention blushy and warm. Maybe it's the excitement of all the novel experiences, but I have the strongest urge to stand closer to Talitha. To feel her skin on mine. To drink in her scent. But I keep my distance. I don't want to seem any more odd than I already must.

I follow her and talk nonstop as she picks a path through small gnarled trees and scrubby brush on the hillside. "What is this place? Who lives here? How did you find it? Why did your dog come here?" The questions spill out of me and bounce around the rocky crevices. From somewhere nearby, faint music and muffled voices travel over the hills.

Talitha presses her finger against her lips. "Shhhh." She slows so we're side by side. She's taller than I am, and thinner. The giraffe to my rhino. She speaks quietly as we walk, her eyes scanning the area around us. "The Wildlands of 'Fith can be a rough place. All sorts of creepy people come through here to slip into the city."

"Oh," I say, edging closer to her side. "How do you know that?"

Talitha smirks. "Because three years ago, my brother and I came in this way."

"You did? You must've have been really young." I have to watch my feet as we pick our way up the steep rocky path in the waning light.

She shrugs. "Not that young. Thirteen when we came. We stayed at the Observatory for about a year before we found a house inside the city."

"The Observatory?"

She points up, and I see a beautiful old building shimmering in the last rays of sun. From here, it looks like a pristine monument to some bygone era on Earth. But, as we get closer, I can make out fractures running through the white walls that show the Observatory's age and state of disrepair.

I hurry to keep up with Talitha. Her long legs lope at a faster pace than my short ones. Plus, I'm not used to the heavy air, dense with water and nitrogen. Even though the sun is nearly down, it's still brutally hot, and I'm sweating through my long underwear.

At the top of the hill, we come out of the woods and rest for a minute beneath the sprawling canopy of a big tree. Talitha takes off her hooded jacket and rolls up her sleeves. Then she flips her head over and catches all her beautiful red hair in a knot on top of her head. I am speechless for a moment. She reminds me of a sculpture made from clay, all smooth curves, no angles anywhere. I imagine placing my hands into the perfect indentation between her ribs and hips. She catches me staring, and I quickly look away.

"What?" she asks.

If I weren't already bright red from the heat, my embarrassment would be completely obvious. "Nothing, sorry, it's just that, um . . . I like your clothes."

Now she stares at me. Mouth open slightly. I look down self-consciously.

"I've never seen a silver outfit like that," she says. "What's it made of? Did you buy it off a Stream?"

"Uh, um," I stammer, then say, "I'm not sure . . ." Because I can't exactly blurt out that it's a MUSC-issued undergarment all Moonlings wear. Even though this girl seems really nice, I don't know if I can trust her yet, and I need to keep a low profile while Dr. Fornax is trying to find me.

"Come on," Talitha says. "I'll show you around."

We stroll past the front of the building. Most of the windows have been replaced by reinforced metal, but it's still quite pretty.

"That's strange," I say, pointing to the copper-colored dome in the center of the roof. "Look at that crack. It looks like one big seam, moving out from the top in a perfect spiral. Like a lotus flower or a pinecone about to open."

"The earthquake and tsunami did some weird things," she tells me. "AutoPods on top of trees. Boats on top of buildings. Houses sliding down hills as if they melted. Construction cranes skewered through skyscrapers like toothpicks in cheese. But look at all the little details that survived." She points to intricate designs in the plaster and metalwork around the entryway—scallops and zigzags and etchings of ancient astronomers and their instruments. "Aurelia takes good care of this place."

"Who's Aurelia?"

"The caretaker," Talitha says. "And if I'm correct, Quasar is probably with her right now. Come on." She leads the way up a winding stone staircase on the side of the building, calling, "Quasar! Quasar, come!"

The dog's sweet little face appears over the edge of a crumbling wall at the top of the steps, and I shout, "That's the dog I saw earlier!"

Talitha runs to him. She tries to catch the dog in a hug, but he's too excited. He hops on hind legs, forepaws on her shoulders, tongue licking at her face.

"Quasar! My lovey! I was so worried about you! I'm so glad you're safe."

I stand at the top of the steps, grinning and envious of Talitha and her dog. This is so much of what it means to be human on Earth, I think. To love something and have it love you back and never feel afraid to show it. The beauty of their reunion makes my chest feel tight and heavy, as if something is trying to break through, like a little green shoot pushing through hard ground after a long-awaited rain.

"Do you want to say hi?" she asks me once Quasar settles down.

I nod.

"Quasar, sit," she says. He plops down and waits politely for a treat.

Talitha hands me a bright orange strip from her pocket. "Mango Bango Oink Oink Jerky," she tells me. "His favorite."

Quasar politely nibbles it from my palm, which tickles. I drop down to one knee and bury both of my hands in his fur. I let him nuzzle my ear and pull in his burnt-sugar smell. "Hello! Do you remember me? I look a bit different now. So nice to finally meet you."

He leans in and pants happily.

A shadow passes over us, and Talitha says, "Hey, Aurelia."

I look up to greet the caretaker, then I gasp and topple backward onto my butt. "Oh, my gad," I cry when I see a half-human-looking AI robot staring down at me. "She's . . . it's . . . that's . . . not a human!"

"I am Aurelia 8.1," the robot says. Her large blue-lit eyes blink in her sculpted faceplate. She bends at the waist and extends an arm to me.

"I thought these kinds of bots had been banned," I say, my heart still fluttering in my chest as Aurelia helps me up.

"Brain uploads and the development of strong AI were banned on parts of the Earth due to fears of a hostile superintelligence takeover," Aurelia explains.

"Yeah, but that's mostly in Merica," Talitha says with a laugh. "You guys hate science over there."

I walk in a slow circle around Aurelia, whose head spins 180 degrees to follow me. "Tell me about yourself," I command, and Aurelia complies.

"I am Aurelia 8.1. I was developed by Zaniah Nashira—"

"Zaniah Nashira! THE Zaniah Nashira?" My voice is too loud, and my entire body trembles when I hear her name. I can barely contain my excitement. "Is she here?" I ask the robot. "Can I meet her?"

"Zaniah Nashira perished in the Great Tsunami," Aurelia explains.

"What?" My heart falls. I bury my fingers in my hair and hold my head as the sadness hits me hard. The one person in the universe most like me was snatched away by some capricious natural disaster before I could ever meet her. "How can Zaniah Nashira be dead?" I cry.

"Who the heck is Zaniah Nashira?" Talitha asks.

Aurelia tilts her head up to look at Talitha, who is taller by at least a foot. "Zaniah Nashira was an Earth-born human whose parents died during the Battle of the Colorado River. Brilliant as a child, she was recruited by MUSC when she was ten years old. Her research was used to develop a sophisticated brain-to-brain interface program, the breakthrough technology that enabled the creation of ExploroBots—"

"Whoa, whoa, whoa," says Talitha. "Are you telling me that the person who made you, Aurelia, is the same person who invented ExploroBot technology on the Moon?"

"This is terrible," I say, my heart broken.

"Awful!" says Talitha. "Just horrifying!"

"Wait," I say. "Why are you sad? Didn't you know she was dead?"

"I don't care about her," says Talitha, a sick look on her face. "I'm upset that the person who made Aurelia is the same one who invented ExploroBots!" She crosses her arms tight against her chest. "Do you know what ExploroBots are?"

"Yes, I think so," I whisper. A chill passes over my body, and I stiffen, wondering what Talitha might think of me if she knew where I'm from.

"Well," she says, eyebrows up, "don't you think what MUSC does to soldiers from Earth is horrendous?"

"Well, actually, yes," I tell her honestly, without hesitation. "I think it's the worst thing in the universe."

Talitha's face softens, and she drops her arms to her sides. "Me too," she says quietly. "Me too."

"Talitha," Aurelia says, "have you come for a viewing tonight?"

"What's a viewing?" I ask, relieved to change the topic away from MUSC.

"Through the telescope," says Talitha. "Come. We'll show you!"

Quasar, Talitha, and I follow Aurelia across the large stone terrace overlooking the half-lit city below. "Whoa," I say, slowing down. "Look at that!"

Talitha stops and points to landmarks. "See how the lights dot the darkness south and east of the 101 ET3 Tube? That's where the Re-Construction crews have made progress over the years. Those dark areas haven't yet been reclaimed. People call them things like Drowney, Torrents, and Miracle Mire. Of course, those names are only funny if you weren't here during the Great Tsunami."

"Were you here?" I ask.

Talitha shakes her head. "We came after." She waves me on.

We circle a promenade around the main cracked dome of the building. Up close, the walls look like an old-fashioned wedding cake covered in white icing and topped with green patinaed metal leaves, most of them intact, thanks to Aurelia's persistent care.

As we walk, Aurelia spouts her knowledge. "The viewing tonight will be from the Zeiss twelve-inch refracting telescope manufactured in Germany from 1931 to 1934. This is the oldest continuously operated telescope in the world."

While Aurelia chatters about the telescope's equatorial mount meant to compensate for the Earth's rotation, I don't really listen. Instead, I'm taking in the sky that's faded from blue to dark gray now that the sun is gone. But the moon isn't visible just yet. Somewhere it hides, like me. Looking for it now, I understand better the pull between the Moon and Earth year after year—each one slowed by the other's gravitational force, as if they are slowly trying to reunite.

Aurelia leads us through a heavy steel door into a tiny room beneath a small dome to the left of the promenade terrace. Inside is nothing more than a looming gunmetal gray telescope beneath arching waffled windows and three ancient clocks on the wall, labeled Pacific Time, Sidereal Time, and Universal Time.

"Why's that the only one that works?" I ask, pointing to the side-real clock with a second hand that still spins. The hands on the other two have stalled at different times.

"It's the only one that remains relevant," Aurelia says. "The other two went obsolete when the world economy broke apart."

"I never noticed those," Talitha says, peering at the clocks. "What's side-real time?"

"Si-deer-ree-al." I correct her. "It counts star days, not solar days. Astronomers use it to tell time by measuring the rotation of the Earth relative to a distant star instead of the Earth's relationship to the sun."

"Why?" Talitha asks. "What's wrong with the sun?"

"Nothing's wrong with it," I say, as overhead, the roof of the domed room slowly spins around us and a slot in the ceiling slides open to reveal a slice of the starry sky. "But it's kind of a lie to say the Earth spins once every twenty-four hours. That doesn't account for the planet's elliptical orbit or the rate at which the Earth rotates on its axis."

"So what?" says Talitha as Quasar spins in his own little circle, then settles on the hard concrete floor. "Why does that matter? I thought time was just an illusion. Isn't that what someone smart once said?"

"Yes, but . . ." I think this over and try my best to explain. "When you track time using the sun, stars appear in the sky four minutes earlier every day. But, when you use sidereal time, stars appear in the same place, at the same time each and every day. That way you always know where to point your telescope without worrying about where Earth is in its orbit."

"So, sidereal time gives you what seems like a fixed point of reference?" Talitha asks.

"Yes!" I exclaim. "Exactly. You're so smart!"

"No, not really," she says, and color rises to her cheeks.

"What would you like to view tonight?" Aurelia asks.

"Let's look at us," I say, and smile at Talitha. "Aurelia, please locate Ursa Major!"

Bolts as big as my fist groan, and gear wheels with teeth like some prehistoric plant eater grind as Aurelia moves the telescope into position for Ursa Major.

I follow Talitha up the creaking steps to the viewing platform. "You go first," I say.

She presses her head against the eyepiece. Her hair comes out of its knot and falls around her face. I reach to brush it away.

She glances at me.

"Oh, sorry," I whisper.

"That's okay," she says with a smile, as she twists her hair into a low bun at the nape of her perfect neck.

When she puts her head down again, I sigh and feel my body tingle.

"What am I looking at?" she asks.

"Do you see the Big Dipper?" I say. "It looks like an upside-down pot with a long handle."

"Yes."

"It's also called Ursa Major. The great bear. Now follow the line of stars down the handle—Alkaid, Mizar, Alioth, those make up the tail of Ursa Major. And around the bottom of the dipper, which is the back flank of the bear, Megrez, Phecda, Merak. Then go straight down from Merak to the front paw of the bear to the star on the toe. That's you!" I lay my hand on the small of her back and lean closer to her ear so I can pull in the scent of her hair. She smells of jasmine and grass. "That's Talitha."

She turns her head just slightly so our faces are inches apart, and a shiver goes down my spine. "Beautiful, isn't it?" I ask her.

We both inhale at the same time, then hold our breath as we gaze at each other, while overhead our stars twinkle in the dark sky.

"Talitha is also known as Iota Ursae Majoris," says Aurelia. "It is forty-eight light years away and has a luminosity nine times the sun."

Talitha's eyes seem to linger on me, and for a split second I think maybe she feels the same way I do. I inhale, trying to form a question, but then Aurelia says, "The Moon may provide more interesting viewing tonight." She shifts the telescope beneath our feet, knocking us off balance and breaking the moment that passed between Talitha and me.

"Thanks a lot, Aurelia," Talitha says sarcastically, and I laugh.

"You're welcome," says Aurelia because, like all robots, intelligent or not, she doesn't register the subtleties of human humor.

"Your turn," Talitha tells me.

We pass each other on the small platform, our hips and shoulders brushing. My temperature rises. If Darshan were with me, he'd ask if I'm all right. And what could I tell him? Nanobrains don't understand physical attraction. And neither did I until this moment. Whatever I've felt for Kepler before was nothing of this magnitude.

To keep myself from staring at her, I peer down into the eyepiece. "There it is!" I say as the waxing gibbous Moon comes into view and guilt washes over me. Guilt for going against Dr. Fornax's orders. Guilt for upsetting my mother. Guilt for getting Kepler in trouble. And mostly, guilt for enjoying this moment while they all fret about me from 384,000 kilometers away.

"During the last quarter waxing phase, the day side of the Moon is illuminated by the sun, so it appears humpbacked in the sky," Aurelia explains. "Starting at the southern pole of the crescent, you will see the terraforming of TourEsa simulators. Moving northward, find the towers and ever-glowing billboards near the Golden Spike and Jade Rabbit casinos."

"That's where all the Yoobies go on their outer orbit vacations," Talitha says with disdain. "So decadent!"

And where most of my cohort is right now, I think with the same amount of contempt.

Aurelia keeps right on going. "Because of the position of the Moon in relation to the Earth and sun, tonight you will have the most luck viewing Lagrange Point 1—the equatorial point closest to the Earth."

She continues to zoom in with the telescope, and then I see it. "MUSC," I whisper when I see my home.

"Yes," says Aurelia.

I gaze at it from afar, wondering how much trouble I've caused. My actions were so impulsive. So stupid and self-centered.

"First inhabited by ten people on the surface, MUSC is the oldest, most continually inhabited off-Earth colony." Aurelia blathers out our history. "After six decades, MUSC instituted ExploroBots to begin construction of SkyLabs and domiciles that are connected to the Moon's surface by six balancing legs and a nonrotating elevator shaft. SkyDocks and Shuttles offer easier and more cost-effective transportation options between the Earth and Moon."

"My father helped build that," says Talitha.

I pop up and stare at her. "What? How?"

"He was a soldier, but then . . ." Her words catch in her throat.

"An ExploroBot?" I ask, my voice barely audible.

"He died in the Hetch Hetchy Aqueduct Battle. MUSC bought his body from my mother." She shakes her head but doesn't go on.

I want to pull her close and hug her tight, but I know I can't. Instead I lay my hand on the small of her back. "I'm sorry, Talitha. So very, very sorry."

TALITHA NEVA

WILDLANDS OF 'FITH, EARTH

WHEN WE'RE DONE with the viewing and have said good-bye to Aurelia, Uma and I stroll down the Observatory steps beneath the light of the Moon and stars. We cross a brown patch of ground (once a bright green lawn) lined with long-dead street lamps and head over to where Quasar sniffs the brittle grass around a fallen obelisk.

"Thank you so much for letting me come with you," Uma says, turning in slow circles to take in the surroundings. "I understand why you and your brother stayed here. It feels almost cozy tucked into these hills overlooking the city. Safe. Like no one or nothing could find you."

"Aurelia says that the best life is a life well hidden," I tell her. "But I'm not so sure about that. She also claims that a long time ago the Observatory was open to the public and people flocked here to look up at the planets and the stars, but I doubt that's true."

Uma stops. "I don't know. She might be right! Maybe once, some girl from the past stood in this exact spot and imagined a future when people would move up there." She points to the yellow-bellied moon hanging in the sky. "And now the future that she imagined is our past."

"Do you ever think there could be another version of the world?" I ask, feeling shy, afraid Uma will think I'm strange for such thoughts.

"Actually," she says, turning to me with wide eyes, "I think about that kind of thing a lot! Like maybe there are all these other realities happening at the same time. And if you could see them all, time would look like a tree branching out with different possibilities."

"Yes!" I say as a little shiver of recognition reverberates through my body. I step closer to her. "And maybe you could find a branch where a different past leads to a different version of today. Like, my mom claims that if some elections had come out differently in the past, there could still be a United States."

"Or maybe in some different version of the world, people listened to scientists, and they stopped the Earth from slowly dying, so nobody had to go the Moon," says Uma.

"Or maybe none of this is real," I say with a laugh. "Maybe everything's an illusion and our memories are lies. How do we know this isn't all a dream?"

"Because I can see this world and touch it," Uma says. "And I can describe it. There's a tree." She points to an ailanthus tree. "And a rock." She points again. "And you beside me." She pokes my shoulder.

"But maybe we only see the world we can describe," I say with a laugh.

"Well, there's one thing I know for sure," Uma says. "I'm real." She reaches out slowly and takes my hand, then presses it against her sternum. I catch my breath when I feel her skin against mine. "And so are you." She lays her other palm on my chest. "Feel that?" We're both quiet for a moment as we breathe, our hearts beating in a syncopated rhythm.

I wish right then that this moment could be my past, present, and future so it would never end.

"Then the only questions are, who are we, and why did we meet?" she asks, and drops her hand. Her warmth lingers on my skin and makes me blush. She looks back up at the sky.

"Maybe there are little portals between different versions of reality, and sometimes without realizing it, we step through one of those doors. Like when you came into the bush," I say.

"Maybe a door between our worlds flew open?" she asks. I nod. "And there you were?"

"Yes!" Butterflies whiz through my belly. "There you were, too."

Uma bites her lip and walks around the fallen monument to astronomers, kicking glittery stones from the crumbling statues. A dozen different pasts, presents, and futures whiz through my mind as I watch her. Is there a reality in which we never met or one in which we did but we'll walk away from each other and never see each other again? Or will I find a way to keep her near me tonight? Will we ever kiss? Is that a future that's already in my past? Or a past that's in my future?

Only one of the spotlights on the lawn still works, so Uma squints in the weak light, reading off the names of long-dead astronomers below each figurine on the ground. "Hipparchus, Copernicus, Galilei." Then she stops, gasps, and points to the carving of a man holding a compass. "There's Kepler! How funny. That's the name of my best friend."

Quasar ambles over and nudges me. "Poor pup." I squat down beside him, and he slings a paw over my arm as I scratch the thicket of fur on his chest. He's full of burrs and dried leaves from burrowing under the barrier and traipsing through the Wildlands. I feel around in my pockets and inside the red knapsack for a crumb of jerky, but I'm out. "He's probably famished."

"Me too," says Uma. "I feel like I haven't eaten in days."

"Well . . ." I debate about what to do. I need to look for the Moonling right away. Those MUSC SecuriDrones can't be far off, and if they find the runaway before me, I don't know what D'Cart will do with Castor.

That thought stops me cold. I imagine him locked inside the tiny room, pacing like a caged wolf, looking for a way out. I have to find the Moonling and get back quickly before he does something stupid. Then again, he told me to try Lost Feelies first and we are starving, so I say, "We could go get some food together if you want." I hold my breath, afraid that she'll say no.

Uma lights up. "That would be amazing!" Then her face falls. "Oh, but . . ." She trails off and looks away.

"Sorry," I say. "I'm sure you have lots of things you need to do, and I—"

"No, it's not that." She wraps her fingers lightly around my wrist. Her hand is warm and soft. "It's just that . . . Well, this is embarrassing." She loosens her grip on me, but I quickly lay my hand on top of hers to keep her close.

"Don't be embarrassed," I tell her. "What is it?" I feel a little queasy. Sure that I'm coming on too strong. But Uma leans in closer. She stands on tiptoes so her lips are near my ear. Her breath on my cheek sends a ripple over my skin like a breeze on still water. I could turn my head a few degrees, and my mouth would brush her forehead.

"I don't have any currency," she whispers, then drops down to her heels.

"Don't worry about that!" I reach inside the red knapsack again. "I can get us just about anything with this." I hold up Castor's data scanner—our ticket to everything in AlphaZonia.

With my old device stowed inside the knapsack and the Wearables back on, I lead Uma and Quasar down the hill to Lost Feelies—the Yoobie neighborhood closest to the edge of 'Fith with good food and possible MUSCie sightings.

Uma sticks close by when we emerge from a quiet side street onto a busy promenade lined with automated food marts and filled with chattering, nattering people Streaming under filtered streetlights. "That's a lot of people!" she says.

"Everybody comes here," I tell her. "Yoobies, tourists, sometimes even Moonlings." I pause for a second and consider telling her that I'm looking for a Moonling runaway, but she shrinks away as if afraid.

"Is there lots of security around here?" she asks.

Her sweetness and innocence make me feel mercenary, so I keep my true objective to myself. I'm afraid she won't like me if I admit what I'm really up to. "There are no SecuriBots, but don't worry!" I reassure her. "Moonlings won't hurt you. They're odd-looking, but mostly they keep to themselves. We're safe here."

I pull her into the flow of bodies and head for my favorite place—a white boxy building with red letters spelling out FOODINI MART flashing above the entrance. Quasar parks himself beside the building to wait while we go inside.

I step up to a bank of screen pads over square cubbies. "If you have a TFT chip, you can experience what D'Cart recommends to eat, then think your order, but we'll have to do it the old-fashioned way."

I hold up my TouchCuff next to the screen and hear the subtle click of recognition. An automated voice says, "Welcome, Jubar Thrashman. What would you like to eat?"

Uma glances at me, perplexed. I hold my breath, afraid of what she'll think. But she gives me a little nod, as if an understanding has passed between us, and she says, "Yeah, Jubar, what's for dinner?" with a wink.

Grinning with relief that she's willing to go along, I explain the system to her. "This is a 3-D food printer. There are tons of options. First, you choose the size of the portion that you want. One-Bite Snack, Make Mine a Meal, or Behemoth."

"Let's make it a meal," she says.

"Next you choose the ingredients you want."

"Whoa," she says when all the options show up on the screen. Four kinds of kelp, six types of ground insect pulp, nine legume purees, dozens of veggie pastes, and three faux meat mashes.

"I like these best." I choose pea protein, beet paste, and ground grub worms. "Next, choose the shape you want." I pick the outline of a burger.

On the screen, we watch a three-armed robot holding green, red, and white squirty tubes lay down layer after layer of nutritional pastes. First, white circles of grub worm form the bottom bun. Then a red beet patty is built on top of that. A thin swirl of green pea paste comes next. And finally, another white paste bun on top. When it's done, a convection light zaps my order to cook it, then the robotic arm slides it forward into the cubby. I tap the screen, which lifts up like a door so I can take out the tray of food.

"Your turn!" I tell Uma.

She chews her thumb as she studies the screen. "There are so many options. I don't know what to pick!"

"How about . . . a neat-meat flower bouquet with green algae foliage?" I suggest.

"Okay," she says uncertainly, then watches with astonishment as swirls of umami-flavored paste form roses on bright green stems with delicate leaves.

"It's beautiful!" she says when her dish slides out.

"Let's make something for Quasar."

"Here, let me!" She chooses a Behemoth chixen-flavored bone-shaped biscuit.

"He'll love it!" I say when we remove it from the cubby.

We take our food outside to the center of the promenade where other people chow down, and find an empty table.

"Where's Quasar?" she asks.

I elbow Uma and point to a knot of people. In the center of that knot are two tourist girls fawning over the dog. They squee and squinch and take pix with their FingerCams each time he sits up, rolls over, or dances on his hind legs for the food scraps they hold out to him.

"Plutes," I say, nodding at the girls. "From the Distract, on the other side of Merica."

"How can you tell?" she asks.

"See their elaborate body paint under their dresses? And those FingerCams? They come here in their flying cars."

"Look at Quasar go! He can work a crowd better than any human I've ever seen."

What Uma says gives me an idea. I climb on top of a bench to scan the crowd for MUSCies, hoping Quasar's antics have enticed them over, but no luck. There's not a single telltale hood anywhere along the strip of food marts. I climb back down and whistle for Quasar. He leaves the girls and trots to our table for his dinner, which Uma gives him along with a pat on the head. The Plute girls follow.

"So . . . does this dog, like, belong to you?" the tall one asks.

I nod as I take a big bite of my burger.

"I would one hundred percent, literally, like, buy him from you right this second. How much do you want for him?"

"He's not for sale," I tell her as I chew.

"No but, she means, like, name your price, and literally, she will pay it," the shorter one insists.

"I understand what she means, but like, literally, one thousand percent, my dog is not for sale," I tell her, mocking her silly diction. "Not everything is a commodity." They look at me blankly. "Although you can pay me for all the pix you took of him with your FingerCams."

The tall one scrunches up her face, and the short one sneers. "Um, noooo," they say together, then walk away.

Uma laughs, then takes a big bite of her meaty roses. "Hey," she says with surprise. "This is pretty good!"

"We can build some dessert next, if you want."

"That sounds fun," she says, and I realize that I'm having fun, too. Which feels strange. I've never been anywhere in AlphaZonia just for fun. Usually Castor and I are skulking around, scavenging what we can, then slinking away into the dark before anyone notices us.

"And then what?" Uma asks as she finishes off her dinner. "What will we do next?"

"I'm going to go to a place called Soggywood," I tell her, leaving out the reason why. "You can come with me, if you want. It's a crazy place if you're up for some adventure."

"Yes!" says Uma with a huge smile. "Anything with you."

THE THROBBING MUSIC hits me beneath my sternum before we exit yet another stolen AutoPod. This car didn't call her Jubar Thrashman or Braga Tralluri. This time she's Rensealer St. Barnabas, but I don't really care. If it weren't for Talitha (or whoever she is), I'd be quivering in a bush somewhere, hiding from Dr. Fornax.

"Why is this called Soggywood?" I gape at the holo displays dancing on the front of every sleek building lining the street, luring the sparkling crowds inside. Big groups of people pass us. They all wear funny jumpsuits, the women's formfitting and printed in intricate designs, revealing patterns of skin like leopard spots or zebra stripes or leaves, and the men's with silver mesh sleeves. No one seems to notice us. Like MUSCies, they're too preoccupied with what's happening inside their minds to notice two out-of-place girls. I start to relax. Clearly, there are no MUSCies here who will see me.

"What should we try?" Talitha sweeps her arms out.

I stand there befuddled by all the choices. If you added up every moment of fun on MUSC from the time the first inhabitants landed to the present, that wouldn't equal the amount of fun people are having right here, right now. Finally, I point to the place directly in front of us.

"What about that—Best Stream Memes of the Week?" A two-story holo of a girl about our age with orangey-yellow skin, pink hair, a pig nose, and little piglet angels circling her head dances next to some guy farting rainbows while the words *Well, slap my ass and call me Jimmy* play over and over.

Talitha doubles over laughing. "No way! Castor would be so proud. He made that meme at the Pink Palace last night! I have to get a vid for him." She blinks to capture the loop. "I think we can find something better, though."

We walk a bit farther and stop in front of a place with a holo of two people sitting cross-legged, staring blankly but intensely at each other while a quiet crowd looks on. "Competitive meditation, ugh," says Talitha. "All you do is watch their brain waves. Snoozefest!"

"What's that?" I motion across the street to a line of people entering a dark cavern on the left side of a circular building, then exiting on the right by pushing through silky pink fabric beneath the projection of two long legs squatting. Each person emerges covered in some kind of shimmering slime and smiling beatifically.

"That's a ReBirth Spa," Talitha says. "It's meant to re-create the peace and comfort of the womb. No devices, no lights, only the gentle echoing sound of a distant heartbeat. At the end you're covered in a restorative gel made from krill. It's supposedly a transformative experience and great for your skin, but dead boring and a little creepy, if you ask me."

We both look around. There are so many options that it's almost too much. Mostly I want to crawl back into a Pod and go somewhere quiet where I can talk to Talitha under the starry sky. But she has a different idea.

"There!" She snaps her fingers and points diagonally toward the place with the throbbing music. Pulsating red, blue, and green light beams crisscross the sky above a rotating structure that's a vague replica of a MUSC station. "Do you like to dance?" she asks as she pulls me across the street with Quasar at her side.

"Well, uh, um, I've never really tried—"

"Now's your chance!" she says. "This is a CelebriStreamer MashUp Dance Party!" We step inside what looks like a Travelator Capsule that slowly goes up two stories and stops. We exit onto a rotating circular balcony. The bass of the music hits me between the hip bones and makes my ears buzz.

"It's so loud," I shout to Talitha.

"Usually sound is only pumped in through HearEars, but this place goes old school."

Overhead lights swirl across the ceiling like the aurora borealis. Down below us, on a dance floor, a mosh of sweaty bodies smash and crash together. Arms in the air. Butts in the air. Hair whipping everywhere. Talitha points into the center of the space, eye level to us, where a clear bubble floats by with a person inside who wears long, tall, sparkling magenta boots with platforms as high as small cars. They're bouncing along to the driving rhythm of the song pervading the entire club. Then another bubble floats by carrying a person dressed like a black-and-white space harlequin with half white hair and half black. A different song starts up and collides with the first one as the bubbles bump into one another.

"What are they doing?" I yell to Talitha over the thunderous, dissonant music.

"They each pick a song," she shouts close to my ear. "Then they mash them together, layering tracks over tracks to make one song. And when the crowd is happy with that, their bubbles join."

She holds up a finger for me to wait, and within seconds, a new song resolves as the rhythms of one song meld with the melody of the other. I look up to see the tall booted person and the harlequin dancing together in one giant bubble.

Below us, a circle of light beams up from the floor, enclosing a gnarl of dancing people who are lifted toward the ceiling on a spinning platform. They dance with a fierceness of display, all eyes on them, flinging rainbow drops of sweat and spit in the vibrant swirling lights. The platform skates around the bubble in the air.

"Get ready!" Talitha takes my hand.

"For what?" I yell, bracing myself, though I don't know what's coming.

"Here we go!" she shouts.

The platform swoops toward us. Talitha takes a half step back as the railing in front us disappears, then she jumps from the balcony, pulling me along through the air, so that we land, teetering on the edge of the floating dance floor circle. My heart pounds in my chest and fills my ears, then is replaced by the roar of cheering from the dancers that we joined.

"What do we do now?" I yell.

"Dance!" Talitha screams as we're sucked into the center of the gyrating bodies. "Just dance your ass off, girl!" She grabs my hands, and we move.

I forget about my body. Forget where am I and who I am, and let the chaos of the mashed-up music charge into my brain and take over my limbs. I thrash. I jump. I wiggle and shake, hot and sweaty next to Talitha. Our sweat mingles. Our fingers intertwine. My thighs rub up against hers. Our bellies touch through the thin fabric of our clothes. This is what the Earth is. This is what I've missed. Getting caught up in a moment with no worry about what comes next or what came before. Just letting everything go so that I'm entirely lost in this exact moment of time and space.

Our dancing disk makes it back to the ground, then another lifts up, and another. People leap from the balcony. The crowd cheers. More bubbles with different Streamers float in and out, mashing up their music.

I love being lost in the happy chaos of it all until I turn and see, leaping over our heads, two MUSCies in travel suits and hoods. My scream is lost in the cheering of the crowd. I yank Talitha into me.

"I have to go!" I shout.

She puts her arms around my shoulders and continues to dance with me close. "Go where?"

"Just out!" I say, but she doesn't hear me.

She tosses back her head and laughs, then stops and points to the MUSCies dancing on the spinning disk above us. She says something that I can't make out.

"I have to go now," I scream, and shrink down, looking for a way to worm through the tangle of bodies.

"Bathroom?" she yells, and I nod—anything to get out of here. She points me in the right direction, and I run.

I hide in a bathroom stall, too afraid to even pee. What are the MUSCies doing here? Who are they? I didn't get a good look. Could they be looking for me or just here to have a good time? And why did Talitha look so interested in them? I thought she hated people from MUSC.

Mostly, I know I need to leave. I slip out of the building, wishing I knew how to hijack a Pod, even though I have no place to go. I end up standing on the sidewalk, Pods zipping by, people swarming from one club to the next. I have no idea what to do. I have no currency. No map. Then I see a flash of brown and bright eyes in a small dark alcove between two buildings.

"Quasar!" I call.

He yips. I duck into the space and hug that dog tight while we both wait for Talitha to come out and find us.

TALITHA NEVA

ALPHAZONIA, EARTH

THE MOONLINGS TELL me nothing. Maybe it's because the music is so loud, or maybe I seem strange, dancing up to them and asking, "How are you enjoying your time on Earth?" In response, they both stare at me with their strange, large eyes through the clear faceplates of their hoods.

"Do you come down here often?" I shout as I sway in time to the beat, smiling ridiculously so they know I'm friendly.

They look at one another, then back at me. The taller one says through a communicator vent, "We do not seek sexual experiences or mind-altering substances."

"Jeez!" I step back, bumping into the Yoobie behind me. She elbows me hard in the kidney. "Ow!" I yelp, and bounce forward again, stepping on the toe of the other MUSCie, who jumps away. "I wasn't offering you those things," I say. "I was being *nice*."

"Thank you for your interest in us," the first one says robotically, then they both turn away as if I'm not worth their time.

I shake my head and walk away, disgusted by their assumption. Who do they think they are? As I thread my way through the crowd, looking for Uma, I mutter in frustration. I don't know how D'Cart expects me to find this supposed rogue Moonling without any information, or at least a description. Then again, why would a runaway show up at an Earth club? That person is probably hiding out in the desert somewhere waiting for the Drones to give up their search. That's what I would do if I showed up on Earth and wanted to hide.

I don't find Uma in the bathroom or at the food and drink vendors. Nor do I spot her on the dance floor, curls bouncing, reflecting light in her cute little silver shirt. Right then, I want more than anything to be with her. At least she's nice and understanding and talks to me like a human being, unlike those MUSCies, who treated me like trash.

After a few minutes, I grab some Gem Water from a vendor and leave the club, hoping she's waiting for me outside. As soon as I hit the fresh air and relative quiet of the street, I hear Quasar's bark. A happy yip to tell me where he's hiding. I follow the sounds to a small cubby between two clubs, where I find Uma sitting, knees to chin, with her arms around Quasar's furry neck.

"There you are!" I say, and squat down to face her. "I was worried that I wouldn't find you. Are you okay?" She nods but looks miserable. "Want something to drink?" I hand her the glimmering bottle of bright blue Sodalite Gem Water.

"Thank you for choosing me," the bottle announces when Uma uncaps the top. "I will cool your body and promote truthfulness."

"Uh-oh," she says, and gives me a quick side-eye glance. "A truth serum?"

"Nah," I say, and snuggle in beside her. We pass the bottle back and forth, taking turns sipping. "What happened in there?" I ask. "Why'd you leave?"

"I'm sorry," she says. "I'm just exhausted. It's been such a long, strange, crazy day. I got overwhelmed. My head is pounding, and my stomach is in knots—"

"Do you want to leave?"

"Truthfully?" she asks. "More than anything!"

"Guess that water worked, huh?" I laugh.

"I want to go somewhere quiet," she says, then adds, "But, the thing is . . ." She hesitates, then sighs. "I don't want to be alone, and I don't have anywhere to go."

"Come home with me," I blurt out, then feel myself blush.

Uma looks at me. "Really? Could I? Will your brother mind?"

"My brother is . . ." I stop and chew on the side of my cheek for a moment. My brother is what? Indisposed? Locked away? Waiting for me to find a Moonling so he can be set free? I feel bad for poor Castor, I really do, but I'm also exhausted and ready to call it a night. Plus I have no idea where else to look for a Moonling this late. Mostly, I hope when this is over, Castor will rein in his risk-taking so we don't end up in this kind of mess again. Of course, I can't admit any of that to Uma, so instead I say, "He won't be back until tomorrow." Then I quickly add, "And anyway, he wouldn't mind if you're there. He'd like you."

She smiles and gives my hand a squeeze. I squeeze hers back and say, "Come on. Let's get out of here."

We Jack-a-Pod to our house on Heather Drive—one of the few still standing this high up in the Hills. To me, it's always looked like a strange white mushroom growing among the rubble of fallen neocastles built during the heyday of Hollywood so long ago.

"This is yours?" Uma asks, eyebrows up, when we get out of the Pod.

"Well," I say with a chuckle, "as long as no one comes back to claim it, it is."

The front door opens for me, and we're hit by cool, dry, stagnant air inside the darkened vestibule, which is a relief from the late-night mugginess outside.

"The first year we were here, Castor and I sniffed all around these neighborhoods, looking for someplace we could stay once we left the Observatory. When he found this place, we knew we'd hit the jackpot. It's self-sufficient, solar-and-wind-powered, and survived every post-quake landslide. We've been here ever since."

We follow Quasar through the mishmash of things that are not ours—white fluffy cloud sofas and chairs levitating above their magnetic bases mixed with junk we dragged up from the city streets and Santa Monica Basin and all the stuff Castor makes—his 3-D printers, toy rocket prototypes, and makeshift lab experiments. I toss Castor's knapsack on the kitchen counter, then fill a bowl with water for the dog, grab two Lemon FizzBomb drinks for us, and say, "Let's go out in the garden. It's nice out there this time of night."

Out back, on the patio, Uma and I sit in side-by-side lounge chairs while Quasar sniffs along the defunct pool filled with dried palm fronds and decaying leaves. He trots up half-crumbled stone steps to nose around a purple bougainvillea vine where every morning hummingbirds dart like tiny fighter jets.

"Tell me more about you," says Uma when we're settled.

"What about me? What do you want to know?"

"Everything," she says, and smiles. "Where you're from. What your childhood was like. How you got from there to here."

I take a deep breath and let it spill. "The truth is, I'm nothing but an undocumented guttersnipe from the Wastelands who snuck in with my twin brother and stole everything we own."

"A guttersnipe!" Uma bursts out laughing. "Sounds like some weird creature that evolved out of the muck after the tsunami."

"Maybe it is," I tease, and hunch over with my teeth bared.

"I know what's it like to leave the place you're from," Uma says.

I look at her and nod. I know Uma's not a tourist. Otherwise, she'd have a device and currency and a place to stay. I'm not sure what she is or why she's here, but I don't need to know until she's ready to tell me. Right now, I love lying beside this girl where no one can bother us.

"Tell me more," she begs. "Where did you grow up?"

I tell her as much about my life in the Wastelands as I can. She listens, rapt, to the story, then stops me after a while and says, "Okay, so let me see if I've got this straight. You and your brother have a parody Stream called NayRay DeDumpingCart that you started when you were twelve?"

"That's right."

"And when you got enough followers, you snuck into AlphaZonia to Stream from inside the city so you could hack product links and make money?"

"Yep. That was Castor's idea. I thought he was crazy, but as usual, he was right. Our fan base grew once we got here, and he's brilliant at finding ways to squeeze currency out of followers."

"I watch Streams all the time. I can't believe I've never seen yours. You have to show me!" says Uma.

"Oh, no," I groan. "It's too embarrassing."

"Come on," she says, and cuddles closer, so her knees are touching my thighs. "Show me."

"Fine." I grab an old refurbished tablet Castor left on the table and command it to project our Stream onto the deck. Grainy, poor-quality holos of our archived Streams from the past few months appear. Except for the night at the Pink Palace. Somehow that one is missing.

"Go back," says Uma. "Way, way back to the beginning. I want to see how you started when you were twelve."

"Oh, god, this is going to be embarrassing," I say, but I scroll all the way back through the archives to my preteen self because I like seeing Uma happy. Then, there I am. As scrawny as a hungry pup. All eyes and teeth beneath a mess of dirty red hair. My ribs stick out and my hip bones are sharp beneath a thin gray men's T-shirt I fashioned into a dress with a bungee cord belt, filthy pink rain boots, and bright green rubber gloves. My skin is sunbaked two shades darker than I am now.

"Look at you!" says Uma, pointing at the holo of my former self. "You were so adorable!"

"What a wreck!" I say, laughing. "I want to comb that girl's hair and wash her face!" I reach out toward the younger me, but of course, my hand goes right through the projection.

"Play!" Uma commands.

"Hey, you guuuuuuys." My younger self singsongs the words just like every CelebriStreamer does. "It's me, NayRay DeDumpingCart. And I'm here at, well, duh, the Dumps!" I throw up my arms just as Castor pulls the camera back to show me standing in the shadow of a huge pyramid.

Uma gasps. "Is that . . ." She leans closer to the image on the deck. "Garbage behind you?"

I nod.

On-screen, the younger me draws in a long, deep breath, then lets it go. "Aaaaaah. Can you smell that? Freshly delivered from the Yoobies." I look at the camera and wink. "Let's see what we can find!" I scurry up the trash heap like a mountain goat. Castor stays close, keeping the camera trained on my narrow back. Suddenly, I stop and whip around with the exact expression D'Cart uses every time she unveils an amazing new product to experience with her TouchyFeely-Tech followers.

"Oh, my gawd, you guys," the younger me coos. "Can you feel that?" I plunge my arm shoulder deep into the mountain of garbage. "The slimy ookiness of trash against your skin? And what's that smell?" I take a long, deep breath. "Rotting food and the desperation of the Wastelands?

Aaahhhh! That's the magic of TouchyFeelyTech! Now look at this!" My NayRay self pulls out a titanium alloy hubcap and plops it on top of my head. "This hat is SOOO gorgeous! And comfy, too! Can you feel how light it is?"

Uma is laughing so hard, she has to wipe tears from her eyes.

"I don't know why we have so many followers," I admit. "The whole parody thing is ridiculous."

"No it's not!" Uma protests. "It's smart. At least the way you do it. And clearly people love it! How did you come up with it in the first place?"

"I always pretended to be different people. Then Castor found a bunch of defunct tech in an electronics dump and wired it all together so we could Stream."

"He sounds really smart."

"He is. He probably could've gotten a scholarship to MUSC if my father hadn't . . ." I stop.

"Oh, Talitha." Uma looks at me.

"Never mind! It doesn't matter. MUSC is another stupid place full of elites. Yoobies! MUSCies! They're all the same."

"Talitha, listen," she says, then stops.

"Yes?"

"I should tell you something . . ."

"Okay," I say, and wait for her to go on. But our little reverie in the tiny oasis of my garden is interrupted when Quasar bays and runs toward the back gate, his teeth bared as he snarls.

"Oh, no!" I yell, and reach for Uma's hand. I pull her off the lounge chair and run behind the date palm tree, where we crouch.

"What's happening?" she whispers, her hand hot in mine.

"I don't know," I whisper back. "Nobody ever comes up here."

I look for something blunt and heavy to defend us against an intruder, but there are only wispy dried palm fronds littering the ground. Quasar continues to snarl and bark, making himself sound ten times more ferocious than his tiny body could ever be. I hear footsteps crunching through the gravel around the side of the house.

"Who is it?" I yell, my voice as deep and menacing as I can manage. Uma tucks herself close to my side as we grip one another tight. The gate swings open, and I shout, "Stop right there!"

"Talitha?" Someone peeks around the corner of our house, then jumps back when Quasar lunges. "Call your dog off, god damn it. It's me, Mundie," he says, annoyed.

"Mundie?" I step out from behind the tree, still holding Uma's hand. "Quasar, come. It's okay."

Mundie comes into the garden and stops short, then backs up two steps when he sees us. Quasar tangles around his legs, sniffing intently to make sure that he's safe.

"Who's that?" Mundie demands, finger pointed at Uma.

Uma and I both stand up straight. She drops my hand and steps behind me into the shadow.

"Just a friend," I say.

"I've never seen her before," says Mundie, rudely.

"She's not from here. Is everything okay? Why are *you* here?"

"Didn't know I needed an invitation." Mundie strides forward. "I need to speak to you." He bugs his eyes out in Uma's direction and adds, "Alone."

My heart climbs up in my throat at the thought of Castor in more trouble. "Hey, Uma," I say, my voice a little shaky, "why don't you go inside and wash up before bed?"

"She's staying here?" Mundie snarls.

"You sure you want me to go inside?" Uma whispers into my ear.

"It's okay," I assure her. "Mundie is a friend," I lie, and try to smile, but it feels more like a grimace. "We grew up together. I just need a few minutes alone with him."

"Okay." She reaches for my hand and gives it a squeeze before she turns to go. "But I'll be right inside." She stares hard at Mundie, who squints at her, trying to get a good look at her face in the dim light.

Once Uma's through the patio doors, Mundie stomps toward me. "What the hell, Talitha?" he demands. "Who's that girl? Why were you holding hands?"

"I wasn't holding her hand!" My cheeks burn with guilt, even though I've done nothing wrong. "We were scared. I didn't know it was you. Quasar was barking his head off. You could have pinged to let me know you were coming."

"I did! A thousand times tonight. But you never answered."

"Oh, right," I say. "I wasn't using my device. I have on other Wearables. Still, why are you showing up here late at night?"

We stand on either side of the table. He stares at me for a moment, then says, "Who is she?"

"Just some girl," I tell him. "I found her in the Wildlands. She had no place to go. I felt sorry for her." I burn with shame for lying. What if Uma overheard me? "How's Castor? Is he okay?"

"He's fine." Mundie moves around the table, closer to me, but I sidestep him and move closer to the door. "But D'Cart has something else she needs you to do."

"Oh, good," I say, relieved. "Finding that Moonling is impossible. What's she want instead?"

"She needs you to get something for her from the MUSC Dump out in the Wastelands."

"The Dump!" I grimace. "Why doesn't she send a robot for it?"

"Because she wants you to get it, and if you don't, then she won't release Castor, so . . . you'll do it?" He reaches out his inordinately long arm and lays his hand on my shoulder. "Right?"

I look down at his hand, not liking how it feels to be touched by him, but once again, I know what I have to do. "I don't have much of a choice, now, do I?"

TIME STAMP

Moon
Day 1, Month of Sol, MUSC Year 94

Earth
June 19, 2XXX

UMA JEMISON

ALPHAZONIA, EARTH

WHEN I WAKE up the next morning, I roll over and search for Talitha's body next to mine in the ocean-blue sheets, but the double bed is empty. I smile at the memory of lying beside her last night. I woke once to find her arm slung over me with Quasar at our feet. A little stuffed toy that looked just like him was wedged betweed us. Moonlight spilled into the room and illuminated her face, so peaceful and sweet in her sleep. I could have moved away, but I didn't. I snuggled closer.

I sit up now and stretch, feeling more refreshed than I have in months, or possibly years. Each day on MUSC, I wake with a heaviness that I can't shake. By the end of every day, gravity feels stronger. But today, I feel light and happy and ready to go. I bounce out of bed, dress quickly in borrowed clothes Talitha left for me—a soft red tank top and tie-waist striped shorts—then pad out of the room to look for Talitha.

The front door to the house is wide open. Sunlight streams into the vestibule, warming my body as I step into the driveway, where I find Talitha loading bags into the back of yet another AutoPod. This one green.

"Are we going somewhere?" I ask, half joking.

Talitha spins. "I'm sorry, Uma. I've had a change of plans." She shuts the hatch of the Pod and comes around to the front of the car. Quasar trots after her like a dog-shaped shadow.

"Oh," I say quietly, feeling stupid. Clearly I misread the situation. The lightness I felt a few moments ago evaporates in the heavy air. "Sorry, I—"

"It has nothing to do with you. I have to go out to the desert for a bit."

"Okay." My voice is small. I wish I could hide my disappointment better, but I can't. I start to sweat and tug the tank top away from my skin. "Is everything all right?"

"Yeah . . . yeah . . . it'll be fine," Talitha says uncertainly, and keeps her distance. "I have to . . . um . . . pick something up for someone, and . . ." She trails off, then stands mute, as if there's more she wants to say but can't.

"I see," I say, but I don't really understand, and my heart sinks at the thought of saying good-bye. "I'll go change—"

"No wait! Listen . . ." She steps closer. "I don't want to leave. I *have* to. It has to do with my brother, and . . ." She hangs her head. "I can't tell you more, but you can totally borrow those clothes! I'll see you again. I won't be gone that long, and as soon as I get back, I'll find you and—"

"I don't know where I'll be," I say honestly, backing toward the door.

"I'm sorry I can't let you stay here." She looks pained.

"I don't expect you to," I tell her. "I'll get my stuff . . ."

She follows, saying, "It's just that . . . well, with Mundie snooping around, I don't think you'd be safe here. But since I have the AutoPod, I can drop you off anywhere before I leave. Where do you want to go?"

I say the only thing place I can think of. "Pink Palace, I guess?"

Talitha hesitates. "Why there?"

"There's something I need." I chew on my thumb as I try to form a plan.

"You're sure . . ." Talitha says, seeming wary.

"Yes," I tell her. After one day, it's clear that without Talitha as my guide, I'll need my device to get around. Maybe I can find a way to cloak my location from the Drones. "I'm certain."

⚭

The drive down the winding hills from her house is gorgeous in the daylight. I sigh and say once again, "You're so lucky to live here."

"I'm not sure luck has much to do with it." A strangled laugh escapes her mouth. "Or if it did, my luck may have run out."

"What's that mean?" I ask, looking at her.

"Nothing," she mumbles. "Do you know what was lucky, though?" She catches my eye. I shake my head. "Meeting you."

My heart skips. "I wish we had more time together," I admit, and move a little closer to her.

"Me too!" she says, half smiling and half looking like she might cry. "This sucks! I really don't want to say good-bye to you."

"Me neither!" I tell her.

"Look!" She grabs my hand. "I know this might sound crazy, but do you want to come with me?"

"To the desert? But it sounded like you have something important to do for your brother. I wouldn't want to get in the way."

"It'll be fine!" Talitha assures me. "You can stay in the car while I do my errand, then we'll come back here together."

"Yeah, but . . ." I shrink away, remembering what Burnell Chen-Ning told me on the Shuttle: *Just stay away from the Wastelands, and you'll be fine.* "I'm not sure I should . . ."

"Yeah." She slumps and lets go of me. "Probably not. It's not that safe out there, I guess."

Then again, as I look out the window and think about reestablishing a connection with Darshan, I'm not sure that I'll be safe here, either.

The Pod rounds a curve and starts up the long driveway to the Pink Palace. My heart races at the thought of not seeing Talitha again. In a few minutes, we'll have to say good-bye. Should I go with her, I wonder? Take another leap, like I did when I stepped onto the Shuttle or when I threw my device away and ran into the bush? I look out the window at the trees and sky and contemplate my choices. Stay here, alone, trying to find my way under the radar, or go out to the desert, which might be dangerous, but at least we'd be together.

As the Pod nears the Palace portico, I do a double take when I see two MUSCies in their protective gear standing by the purple blossom bush. I glance at Talitha, but she's busy looking at something on her Lenz. Then a third MUSCie emerges from the green leaves, carrying something blue and white and large and floppy. The sun hits the person just right as we zoom past, and I see Burnell Chen-Ning's face inside the hood.

Quickly, I grab Talitha by the shoulders and dive onto her so we're both lying on the seat out of sight. "I changed my mind! I want to go to the desert with you!"

"What?" Talitha stares up at me, then laughs. "Are you sure?"

My heart beats so hard I wonder if she can feel it against her chest. "Yes, I'm positive. Turn the car around! Now!"

She commands the car to U-turn, and I hug her fiercely so we both stay down as the car loops around the portico and heads back the way we came.

"I have to reprogram this thing!" She laughs and struggles to sit up so she can command a new location to the AutoNav. I wrench around and glance out the back window. The last thing I see as we speed from the Pink Palace is that boy Mundie from last night striding out onto the lawn toward Mr. Chen-Ning, who holds out my flight suit, like a husk that I shed.

◯◯

My heart doesn't stop beating a million miles a minute until the Auto-Pod pops out of the San Gabriel tube, leaving AlphaZonia behind the craggy mountain range that separates it from the Wastelands. Only then do I stop checking the sky every few seconds for MUSC drones on my trail. But the image of Burnell Chen-Ning holding out my flight suit as he walked toward Mundie plays over and over in my brain. I wonder how much they know and whether Mundie got a good enough look at me last night to put the pieces together. Mostly, I worry about whether they found my device—my ticket back to MUSC, unless I'm scooped up by security before I get to it on my own.

Out here, I feel safer, though. There are no Pods in front of us and none behind. There are also no more palm trees, green lawns, or blooming flowers. The entire landscape is brown and bristly. The hills are sparsely covered with strange, spiky plant life. In fact, the area is so burned out and empty that eventually the AutoNav disengages and Talitha uses voice commands to tell the car where she wants to go.

"How do you know where you're going?" I ask as she navigates turn by turn down more and more desolate roads.

"Just follow your nose!" She laughs. "And I mean that literally, because we're heading for the Dumps."

"The Dumps?" I repeat, and swallow down my discomfort.

She takes a left onto a bumpy dirt road, and immediately we're hit by a wall of stink. The festering aroma climbs into my nostrils and sticks to the back of my throat. I gag and gag again. Only Quasar seems intrigued by the symphony of scents. He sits up tall in the seat and sniffs at the air with relish.

"Eventually you get used to it," Talitha says.

I press the bottom of my tank top against my nose. "You sure?"

"Sad but true."

We take a right and enter the shadow of a mountain. Overhead, small white birds dart and laugh as big black ones fly in lazy circles.

I look more closely, then blurt out, "Those aren't real mountains!"

"It's the trash," Talitha says. "Everything the Yoobies no longer want or need comes here."

"I can't believe there's so much." I take in the enormity of the mountain chain.

"I can," Talitha says. "The Yoobies are completely self-centered. As long as they can shove all of their trash out of sight, the world is a shiny, happy place to them, no matter what the impact is on everybody else. No more trying to reduce, reuse, and recycle for them. The planet's dying anyway. They figure they might as well wring every last ounce of resources out of it while they can."

"What are those?" I point to a parade of what look like giant metal sea serpents rising and falling through the heaps of garbage. Quasar puts his paws on the window edge and barks.

"WRMS," Talitha tells me.

"That ain't no worm," I say.

"No, Waste Reorganization Management Systems. They move through the Dumps, grinding and compacting trash to make room for more. You have to be quick when you scavenge. The best stuff doesn't last."

She tells the car to turn at a lone wind turbine, spinning for no reason, then drives for several minutes. We pass a dry lake bed where rotten piers poke out like the finger bones of a skeleton reaching for the hulls of boats baking in the heat. Then we pass rows and rows of tract housing that must have fallen like dominoes during the massive quake.

Finally, we come to a short, squat, windowless building in the middle of nowhere. It looks as if some giant hand from the sky plunked down a white box in the desert. The only sign that anything might be happening inside is a thin line of putrid smoke snaking up from a vent on the roof.

When Talitha commands the Pod to stop, I see the words SCIENCE WILL SEE US THROUGH emblazoned on the side of the building beneath a MUSC logo. I plaster myself against the back of the seat.

"What is this place? Why are we here?" I ask, starting to panic.

"It's the ExploroBot Creation Center, where MUSC turns soldiers into technoslaves."

My heart is in my throat, and I'm sweating through the borrowed shirt. "I can't go in there."

"Of course not," she says as she pulls on the tall boots and long gloves she packed into the backseat of the Pod. "That place is locked down tight and fully automated. No humans allowed. At least no live ones." She snorts at her own dark joke.

I turn to face her in my seat. "Talitha, I . . ." I search for a way to tell her who I really am and why I have to get out of here. "I can't be here."

"Okay, so come with me," she says breezily. "It'll only take a few minutes." She shoves a set of boots and gloves at me.

"No, stop! I need to tell you something," I say slowly.

"Well, it's going to have to wait." She commands the door to open and gives me a tight smile. "The trucks with bodies will arrive soon, so

I have to take care of this now." She straps the red knapsack to her back and steps out of the pod. Quasar hops after her and trots happily away.

I sit there dumbfounded for a few seconds, then I realize that staying on my own this close to anything MUSC-related scares me more than heading off with Talitha and her dog.

Quickly, I pull on boots and gloves, then run after her with my head ducked. I catch up to her and ask, "You can just march right in here?" I twist and turn, looking over each shoulder as we stroll past the building. "There's no security to stop you?" I scan the sky for drones.

"Hell, most people want nothing to do with this place. Including me." She shivers. "Castor liked it, though. Claimed he could find stuff here he'd never seen on Earth."

Behind the building, I stay close to her side as we hike up the first rolling heap of trash. The late-morning sun paints the pale blue sky with streaks of pink and orange clouds. Quasar snakes his own path far from us, nose down, ears up. In the distance, packs of dogs romp over the hills, ripping open bursting bags to lap up the slurry of gad knows what. Puppies play tug-of-war over shreds of fabric and chase the rats and mice that also feast on the trash.

Below my feet I see mostly medical waste spilling out of bright red bags. Plastic tubes, empty vials, shiny slender syringes glinting in the sun. Scissors, suture kits, rolls of bloodied gauze. I step over an unopened box of antibacterial bandages that have expired. "What a waste," I say, and kick them away.

"Rhetorical remark!" Talitha laughs.

When I look at her funny, she says, "Hey, you've got to have a sense of humor here and appreciate the absurdity of it all, or you won't last a minute. It's just too damn sad if you don't." Then she heads up toward the crest of the mound and calls, "I have to go to the other side."

I try to follow her, but I'm slow and I have to stop several times, hands on knees, to catch my breath.

"I'm coming," I call after her.

"Take your time," she calls back. "Or just stay there and wait for me. I won't be long. Promise!" She disappears over the ridge.

When I'm about halfway up the mound, I hear Quasar yelp. I stop and scan the area, my hands covering my eyes to block out the glare from the sun. I find him farther down the mound facing off with a pack of dogs.

"Hey, hey! Quasar!" I yell and wave my arms. I move toward him, but I'm slow on the unstable garbage beneath my feet.

Above me, Talitha appears, casting a long shadow. "What's wrong?" she yells.

I point to the dogs.

"Oh, no," she says. "He's bound to get into a fight. Quasar! Come on! Come here, boy!"

He lurches, as if to turn, but his back right leg is caught. He growls and snaps at his foot.

"He's stuck, I think. I'll get him." I start to jog toward the dogs, since I'm closer than Talitha.

"Thanks! And be careful," she calls after me, and then heads back down the other side.

Suddenly, behind the pack of dogs, giant WRMS erupt like parasites from infected skin. I stop and gasp as all of the dogs scatter except Quasar, who's stuck in the dark shadow of the WRMS. I scream and run toward him.

One of the WRMS rises and curves into an *S*. Quasar yelps and shakes fiercely, but he can't get loose and I'm still far away.

It plunges down like a fairy-tale serpent in the sea and rises again, this time only a few meters from Quasar. He frantically chews at whatever's got ahold of his foot.

"I'm coming! Hold on!" I shout, trying to find firm footing on the ever-shifting surface of this trash mountain.

He turns and gnashes his pointy canines at the mechanical worm, but he's no match for its circular maw with rows and rows of grinding teeth.

"Talitha!" I scream. "Help!"

UMA YELLS FOR me, and I run. At the crest of the ridge, I see what's happening, then fling myself over, slip, and roll while shouting, "Stop! Stop! Stop!" Yet everything keeps going.

On all fours, I watch one of the WRMS loom above Quasar, preparing to dive deep. Uma's scrambling to get near him. I'm close enough to see them clearly, but I know I can't reach them in time. Quasar curls up as small as he can get, closes his eyes, and braces for disaster. Just then, Uma darts beneath the grinding machine's shadow and snatches up my dog. A metal grate hangs from his back leg like a manacle. They roll, Quasar cradled in her arms as the giant WRM plunges into the very spot where they had just been. It threads into the mountain, leaving only a dark hole sucking trash. I scramble to my feet and bolt toward them.

"Whoa! Whoa! Whoa!" Uma hollers. She holds Quasar tight as they slip and slide into the hole the mechanical earthworm left behind.

"Dig in your feet!" I shout to her, but it's too late. They are sucked down along with the bags of bursting garbage cascading past them.

"No!" I scream. On the ground, I see a long black hose. I grab it and run toward the gaping hole. While imagining where they might be, I throw it blindly over the precipice. The hose becomes a dark *S* written in the sky, then plummets.

"Grab on!" I shout as I fling myself down to peer over the edge.

Below me, at least twenty feet, Uma clings to some kind of conveyor belt hull stuck in the side of the hole as more trash rolls past. The hose lands close enough that she can grab it with one hand while still holding Quasar tight with the other.

"Hold on!" I shout to her. "I'll pull you up."

She twirls the hose around her wrist and wraps one leg, ankle to knee, farther down. The sides of the hole give way. She screams as she and Quasar dangle.

"I've got you!" I shout.

"Pull us up!" she yells.

"I'm pulling!" I grunt and groan as I tug with all my strength. Quasar tries to help, scrambling for a foothold with his tiny paws.

"It's working," Uma shouts. She gets the tips of her boots lodged into the sloping side, and slowly they scramble up. I hear her talking to Quasar. "It's okay," she says, her voice calm and strong. "Talitha's got us now. We're going to be fine."

When they're near the top, I dig my feet in deep and give one final, giant tug. Uma pushes off the side of the hole with her feet, and they both bolt upright onto me. The three of us tangle up and fall over, rolling the other way, down the hill, bumping over red bags of medical waste until we smack into a retaining wall and come to a sudden stop.

"Oh, my gad! Oh, my gad!" Uma screams.

"Stupid WRM!" I yell. "It's supposed to stop if a human's near."

"Probably thought we were dogs."

"It should stop for dogs, too!" I scream with fury at their disregard for Earth life.

Uma and I are covered in slime and grime, but Quasar is ecstatic. He licks our cheeks and hands and necks as if we are delicious.

"Stop! Stop!" I tell him, laughing and crying. "You have to hold still."

"Easy there. Easy," Uma says, trying to calm him.

"Hold him tight," I say. "I've got to get this thing off his leg."

Uma presses Quasar against her chest so he can't move, then I wrap my fingers around his muzzle with one hand and grip the manacle hanging off his leg with the other. "One, two, three!" I say, then I twist and tug.

Quasar yelps in pain.

"You got it!" Uma says.

I toss the horrible biting jaw away. "Dumb thing!"

Quasar looks up. Surprised. He blinks, then whimpers and starts to lick his wounds.

"Is he going to be okay?" Uma asks.

"His leg is messed up. Bleeding badly." I examine the chewed-up skin. Muscle and tendon are exposed, and the bone is crooked. "This place is crawling with horrible bacteria."

"Wait!" Uma hops up. "Stay here." She hands Quasar to me, then runs over the shifting ground, searching frantically for something. She returns a minute later with a roll of bandages.

"Expired or not, they'll help stop an infection from forming," she says. "Hold him steady, and I'll wrap his leg."

When she's done bandaging him, I say, "We have to get him to my mom." I hoist him up to my shoulder and stand.

"Your mom?"

"She lives near here. She grows lots of herbs and makes her own medicines. She can cure about anything."

Quasar pants heavily from my shoulder. Uma stands beside us and rubs his back. I look at her. Beautiful, even covered in grime. "You saved him," I say, suddenly overcome with a swell of gratitude and awe.

"And you saved me," Uma says.

We look at each other, then we both move forward. Our lips press hard together. I wrap my arms around her shoulders, with Quasar in between us, and we kiss, tongues entangled beneath the strong sun.

While Uma carries Quasar to the car, I run back up over the ridge to the pit on the other side, where the goo is contained in a half-buried tank. I know what D'Cart wants, although I don't know why. I hurry from barrel to barrel, reading the labels sticking up a few inches from the ground, until I find the one Castor has stolen from many times while we were here. I open the knapsack and take out the extraction kit I found at our house. With the hand drill, I bore a hole in the top of the thick metal barrel, then set up the siphon system—a long tube with a pump that draws the goo out into a canister. When the can is full, the pump stops. I withdraw the tube, then replace the metal disk to seal the top of the barrel with Castor's special glue. I put the extraction kit and canister back into the knapsack, then hurry to the AutoPod so we can get the hell out of here before the blue MUSC trucks arrive.

CASTOR NEVA

ALPHAZONIA, EARTH

THAT AFTERNOON, WHEN the door to the tiny room opens, I sit up from where I slept on the floor, expecting a DomestiBot with my lunch, but I see Mundie in the hallway, arms crossed and scowling, and my heart sinks.

"Did Talitha come back? Are you here to release me?" I ask, hopefully.

"As if!" He walks in and plants himself in a chair to stare at me.

"Aw, come on, Mundie!" I get up and drop into the other chair, then put my feet up on the table between us. "I've been in here for two days."

"Yeah, and it stinks in here," he says. "But you're being fed." He nods to the empty plate from this morning's breakfast.

"You can't keep me here indefinitely," I say.

"Actually, I could," he says. "Who, other than your sister, would be looking for you?"

"I know people," I say angrily.

"No you don't," says Mundie.

"My mom!"

Mundie scoffs. "I know your mom." He stares at me, one eyebrow up. "She won't come here. Not even for you."

I drop my gaze between my feet to the flat beige carpet, because I know Mundie's right. My mother loves me, but she's not a fighter. She flees from trouble and hides. I've spent my life trying to push those instincts away. I sigh. Annoyed more than anything.

"You know, Mundie." I stand and spin my chair around so I'm beside him. "We're from the same place. Wastelanders like us should have each other's backs."

"When have you ever had my back?"

"When have I not?"

"You've spent your whole life ignoring me, and now all of a sudden we're friends? I don't think so."

"I never did anything to hurt you," I point out.

Mundie unfolds himself from the seat and stands up tall, towering over me like a menacing stork. "You keep Talitha away from me."

"You do that yourself!" I say.

He winces at the jab. Then he reaches down to grab my arm and yanks me from the chair. I struggle to get out of his grip, but Mundie's strong, and I realize I should try less to piss him off, so I add, "Besides, I don't care who she's with."

"Just as long as it's not me?" He drags me out the door, where a SecuriBot waits.

"Where are you taking me?" I ask, because there's no use arguing with Mundie about Talitha. He's going to think what he wants to think.

"D'Cart wants to see you again. Don't ask me why. I think she should let you rot."

I follow him to the elevator, and the bot follows me. Being out of that small room is a huge relief. Of course, the first thing I do is look for ways to escape, but there are none this high up in the Palace.

Inside the elevator, Mundie slouches against the wall. "I've done everything to show Talitha how I feel," he complains. The doors close. "Upper lab," he says, and we ascend toward a higher floor. "You guys were my best friends in the Dumps when we were kids."

You just followed us everywhere, I think. While Mundie carps on about Talitha, I try to make a plan. Could I shove him out of the elevator when the doors open, then command it to the lobby? What about the SecuriBot?

"I came to AlphaZonia because she was here. I got a legit job so I could stay," he says.

Or maybe I could step out with both of them, then dart back in before the doors close again?

"I show up at your house! I bring her presents!"

No. They'd have security waiting for me at the bottom.

"I even talked D'Cart into letting her go when you guys got caught!" Mundie says. "And I offered to help her, but all she wanted me to do was keep you safe."

"So why don't you?" I say.

"I haven't beaten the crap out of you—that's something," he says.

The elevator stops, and we exit into the most amazing laboratory I've ever seen. I shake off Mundie's threat as I gape at the white walls lined with holos of design plans for all kinds of crazy contraptions. Behind a long bank of windows, assembly lines of 3-D printers and robots crank out products. D'Cart claims she invents everything she sells, and after seeing this, I believe her.

"This place is incredible," I whisper, but Mundie's not listening to me.

"The Yoobies don't like me because I'm not one of them," he whines as we walk through the lab. "The only thing I have in common with the stupid Yoobies is the TFT chip inside my head." He bangs a finger against the side of his skull. "And Talitha just ignores me. You hate my guts. I'm barely above this SecuriBot." He reaches back and slaps at the faceless machine beside me.

"Listen." I sidle up to him when we pause outside a closed door at the far end of the lab. "When I get out of here, you and Talitha and I should find a way to work together. Maybe we could even find a house . . ."

Mundie looks at me. "Shut up, Castor."

"Jeez, Mundie, I'm trying to be nice and—"

"I'm not an idiot," he says. Then he opens the door and shoves me inside the room.

I trip, head down, arms out, and land against a desk. I look up to see D'Cart blinking at me from the other side. But she looks different. The over-the-top hair and makeup are gone. No froofy pink clothes. Her face is scrubbed clean, her hair is pulled back tight, and she's wearing a white lab coat.

"You make quite an entrance," she says.

I straighten myself up. "Mundie pushed me."

"Boys . . ." she says, but trails off.

Behind her is a life-size hologram of a girl about my age, with dark curls and a wide smile in a MUSC-issued uniform.

"Why am I here?" I ask.

UMA JEMISON, AGE 16, scrolls beneath the hologram girl's face.

"Good news," D'Cart says with a smile. "Looks like we found the Moonling."

UMA JEMISON

WASTELANDS, EARTH

I HOLD QUASAR on my lap on the drive to Talitha's mother's house. I duck down when we pass a line of automated blue trucks with the MUSC logo on the side.

"Just in time," she says, and draws in a ragged breath.

Quasar is so exhausted by the pain that he sleeps fitfully, whimpering now and again, as I watch out the window with fascination. The landscape feels oddly familiar to me, and I wonder if my parents lived near here when I was small.

"Is this where you grew up?" I ask.

"Sort of," Talitha says. "Before my dad died, we lived in Palmdale, which operates more or less like a town, or tries to, anyway. They siphon water from the lakes up in the mountains, set up solar panels for power, barter for fresh food with farmers, and try to run a school. But after my dad was gone, Mom moved us out here. She thought leaving would be the answer to all her problems, but really she just traded one set of troubles for another."

"I know that kind of trade-off," I mutter.

At an old water tower with the word *Palmdale* in faded blue, Talitha turns right, onto a long, dusty road. After a few minutes of riding in silence, we pass beneath an archway constructed of chicken wire, old fence posts, car parts, blank screens, pipes, tubes, wire coils, and a thousand other things that I can't name. We pass a sign made from a cacophony of spinning, shiny found objects.

" 'Calliope,' " I read. "Is that the name of this town?"

"Town?" says Talitha with a laugh. "It's more of a conglomerate of people who don't like to follow rules."

Since the sun is directly overhead, the heat has become intense, and only a few people are out. Slowly, our Pod creeps past the oddballs on their strange patchwork bikes—the favored mode of transport here, except for the one guy who walks by on stilts. A thick film of dust swirls around the Pod, turning the windows nearly opaque. I can see just enough to make out the giant word sculptures welded from discarded objects that line either side of the main road. I read them aloud, "LOVE. TOLERANCE. ACCEPTANCE."

"Yeah, well," says Talitha, eyebrows up, "That's a nice message, but it ain't all you need!"

Quasar perks up and gives a weak bark as if in agreement. Outside, a pack of dogs lift their heads from where they lie inside a half-buried sea-foam-green convertible car sticking up from the sand.

"He knows we're home," says Talitha.

"That's a good sign." I pat him on the head.

At the end of the road, we skirt around concentric circles of shacks surrounding some kind of yurt covered with wind chimes and shiny spinning sun catchers.

"That's the ayahuasca temple," says Talitha.

"Is that the name of their god?" I ask.

Talitha laughs. "Sort of. I mean lots of people out here worship it, but it's a drug, not a god. People make a tea from a plant that they think allows them to communicate with nature."

"Does it?"

"Who knows?" she says. "But I'd never do it, even if it did. The people drink the tea, then shake and sweat and vomit and shit themselves in the process."

"Willingly?" I ask, trying to imagine why anyone would put themselves through such torture.

"Yep."

"Does your mom do that?"

Talitha shakes her head as we pass by the colorful houses radiating from the temple. "I think she probably used to, but not anymore. Now she grows and sells the plants they use to make the stuff."

We keep driving, all the way to the outskirts of the orderly shacks to yet another dusty path. Out here, even the voice commands won't work in the Pod, so Talitha physically handles the steering wheel and pushes the pedals with her feet. She turns left at a boulder painted with a giant lizard. We pass a smattering of old campers, gutted buses, and makeshift yurts.

"Does she live here?" I ask.

"No way," she tells me with a grin. "That would be far too mainstream for her."

A few more minutes, and we turn down the last road, nothing more than a shallow depression in the compacted sand. Up ahead, in the wavy lines of heat rising from the dust, I see a sparkling shelter.

"This is where my mother lives," Talitha announces.

She parks in a clearing in front of her mother's "house"—three enormous shipping crates, one blue, one yellow, and one red, stacked then welded together into an asymmetrical living space. The yellow sits atop the blue, and the red one is turned up on its side like a tower. There's a small porch tacked onto the front with the only blooming bougainvillea bush for miles. The walls are covered in a beautiful sparkling mosaic made from broken glass and flattened metal and tiny motherboards from long-dead machines.

I climb out of the pod with Quasar in my arms. "It's so gorgeous and lush!" I say, pointing to the succulents and flowers growing around the edges of a saguaro cactus fence—prickly sentries standing guard. "How does she grow this stuff?"

"Castor," says Talitha, admiring the space. "He diverted water from a lake up there." She points to the bluff behind her mother's place. "Don't ask me how. Out back, there's a recycled water greenhouse where she grows fruits and vegetables for herself and the ayahuasca plants that she sells or trades for other goods."

With Quasar squirming in my arms, I follow Talitha to the front door.

"Locked," she says, annoyed. We walk around to the back and find it locked as well. "My mom likes to say everyone in Calliope is well-intentioned and honest, but she's no fool. She knows there are as many thieves, cheats, and liars here as anywhere else."

"Did you let her know we're coming?"

She laughs. "My mother doesn't believe in using a communication device."

My eyes bug out.

"I know. Weird. But I'll bet you anything she'll claim she felt our presence when we see her."

I blink at her, not knowing what to say.

"She thinks she has a sixth sense. That she's tapped into the universe in a way that's unexplainable by science." Talitha rolls her eyes, but I'm fascinated. "If you haven't realized yet, my mom's a little kooky."

"From the looks of this place, I'd say she's amazing."

"She's going to love you!" Talitha says with a snort as she takes Quasar from my arms.

In the garden behind the house, Talitha lays the poor pup on a soft braided rug beneath a colorful swinging hammock rigged up between a fan palm and a big metal post. Next to it is a stack of tires made into a chair. She goes around to the greenhouse and returns with water for all of us and a handful of sticky dates to eat.

I devour the fruit, spitting the pits into my palm. Talitha stretches her arms overhead and says, "Do you want to have the first shower?"

"Shower?" I say, my mouth agape. "What kind of shower?"

"A real one," she tells me. "None of that ionized cleaning spray out here. Just pure, clean, stolen water."

Inside the small shower stall behind Talitha's mother's house, the rush of real water over my head is one of the most glorious things I've felt in years. Well, besides my feelings for Talitha! Being with her, I'm free and happy in a way I've never been. On MUSC, I constantly worry what people think. How they judge me for being a Zero Gen and whether I'm setting a good example so Second and Third Gens know that people from Earth are just as capable as anybody else. But here on Earth, with Talitha, I don't have to think about any of that.

I close my eyes and tilt my head back so the water rushes over my face. I can almost imagine that I'm diving into the ocean, just like in my swimming dreams. The water spills over my forehead and cheeks, down my shoulders to form rivulets that cascade over the naked skin of my belly. My skin drinks it in. My hair absorbs the moisture like a desiccated sponge. I feel like a dormant desert plant coming back to life in a sudden rain. I think of that weird ReBirth Spa we saw last night, water baptisms by religious sects, the sodalite truth Gem Water Talitha gave me, and this oasis in the desert. Water is a purifier, and it's time that I come clean. Today I will tell Talitha who I am.

I find fresh clothes (a soft yellow shirt and cotton shorts) warming on a rock outside the small shower. I dress, then find Talitha waiting for me in the hammock. She has wet hair and is wearing clean clothes, as well.

"Want to join me?" she asks.

My heart zings, and my skin prickles at the thought of being next to her, but I try to play it down. "Is there room?"

"There's plenty of space!" She wriggles over.

The hammock wobbles precariously as I climb in. Talitha laughs and clings to the webbing like a trapped bug. We rock and nearly tip over the opposite way.

"Whoa! Whoa! Wait!" Talitha says, both of us giggling. I adjust my body, and we tilt the other way. Her body rolls into mine. I could keep jostling like this, bumping up against her all day. But finally, we settle. Lying side by side, no dog in between us. This time our shoulders, elbows, and knees are pressed together.

"This is nice," she says, and reaches for my hand. We intertwine our fingers. I wish my hand was less sweaty and that my heartbeat wasn't so loud.

"Yes," I croak. "It's glorious." I gaze up through the palm frond canopy overhead at the bright blue sky.

"Talitha," I whisper a few minutes later when I build up my courage to tell her where I'm from and what I'm doing here. I turn to face her, ready to tell her everything, but her eyes are closed and her breathing is even. "Are you asleep?" I whisper.

She doesn't respond, and I don't have the heart to wake her. She looks so peaceful, and beautiful, asleep in the dappled sun. There's time. I can tell her later. For now, I lean over and kiss her gently on the forehead. Then I lie back and close my eyes as the heat of the day, the warmth of Talitha beside me, and the gentle rocking of the hammock lull me off to sleep.

TALITHA NEVA

CALLIOPE, EARTH

HOURS LATER, I wake to the unmistakable sound of my mother's buzzing motorbike. I sit up, rocking the hammock where Uma sleeps beside me. She opens her eyes, startled, and cries, "Are we landing?"

I look at her and laugh. "You okay?"

"Oh, gad," she says, clutching the edge of the hammock with one hand and my thigh with the other. "I didn't know where I was just then."

"Calliope," I remind her. "My mother's house."

"Right," she says, then sighs. "The best place on Earth."

"Wow," I tell her with a chuckle. "My mother will be honored that you think so." I sling my legs over the hammock edge and offer Uma my hand as I say, "And here she comes now."

Together, we walk to the front of the house. In the distance, I spot a wavering image coming down the road—a fat-tired, rainbow-colored motorcycle shimmering in the early evening sun. I wave my arms overhead. My mother stops, puts one foot on the ground, lifts her sand goggles, and shades her eyes to see.

"Mom!" I shout, hands cupped around my mouth. "Hey, Mom! It's Talitha!"

My mother whoops and gets back on the bike to blitz toward us with a sand trail swirling in the air behind her. She arrives looking how she always does: bikini top, many-pocketed shorts, and worn boots. She steps off the bike, pushes her thick-rimmed black goggles to the top of her head wrapped in colored silks, and reaches for me.

"Talitha, darling girl child!" She pulls me close. For a moment I am soothed by her smell—desert sage and lavender. The comfort of her hug, like everything else about her, makes no sense. For someone so thin and bony, her embrace is always warm and soft. "I knew you were coming."

I glance over my shoulder and wink at Uma, who stands shyly by the bougainvillea bush. "No, you didn't, Mom." I start to pull away, but she squeezes me tighter.

"Last night I dreamed of Hala Bashi, the red-haired Uighur warrior," she tells me.

"Mom," I say. "We aren't Uighurs and I'm not a warrior."

"But you are my fierce red-haired girl, so it was a sign." She buries her fingers in my damp hair to massage my scalp, which makes it impossible to stay annoyed with her. "Is Castor with you?"

I shake my head.

"Oh," she says, clearly disappointed, but not surprised. Castor rarely comes to visit, and I offer no other explanation because I don't want to worry her. Not yet.

Then Mom notices Uma. "And who's this?"

"Don't you know?" I ask, because I can't help baiting her sometimes. "I thought you dreamed of us?"

"Hmph," my mother says. "Talitha is no fun. But you!" She walks toward Uma with her arms wide open. "I can tell that you are someone special who came from far, far away. I'm Rhea. What's your name?"

"I'm Uma. Nice to meet you." Uma holds out her hand like a regular human being, but my mom chooses to hug her anyway. Way too tight. I half bury my face in my shoulder as I laugh at Uma stiff in my mother's arms.

"Mom." I lay my hand on my mother's back. "We need your help."

She lets go of poor Uma and turns to me. "Why? What's happened?"

"Quasar," I tell her. "He's hurt."

We hurry to the back garden and find our pup on his side panting beneath the hammock.

"Oh, dear!" Mom drops down on all fours and crawls toward him, head bowed as if in submission. "Beloved totem creature. Who did this to you?"

"WRMS," I tell her. "Uma saved him."

"No, well, I . . ." Uma blushes and brushes away my compliment.

"He was stuck in something nasty."

Quasar growls halfheartedly at my mother as she unwraps the bandages. "Where are these from?" Mom asks.

"We found them in the Dump," Uma explains. "They're expired, but they were still sealed and sterile."

"Are there more?" Mom asks. We shake our heads. "You did well." Mom strokes Quasar's head as she coos into his ear. "And I have just the thing to patch this pup right up!" She scoops him into her arms. Quasar trusts her so implicitly that he doesn't make a sound. Just licks her nose in a friendly greeting.

Inside the greenhouse, moist with humidity, my mother lays Quasar on a clean metal table and begins gathering up leaves from various plants surrounding us.

"Now, listen carefully," she says. "Go out back to the tilapia tank and kill two fish. Then bring me the skin for his leg. We'll fry up the meat for dinner."

Uma looks at me, bewildered. I beckon for her to follow me outside. "My mother might sound a little strange, but she knows what she's doing."

"If you say so," Uma says.

Out back, by the three aquatic tanks, old swimming pools half buried in the ground inside locked, reinforced cages, I grab a net. "This one is filled with mussels," I explain, pointing to this first one. "This one has different types of seaweed, and this one is full of fish." I point down at the dozen circling tilapia. They take turns popping their heads out of the water, mouths opening and closing in anticipation of a feeding.

"But why . . ." Uma starts to ask.

"Shhhh," I tell her as I concentrate. As soon as my shadow looms over the tank with the net, the fish dive deep and swim faster. "They're wriggly little buggers," I whisper. "You have to anticipate where they'll go if you want to catch them."

I watch the fish, zeroing in on two swimming side by side in a figure eight pattern. I let the tension in my body go so I'm nice and relaxed as I drop my shoulders and lift my sternum. I imagine that I am the fish, then I dip my net just ahead of where they're going. I snag both fish with one quick flick and pull them up dripping and writhing.

"Whoa!" says Uma, impressed, until I slam them on the chopping block and bash their heads in with a hammer. Uma gasps and hides her eyes.

"Sorry," I say. "Did that scare you?" I take a sharp knife from my mother's tool cabinet above the chopping block. I scrape away the scales, then quickly gut the fish like I was taught when I was seven.

"I've never seen an animal killed before," she says, peeking out at me.

"But you eat meat, right?"

"Sort of. I guess. I mean, some kind of processed patties. Probably grown in a lab somewhere."

"This will taste ten times better, I guarantee." I flay them and re-move the skin, which I lay across a clean metal plate. "Take this to my mother, please."

I chuckle as I watch Uma carry the plate away from her body as if the skin might come back to life and grab her. Then I get back to fillet-ing the meat for our dinner.

When I join them in the greenhouse again, Quasar is lying content-edly as Mom finishes wrapping his leg in fish skin, making him look part reptilian.

"Tilapia is disease resistant, and the collagen will help regrow his skin while keeping infection out," Mom explains to Uma. "But what-ever you used on him saved his leg. The muscle bands are reattached and healing, and the fractured bone has already fused. It's amazing."

Uma looks slightly embarrassed. "Well, you know those people up on MUSC probably have medicine that's light-years ahead of what's down here."

"MUSC?" Mom rears back with revulsion. "Were you at the MUSC Dump?"

"I had a job to do," I say defensively. My mother looks betrayed. "Someone hired me to go there and pick up something important. I didn't have a choice."

"One always has a choice," my mother says, and turns away to wash up.

My face burns, and I tremble. I almost blurt out that I did it to save Castor, but I keep my mouth shut. There's no use causing more drama, especially in front of Uma. Instead I lean down and kiss the white star on Quasar's forehead, which calms me enough that I can let it go.

After a dinner of fried tilapia, nopales, greens, and cherries, Uma and I lie tangled on an old springy mattress surrounded by rosebushes in my mother's garden.

"A literal bed of roses," Uma says, delighted.

"My mother can never pass up a pun," I say.

One of my long legs is wrapped around her strong, compact calf. Her right arm rests behind my neck. We hold hands, fingers laced together and resting on our hip bones. Overhead, stars speckle the night sky like scattered quartz, but the Moon is still hidden behind the mountain.

"Is it true that when you look at a star, you're seeing light that's no longer there?" I ask.

"Theoretically, yes," says Uma.

"So we're actually seeing into the past when we look up?"

"Sort of," she says. "See, light travels at about three hundred thousand meters per second so if you think about stars that are really far away, like the Eagle Nebula, it takes seven thousand years for that light to reach us on Earth. Theoretically, stars in that nebula could have died before the light gets to us, so what we see is the light that started out seven thousand years ago but just got here now."

"Wow," I say, still staring up. "If that's true, then there could be a new star whose light hasn't reached us yet."

"That's right."

"Like us," I say dreamily.

Uma lifts her head to look at me. "Huh?"

"I mean, sometimes I feel like a star that's been beaming my light out into the universe for a long, long time, only nobody has ever seen me—until now." I squeeze her hand.

"Awww," Uma coos. "That's so sweet! I love how you see the stars as something beautiful to be contemplated, not as utilitarian objects for fuel and exploration. So many people look up and see the planets as places to be conquered."

"Who says I'm not going to conquer you, Ursa Major?" I grab her wrist and roll over so I'm on top of her. "I've been dying to kiss you again."

She smiles up at me and lifts her face to mine. "Go ahead."

We kiss like we did in the Dumps, only this time her mouth tastes of mint and honey from my mother's sun tea and her skin smells like lavender and sage from my mother's soap. When we pull apart, my lips pulse in time with my beating heart.

I roll onto my back next to her, warm and buzzing with happiness. "Show me our constellation again."

Uma lifts my arm so we're both pointing at the sky.

"First, you find the Big Dipper."

"I see it!"

"Follow the line of stars down the handle." We trace the arc as she says each name. "Alkaid, Mizar, Alioth." Then around the bottom of the dipper. "Megrez, Phecda, Merak. Straight down from Merak on the front paw of the bear. There!" She jabs my finger in the air. "Iota UMa. My Talitha."

"I've always been a part of your constellation."

"Yes," she says, and we kiss again. "You are my sidereal time."

"Your what?" I say with a laugh.

"Remember, the clock in the Observatory?" She props herself up on one elbow to face me. "You are my star. My point of reference."

"That's so . . ." I try to find the right word.

"Dorkbottish?" she says, cringing a little.

"Yes," I say, and laugh. "But also incredibly sweet." I bring her knuckles to my lips.

She smiles big. "Did you know that in a vacuum, light from a star could travel forever?"

I shake my head.

"It's true!" Uma lies back again and stares up at the sky. "Right now, I feel like Calliope is our vacuum, where your starlight and mine could go on and on, side by side, without interruption to the end of time."

"How do you know so much?" I ask.

"Well," says Uma. She pauses to take a deep breath. "Remember how I told you that my family moved when I was young?"

I nod.

"We actually started out someplace near here, I think."

"No way!"

"I don't know exactly where we lived, but it was somewhere in the Wastelands. A place that used to be called Hesperia, I think. The few pix and memories I have looked a lot like this area."

"I wonder if we ever saw each other." I try to imagine my filthy toddler self, running wild with Castor, passing by a tiny, perfect, curly-headed Uma.

"Maybe." She chuckles. "Do you think we waved at each other?"

"I probably threw trash at you," I say. "I was kind of a hellion."

Uma laughs. "I bet you were adorable."

"If you like filthy little guttersnipes."

"I do!" she says, and pecks me on the cheek.

"Why'd your family leave?" I roll over to face her, but she keeps her eyes focused on the starry sky.

"My parents wanted more for me. An education, mostly."

"Yeah, good luck getting one of those out here! So where'd you go?" I snuggle closer, laying my head in the soft spot beneath her shoulder.

"Well . . ." she says. "I've been wanting to tell you that—"

The back door of the house squeaks open, and Mom marches out, calling my name while holding Castor's red knapsack in her hands. "Something in here is beeping." Mom shoves the bag at me.

I heave myself up and sigh at my mom. She has the timing of Aurelia. I dig through the knapsack, past the Kinematic Jumpsuit, the razor, the Wearables, Castor's jacket, one of his old hats, and the canister of goo. At the bottom of the bag, I uncover my device, which beeps and blinks furiously. Thinking it might be Castor, I hop up and strap it on my head, but the image on my Lenz is fuzzy.

"Castor? That you?"

The audio is too distorted to hear properly.

"Wait, hang on, let me get better reception." I look over my shoulder at Uma, sitting up, hugging her knees. "I'll be right back!" I call to her, then I jog up the bluff behind my mom's place to find a stronger signal. At the top, the static clears, and I see Mundie, hunched in the curve of a kidney-bean-shaped table. Behind him is a white wall painted with bright green leaves. Seeing him makes my stomach squeeze, and every ounce of relaxation and happiness I felt in the last hour with Uma flies away.

"Where the hell are you?" he barks. "Why didn't you bring us the goo?"

"I got the stuff, but I ran into a problem," I explain as I pick my way down the bluff toward Uma. "I'll bring it first thing in the morning. What's the rush, anyway?"

"You're the one who was in such a hurry to get your brother back. Or are you having too much fun with your little girlfriend to worry about Castor anymore?"

"Listen, Mundie!" Now that I have the goo and I know Castor will be safe, I don't have to be so nice to Mundie anymore. "I'm really sick of—" But then D'Cart enters the frame of my Glaz in a flutter of salmon-colored gossamer. I skid to a stop, sending tiny pebbles rolling down the steep hill.

"Hello, Talitha," she says.

I stand dumbfounded for a moment before I can say hello, my voice too high and squeaky. "I'm sorry I didn't make it back yet. I had a problem and then it was too late to head back, but I have the stuff, and I'm coming first thing in the morning."

"How lovely," she purrs. She leans forward and rests her elbows on the table, making a tent with her fingers in front of her face. "And I hear from Mundie that you've met the MUSC runaway."

I scowl at him. "I never said that. I went to Lost Feelies and Soggywood. I talked to a couple of Moonlings at a nightclub but I didn't learn anything—"

"She's talking about the girl who was at your house last night," Mundie says.

"No," I say slowly, angry that Mundie can't let the Uma thing go. "She's from Merica."

"No," he says even slower and haughtier. "That girl ran away from MUSC. She's the one you're looking for."

I shake my head. "You must have confused her with someone else. You saw her, Mundie. She's not a Moonling."

From the shadows on the bluff, I look down at Uma waiting for me in our bed of roses. In that moment, I wish more than anything that a door between two simultaneous realities would open and Uma and I could step through into a different version of the universe where we have a little house in our own small starlit vacuum.

"She's definitely from Earth," I add defiantly. But even as I say this, something niggles at me. The strange silver clothing, no device, a family that moved from here to get a better life, all the things she knows about MUSC and the Moon and the stars.

"Is this her?" D'Cart sends a feed to my Glaz. A holo of Uma stares at me from some other time and place. It's definitely her. Same corkscrew curls, same gold-flecked green eyes. The only difference is the slight look of sadness on her face instead of her happy, eager smile. UMA JEMISON, AGE 16, scrolls beneath her image.

"That's her," says Mundie. "That's the girl I met at your house. She's lying if she told you she's from Merica."

"I'm not surprised." D'Cart sniffs. "MUSCies can't be trusted. Never could. They're an immoral lot."

"But . . . but . . . but . . . she can't be one of them," I say.

"She was born on Earth. In the Wastelands, in fact," says D'Cart. "A place called Hesperia. She won a scholarship to MUSC as a child."

I can't talk. Can't move. I feel like I'm being sucked into another gaping hole, about to be buried beneath a heap of garbage.

"Since we know who she is and you've already befriended her, now all you have to do is bring her in," says D'Cart, as if this should be easy.

"No," I say. "Mundie told me if I bring you the goo, you'll let Castor go."

"Well . . ." D'Cart thinks this over. "Mundie was wrong and the situation has changed. Now, I want the girl and the goo."

"You can't just change our agreement," I insist.

"Yes, I can," D'Cart says simply.

"Do you know where she is?" Mundie asks.

I open my mouth to answer, then close it again. I work to put the puzzle pieces together. Why didn't Uma tell me where she's from and why she ran away? What's she running from? Is that why she left the club when the other MUSCies showed up? Are her feelings for me real, or am I simply a convenient way to get around without being caught? Anger builds in me as the questions mount.

"Well," says Mundie, impatient as a hungry snake. "Do you know where she is?"

I swallow hard. My mother's words echo back to me: *Whatever they want, there will be more in it for them than there is for you.*

"I don't know where she is," I manage to say.

"That's too bad." D'Cart shifts. "I thought this might be easy." She leans back but keeps her eyes trained steadily on me.

"I can bring you the goo first thing tomorrow," I say again. "And if you release Castor, we can look for the Moon girl together. With both of us looking—"

"Nice try," says D'Cart. "But that's not going to happen."

"But, but, but . . . what if I can't find her?" I ask. My eyes sting, and my throat feels as if it's going to slam shut.

"Then Castor will be on the Shuttle in her place," says Mundie.

"What?" I say.

"Not exactly in her place," D'Cart says with an odd little laugh. "ExploroBots travel differently than MUSCies, you know."

"ExploroBots?" I bark. "What are you talking about?"

"Talitha, wake up!" Mundie says, and snaps his fingers at my face. "If you don't bring the goo and the girl, D'Cart will sell Castor off as an ExploroBot and send him to the Moon."

I feel the blood draining from my face. Stars swim in the dark sky above. I have to squat to keep my balance. "This makes no sense!" I say, breathy and confused. "You said you hated the ExploroBot program. You said it's wrong and immoral!" I nearly shout at D'Cart, then lower my voice, since sound carries out here. "You said you wanted the Exploro-Bot program to end."

"That's true," says D'Cart. "The ExploroBot program is a travesty. A gross misuse of excellent technology. But I need a person on the next MUSC Shuttle. So it can either be your brother with the ExploroBots or the Moonling who's going back anyway once they find her."

"But, why?" I ask, my heart breaking at the thought of choosing between my brother and a girl I fell in love with yesterday.

"I have some unfinished business with MUSC," D'Cart says.

"You're putting me in a difficult position," I tell her.

"No," she says firmly as she rises and walks away. Then she turns and says over her shoulder, "I'm giving you the chance to save your brother."

"How could you be a part of this?" I hiss at Mundie as D'Cart leaves the room. "You said you would take care of him."

"I'm trying to help you get Castor back!" Mundie says to me.

"No," I say. "You're trying to keep me apart from Uma!" Then I disconnect.

I stay up on the bluff, slumped against a rock, knees up to my chest, head buried under my arms, for at least an hour, trying to figure out what to do. Overhead Ursa Major sweeps slowly across the sky, with Talitha eternally locked on the big bear's paw. Or am I under her thumb? Uma said I was her point of reference. Her constant in the universe. Sidereal time, my ass! She's been using me to get around.

Part of me wants to spring down the bluff and confront her. Tell her that I know the truth about her and demand to know why she lied to me. But I can't. Because if I do, she might take off, and then I'll lose my chance to get my brother back. I could never live with myself or face my mother again if Castor died in the same way as my father.

But I can't face Uma now. I won't be able to look her in the eye. She trusts me. Thinks we're on the same side. And I have to keep it that way until I take her in. Because as D'Cart said, *the situation has changed.*

I hear someone crunching up the path, and I scramble to disappear into the shadow of the boulder until my mother whispers, "Talitha, are you okay? Was that Castor on your device? You've been gone for over an hour. Where are you, girl?"

"Here I am." I step out.

"Why didn't you come back?" She reaches to push my hair behind my ear.

"Just watching the stars," I lie, and look away so she can't read my face.

"You can see so many more out here than in the city, I bet." Mom settles herself against the rock. I slide down to sit beside her but keep my eyes on the ground.

"What's troubling you?" she says.

I know Castor's right, I'm an excellent liar, but I've never been able to fool my mother, so instead of telling her the truth, I say, "It's nothing for you to worry about. I can handle it."

"I know you can handle it," says Mom. "You're capable of handling almost anything. Always could. Since you were tiny. But that doesn't mean you have to do it alone." She lays her hand on my knee. "Please tell me what's going on."

I take a deep breath and choose my words carefully. "Mundie called. Castor got caught stealing from the AlphaZonia CEO."

Mom gasps and covers her mouth with her hand. "Is he okay?"

"For now," I say. "He's being held at the Pink Palace."

"We have to go get him!" she says, but doesn't move.

"It's okay," I assure her. "They offered me . . ." I hesitate. "A job. If I take it, they'll release Castor."

"Is it difficult or dangerous? This thing they're asking you to do?"

Tears spring to my eyes. I'm glad it's dark, so she can't see me cry. "Yes," I manage to croak out. "Both. And it's the hardest thing I've ever had to do, but I have no choice."

"We always have choices."

"Mom!" I cry. "If I don't do it, they won't let Castor go!"

"That may be the case. But remember what I've always taught you.

Whatever they're asking you to do, there's more in it for them than there is for you. So be careful what you relinquish in exchange for your brother."

"I know, but . . ." I swallow hard. "Mundie said—"

"Mundie, hmph!" says Mom, and crosses her arms tight. "I never did like that boy. Always following you and Castor around like a hungry dog, ready to bite you the minute you offered a hand. And now he works for D'Cart and has Castor in a corner? Doesn't surprise me in the least. People in AlphaZonia don't care about people like us."

I sit back, waiting out my mother's rant—the same one I've heard all my life, but now that I've lived in AlphaZonia, I actually understand what she means.

"The rich fear the poor, always have. Which is ridiculous, because the wealthy have done far more harm to us than we've ever done to them. False privilege!" she spits. "That's what it is! They think because they have more possessions, they have more to lose. They used to build walls and gates to protect their kind, but then they saw an easier way to keep us out. Let the rich buy their way in to exclusive societies that we can't touch. But they're no more deserving than we are. Strip away all their stuff, take away the chips inside their brains, and what's left? A human being! And every human deserves a decent life."

She turns and looks me in the eye. "You and your brother included. Which is why I raised you here. Away from all that nonsense. But you went back."

"Don't," I warn her. "You know this life wasn't enough for Castor or me."

"You'll never be a Yoobie. Even if you work for that horrible woman RayNay DeShoppingCart and get a chip inside your head," Mom says.

"I don't want that," I tell her. "But I have to make sure Castor is safe."

"Of course you do, but you must be careful. The deal they're offering will be lopsided."

I draw in a sharp breath, because I know she's right, but I don't see a way around it.

"I should come with you," Mom says.

"You don't want to do that," I say, and my mom looks away. "And that's okay," I assure her. "Honestly, Mom, the thought of you in your sand goggles and turban traipsing around the Pink Palace is almost funny." I snort a strangled laugh.

"I can look different," she says, slightly offended.

"But you'll still be you. Which is perfect and wonderful, but this time I have to acquiesce to D'Cart's demands, no matter how hard that is."

She sighs. I see a trace of relief in her eyes that she doesn't have to leave her oasis in the desert, but she grabs me by the shoulders and says, "You must be careful! Talitha, promise me you'll be careful."

"I always am," I assure her. "Remember? I'm not the risk taker."

"I want you to let me know as soon as everything is okay," she says.

"How?" I almost laugh. "You won't use a device."

"Don't you have something you could give me? A way to let me know?" She searches my face, and I see that she's sincere.

"Will you answer if we call?" I ask.

"Yes," she says. "I promise."

I take the device from my head and hand it to her. "Keep this with you," I say. "I'll call you as soon as I know something."

My mother and I walk arm in arm down the bluff. We stop by the outdoor bed where Uma has fallen asleep, beautifully bathed in the moonlight with Quasar tucked against her side.

"What about sweet Uma?" Mom whispers. "Will you take her with you?"

"Yes," I say, and swallow down the nasty taste that's crept up in my mouth. "I need her."

"Yes," says Mom. "You've found someone special."

"No." I feel a deep pit open in my chest as if my heart has imploded like a dying star. For a brief moment in the time line of my life, I thought I'd found someone who understood me in a way no one ever could, but now I know the truth.

I look at Mom and say, "She's not the person I thought she was."

TIME STAMP

Moon
Day 2, Month of Sol, MUSC Year 94

Earth
June 20, 2XXX

UMA JEMISON

CALLIOPE, EARTH

THE NEXT MORNING, Talitha walks from the house to the Auto-Pod and fills the hatch with a box of fruits and veggies from her mother's greenhouse without a word to me.

"Good morning," I chirp from the stack of tires where I sit with a mug of sweet mint tea. I'm dressed in a cute green shirt with a frog on the front and a pair of Talitha's lightweight baggy pants. Quasar sleeps at my feet, his three good paws twitching as if running in his dreams. "Need any help?"

"Nope," she says without eye contact, then passes back to the house again.

When she comes outside with another armload of stuff, I say, "Can I get you some breakfast?"

"Nope." She dumps her knapsack, a jug of water, and a pile of clothes into the car.

"Not a morning person?" I joke, but it lands flat. She walks by again without a smile.

Her mother stands in the doorway, watching us as she sips her own steaming cup of tea. When Talitha is inside the house, Rhea comes to lean against the fan palm shading me. She's in a silky kimono, with her long dark hair down around her shoulders. She looks both younger and older than she did last night.

"Did I do something wrong?" I squint up at her and ask.

"She's fretting over her brother," Rhea tells me.

I watch a lizard tiptoe across the rocks. Hummingbirds busy themselves among the red and orange trumpet vines climbing up the fence. I peer down on these minuscule life-forms as I once peered down at the Earth from MUSC, wondering what the humans below were thinking. Now I'm here and I still don't know.

"I wish we could stay here longer," I admit. "This has been such a nice respite from the rest of life."

"You don't have to leave," says Rhea.

"That's kind of you," I tell her. "But I want to help Talitha."

"She might not take your help. She won't take mine." Rhea's quiet for a few moments, sipping at her tea, before she adds, "Castor and Talitha have always been incredibly close. They have a twin language they use to keep secrets from me." She chuckles. "When they were little and it was just the three of us, I felt excluded sometimes, but in my heart I know they have a deep bond that is very special. They might squabble like two ravens, but nothing will ever come between them."

"I've never had a connection like that with anyone," I admit.

"I did once," says Rhea.

"Your husband?"

She nods as the lines on her face settle into well-worn paths of pain.

Last night, lying under the stars with Talitha, I thought maybe I might have found that kind of bond, but this morning, I'm not so sure.

"I wish I knew what they were up to," Rhea says, mostly to herself. She drains her tea and pushes off the fan palm to pace over the rocks in her bare feet. "But I suppose this is another instance when I have to let them work things out for themselves."

"You understand them so well. And you're so accepting," I say.

That cracks Rhea up. "I'm not sure they think that, but it's nice of you to say." She comes to sit beside me on the tire stack. "What about your mom? Does she understand and accept you?"

"Well . . . that's a tricky question. I know she loves me very much and wants what's best for me, but . . ."

"It's hard to be a parent." Rhea stares into her empty mug. "Especially when you can't give your children the life that they deserve."

"I miss my mother. That much is certain."

Rhea puts an arm around me and says, "I'm sure she feels the same."

"I think she's mad at me." I scan the sky for a faint morning trace of the nearly full moon, but it's tucked away for twelve hours in the never-ending do-si-do with the Earth.

"That will pass," says Rhea. "It always does. But find a way to let her know you're okay." She squeezes me gently. "Will you?"

"I'll try," I say.

Talitha comes outside again, this time with a brown canvas hat pulled low on her head so I can barely see her eyes. "Ready?" she asks as she marches past.

I hop up from the tires, which wakes Quasar. He stretches with a tiny yowl of pain.

"Poor pup!" I drop to my knees beside him. "I hate to say good-bye to you." I lean down so I can kiss the white star between his soulful brown eyes.

I know it's much worse for Talitha. She hugs him tight. He licks away the tears on her cheeks. "Take good care of him until I get back," she tells her mother.

"He'll be fine," says Rhea. "And I can send you updates on that thingamabob communicator you gave me last night."

Talitha rolls her eyes but then stops herself and pulls her mother into a long, fierce hug. "I love you, Mom," she says.

"I love you, too," says Rhea.

I feel a deep, dull ache inside of me as I watch Talitha with her mother. Rhea's right. I need to at least let my mom know that I'm okay. I resolve right then that when I get back to AlphaZonia, I'll find a way to contact her, even if only for a few moments.

I take one last look around. "You have something very special here. I'm going to miss it."

"You're welcome back anytime," Rhea tells me. She opens her arms, and I gladly accept a strong hug from her. Before she lets me go, she whispers, "And get in touch with your mom, okay?"

"I will," I say. "I promise."

When I let go, I see Talitha eyeing us, her stare as stony and cold as a Moon outcropping, and I wonder what happened to the wonderful, warm girl I met yesterday.

The ride out of Calliope is somber.

"Are you sad to leave?" I ask Talitha as the AutoPod speeds across the barren landscape of the desert. The early morning sun washes out the surroundings to a hazy yellow.

"Not really," she says while keeping her gaze trained out the window. Then, silence again.

This goes on. Me asking a stupid question, her barely answering, until we enter the San Gabriel tube. I'm sick of the awkwardness between us, and the darkness of the tunnel emboldens me, so I turn to her and say, "Is everything okay?"

Talitha sits back and pulls her hat down lower on her head, covering up her eyes and refuses to answer.

"Please tell me what's wrong. Did I do something to upset you?" I reach out to touch her arm.

She moves away so her back is against the door, and she looks at me intensely from under the brim of her hat. "Tell me more about you. What was your childhood like? Where'd your family go when you moved?"

The questions sound more like demands. The whole situation feels odd, especially after how cold she's been all morning, but I try my best to answer, thinking it may appease her.

"My parents are kind of like your mom," I tell her. "They thought changing where we lived would solve all of our problems, but there were new problems where we ended up. At first it was okay because at least we were together."

I stop and take a breath, debating how much I should say. Last night I was ready to tell her everything, but now I'm not so sure. The way she's looking at me has me spooked—as if our connection fizzled once the sun came up.

"We have one thing in common, you and I," I venture. My heart speeds up, and my palms get sweaty.

"Oh?" she says as if she doesn't believe me. "What's that?"

"My dad also died when I was little."

Talitha's eyes widen, and her jaw goes slack. She pushes the hat back on her head, so I can see her face clearly.

"I didn't tell you before because . . . I don't know. I don't like to talk about it."

She continues blinking at me as if she can't find any words.

"It happened when I was ten," I say. "And, you know, after that, everything changed."

"Oh, Uma," says Talitha. She rubs her hands across her tired face. "I'm so sorry. I didn't know."

"Of course you didn't." I try to smile, but I can't. "I didn't talk about it."

Talitha stares into the darkness outside the window. "I don't like to talk about my father either. When people find out, they don't know what to say."

"Or they say something stupid, like 'Do you miss him?'"

Talitha gives me a sad laugh of recognition.

"What kind of question is that?" I ask. "You sound like a monster if you say no, but saying yes isn't exactly true."

"I know what you mean," she says, finally looking at me how she used to.

The Pod exits the tunnel, and we're back inside the boundaries of AlphaZonia, which is a lush paradise compared to the stark beauty of the desert.

"For me," she says. "It's more like I miss the idea of him, because the truth is—and this part sucks—I don't remember him all that well. I was only five when he died."

"Even though I was ten, the stuff I hang on to is small," I admit. "Like, how he'd scoop me up and I'd curl on his lap while he read to me. I never felt safer than that."

"I liked to rub my dad's cheeks," Talitha says dreamily. "They were rough with beard scruff when I kissed his face. It hurt, but it was also comforting in a way because it meant that he was there with me."

"My dad smelled like a certain kind of soap, and even now when I get a whiff of it, sadness wraps around me like a big heavy coat."

"Missing someone is a strange sensation," says Talitha. "Like a limb is gone, but you've learned to live without it."

I think of Talitha's father then—an ExploroBot encased in a silver suit. I wonder which people from which cohort on MUSC controlled his reconstructed body with their minds. The whole thing makes me dizzy with nausea.

"How'd your mom take it when he died?" Talitha asks me quietly.

"I think it was harder on her than on me," I admit. "She's really isolated where we live. She works a lot, so I don't see her much, and she doesn't have many friends. At least I had Kepler. He's my only true friend."

"The only one?" she asks.

"Yeah, pathetic, I know, but the thing is, I don't really fit in with the other people there. Most of them look down on me and my mom because we came from here. Kepler's the exception. He likes me for who I am. He's a good guy. You'd like him."

Talitha inches closer. Her hand lies next to my leg on the seat. I want to grab it. Feel her warm fingers in mine again, but I don't. Not yet.

"Is that why you ran away?" she asks.

I sit, dumbfounded as we stare at one another. "How did you know I ran away?"

"I know where you're from," she says, her voice hushed and angry. Her chest heaves as if she's squishing down the urge to scream. "You should have told me."

"I wanted to tell you but . . ." I hang my head, unable to look her in the eye just then. "I was afraid you would hate me if you knew."

Talitha says nothing.

"I didn't mean to run away," I tell her honestly. "I just wanted a break. I've spent my whole life being watched and judged. Compared to people I'm nothing like. I've been promised a trip here since I was little, and then it was taken away from me for no good reason.

"My mother says life is a series of trade-offs and I should be grateful for what I have, but I'm tired of being the one who's always giving something up. My family had to work for everything we have. When I look at the people around me at MUSC who have more than I have, I wonder, what did they do to deserve it? Why don't I deserve the same? And why could something I wanted, and worked so hard to get, be taken from me so easily? I couldn't accept it. When the chance to leave came, I took it."

"Oh, Uma," Talitha says. "I wish I'd known . . ."

I shrug and laugh half-heartedly. "The funny thing is, I'd barely ever broken a rule before that. I planned to be here for a few weeks, then go back and face the consequences of leaving. I figured it would be easy. But . . . I didn't know I would meet you."

Talitha pulls away. "What do I have to do with it?"

"You changed everything," I tell her. The pitch of my voice is too high and too desperate, but I can't stop the words from spilling out of me anymore. "I've never felt this way before. About anyone. I told Dr. Fornax that I felt drawn to Earth, and now I know why. There is a pull between us. Like the Earth and Moon. I know you feel it, too. I want to be close to you and look at you and ask you questions and listen to your voice and take in everything you say. You make me curious about the world. You make me want to experience everything!"

I toss my arms out to the sides, motioning to the city whizzing by in a green and silver blur. "When I'm with you, I feel like a spoiled, greedy little brat who thinks she is entitled to everything she's ever wanted."

"No, Uma," Talitha says. Her anger seems to break a bit. "That's not greedy. You deserve to get what you want."

"And what I want is you." I lean forward and lower my voice. "When I kiss you—" I inhale sharply at the memory of the taste of her. "The world seems possible to me in a way it never did. I broke a lot of rules when I ran away, but the truth is, I don't regret a thing, because it means

I got to be with you. At least for a little while." I tilt my head to the side and begin to close my eyes, but Talitha rears back stunned as if I've slapped her.

"I can't . . ." she says.

My face burns, and my guts churn. "I'm sorry." I shrink down in my seat. If I could stop the Pod and jump out right now, I would. "I thought you felt the same—"

She grabs my hand, sending a tiny jolt across my skin. I look down at her fingers on mine. It's hard to tell where my hand starts and hers ends. Our skin is nearly the same tone now since mine has become burnished in the strong sun of the Earth.

"I do feel it," she says. "It's just, everything is a mess! It's all so complicated right now. My brother . . ." She stops and searches my eyes. "I have to help him and . . ." Her face crumbles. "And to do that . . ." She hesitates and gulps. "I can't . . ." She stops and grimaces as if she's fighting something that she can't let out. "I can't explain it all."

"It's okay," I say gently, and stroke her arm. "You don't have to explain to me."

"I wish I could." Talitha draws in a ragged breath and squeezes my hand. "I wish we could tell each other everything."

"Do you know what I wish?" I ask. She shakes her head. "I wish that door in the multiverse between your world and mine had opened at a different time. A time when both of us could do whatever we wanted in life."

"Same," she says.

I take a deep breath, and I look out the window again. The Pod has slowed, and I realize we're pulling into the long, winding drive of the Pink Palace. I sit back, confounded.

"Talitha," I ask, "what are we doing here?"

TALITHA NEVA

ALPHAZONIA, EARTH

"I'M SORRY, UMA," I say, and hear the tremble in my voice as the AutoPod meanders up the Pink Palace drive. "There's something I have to take care of here."

"Please, stop! Let me out, okay?" Uma claws at the door, but it's locked tight on my command. "I'll wait for you down here away from the grounds."

"No," I say, and lay my hand on her arm. "I need you with me."

"Yeah, but . . ." She looks around. "It's not safe—"

"I have to make a trade with D'Cart to get my brother back."

"The stuff you got at the Dumps yesterday?" she asks.

I nod and bite my bottom lip to keep it from quivering as the Pod pulls to the side of the drive. We idle near the hedge of purple-blossoming rhododendrons and giant palm bushes.

"But why do I have to be with you? Do you need me to help you carry it?"

Uma searches my face, trying to understand. I feel terrible and can barely look her in the eye. I know I should be loyal to my brother, but betraying Uma is too harsh a consequence. If I don't do it, though, I'll be the reason Castor is shot up to the Moon. My mom's words come back to me again, *We always have choices*. There has to be another way. A way to save them both. I just don't know what it is yet.

"Listen," I say urgently. "Will you wait for me here? Please? I won't be long."

Uma takes a long, deep breath, then squares her shoulders and sits up straight. "Okay," she says, but I hear the uncertainty in her voice. "If that's what you need me to do, then I'll wait for you here." Then without warning, Uma darts forward to kiss me.

That kiss catches me off guard. I press my fingers to my buzzing lips to seal in the feeling before I turn away and climb out of the Pod. I can't say anything just now because my voice might give away my near panic and spook her into bolting.

"Talitha," she calls after me. I hesitate, then turn around and see fear in her eyes. "Please hurry!"

I run away with the canister of the goo in the red knapsack bumping against my back and Castor's hat pulled low on my head.

Once again, I stand beneath the black-and-white-striped awning of the Pink Palace portico, where I don't belong. The last time I was here, with Castor, my heart pounded, my palms sweated, and my hands shook, because I was certain someone would realize we were imposters. This time, I'm not trying to be anyone I'm not. I'm a thief and a liar, and I'm here to make a deal. But like last time, the closer I get to the door, the more I want to run away from the terrible choice I have to make. Give up Uma to save my brother or save Uma and never see my brother again. Last night I felt certain about what I should do, but now neither option is acceptable. When I get to the door, a red SecuriBot wheels out to stop me.

"I'm Talitha Neva, here to see D'Cart," I announce.

"Talitha Neva is not on the approved guest list at this time," the robot says.

"She is expecting me," I insist. "She asked me to come."

"Talitha Neva is not on the approved guest list at this time," it repeats.

"Ping Mundie," I request, but the robot tells me once again that I'm not on the list.

"Damn it, nanobrain!" I growl. "Go get Mundie, or I'll pull out your CPU and shove it up your—"

"Talitha?" Mundie pushes through the door and stands next to the SecuriBot. He's flushed and out of breath. "I saw you on the security cam and ran up here." He peers around behind me as if I've hidden something in the potted plants. "Where's the Moonling? Did you bring her?"

"I have the goo." I wrestle the knapsack off my back and take out the container with shaking hands.

"But where's the girl?" Mundie reaches for the canister.

"No!" I snatch it away. "Before you can have this or the Moonling, you have to . . ." I pause and look around for anything to buy me some time while I think of a decent plan. "Let me see Castor."

"That wasn't the deal," Mundie says, arms crossed.

"Well . . . as D'Cart said last night, the situation has changed, and . . ." I take a deep breath to calm my shaking hands as I clutch the container, my only bargaining chip. "I want to make sure that my brother's safe before I'll give you anything."

Mundie shakes his head.

"I'd be a fool to give you everything right now. For all I know, D'Cart could have conscripted Castor into a ReConstruction crew or sold him off to MUSC like she threatened."

"He's here. You just have to trust me," Mundie says.

"Trust you?" I snort, which makes Mundie flinch. "You lied to me. You said you'd keep him safe."

"No," Mundie says, shaking his head. "I said I'd try."

"You should have tried harder." I take a step closer, leaving enough distance between us that he can't grab the container. "You owe me this," I say quietly.

"I don't owe you anything!"

"You're supposed to be my friend!"

"I wanted to be more than friends, and you know it!" Mundie stamps his foot, which makes me jump back.

We stare at each other, then I inch closer. "After everything we've been through?" I ask, knowing more clearly what I have to do. If I can parody a CelebriStreamer, then I can pretend to be a girl in love with a boy. It's just another character. I soften my face and look at him pleadingly. "The late-night talks beneath the stars? The time you kissed me?" I say the things I wish I could say to Uma. "Those mean nothing to you?"

"I saw you with that Moon girl," Mundie says. "The way you held her hand so tight. How you looked at each other. You've never looked at me like that."

"She means nothing to me," I lie. "I'll bring her to you, but only after I have ten minutes alone with Castor to make sure that he's okay."

Mundie sighs and shakes his head as if he's fighting with himself. "You can see him on your iEye—"

"No! Not good enough. I want to see him in person. Please." I reach out to stroke Mundie's arm. "What's it going to hurt?"

He sighs and says, "Okay, but—" Then something strange happens to his face. It goes weirdly slack, as if he's not in control of the muscles anymore. His eyes are blank as if he's dazed.

"Mundie?" I withdraw my arm. "Are you okay?"

Without a word, Mundie turns on his heel and walks back toward the door.

"Mundie, wait. Where are you going? Should I come with you?" I take a step, but the SecuriBot blocks my path.

"Mundie, come back!" I yell, but he doesn't flinch or slow down. The door opens, and he walks inside, leaving me stunned and confused.

Now I have no idea what to do. The one thing I thought I could count on, Mundie's feelings for me, didn't work. Trying to trade the goo for a chance to talk to Castor didn't work either. I feel sick. The only choice I have left is giving up Uma to get my brother back.

AFTER A FEW minutes of waiting for Talitha, I peer out the window and tell myself I'm being silly. The MUSCies who are looking for me have come and gone. The Pink Palace might even be the safest place for me, since they've already looked here. Plus, if I can find my device, this may be my only chance to check in with my mother. The truth is, I never imagined I'd be on Earth without out daily check-ins. I wanted to share everything with her. I know she's got to be furious with me for all the things I've done wrong, but Rhea's right—she's probably also worried sick. It's possible Mr. Chen-Ning found my device when he was here; then again, I only saw him carrying my flight suit, so I might get lucky. I know it's risky, but if I can connect with my mom for a few moments, then toss my device away again and leave, I should be safe.

I figure it'll take Talitha at least ten minutes to drop off the stuff and collect her brother, so I hop out of the Pod. Birds busy themselves on the dewy grass. Sunlight filters through the palms, and the sweet smell of honeysuckle permeates the air, cool from the night. Still, I feel uneasy. I run for the bushes, looking right and left for any bystanders, but there's no one else around.

I find a break in the branches where I pushed my way through two days ago and wonder if there really is an invisible portal that opened between Talitha's world and mine. I know it's silly, but I like the idea and wish I could find that portal again to step through anytime I wanted to be with her, because at some point, I have to go back to MUSC, and she won't be able to go with me. So what will we do then? I have no idea.

Behind the bushes, the ground is soft and damp. The air is moist. I search the area where I think I threw my device. If I remember correctly, it smacked the wall with a crack, then fell in the dirt. For all I know, it could be in a dozen different pieces. A flash of light catches my eye. I look up and see that, hanging over a branch at eye level near the wall, is my device, almost as if someone has picked it up and placed it there for me to find.

"No way," I say, and can't believe my luck as I strap it to my head. Darshan immediately comes online. I never thought I'd be happy to see him, but I am. *Darshan*, I command, *ping my mother*.

Pinging your mother, he confirms.

I wait, breath held while I pace. I realize then that I don't know what time it is on MUSC. I've completely lost track of the days and nights up there. Then again, my mother won't care. Day or night, she'll be relieved to hear from me. Even if I only leave a short message.

My device pings and pings, no doubt working hard to reestablish a connection with the MUSC satellites. I get worried then. What if she doesn't answer? What if Fornax has locked her up until I return? Or worst of all, what if she doesn't want to speak to me? I feel light-headed as all of the problems I've caused line up in my brain. But then, to my relief, she appears.

"Uma!" she cries, peering into her Lenz, searching for me. "Is that you?"

"Mom!" I yell. "It's me, and I'm okay! I just wanted to . . ."

I see her lips move, but I can't make out what she's saying because of some racket overhead.

"Hang on. Just a sec!" I try to move away, but the loud, driving noise won't stop. Then the dry leaves in the bush begin to lift up and swirl past my head. The branches around me bend. A strong wind presses down, tossing dust and dirt in my eyes.

"What the hell?"

I throw my arm against my forehead to block the light and dust and look up to see what's happening. Overhead, I see the silhouettes of four drones descending toward me, and I scream.

"UMA! START THE car!" I run toward the AutoPod as four red Se-curiDones the size of vultures hover in a diamond formation over the rhododendron bush. "Start the car! Start the car!" I yell, waving my arms in the air to get her attention.

Overhead, the drones plunge straight down into the bush. Branches shudder and shake. Small birds fly up and dart away. A whirlwind of leaves ascends. Then I hear screaming.

I watch, mouth agape, as the drones emerge from the top of the bush carrying a screaming person splayed out like an *X*, one drone on each wrist and ankle. I sprint for the car, commanding the door to open, hoping that Uma's safely hidden, but when I get there, the car is empty.

"Oh no! Oh no!" I look up in the sky, realizing with horror that the drones have Uma. "No!" I shout, and bolt across the grass, waving my arms. "Uma! No! Let her go! Help! Someone, please, help!"

Uma's terrified screams echo off the Palace walls and reverberate through the air. The drones hover for a moment above the trees. Palm fronds whip like a hurricane is coming.

The commotion brings Mundie outside again. "What is it?

What's going on?" he shouts over the noise as he runs across the lawn toward me.

"They have Uma. Stop them!" I shout. "Make them stop!"

"You idiot!" Mundie screams at me. "You had her, and you lost her!"

I turn on him, blind with rage. I toss my knapsack off my shoulder and throw the container of goo aside, then run full force at him with fists closed. I swing wildly, catching him on the shoulder with one hand and the bottom of the jaw with the other. He jumps away, but I charge at him again, head down, shoulders rounded. I knock him to the ground, where we roll.

"This is your fault!" I scream at him. "You wanted this to happen. You led me here!"

Mundie is taller and stronger than I am. He pushes me off like a bug, then backhands me across the cheek. I roll into a ball and groan. The slap leaves me seeing stars.

"I did everything for you!" Mundie stands over me and shouts. Spit flies from his mouth. "But I was never good enough, was I? Well, you can kiss it all good-bye now. Castor." He points to the Palace. "That girl!" He points to the sky. "Just like your dad. They're going to the Moon." He swoops down and grabs the canister of goo off the grass, then he storms back toward the Palace. "And you'll be all alone!"

"Mundie! Stop! Please!" I push onto my hands and knees. Above me, the drones make another quarter turn and hesitate. Uma screams and screams. "No, please no," I say, horrified and helpless as they lift up all at once and carry Uma away over the Palace.

I double over and vomit, then vomit again in the grass. I failed. Failed everyone I love. The doors to the Palace are shut tight with Castor and Mundie inside. Both Uma and the goo, my only chances to get my brother, are gone. I have nothing. Mundie's right; everything I love is stolen away by that horrid sterile rock in the sky.

"Take me," I moan into the grass. "Take me instead."

I cry this way for several minutes until I listen to the words I'm saying and I stop. I sit up on my knees. "It should be me," I whisper, and pull myself together. "I should be the one to go, not Castor."

I grab my knapsack and scramble to my feet. No one is around. Mundie is inside. The Palace SecuriBots and MUSC SecuriDrones are gone. There are no Yoobies in sight. I plunge headfirst into the bushes. As if I'm going back in time, I skitter past the place where the doors between the multiverses opened and I met Uma for the first time, past the place where Quasar waited, past the place where Castor talked me into the worst idea of his life. Then I make a wide circle, skirting the security wall once again, only this time in the opposite direction so I can return to the rear of the Pink Palace, where Mundie released me two days ago.

Lifeless bots stand dead-eyed on the rear loading bay. I find a bot that's missing a wheel on one side with a crazy tangle of blue, red, and black wires sticking out of an open panel on its back. I pull two pins from my hair, twist them together, and jimmy open the CPU panel on the head. Kids like Castor, Mundie, and me learned a long time ago how to gut a robot in two minutes flat. And that's all it takes for me to have my fists full of the motherboard, a handful of circuits, and the navigation system. I'm like a wolf, going for the heart and liver first, leaving the less valuable pieces for later vultures.

Next, I dismantle a service robot, removing its torso from its wheelbase. Then, hands out in front of me, I search for cloaked furniture. I ram my knee into an invisible chair, then hop around and curse until I run into two small cloaked end tables near the trash. If I hold them in the right way, I can see their pieces clearly. I wrench off the legs so I have the seat, seat back, and two tabletops. As I turn them over in my hands, I see they are made of a thin two-way mirror. From the back,

I can see through them, but from the front, strong light reflects so they appear to blend into their surroundings.

Working quickly, I bang out a crude contraption with whatever scraps I can find. I wire everything together with the stolen nav system and CPU board, then connect the whole thing to the iEye, wrist cuff, and shoe insert Castor set up for me at the party. When I'm done, I have a makeshift mover, a cloaked box just big enough for me to sit inside and drive. I drag it over near the garbage dumpsters, climb inside, and wait.

Although it seems like hours, it's probably not that long until I hear the trash trucks. My heart races at the familiar sound. I wait, barely breathing, hoping for a bit of luck. Soon I hear the *squonk* of the rear kitchen doors. I cup my hands around my eyes and peer through the mirrored surface of my mover. I see a CleanerBot wheeling barrels of garbage down the service ramp toward the dumpster as the automated trucks pull into the back of the lot. Once the CleanerBot is past me, I make my move. Pushing full throttle, I propel my small wonky device through the open door into the automated kitchen. Inside the Palace, I connect the nav system to a map of the interior displayed on my iEye and set a course for the nearest service elevator.

As I pass ChefBots, I go undetected. Then again, these bots aren't concerned with security. I may not have as much luck once I'm beyond the kitchen. My little mover pushes through the swinging doors and bumps along a carpeted hall. Up ahead, I see an intersection. I check the map on my iEye. I need to turn left to find the service elevator that will take me upstairs where I hope to hell Castor's still being held. But, as I near the junction, I hear a whoosh and a muted roar. My heart jumps into my throat when I slam into something and stop. Since no one is around, I pop up out of the mover and see an automated vacuum disk bumping me.

"Move it," I whisper. It backs up and rams into me again. "Damn it. Move over," I growl, but it blocks my path, too stupid to know how to go around. It's in the center of the hall, taking up too much space. I can't get past it, and it won't go around me because it doesn't see me. This is ridiculous! I won't be thwarted by a vacuum!

"Come on, you stupid bot, get out of my way." I jump out of my cloaked box and bend down to pick it up, but from the other direction, behind the sweeper, I see a line of people.

"Oh, shit," I say aloud, and drop the vacuum. It rights itself and trundles off. Mundie's at the front of the line, flanked by four Yoobies, two on each side. I brace myself against the wall, ready to fight, ready to run, ready to beg Mundie to let me go. But he doesn't notice me. In fact, he doesn't even blink. Not a single Yoobie bats an eye or makes a sound. They march single file, as if nothing else around them exists. They are dead-eyed and uncharacteristically quiet, which is eerie. Yoobies are never quiet. Never not talking about themselves.

"Mundie," I whisper as he gets closer, but he doesn't flinch.

I don't know if he's decided to let me go or if he's not in control of his body, but either way, it doesn't matter. I abandon my mover and run for the service elevator.

On the fifth floor, I dart for the room at the end of the hall. Using the security code from the CleanerBot's CPU, I command the door to open and hold my breath, afraid they've moved him someplace else. But no. I'm in luck. My twin jumps up from a chair, and we run to each other.

I'M FLOATING. WITH Kepler. By my side. He has my hands. Pulling. Pulling too hard.

Slow down, I tell him. *We're going too fast. I'm going to be sick.*

Uma! Come on, he says. *The parties are starting.*

I don't want to go to the parties. I want to stay here! I insist. *There's someone that I like. A girl with hair the color of Mars.*

No. I jerk awake and scream. I'm not on MUSC. Not floating with Kep. I'm in the air, terrifyingly high above a ruined city. Buildings, trees, and a patchwork of roads are splayed out beneath me like a holo map. My stomach squeezes. My head spins. The edges of my sight blur. Everything goes gray and fuzzy. I open my mouth to scream again, but no sound comes out. In the strange silence of the sky, I hear my name. I whip my head side to side, trying to see who's calling me.

"Uma! Uma!"

I focus in. My Lenz is pressed hard against my face by the wind, but I can make out my mother's fuzzy outline too close to my eye.

"Mom!" I scream and writhe. "Help me! Help!"

"Stop screaming, stop!" she shouts. "Calm down. Where are you? What's happening?"

"Drones!" I shout, trying to form sentences but failing. "On my wrists. My ankles." I look up. I'm splayed out. A big X. A target moving across the sky between four red, faceless, mindless SecuriDrones with four propellers each. The MUSC logo stamped in silver shines across their flanks. "Picked me up," I pant. "Carrying me too high. I'm going to die! They're going to drop me!"

"No," Mom says. "They've got you. You're safe. Calm down."

"Safe!" I glare at her. My anger makes me focus. "Did you know? Did you know they were coming for me? Are they taking me to the Shuttle? I don't want to go back yet!"

Mom grimaces, then shouts, "Why? What's down there that you love so much?"

"Talitha!" I shout with all my might.

My mom rears back, her eyes wide and her mouth open. "Talitha? What's that?"

"A girl," I whimper, so frightened of the height and the speed and of where the drones are taking me. "Her name is Talitha, and I love her, and I think she might be in trouble. She needs me, Mom. I need to know she's okay before I come home. Don't let them do this. Don't let them take me away from here. Not yet!"

It seems to take a moment for all my words to sink in, but then my mother says, "Then fight!" Her face is fuzzy on my Lenz, but I can hear the fierceness in her voice.

"Fight?" I say.

"Yes! We raised you to be a fighter, Uma. So bang your feet together. Knock those drones off course. Do something! Come on, Uma! Fight! Fight for what you want."

I do what she says. With all my strength, I jerk my legs. For a second, the drones falter. I scream as we plummet, but then they right themselves, and I buck again. I jerk my legs to crash my feet together, knocking one propeller off the drone on my right foot. It falters and swoops. I scream again, sure that I'm going to fall, but I don't fall, and I realize that the drones are powerful but light. Again, I smash my legs together. Another propeller whips away into the air. We drop another few meters. I smack the drones against one another over and over, knocking propellers off, and we descend.

"It's working!" I shout to my mother.

"Keep going!" she shouts back.

I crash my legs together one more time, and the drone on my left leg hisses, sparks, and detaches. My left leg flops, and I cartwheel through the air, screeching like a bird in death throes. The falling drone spins out of control, zigzagging, and crashes into a palm tree, sending a plume of smoke and fire into the air.

When I'm upright again, I use my free leg to kick at the other drone on my right ankle. I knock the two remaining propellers off one by one until that one detaches, which leaves me hanging by my arms, legs dragging down. Pain sears through my shoulders. I pull down hard on the left side, trying to ease the pain, and my body arcs wide to the left. I pull down hard on the right side, and I arc to the right.

"I can steer!" I yell. "I can control them."

"Yes!" my mom shouts. "Keep going."

I pull left and right, sailing now through the sky, trying to set a course. "But I don't know where I am."

"Get the ocean on your right side, then you'll be heading south," Mom says.

I pull left and right, reorienting myself until I see the enormous swath of blue water meeting the sky at the horizon. Despite my terror, I'm amazed at how beautiful it is. The blue goes on forever.

"I did it!" I shout. "I'm heading south, back toward the city."

But the drones attached to my arms begin to grind and buzz. My weight is too much, and we're losing altitude. The tops of trees are getting closer to my toes.

"Find a landmark!" my mom shouts at me.

"Everything looks the same!" I shout back as I scan the endless tangle of roads below, each dotted with the rectangular tops of houses, surrounded by patches of green. But then something catches my eye. A flash of pink in the center of a giant swath of green. I pull as hard as I can on my right arm and swing around so that I spiral, down and down, bringing myself closer to what has to be the Palace. As I descend, I see the black-and-white stripes of the portico and then, behind the pink building, a huge blue rectangle in the middle of the enormous lawn.

The right drone whines, high-pitched and persistent. Dark smoke trails behind it, marring the sky. "I have to get lower," I tell my mother. "Closer to the ground. Find a safe place to drop, because these drones aren't going to last."

I pull harder into the spin, willing myself down. "Maybe I can set down on the roof?"

"Be careful! Oh, my gad, be careful!" my mother shouts, the panic rising in her voice as I feel more in control.

I swoop down, over the top of a row of trees, so close that palm fronds brush my legs. The drone on my right arm pops. Sparks rain down on my arm and sizzle against my skin. I jerk and yowl in pain. The drone releases its grip on me and plummets to the ground, sending me careening out of control. My legs kick and flail as I flounder, held by one drone on my left arm. I scream and squeal, trying to gain some control, trying to get close enough to the ground so that I won't break every bone in my body when the last drone dies. It screeches as the motor burns out while trying to keep me aloft. Down and down we fall, too quick, too hard. The green grass comes up fast; the blue of the swimming pool fills my vision.

Then I know what I have to do. I shake my arm wildly, trying to loosen the drone's grip, trying to time it just right, sure I'll get it wrong and splat onto the hard ground. "Now!" I yell, and yank one more time.

The drone's grip fails, and I'm free. Falling through the air. Screaming for my life. Hurtling toward the Earth. Toward the water. I tuck my body, close my eyes, and brace myself for impact.

CASTOR NEVA

ALPHAZONIA, EARTH

AFTER TALITHA EXPLAINS everything to me—who Uma is, what D'Cart asked her to do, what Mundie said, how she got back inside the Palace, and what we should do now—we sit across from each other, both with our hands folded on the table, left index fingers on top. My mother swears we held hands in the womb. I came out first. She says Talitha held my ankle when she followed me into the world. But my mother makes things up.

"You're sure?" I ask.

"Yes," says Talitha with more certainty than I've ever heard in her voice.

"But what if—" I start to say.

"No *what if*s." She reaches into my knapsack and pulls out the electric razor. "Shave it."

I stand up to do what she asks. "Told you it would come in handy," I joke, because otherwise the reality of our situation is too painful. The razor buzzes in my fist. I start at the top of her left ear and push back. I work methodically, in strips, from left ear, over the crown of her head, front to back, left to right. She watches the persimmon-colored curls fall to the floor around our feet. When I'm done, I step back and run the razor over my face and neck until my skin is baby soft and smooth like a girl's.

Talitha's hand shakes as she rubs the top of her newly shorn head. "I feel half naked."

"You look like a different person."

She looks up at me. "But do I look like you?"

I nod. Then I look away, too shaken by the resemblance. I squat and gather up the hair. "I can sell this," I say, fists full, as if that's the most important thing right now.

"We have good hair," she says, and helps me clean up the mess. We quickly stuff all but two handfuls of my sister's locks into my knapsack.

"Clothes," she says when the floor is clear.

It's been a few years since we've dressed in front of one another. Being naked together used to come so casually to us. Bath time when we were kids. Skinny-dipping when we were lucky enough to find an arroyo after a rare rain. We shared everything when we were little. All clothes were communal—shorts, skirts, dresses, tops—we each wore both. But now we are shy. We kick off our shoes and socks, then avoid each other's eyes as we strip off our pants. Left leg, right leg. We are mirror images. We trade pants. Mine are baggier, but hers fit me in the waist just fine.

Next our shirts. Arms crossed at the belly, then a quick tug up and over our heads. The way our mother taught us. Other than her tiny breasts and the slight slope of her hips, we are the exact same size and shape, with ribs showing above the flat planes of our bellies.

"I forgot you have an innie," she says, and points at my belly button, then to her own outie.

"Yeah, it'll suck if our belly buttons give us away," I say, and almost laugh, except it isn't funny.

Talitha wriggles out of her bra beneath her tank top and hands it to me. "Use your socks," she says.

"Huh?"

"Stuff them in the bra."

I do what she says, struggling to snap the contraption in the back, then I fill the small cups with my wadded-up socks. She turns her back to me and takes off the tank top. With her teeth, she tears the stretchy fabric into two long strips, which she wraps around her chest.

"Help me," she says over her shoulder. "Make it tight."

I pull the ends as hard as I can. "Can you breathe?"

"I'll be fine," she says.

I tie the ends together.

We each put on the other's shirt. Hers is warm and smells like our mother's sage and lavender soap. She pulls up the hood to my jacket just like I do. I leave her shirt billowy and untucked like she does. We look at each other, and Talitha breaks first. A snort.

"What?" I ask, looking down.

"You with boobs, that's what!"

"Feels nice!" I say, and lift my sternum. "Good thing yours aren't bigger."

"I like being a boy." She laughs and runs her hand down her con- stricted chest. "Now the hair."

She pins some of the shorn hair to to the inside of that hat she was wearing and sets it on my head so that her curls falls around my shoul- ders.

"How do we look?" I ask.

"We'll pass," she says. "Last thing—I gave Mom my device. You have to contact her and say that you're okay once you get out."

"Will she answer?"

"She promised."

I feel a fist in my throat. "You don't have to—"

"Yes, I do," Talitha says, then corrects herself to say, "I want this." She takes a deep breath. "You should leave."

Emotions I have no names for well up in my chest. I try to fight them down, but my voice trembles when I say, "No. Let's try to get out. Both of us. Together."

Talitha shakes her head. "Too risky. At least this way—"

"But—"

"Castor . . ." She lays a hand on my chest and pushes. "Go. Please."

I reach down and take her hand. We weave our fingers together. Each of us fighting to get the left index finger on top.

"Tell Mom I love her." Talitha swipes at a tear on her cheek. "And take care of Quasar."

"Of course," I whisper. I step in to hug her, but then we hear footsteps outside the door.

"Oh, no," she says. We squeeze hands and stare hard at each other, then jump apart just before the door opens and Mundie steps inside. He stops and glowers. "You," he spits at me, thinking that I'm my sister.

Talitha tightens her shoulders and holds them up, hunched forward just a bit, closer to her ears in a protective stance like I would. In a lower voice, more angry than her own, she says, "I knew she'd find a way to see me."

Mundie ignores her and turns to me. "The deal is off. You know that, right?"

"I know," I say, more whispery. I wiggle my shoulders to loosen up, then drop them down and back as I lift my sternum so I stand proud like my sister. "Just wanted to say good-bye to him." I glance over my shoulder at her one more time. She was Talitha when she walked in here, and now she's staying here as me. I lift my chin, grab the knapsack, and walk past Mundie like Talitha would.

"I'm letting you go," he says. "As a favor."

I nod, then before he can reconsider, I get out the door and sprint.

I've been in and out of the room enough to know my way around. I head straight for the stairwell. Robots can't do stairs, and I'm faster than Mundie if he changes his mind. I charge down and around stairwell after stairwell, taking steps four and five at a time, jumping to landings, ignoring the pain shooting up my ankles into my knees. I'm not going to stop. I owe it to Talitha. I'm getting the hell out of this place and finding a way to get her back.

Once I hit the second floor, I burst through the door into the hall. I won't go all the way to the first floor because SecuriBots will be waiting for me. Instead, I charge through the hall as fast as I can, toward the French doors at the end. Sunlight streams through the windows, so I know I'm heading in the right direction—toward the back of the building in the west where the sun is starting to set. I hit the doors, slam them wide open, and keep running across the balcony where D'Cart greeted everyone that night at the party. I jump. My right foot hits the stone parapet at the end of the balcony, and I take a giant leap, propelling myself into the air. My body flies, arms and legs still running. Unless I've horribly miscalculated, I should be heading for the deep end of the pool.

I hear screaming as I fly and wonder if it's me. Then I see something horrible.

Another body, falling from the sky. Twisting and turning, hurtling out of control in front of me. It hits the water just seconds before I do.

I plunge in feetfirst and sink, arms overhead, clothes billowing up and covering my face. I blow out, then save air until my feet hit the bottom of the pool. I push off, driving my arms down so I dart back to the surface quickly. I inhale hard, sucking in air, then look down, trying to find the other person in the pool. I see the dark shape, writhing, wriggling, like a dying eel below me. I take a deep breath and dive.

The person fights, but she's stuck, tethered to the bottom of the pool by a pant leg sucked into the drain. I bob to the surface for another gulp of air and dive down again, pushing hard with my arms to reach the bottom. I look at the girl. Dark hair floats up around her head. She's wearing Talitha's green shirt with the frog on the front. Knowing I'll never get the pant leg out of the suction of the drain, I loosen the waist of her pants and strip them off her body, pulling her shoes off, too. I wrap my arms around her legs and push off the bottom as hard as I can, with her sitting on my left shoulder to drive both our bodies toward the surface of the water.

I EXPECT MUNDIE to figure it out and go after Castor, but he stands in the doorway and watches the person he thinks is me run away. His shoulders slump. I see resignation in his eyes, which are alive again, unlike when I passed him in the hall.

"Your sister's a bitch. And a tease," he says. "Led me on for years, but I don't care anymore. She's a lesbo, and I'm not into that."

I could almost feel bad for Mundie if he weren't such a jerk. He would have been better off living in Merica, where people think like he does. Instead he came to AlphaZonia and made himself miserable, so it's easy for me to stay put against the wall, my arms crossed defiantly, sneering at him as I imagine Castor would.

"But at least I'm getting rid of you!" He reaches out and grabs my shoulder. My heart catches, and my palms sweat, I'm so afraid he'll know it's me. But in his anger, he doesn't seem to notice.

Please, Uma, please be on that Shuttle, I think to myself as Mundie shoves me into the hall and marches me toward the elevator.

"TFT Implant Center," he commands, and we travel down to a lower floor. We exit into a pristine patient ward in what appears to be an automated hospital. MediBots zip along the corridor and disappear into quiet rooms. I peek inside one as we pass and see a young Yoobie guy in pale pink lying passively on a bed, laughing at an external Stream projected on his wall while three MediBots prod and poke him.

"Are all these people getting TFT installed?" I ask as we walk past dozens of these rooms.

"Duh," says Mundie.

"Am I getting one?"

He shrugs and says, "It's not so bad. I have one."

I wonder if the dead-eyed people I saw earlier with Mundie were patients here.

At the end of the hall, he dumps me in an exam room where a SecuriBot snakes out two tentacles and straps me to a gurney. The room is small and cold. The bright overhead light reflects off the silver surfaces of a sink and metal countertop. I shiver but don't struggle, because there's no use. Whatever's about to happen to me can be no worse than what Uma's going through. I have to be strong for her and make it onto that Shuttle.

A person walks in that I don't recognize at first, then I realize that it's D'Cart. She looks nothing like she usually does. Instead of her trademark flowing pink silk clothes and glammed-out hair and makeup, she's in a crisp white lab coat, hair pulled back tight, face scrubbed clean. She pulls on gloves, then takes a thin patch out of her pocket.

"I'm sorry your sister chose the Moonling over you," she says perfectly pleasantly as she walks toward me.

"MUSC drones got the Moon girl," Mundie says, and D'Cart blinks with surprise. "Picked her up a while ago and carted her off like vultures with a hunk of meat."

D'Cart shudders. "Cruel people. Hauling her back up to the Moon,

I suppose. Poor kid. I was just like her once. Dying to get out of there. At least I get to go back on my own terms." She grins and comes at me with the patch.

"What's that?" I ask, instinctively pulling away, but I don't get far with the straps holding me in place.

"Just a little oxymorphone mix to make your flight more pleasant." She pushes up the left side of my shirt. I flinch, afraid that my outie belly button or the small mounds of my breasts beneath the binding will give me away, but she only exposes my hip, which she rubs with a cold, wet swab before she pulls the backing off the patch and slaps it on my skin. Immediately, my belly feels warm and my legs get heavy. That sensation continues to radiate through my body, and I feel myself relax, despite my fear and uncertainty about the situation.

"There's enough anesthesia in there to keep you comfortable for the entire flight, plus a nice strong dose of a benzodiazepine to erase your memory of this. You won't notice a thing once you're under or have a clear memory of what happened here when you wake up," she says, as if that should be comforting.

She picks up a small machine from the countertop and sets it on my chest. Two clamps reach out and attach themselves to my temples as a thin black cable snakes forward and stops in front of my right nostril. "You know what this is, don't you?"

I whimper but can't shake my head.

"It's one of my finest EndoscoBots!" she says proudly. "Normally I'd attach a drill to the end so it could bore a hole through the transnasal corridor and insert a TFT web in your brain, but I have something different in mind for you!"

She withdraws a box from her pocket, then uses a set of tweezers, the kind I've seen Castor use many times on the Yoobies during a Dopa-Hack, to pluck out a small silver disk.

"Isn't it cute!" She holds it up to admire. "I stayed up all night making this pump." She attaches it to the end of the black cable, which sways in front of my face like a cobra waiting to strike.

"I've had this idea for a long time," she says. "But I couldn't figure out how to spread my little cyber critters to the MUSCies. Their security is airtight. All of them walking around with those stupid hoods." She rolls her eyes. "Until the Moonling showed up. Then I knew, if I could infect just one person with the right stuff . . . Actually, I wish it had been the Moonling," she says. "Then again, you are the perfect person for this job. Do you know why?"

I shake my head, which makes the room spin.

"Once I load you onto the Shuttle, you will be untraceable. Like all Wastelanders, you're a nobody. An undocumented person who doesn't belong anywhere. That's what I was, until I made myself into someone else. No one but your sister and your mother will ever miss you."

"Mastream!" I slur. "Flowers. No. Fallers. Ugh." My tongue feels fat in my dry mouth, and I can't get the words to come out right.

"Your stream? Your followers? Oh, please!" says D'Cart. "Streams die all the time. The people of Earth have the attention spans of gnats."

Mundie laughs.

D'Cart scowls at him, then leans down close to my ear. "I wish I could have sent dumdum over there in your place." She jerks her thumb toward Mundie. "But I already put a chip in his brain, so the virus would have shut him down, and I'm going to need him. Such a shame to waste a brilliant mind like yours. I always knew you were special, Castor. It's amazing how with no education at all, you can put things together in new ways to make something novel. That's the sign of genius. And this . . ."

She holds up the canister of goo Mundie stole from me. "What you did with this is pure brilliance!"

With the tweezers, she plucks out tiny glimmering balls of goo that she inserts into the minuscule pump, one after the other. "Who knew the way to spread my virus was under our noses all this time?" She tosses her head back and cackles. "Get it? Under our noses? But it's ironic, isn't it? Me using your stolen tricks against you to get back at MUSC?"

Next, she takes a vial and a syringe from her other pocket. "Now for the virus." She pulls the cap off the needle with her teeth and spits it on the floor, then inserts the tip into the vial. "I've had this ready to go for years."

Slowly she draws the liquid down into the syringe, then flicks it to loosen an air bubble. The needle glints in the cold white light. My heart is in my throat as she comes toward me, but my body is too leaden to move away. Instead of injecting me, she inserts the needle into the tiny pump and loads it with the liquid.

"There it goes," she says, and shakes the snaky robot arm to mix the goo and the liquid inside the disk.

"Now, with every breath you take, my itty-bitty cyber warriors will hop on the backs of the bacteria filling up your respiratory system. And when you're on board, breathing and coughing and sneezing, our little friends in here will circulate through the Shuttle's air system, get up the noses of the MUSCies, sliding right up inside their neural webs, and BOOM! I'm in business."

"Bzzniss?" I ask.

"Expansion! Colonization! A new destination for my followers," she says excitedly. "And no more ExploroBots." She takes my hand in hers. "Together, we're going to end that travesty. Now, are you ready?"

"No, please," I moan.

"First, a little spritz of local anesthetic so you won't feel a thing." She shoves a small nozzle up my nose and squeezes a mist into my airway. Immediately, the front of my face goes numb. Then the clamps on my face tighten so I can't move my head while, slowly and carefully, the snake-like cable enters my right nostril and pushes the pump deep into my sinus.

"Don't worry!" D'Cart pats my arm when I gag and sputter. "We're just installing it in the middle nasal meatus, snuggled up between the two layers of the nasal conchae. No long-term harm done to you. Once the goo runs out, the device will shut down and you'll sneeze it out or swallow it."

The cable retracts from my nostril. I feel my nose running. Something drips onto my upper lip. She wipes it away with a soft cloth.

"It's working," she says, sounding giddy.

"Now listen, Castor." She leans in close. "If you're half as smart and resourceful as I think you are, you'll probably survive. You have no implant, so the virus won't affect you, and you're hardy enough to fight off the bacterial infection. All you have to do is stay alive once you get to MUSC."

A sick feeling washes over me.

"And if you do, you can join us. You'd truly be an asset to my organization when we get there."

"Gewhere?" I ask, unable to make my numb lips form clear words.

"MUSC," she says like I'm stupid.

"Idonunnerstan," I say.

D'Cart pats my arm. "I don't expect you to. You're a pawn in a bigger battle, and I'm not who I seem to be."

I blink and try to focus, but I feel myself being pulled under, and I'm uncertain if I'm hearing her right or if the drugs are making me hallucinate now.

"But if you do make it through all this, here's a message for you to deliver." She leans down and grips my face between her cold hands so we're eye to eye. "If you see Valentina Fornax up on the Moon, tell her Zaniah Nashira is coming back and MUSC will soon be mine."

She steps away. My vision blurs. Then Mundie is close to me. "You know, Castor, with both you and the Moon Girl out of the way, I'll finally have Talitha all to myself, and when I find her—"

"No," I say. I look him straight in the eye and muster up all the reserves I have. "I'm T'ltha." Mundie blinks at me, and I try again. "'M Talitha."

"No you're not," he says, but I can hear the panic rise in his voice as he begins to suspect the truth.

I start to float away. Above my own body into the bright white light of this room. I hear myself laugh, sloppy and sad. "Mgointothemoon."

"No, no, no," says Mundie. He pats at me as if I'm a dog, starting at my shoulders, past the flattened mounds of my small breasts. My stomach clenches as he violates me with his touch.

"Quasar," I growl sloppily. "Attack." Then I remember, Quasar isn't here. Soon I'll be floating in the sky. Weightless like my father.

"This is the wrong one!" Mundie cries. "The wrong twin. It's the girl. This is Talitha."

"Doesn't matter." D'Cart snaps off her gloves and tosses them away. "All we need is a host. Boy, girl, human, Moonling, any warm body will do." She turns away. "Have the SecuriBots take her to the ExploroBot Creation Center in the Wastelands. There's an AutoTruck waiting there for her."

SWIM, MY FATHER tells me. *Move your arms and legs and swim.* The tide pulls me back, away from him, and I'm out of air. My lungs burn, and my body is too heavy to move. *Swim,* he yells again. Above me I see wavering light. Blurry blue and yellow. That way is up. I need to go. I make myself move. I claw at the water. Something below me lifts my body until my head bursts into the air and I gasp. I sputter and choke as someone or something tosses me up and out of the pool and I roll face-down on concrete, gasping like a dying fish. A person climbs up beside me and stands over me, dripping.

"Are you Uma?" a deep voice asks.

I flop to my back and squint up into the light where I see Talitha's face. I think my eyes must be playing tricks on me. I can't talk. Only cough and choke and nod.

"We have to go." The person with Talitha's face reaches down and pulls me to my feet. I'm barefoot. My pants are gone, but this person doesn't care. "SecuriBots!" he yells in an unfamiliar voice. "Run!"

My arms and legs are waterlogged and heavy. My shoulders ache, and my arms tingle from where the drones carried me. But I do my best to follow across the grass, away from the pool, away from the Palace, away from three red robots now in pursuit.

"Who. Are. You?" I manage to get out.

"I'm Castor," he says, and pushes me to go faster.

"Twin?" I gasp.

"Yes."

Behind us the red SecuriBots wobble up the hill, wheels uncertain on the uneven terrain. Castor darts away and scoops up something shiny from the ground as we run. "This yours?" he asks when he returns to my side.

I feel slapped stupid. I can't understand.

"Is this yours?" he asks again, shoving it at me.

I recognize it. My device in three pieces. Fallen from the sky. "Yes." I gasp for air.

Castor swings a red bag off his shoulders. Talitha's knapsack! He unzips it as he jogs and shoves my device inside. Ahead of us, I see the ruined remains of a smoking MUSC drone. One propeller still turns. Castor swipes that and bags it, too.

"Keep going!" he says when I slow down. He grabs the corner of my shirt and pulls me forward. We climb a hill, pass a pond, and follow the curve of a small stream to the right, toward willow trees and the security wall. The robots have spread out. Triangulated to cut us off. One goes into the stream, spraying water left and right as it speeds toward us.

My lungs burn, my legs are jelly. "Can't!" I gasp.

"Yes you can!" Castor shouts. "Talitha will be waiting for you. You have to get there."

"Where?" I beg.

He shoves me into the stream ahead of the robot and yells, "Duck!"

I dive under a low branch. Through a face full of water, I see a small grate where the stream flows out of the wall ahead of us.

I hear the SecuriBots thrashing through the branches behind us. Castor slides past me and kicks at the grate. "Help me!" he yells.

I grab a heavy stick from the bank of the stream and crawl forward to bash at the grate until it pops open. "Go! Go! Go!" Castor yells, and pushes me through the hole.

I look over my shoulder as I slide through the opening. One red robot has made it through the branches. It shoots out two tentacles, but Castor dives headfirst through the hole just as the tentacles splash into the water where he crouched a second ago.

Safely on the other side, we scramble to our feet and run out of the stream, go through more trees, and pop out onto the side of a road. The road Talitha and I ran up days ago. Castor shouts, "Jack-a-Pod!"

I double over, sure I'm going to vomit, worried I'm going to pass out.

"Come on! Come on!" Castor shouts, dancing from foot to foot as he scans the road just like Talitha did before.

Below us, at the bottom of the hill, a red SecuriBot zips out of the Palace gates and beelines for us.

"No!" Castor shouts. He reaches into his knapsack and takes out the dead drone, then wings it at the robot. He catches it in the face-plate. It falters, rears back on two wheels, then rights itself again. Castor picks up a rock from the ground and whips it at the Bot, knocking it off course. Then another. I try to help, but my arms are still floppy and my aim is bad. Just then, a blue AutoPod flies down the road. "Pod!" I yell.

"Run!" Castor shouts, and somehow I find one last burst of energy. Barefoot and shouting in pain, I follow Castor across the burning road to the AutoPod that has screeched to a stop in the middle of the road.

∞

Hours later, Castor and I idle in the jacked blue AutoPod behind the MUSC Shuttle terminal. I'm clean and dry and back in my silver MUSC long underwear that I left at Talitha's house before we went to Calliope, plus shoes from her closet and a little stuffed toy that looks like Quasar tucked on my lap. Overhead, the nearly full Moon hangs low in the wee hours of the morning while the Shuttle sits like a proud silver bird, floodlights illuminating the MUSC seal and logo on its side.

Although Castor explained Talitha's plan to me, I'm so nervous that I can't stop shaking.

Your body temperature has spiked to thirty-eight degrees Celsius, Darshan informs me. *Do you require medical attention?*

"I'm not sick," I tell him aloud.

"Huh?" says Castor, who's dozed off beside me.

"Sorry," I say. "Talking to my nanobrain cyber assistant. You're sure you hid my location when you put this thing back together?"

"Yeah," he says, and stretches. "And I hacked some other stuff for you while I was in there. Now you have a blanket override. Figured it might come in handy."

"What's that?" I ask.

"You know, for when he tells you he can't access something or doesn't have the info. It's just a lame layer of security. The truth is, he can access anything in the MUSC cybermind once you change those settings. Just ask him!"

"Wow," I say, looking with newfound respect at Darshan glimmering in my peripheral. "You can really do that?"

"Sure. It's not even that hard. These old models are super easy to break into. Actually, I can't believe they let you have one. Why don't you have an implant like everybody else at MUSC?"

"I always thought it was because we didn't have the money, but turns out—"

"Parents didn't want you compromised?" he asks.

My jaw drops. "How'd you know?"

"That's what I'd do if I had a kid," he says. "The less connected you are to the cybermind, the more freedom you have in life. You want access to the machine, but you don't want to become a part of it."

"Gad," I say. "Talitha's right. You're brilliant."

The corner of his mouth twitches, just a bit, in what I think might be a glimmer of a smile.

"You want me to change his appearance? Get rid of that goofy old-school British accent?" Castor holds out his hand.

"Sure." I laugh and hand over my device. "And while you're in there, can you make him understand the difference between physical illness and being nervous so he'll stop asking me why my heart is racing and I'm sweating?"

"You mean you want him to read your emotions?" Castor says with a snort as he rustles around in his knapsack. He takes out a palm-size black device with a screen and a few wires that he physically attaches to my device. "I can't help you there! My brain functions more like a robot." He rolls through lines of code on his screen, reworking them as he goes. "Feelings are Talitha's job."

My heart palpitates at the thought of Talitha. "You're sure she'll be on this Shuttle?" I ask, and hold my breath.

"Your guess is as good as mine," he admits.

My heart sinks. "What if—" I say.

"No *what if*s. This is Talitha's plan. We have to trust her, but . . ." He frowns and bites his bottom lip. "I wish I knew why D'Cart is sending her up there." He looks out the window at the Moon. "She said something about ending the ExploroBot program and expanding her empire, but I don't know what that means or how Talitha is a part of her plan, do you?"

"Sorry, I have no idea. But if D'Cart thinks she can take on MUSC, she must be all kinds of crazy. That place is a fortress." I shiver at the thought of Talitha being caught in the middle of some ill-fated plan. "But, Castor, I promise you, I'll keep her safe until she can get back here."

"And what about you? Will you come back to Earth, too?"

"I doubt it." I look away and hug the little toy dog to stop from shaking. "I'll probably be assigned some horrible LWA as punishment and not be allowed to leave again until my mother dies." I gaze out at the vague shapes of cactus and crooked Joshua trees dotting the mountains in the murky moonlight. "I wish I had more time here."

He hands me my device.

"What about you? What are you going to do?" I ask.

He pulls in a deep breath. "First, I'm going to figure out what that loony bird D'Cart is up to. Then I'm going to kick Mundie's ass."

"Be careful," I warn.

"Don't worry. I have backup," he says with a wink.

Out the windscreen, we see a line of blue AutoTrucks with the MUSC logo pass by on the road.

"Time for you to go," says Castor. "Will you be able to get on board?"

"That's the least of my worries," I say with a dark chuckle. "As soon as they know I'm coming, SecuriBots will swarm me like flies." I take a deep breath and steel myself for what's to come. *Darshan*, I command, *alert MUSC that I'm returning on this Shuttle.*

MUSC has been alerted. Shuttle boarding has begun, says Darshan, who now has deep red hair and a flat American accent that makes me chuckle.

"Thanks, Castor," I say. "Now whenever Darshan talks to me, I'll think of you."

"My pleasure," Castor says, then he pulls me in for a quick hug. Despite how much he looks like Talitha, his embrace is nothing like hers. "Take care of yourself."

"You too." I climb out of the car and walk on shaky legs toward the terminal entrance. I go slowly so that I can savor every last moment on the surface of the Earth. I breathe in deeply, drawing the atmosphere into my lungs. Nitrogen and oxygen and argon, true and real. In the distance, I see a small pinprick of light speeding toward the Shuttle site, buzzing like an angry insect, and wonder what it could be.

I stop for a moment to watch the life-support capsules holding the bodies of the brain-dead soldiers unloaded by WorkerBots from the back of the MUSC AutoTrucks onto a conveyor belt going into the belly of the Shuttle. Of course, I want to run to the tarmac, shouting Talitha's name as I rip open each casket until I find her. But then what? We wouldn't get very far with all the MUSC security around. The best chance I have at seeing her again is to follow her plan and get on board.

As soon as I step inside the terminal entrance, two SecuriBots clamp onto my wrists. I tighten my grip on the little toy dog as they escort me up the escalator, over the beautiful babbling stream, away from the green wall welcoming me to Earth.

At the top, we pause, waiting for the boarding doors to open. From here, through the enormous windows, I see the sun casting faint morning beams over the mountains to the east. There's just enough light to see the planet one last time. It's almost hard to look. There's so much I'm about to lose. So much I haven't done and seen. So much I'll never do.

"Good-bye," I whisper to everything I'm leaving behind. Before I look away, I see something very strange. A fat-tired, rainbow motorbike with a sidecar skids to a stop beside the tarmac in a puff of dust. A person climbs off the bike and pushes sand goggles to the top of her head to survey the area.

"Rhea?" I say aloud.

She reaches down and lifts something out of the sidecar. The sand swirling around her is too thick for me to see what it is at first, but as the sand settles, Castor runs toward her from his Pod. She sets the squirming bundle on the ground, and I see clearly.

"Quasar!" I shout, and kick the window. The dog hobbles toward Castor, back paw held delicately in the air. Castor catches him up in his arms and lifts him to his chest while Quasar smothers him in kisses.

The door ahead of me begins to hiss. "No, wait!" I yell, but there's no waiting any longer. My return to MUSC has been set in motion. The SecuriBots pull me away.

"Stop!" I struggle to get another look before I'm dragged inside. Are Rhea and Quasar the backup Castor was talking about? Are they here to rescue Talitha?

"What about me?" I yell at no one. "Don't make me go alone!"

One of the bots backs off, as the other one yanks me through the boarding door, which shuts and locks behind us. I turn and kick at the door, terrified that I've been tricked. Was this the plan all along? To lure me onto the Shuttle with a false story of being reunited with Talitha? Was it his idea or hers?

The other MUSCies stare at me as the SecuriBot drags me wailing to my seat. I must look bizarre to them, real tears shedding from my face, unprotected by a hood. They grimace at me, but I don't care.

From the back of the Shuttle, a man stands up. "Uma?" he calls. I glare at him, then see it's Burnell Chen-Ning.

"Guess you found me," I sneer at him as the bot pushes me into the first seat, then locks my harness into place. Luckily, there's no one across the aisle from me, so I can cry as miserably as I want without anyone looking at me. The bot parks itself in in the bulkhead area in front of me and trains a red visual sensor on my chest to make sure I don't try to make a break. I squirm in my seat to get a look out the window and see whether Castor and his mother have found Talitha, but the AutoTrucks and the cargo loading bay are too far under the belly for me to see from where I sit. Now there is nothing that I can do. No way to escape. No way to know if Talitha is going with me to the Moon. I clutch the little stuffed dog and cry like a small child as the Shuttle engines rev.

TIME STAMP

Summer Solstice

Moon

Day 3, Month of Sol, MUSC year 94

Earth

June 21, 2xxx

UMA JEMISON

MUSC SHUTTLE TO
THE MOON

I WATCH OUT the window of the Shuttle as we taxi beneath the full Moon on the horizon. Some Earthlings call this a supermoon, and tonight I understand why as I watch it full and foreboding on this summer solstice night. I feel its power over me. Calling me back. I doze fitfully through the takeoff and exit from Earth's atmosphere. Through hours of climbing into the weightlessness of space, I dream of searching for something I can't find. I look through every exhibit at a hologram zoo. I hunt through hundreds of petri dishes lined on shelves. I flip through an endless Stream of channels. I go through tunnels and climb mountains and dig through piles of trash, but I can't find the thing I seek. Finally, I wake up, bladder screaming, body stiff and sore. Now that we're nearly home, the SecuriBot's red light is out and my harness is unlocked.

I unbuckle and use the handles on the ceiling to navigate through the aisle toward the lavs in the back. Since I'm calm, none of the MUSCies on board seem to notice me. Most of them are asleep or lost in their work Streams anyway, including Burnell Chen-Ning, who's zoned out in his seat.

In the lav, I relieve myself in a VacuuTube and wash up, then I float out to the snack area, where I stare at a display of drink pouches and packs of freeze-dried food. I know I must be hungry, but I'm too sad to eat. I sigh and start to turn away, then I notice a thin mesh curtain affixed from floor to ceiling between the lav and the snack bar. Affixed to the wall is a small sign that says CARGO HOLD. I reach out and press my hand against the sign, wondering if Talitha could be down there in the belly of the ship after all. What if Castor and Rhea couldn't find her? What if she didn't want to go with them? My heart speeds up. If she's here, I don't have to wait until we land to find her, but I do have to get inside the hold.

I look behind me to make sure no one's watching, then I push the curtain aside. In front of me is the outline of a closed door etched in the back wall of the cabin. I search for a handle or a button to let me inside. I just want to see her. To know if she's here or if I'm truly alone.

Darshan, I command, *open the cargo hold door.*

The cargo hold door can only be accessed in an emergency, Darshan tells me.

This is an emergency, I argue, and wonder if Castor lied about installing a blanket override.

No emergency status has been received from the automated flight crew.

Override, I command, then hold my breath and wait.

After a few seconds, red-haired Darshan says, *The cargo hold door is locked.*

Override lock? I say, uncertain Darshan will be able to do what I ask. But, to my surprise, he projects a hologram keypad on the wall and flashes a series of numbers on my Lenz. I enter the code on the keypad slowly and carefully, then wait, my stomach churning. After a few seconds, the door *wheesh*es open.

Quickly, I pull myself through and propel past stacks of clear storage bins bolted to the walls and stocked with extra food and beverage pouches, travel suits in various sizes, lavatory supplies, and first aid kits. I pass giant floor-to-ceiling containers of sanctioned Earth goods—mostly vacuum-packed, decontaminated fruits and veggies and nuts, bags of irradiated soil, blocks of salt, and a few small luxuries like plant-fiber clothing and bags of coffee.

At the bottom, lining the belly of the Shuttle, I find the Exploro-Bots.

Ten of them hang in life-support jelly bags anchored to the floor by thick black straps. They sway like animal carcasses in a meat locker. Except the ExploroBots aren't dead. And not exactly alive either. They're somewhere in between, which is exactly how MUSC wants them. The vague outline of a human form is visible through each opaque bag, but the gel inside that keeps the bodies in a state of suspended animation is too thick for me make out facial features, and I'm glad. As much as I want to find Talitha, I don't want to look into the eyes of these undead humans. It's bad enough that I can hear their labored breathing through the ventilation filters attached to their mouths. One coughs, and the bag jiggles, which sends a sickening shiver through my body.

My father or mother or I could have ended up here, had we not made it off the Earth in time. Talitha's father was here, and now she may be, too. I shake my head at the stupidity of it all.

If the people before us had taken care of the Earth . . . If they had listened to the scientists calling for action for decades as glaciers the size of large cities sloughed off into the oceans . . . If they had used their resources more wisely . . . If they had stopped consuming so much and caring only about being entertained . . . If they hadn't elected egomaniacs to office who promised the impossible and delivered only benefits for the wealthiest few . . . If, if, and only if. When confronted face-to-face with all this senseless death, I understand why the first humans left the Earth. Because there are no different versions of the world. Where we are is all there is. All other doors have been slammed shut. Once science died and reason was replaced by gut feeling and alternative facts, what was left to do but start fresh someplace else?

I draw in a ragged breath, terrified both of finding Talitha in this state or not finding her at all as I push through the bags, reading the names, serial numbers, and a list of injuries on each one:

ALSOP, 12ksdl393, chest wound, lower left
    extremity amputee
BINLARBY, 45345lkq545, right eye missing, hip
    fracture, no liver function
CZENSKI, 900945isda, partial spinal cord
    severance
GREIG, 57854clik, double amputee to knee
KAOUTHAI, 48482, total spinal cord severance at
    C12
MYEONG, 55098, shrapnel to heart, collapsed
    lung, left arm amputee
PATEL, 45459, renal failure, occipital brain damage
SANCHEZ, 11218, burns to 80% of body surface
TEVALATHIAN, 493406zpyd, internal injuries
VYHOVSKY, 46064, blunt force trauma to skull

I go through twice, listening to the dissonant inhale and exhale of the bodies, the rattle of coughs, but I don't find one labeled Neva. My heart plunges as the reality of the situation sinks into my brain. My stomach ties in knots. My skin prickles with shame as I allow myself to fully comprehend. It was all a ruse. Talitha is gone. I was tricked by her or her brother or both, but what did I expect? Their lives were spent in parody. They are brilliant thieves and masterful liars.

I will return to MUSC, shamefaced and in trouble, my LWA placement in the toilet. And for what? An impulse? A desire? Some feeling that I thought was love? Ha! Kepler and Castor are right. Human emotions are stupid and only get in the way.

And yet I can't stop feelings from burbling up inside of me—sadness and betrayal and anger spill out of me like lava spewing from a volcano. I curl into a ball and wail with my fist pushed into my mouth. I let myself cry for like this several minutes. I don't care if anyone in the Shuttle hears me. I don't care what they think of the foolish Earthling that I am because whatever they think of me is probably true. I am an idiot! An easy mark. How could I ever think a girl as beautiful and conniving as Talitha would love someone as plain and stupid as me?

"Talitha," I moan. "Talitha, oh, Talitha!" until I can't cry anymore, then I float silently away from the ExploroBot bodies. In the silence, I hear a sound. A cry, really. "Uuuuuuu" echoes through the belly of the Shuttle.

Afraid I've woken the dead (or half dead) with my cries, I swim away.

"Mmmmmmm," it says. "Aaaaaa."

I should leave these people in peace. They don't need to deal with my pain on top of their own. But then I hear it again.

"Uuuuuuu. Mmmmmmm. Aaaaaa." And a cough. "Uuuuuuu. Mmmmmmm. Aaaaaa."

My heart jumps into my throat. I brace myself against a wall and listen more carefully.

"Uuummmmaaa."

"Talitha?" I say. "Talitha, is that you?" I push through the bags again, pressing my ear against the ventilation disk of each body until I come to the one marked Tevalathian one more time. I grab it by the shoulders.

"Talitha!" I yell. "Talitha Neva! Is that you?"

The body inside coughs and moans. I grapple to open it. My hands shake violently as I release the flap, and the top opens like a flower blooming. Then, slowly from the bag, a body rises as if from the dead. It is wrapped in a gauzy shroud and covered with thick, opaque gunk. I try to catch it, but it slips through my arms.

I strip off my shirt and chase the floating body through the air, wiping the goo from the face until I see my Talitha!

"It's you. It's really you!" I cry. "I thought I'd never see you again!"

For a few seconds, her eyes flutter open but don't focus. The bright green of her irises has soured to yellow. Her beautiful hair is gone. Her warm brown skin is now ashy gray, and her perfect lips cracked and flaking white. I hold her against my body. She is racked with a violent cough. I press my lips to her forehead, which is clammy and too warm.

I swim through the cargo hold, dragging Talitha's body with me as I make my way back up to the storage bins. I find hand washing cloths in the stash of supplies for the lav. I use six of them to clean her up. As I remove the gauze from her skin, I find a small patch attached to her hip.

Darshan, what is this? I blink on the label.

Oxymorphone and benzodiazepene, he says. *An anesthesia and amnesiac patch that will last approximately eighteen hours.*

With one hand, I press her body against the bins while I pry the patch loose, but it's firmly in place. I keep picking at the edges, pulling to release it, and in the process, I rip off a bit of skin. Blood seeps out and pools on her hip.

"I'm sorry! So sorry!" I cry as I tear open a first aid kit from the supplies. Small scissors, bandages, wipes, tape, and painkillers float past me. I stanch the bleeding and cover it with an antiseptic bandage. Then I search the rest of her body but find nothing else attached.

"It's going to be okay. We're together now. Everything is going to be okay," I say over and over like a mantra, willing myself not to panic.

The Shuttle will dock in thirty minutes, Darshan informs me.

"Holy Mercury!" I say aloud. I can't dock with a half-naked, unconscious Earth girl in the cargo hold. I rummage in the bins for extra flight suits. I put one on, then work up a sweat trying to shimmy the other over Talitha's floating limbs. She is limp and heavy in her drugged state, but after several minutes, I manage to zip her inside a suit.

"Hey, hey," I whisper, and hold her cheeks in my hands so we are eye to eye. "Look at me. It's Uma. I'm here."

Talitha moans. Her eyes open and dart around. I search her pupils for some flash of recognition. She tries to swallow, but her throat is dry. I grab a drink bag from a storage bin and puncture the side with a straw, then slip the other end between her slack lips. I gently squeeze the bag until the liquid rises to her mouth.

"Come on, come on." Once a drop hits her tongue, she purses her lips and drinks. A good sign.

"Okay," I say, relieved. I repeat this action over and over until she turns her head away. She faces me, working her lips, trying to say something.

"What?" I ask. "What do you need?"

Her voice rasps like metal against stone. I can't make out the words.

"What is it?" I ask again, and lean so close that her lips brush my ear. "Are you hungry? Cold? Too hot? Uncomfortable? In pain?"

She strains and coughs, until finally I hear the whisper of one word. "So . . . So . . ." she tries and tries again.

"So . . . what? What can I do for you?" I scramble to understand and anticipate her needs.

She shakes her head and tries one more time. "Sorry," she says. "I'm. So. Sorry."

I hold her close to me. "No," I whisper as I stroke her head. "You don't have to be sorry. We're both here. We're together. Everything is going to be okay."

Please return to your seat, Darshan says from my Lenz. *The Shuttle will dock in twenty minutes.*

I need to get Talitha to a safe place for the docking, so I pull us both through the cargo hold door and into the cabin where we can harness in. This time, my movements are not ignored by the other passengers.

Immediately, Burnell Chen-Ning spots me. "Hey," he says when I pass him. "What are you doing? Who's that? Where are you going?"

I ignore him and keep moving forward. Heads turn, eyes peer up at me, MUSCies shrink in their seats as I drag Talitha's levitating body behind me.

"Is that an Earthling?" Mr. Chen-Ning follows us.

I don't respond. Don't stop or turn around. I keep moving past their murmurs and protests to the two empty seats in the front of the Shuttle. I maneuver Talitha's body down into one of the seats and buckle her in. Then I push myself into the other seat and put on my harness. Out the window, I see the Moon looming larger as we near the MUSC docking site.

Talitha's color is better. Her breathing is smoother, but her nose runs and she continues to cough.

Mr. Chen-Ning floats up the aisle between us. "Did you sneak on with this, er, um . . ." He struggles to find the word.

"Human being?" I say.

"Look . . . Uma . . ." He tries to appear reasonable. "I'm glad you came to your senses and decided to return, and I understand that interesting things happen on Earth during Sol, believe me. But you can't just bring a random Earthling back to MUSC with you. This person is not a souvenir. There are protocols. Rules to be followed. Documentation needed. Bottom line: There's not room for everyone on MUSC."

"Oh, really?" I snap at him. "And how did you earn your place on the Moon?"

"I was born there," he says. "I'm a Second Gen."

"In other words, your grandparents were tough enough to make the trip before you were ever born. And then your parents were lucky enough to be born there, and you were lucky enough to be born there, and Gemini was lucky enough to be born there."

"My family worked hard. We earned our LWAs—"

"Yeah, well, just because you were born on the Moon doesn't make you better than Earthlings!" I bark at him. He backs away, wide-eyed and cowed by my audacity. Obviously, he's unnerved by how unhinged I've become, but I don't care. I'm sick of living under the shadow of Second and Third Gen MUSCies who believe they earned every advantage they were handed.

"Uck," he says, and swallows hard. "I feel sick."

"You should," I say. "Sick of yourself. You personally did nothing to earn your place high above the Earth."

He goes pale, and his eyes grow heavy as if he can't take being yelled at by someone like me.

"Yeah, well . . ." he says, his breathing more labored, "I'm 'lerting the 'thorities there's a sto'way on board," he slurs over his shoulder as he floats toward his seat.

"Go right ahead," I call after him. "And while you're at it, tell them Uma Jemison isn't taking any crap anymore!"

Halfway through the cabin, he slumps in midair and hovers. The woman below him gasps. "What's happening?"

"Did he pass out?" someone else asks.

Suddenly, my anger with Mr. Chen-Ning fades and is replaced by concern. "Is he okay?" I call.

"What did you do to him?" an angry woman seated behind Talitha snaps.

"I didn't do anything. He followed me up here and was yelling and then he got all sleepy and weird," I say.

Another guy unbuckles and rises up to help him. "Burnell? Can you hear me?"

Then the woman behind Talitha swoons. She grabs the armrests of her seat and lays her head back. Her eyes grow heavy, and she begins to slur as well. "I don't feelsogood . . ." Her eyes flutter, then they close.

I undo my harness and rise up to the ceiling again. Now Burnell and the other man float unconscious near the ceiling, and the others on board have grown bleary-eyed and thick-tongued.

"What's happening?" I ask. "Are you all okay? Darshan, help!"

How can I be of assistance? Darshan asks.

"I don't know what's happening," I tell him as I float through the cabin, watching as one by one, each person on board seems to power down into a deep sleep. "Everyone is losing consciousness! Help! Help me!"

Please remain seated, is the only advice dumb Darshan has.

I struggle to get Burnell and the other unconscious man buckled into their seats so they will be safe when we land. Then I work my way to the front where Talitha sits. When I get there, she gazes up at me, fully awake now.

"Uma!" she exclaims, and reaches for me.

I dive down on her. She hugs me tight. My legs float straight up in the air. We smother one another with kisses like two puppies.

"I was so worried about you!" I tell her.

"Me too!" she says. "When those drones carried you off—"

"Castor saved me!" I tell her.

"What?"

"But then I thought that he came and got you. I didn't think you were on the Shuttle, and when I finally found you, you looked half dead."

"I think I was," she says, and rubs her head. "I'm all cloudy, and my body's sore." She sneezes and wipes her nose. Behind us, throughout the cabin, people cough and sniff. I look down at Talitha, who still seems weak and vulnerable. Are people catching what she's got? If so, how long do I have before I go down? I don't want to worry her, so I don't mention the Shuttle full of unconscious MUSCies. Instead I focus on her.

"What happened in the Palace?" I ask, and harness myself in across the aisle from her. "Did D'Cart do this to you?"

She blinks and shakes her head as if thinking hard, but then she shrugs and says, "I don't remember." She sniffles and wipes the arm of her flight suit under her running nose. "I think she was there. Or was it Mundie? Or Zaniah Nashira?"

"You are delirious!" I say. "Zaniah Nashira is dead. Remember? Aurelia told us she died in the Great Tsunami."

"Right," Talitha says, looking sad at the thought of everyone she left behind.

"Hey, look what I have!" I hand her the little stuffed dog.

"Quasar!" She hugs it tight to her chest.

"Look." I point out the window at the docking arm unfolding from the spinning MUSC station. "We're almost there."

Please remain in your seat with your harness fastened, Darshan says. *The Shuttle will begin docking shortly.*

"Wow," she says quietly, and reaches for my hand. "I never thought I'd really be here." She looks at me. "What happens now?"

Before I can answer, the SecuriBot wakes up. Its red eyes light up, and it scans me. Then it twists its head and scans Talitha. "Intruder!" it announces, and a loud buzzer goes off. "Intruder. Intruder."

CASTOR NEVA

WILDLANDS OF 'FITH, EARTH

"CASTOR NEVA?"

I open one eye and squint into a bright light. Aurelia stands over me. The spotlight from her left eye beams into two old restaurant booths pushed together where I lie curled in a ball with Quasar tucked against my side. Just like old times, only now I'm about a foot taller.

"Hey, Aurelia." I stretch my legs one at a time, then without disturbing Quasar, I climb out of the cramped space. I stand there for a moment, taking in what was once the Café at the End of the Universe in the basement of the Observatory and later, the place where Talitha and I made our home for our first year in AlphaZonia. "I haven't seen you in a while," I say.

"We last encountered one another three hundred and fifty-seven days ago," she tells me.

"Really?" I ask. "Has it been that long?"

"Yes," she says.

"Sorry." I cringe, but Aurelia only looks at me and blinks. Then I remember she doesn't care—357 days is a number to her, like any other. "This is why I like you, Aurelia. You know the exact number of days it's been since we've seen each other, but you don't assign emotional value to that number like a human would."

I look around the room for my mom, who collects emotional injustices like seashells, but the booth where she slept is empty. I check the message blinking on my iEye.

Gone foraging for breakfast, Mom says from Talitha's old device. *Be back soon.*

Aurelia scans the rest of the room with her light. "Is Talitha with you?"

"No . . ." I stop because my voice catches. Mom and I tried to find her last night. Tried to intercept the caskets unloaded from the truck onto the Shuttle, but a line of SecuriBots, lights and sirens blazing, chased us off the tarmac. We barely made it to my AutoPod without being apprehended. Then we watched, silently, from a distance while robot arms lifted the anonymous ExploroBots into the belly of the Shuttle.

"Where did she go?" Aurelia asks.

I walk over to the windows at the side of the café. Most of them are boarded up, but a few still have glass. I stare up at the pale blue sky, wondering where my sister is now. "She's on her way to the Moon," I finally say.

"That is unexpected information. Did she travel alone?"

"No," I tell her. "At least she's with her friend Uma—"

"Uma Jemison," Aurelia says. "I met her. She was very sad to hear of Zaniah Nashira's death. Please tell her I was incorrect."

"Um, yeah, okay, but I don't think I'll be seeing her anytime soon." I turn away from the windows to face Aurelia again. "If my calculations are correct, they should arrive at MUSC soon. Tonight, when the sun goes down, my mother and I would like a viewing—"

"I am sorry," says Aurelia. "The telescopes will not be available for viewing any longer."

"Why not?"

"I have been called upon by Zaniah Nashira to launch the *Res Extensa* rocket."

I put my hands on my hips as I puzzle through what she's saying. "Are you okay? You're not making much sense. Do you want me to check your circuitry?"

Aurelia blinks her blue-lit eyes. "I have run a self-diagnostic test. Everything is in working order."

"Okay, but, there's no rocket here. You know that, right? Just telescopes and an old planetarium."

"Incorrect."

"Oh, really?" I laugh. "Since when do you have a rocket?"

"That is a difficult question to answer. Do you mean at what date did I begin assembling the *Res Extensa* or at what date was it completed?"

"How about both."

"*Res Extensa* assembly commenced approximately ten years ago. I completed my task twenty-six days ago. Launch will occur in two hours, fourteen minutes, and nine seconds."

"Okay," I say slowly, wondering if she's been hacked or has a virus or just some loose wiring inside her CPU. "And where is this rocket now?"

"I am unauthorized to tell you."

"Override," I say.

"Your override privileges have been revoked," she informs me.

I step toward her. "Who's been messing with your circuitry?"

"I have," says a voice from the shadows.

I spin around and see a person backlit in the doorway.

"Who's that?" I ask, shading my eyes to get a better look.

The person steps forward into Aurelia's bright spotlight, and I gasp. "D'Cart?" She's in a pink flight suit with silver stitching and boots up to her knees. "Intruder!" I tell Aurelia.

"Zaniah Nashira is not an intruder," says Aurelia pleasantly.

"Who the hell is Zaniah Nashira?" I yell.

"That was my name before I became RayNay DeShoppingCart," D'Cart says as she waltzes toward me. "I built Aurelia many years ago when I returned to Earth from the Moon." She shudders. "Such a horrible place."

I have so many questions at that moment, but the first one I blurt out is, "Then why'd you send my sister there?"

Quasar limps to the end of the booth and stands on the bench, at my hip. A low growl comes from his throat as D'Cart positions herself next to Aurelia a few feet from us.

"Aha! Listen to that! We did have the wrong twin. Mundie! You were right."

Mundie steps through the doorway and walks calmly to her side. I jump, afraid he'll run at me and tear me apart, but he stays still, barely blinking and unfazed by seeing me.

"I should have noticed it was Talitha right away," says D'Cart. "I've practically watched you two grow up. You'd think I could tell you apart. Even with the same bad haircut."

"What's that supposed to mean?" I lift Quasar from the booth bench and inch closer to the windows—our only chance at escape.

"I was here, you know." D'Cart motions all around. "I'd come visit, checking on Aurelia's progress every few days. When you and Talitha arrived, I didn't have the heart to kick you out like I did all the other Wastelanders who've tried to camp out here over the years. You were both so scrappy! Reminded me of me. Then I found your parody Stream, and oh!" She laughs softly. "Well, it was just so funny. Like I told you before, there's no flattery like imitation. Honestly, I felt protective of you and Talitha, which is why I programmed Aurelia to take care of you. I know it sounds silly, but I wanted to see you thrive. Well . . ." She pauses and rethinks this. "Until you stole from me." Her face hardens. "I really did not like that."

"Yeah, so I noticed," I say, and take another step toward the boarded-up windows separating the interior of the Observatory from the Wildlands of 'Fith.

"Actually, now that I think about it," says D'Cart slowly, "you and Talitha trading places is better. I'd like to take you with me, Castor."

"Where?" I ask. A chill settles over me. I don't like the direction this is going.

D'Cart cocks her head and looks at me funny, as if I've missed something obvious and important. "To MUSC. Mundie and Aurelia are coming, too. Plus, Talitha will be there. Well, if the virus hasn't killed her—"

"Virus? What virus?"

D'Cart waves my concern away. "She should be fine. I concocted a little cyber critter to get inside the MUSCies' heads and mess with the wiring of their neural webs. As soon as I get up there, I'll take over their minds, like I did his." She jerks her thumb toward Mundie, who doesn't flinch.

"Mundie?" I say. "What's going on? What's she talking about?"

"He can't really process your language right now," says D'Cart. "He'll only listen to me."

"How'd you do it?" I inch closer and closer to the bottom right window. If I can keep her talking about herself, I might have a chance to make a run for it.

"Ah," says D'Cart, eyebrows up. "Now you're asking interesting questions! Did you know that when I lived on MUSC, I designed the brain-to-brain interface technology that made the MUSC ExploroBot program viable? Valentine Fornax was my mentor, and she took all the credit for my innovations. I never intended for my technology to be used that way. I wanted to help people! I wanted a way for soldiers, like my parents and your father, to have use of their bodies again. But Fornax didn't listen to me.

"She saw a different use for the technology. A way to further MUSC's mission, which is her only concern. She rose up the ranks of MUSC all the way to the top, riding on that high horse, and cast me down, back to Earth, when I objected to them using my BBI to turn humans into cyborgs to do the dirty work at MUSC. And when I return, they'll get what they deserve. The MUSCies will serve us. People like you and me, Castor, we will have our own place to flourish when I take over the survival colony."

I don't wait around to learn more. Instead, I bolt left, shoving through the bottom, boarded-up windowpane I jimmied loose years ago. It was our trapdoor, the way in and out of this burrow where we thought we were hidden. Turns out, we were being watched the entire time.

"Stop him," D'Cart tells Mundie.

I'm slow with Quasar in my arms and struggle to get through the hole now that I'm bigger. Out of the corner of my eye, I see Mundie lurch toward us. Quasar growls viciously and launches himself from my arms.

"Quasar, no!" I shout, half in and half out of the window.

He lands on Mundie, knocking him into the ground, and latches onto his arm, teeth sunk into skin. Mundie yelps and flaps, but Quasar won't let go. His nails skitter across the floor as Mundie tries to get free, but Quasar is unsteady on his hurt leg. One more fierce shake from Mundie flings

Quasar backward, toppling over and howling. I scramble into the room and run for Mundie while Quasar cowers in a corner, whining in pain. Aurelia rushes to him.

"Goddamn you, Mundie!" I roar. "I will kill you." I jump on top of him and pummel him. I hear the impact of my fists on his face, but I don't feel anything in my rage. "This is for every time you followed us and every time you creeped my sister out and every time you . . ."

"Aurelia, subdue Castor," D'Cart commands.

She leaves Quasar and zips up behind me.

"No, Aurelia, don't!" I yell, but her strong hands attach to my shoulders, and she lifts me off of Mundie as if I were a bug being plucked from a branch. She pins my arms to my sides and wheels backward, away from Mundie, who lies on the floor moaning.

"Damn it, Aurelia, let me go! What are you doing?" I kick and squirm, but I'm no match for her quiet strength.

"Now, now, boys . . ." D'Cart tsks at us as Mundie picks himself up. His upper arm is mangled, and blood seeps from one nostril over a fat blue lip, but he doesn't seem to notice. "I can't have you two fighting all the way to the Moon."

"I'm not going to the Moon with you!" I growl.

"Yes, you are, Castor Neva," D'Cart says. "And it'll be the best thing that's ever happened to you. Believe me! Mundie. Aurelia. Let's go. The *Res Extensa* waits."

Without a word, Aurelia lifts me so my feet can't touch the ground and wheels off behind Mundie, who follows D'Cart out of the café.

"Quasar!" I call out. "Aurelia, come on." I wrench my head around so I can see into her blue-lit eyes. "We can't leave him here!"

Aurelia glances at Quasar, who limps toward us, tongue hanging out, ears and tail drooping.

"Always keep Quasar safe," I beg her.

She blinks, as if calculating through a set of algorithms to see which one will override the other. Then she spins, wheels toward the dog, and scoops him up in one arm while holding me tight with the other. She carries us both, side by side, out of the café through the darkness of old space exhibits. Talitha and I used to run beneath the hanging planets here and jump, trying to touch Saturn's rings. We pass by old chunks of meteorites and defunct displays explaining a universe to people who would never get off this planet. Aurelia turns and bumps down the Wormhole Stairway, one of our favorite places to play. At the bottom, in the small cylindrical room beneath a sculpted ceiling, standing waves of sound amplify every movement. I hear the whirl of Aurelia's internal gears. The wheeze of Quasar's painful pants. The fabric of my pants swishing against my skin.

"Aurelia," I whisper. My voice bounces and echoes back. "Please stop. Don't do this. Let us go."

"Zaniah Nashira has asked me to take you to the *Res Extensa*," she says.

"And Quasar?" I ask, bewildered.

"No," she says. "My orders to keep Quasar safe come from you."

The floor drops and I cling to Aurelia as the small cylindrical room descends, like an elevator, through a shaft in the interior of the hillside. When we stop, the wall in front of us slides open and light spills in. I see D'Cart strapped into a reclining seat bolted to the base of the small, round cockpit and tilted back, with a cradle for her helmeted head. Mundie is strapped into an identical seat to the left and behind her. With one arm, Aurelia drops me in a rear seat across from Mundie and harnesses me down, then plunks a helmet on my head, too. She gently lays Quasar in the chair between us and finds a way to strap him in. He licks her hand and whimpers.

D'Cart jerks her head toward us. "The dog, Aurelia?" I hear her say through the speaker in my helmet. "Really? You brought the dog?"

"Yes," says Aurelia. "My instructions are to keep Quasar safe."

"Your instructions?" D'Cart says. She scowls at me, but I keep my mouth shut.

"Well . . ." D'Cart sighs as Aurelia wheels forward and locks herself into place next to D'Cart's seat. D'Cart commands a screen to lower from the ceiling. "It's too late to take him back now. I guess we'll have the first pet in space!" She chuckles to herself, but no one else reacts.

I watch their reflection in a large window that takes up most of the front of the cockpit. Six circular windows evenly spaced around the perimeter of the capsule look out into the darkness of this underground silo.

I look to Mundie, but he stares straight ahead with that same dead look in his eyes. The blood has crusted beneath his nose, and his lip is so swollen that I doubt he'll be able to talk. The wound on his arm from Quasar is still raw and leaking. I have the urge to punch him, but I can't reach.

"Isn't it amazing?" D'Cart says as she runs through diagnostics on the screen. "All these years, Aurelia was down below the surface, building this rocket to the Moon. I uploaded the plans into her CPU years ago, and she patiently, methodically carried them out. Piece by piece. Moment by moment, while the world revolved around her. And no one knew. Not even you, Castor Neva." She wrenches her head around to look at me again. "Your ticket off this planet was right under your feet, and you didn't even know it!"

"I don't want to go with you," I bark at her.

"Listen," she says. "You should be honored that I chose you."

"I'm not," I insist.

"MUSC will be a refuge, you'll see!" she says. "They have the best facilities. We'll do research. Come up with great new products and—"

"What about all the people who already live there?" I ask.

"Most of them will have to go, but we'll keep a few around to serve us. They will be the ExploroBots of our station, and it serves them right, too. Together we can—"

"There's no together. I'm not helping you!"

"Castor Neva!" she says. "I'd think you of all people would see that what I'm doing is for the good of people like you! When everything really goes to hell on Earth, when the resources are truly gone and the fighting worsens or a massive pandemic breaks, I'll have created a safe haven on the Moon. Coming there will be the ultimate reward for my most loyal and elite followers. You should be grateful that I invited you first."

"You don't give a shit about the ExploroBots, do you?" I say. "It's all about better vacations for your followers. You're going to turn the one place in the universe with any scientific purpose into a resort for the most vapid people—"

"You petulant, ungrateful teen! I don't have to listen to this! I'm turning off your mic." She clicks me off.

"You're the worst of humanity!" I yell, but she doesn't hear me.

Deep below us, I hear the muffled rumble of engines boosting. I feel their power vibrate through my body. Suddenly, the capsule lurches upward. I reach for Quasar. I'm close enough to bury my fingers in his fur when he looks at me with worried eyes.

"Hold on to your seats, because here we go!" says D'Cart, as giddy as a kid on a roller coaster ride.

"Look! Look!" She switches one of the screens in front of her to her own Stream. "I launched drones so we could watch the event live with all my followers!"

The screen shows the Observatory glowing white against layers of pink and gray clouds streaked across the early morning pale blue sky. The drone sweeps around behind this fortress sprouting like a black-capped white mushroom from the side of the hill, then it lifts up and retreats to show a wide shot of the front of the building. The three domes glimmer in the rising sun. The smaller two on either side dwarfed by the giant one in the center. How many nights did I spend up there, peering through the Zeiss with Aurelia by my side, waiting patiently for me to get tired of looking up at the Moon, searching for my dad? How many times did I dream that I could build a rocket to rescue him? And now here I am, strapped on board as lonely and helpless as he once was.

The drone hovers over the top of the central dome. A small, dark circle opens in the middle of the roof, which spirals open like a lotus flower blooming, folding back on itself as the shingles retract into the sides of the building while up through the center the tip of the rocket noses out like a sprout emerging from the ground.

"There we are!" says D'Cart. "Wave to the camera! All of my followers the world over are witnessing this historic moment!"

I turn to look out the circular window nearest me as we slowly emerge. I see the fallen obelisk and the parched grass in front of the Observatory. Then I see someone run out from a trail in the Wildlands of 'Fith.

The drone captures the image of the person, too. "Who's that?" D'Cart says. "Zoom in!"

On-screen, we see a bird's-eye view as the drone swoops down toward the ground. The person skids to a stop, throwing an armload of plants in the air and ducking.

"Mom!" I yell, but my voice goes nowhere. I try to blink onto my iEye so I can reach her, but there's no reception. No doubt, it's been blocked by this behemoth that I'm strapped inside. "Mom!" I shout again. I lean over as far as the harness will allow and bang against the window as I yell.

"She can't hear you," D'Cart clicks into my helmet and says as if annoyed. "You know that, right?"

"Stop this! Stop!" I demand, but D'Cart has muted me again.

Then the countdown begins. "Ten . . ."

A long, slender scaffold lifts the rocket higher and higher in the air.

"Nine . . ."

From the window, my mother appears punier on the ground.

"Eight . . ."

Does she know that I'm on board? She claims to have a cosmic connection to Talitha and me. She says it's just how mothers are. They know when their children are in trouble.

"Seven . . ."

On-screen, I watch her drop to her knees, her face twists with anguish, and she beats her fists into the ground.

"Six . . ."

My mother knows. She understands that she's going to lose yet another person she loves to the Moon. Why couldn't I save my father? Why couldn't I save Talitha? Why can't I save myself?

"Five . . ."

The rockets rev and rumble. I feel their power deep in my cells.

"Four . . ."

My mother jumps to her feet and runs for the woods as the doors and windows of the Observatory are blown off.

"Three . . ."

Smoke and debris billow out in gray and white clouds that obscure the fallen obelisk, the trees, and the hills surrounding the Observatory.

"Two . . . one, liftoff."

Inertia presses me hard against the seat as we launch into the sky, trailing a bright fire tail—a daytime shooting star. On-screen, I watch the beautiful old Griffith Observatory crumble to the ground as the Wildlands of 'Fith erupt in flames, and we disappear behind the blanket of sunlight hiding the rest of the solar system from the world's view.

TALITHA NEVA

MOON UTILITARIAN
SURVIVAL COLONY

THREE ARMED GUARDS rush through the Shuttle door the moment we lock in place on the MUSC loading bay. They have the same small-nosed, big-eyed look of all Moonlings and are dressed in the regulation blue and silver tunics, but unlike the other Moonlings I've seen, these people are armed with PEP guns raised to their shoulders.

"Intruder. Intruder," the SecuriBot continues to announce, flashing a red light beam onto our foreheads.

I reach across the aisle for Uma's hand and yell, "Don't shoot!"

The guards stop, in formation. One in the lead, two in the rear. The woman in the front points her weapon at me, then at Uma, then back at me. "It's just a couple of Earth girls. Stand down," she says. The SecuriBot powers off, and the other two guards lower their guns.

Uma opens her mouth to say something at the same moment I sneeze so loud I'm afraid the guards will shoot us. Instead they back away.

"Medevac," the lead one commands. All three unfurl hoods from their tunics, roll them over their heads, and attach them to the necklines of their shirts. The lead guard looks beyond us to the other passengers.

"What's wrong with everyone?" she asks through her communication vent. I can hear the panic rising in her voice as she lifts her gun to her shoulder again. "Are they dead?"

"No!" says Uma, hands still in the air. "Everyone lost consciousness, but—"

"What?" I ask, and try to wrench around to see what's behind us.

"Bring backup," the lead guard barks, and the other two quickly exit the Shuttle. "Get up." She motions to us with her gun. "I'm taking you to quarantine. You can make your statement there."

We unlock our harnesses and stand, clinging to each other. I don't know if it's the lingering effects of the anesthesia or if I'm just scared, but I can barely walk.

"My legs are so wobbly," I whisper.

"It's the induced gravity of rotation," says Uma, propping me up, but I notice that she is shaking, too.

The guard steps to the side, gun trained on us as we pass, but then she stumbles. "Oh, my!" She braces herself with an outstretched arm against the Shuttle wall. "I'm'a'li'l . . ." she slurs, then her knees buckle and she starts to fall. "Dizzy . . ."

Uma darts forward to catch her before she hits the floor, then gently lays the slumping body in the aisle, making sure to keep the gun pointed away from us.

"Should we take it?" I bump the gun with my toe, but I don't wait for Uma's answer. The guttersnipe in me already knows what to do. I grab it and sling it across my shoulder.

"No!" says Uma. "People will think we're guilty of something if we have a weapon. We should just explain—"

"Explain what? Why we're the only two people awake on a Shuttle from Earth. Can you explain that? Because I can't."

"Well, no, but—"

"They'll shoot first and ask for explanations later. If we want a chance to talk, we might have to buy ourselves a little time. With this." I pat the gunstock.

"Do you even know how to use it?" Uma asks, her eyes wide.

"No," I admit, looking it over. It's nothing like the old-fashioned bullet gun my father taught us to shoot in the Wastelands when we were small. My mother threw it out when we moved to Calliope. *Violence breeds violence,* she always said. "But I'll figure it out if I need to."

Uma grabs my hand. "Let's just go before more guards show up."

I look at the small stuffed dog on my Shuttle seat, but I don't go back for it because I understand things just got serious.

I cough and sneeze and wipe my nose as we step into the space beyond the Shuttle. Windows line one wall where bright lights zoom by in the dark sky. A huge blue-and-white blur passes overhead.

"Is that . . ." I reach out and press my hand against a window as I stare into space.

"Earth," says Uma. "But don't look too long. It'll make you sick."

"No," I say, still gazing out, waiting for the Earth to pass by again. "It's beautiful!"

"Come on," she insists. "We have to go."

Slowly, carefully, we creep into a brightly lit corridor, where we find the body of another guard passed out on the floor.

"Uh-oh," says Uma.

"There's the other one!" I point to the body of the third guard being carried away on an automated sidewalk in the center of the hall.

A siren wails, and flashing lights bounce toward us as a squat red armored truck zooms around the corner and screeches to a stop. Uma and I retreat, arms up in the air, hands linked, the gun between my back and the wall.

"I'm a MUSC citizen!" Uma cries when four guards spill out of the truck with PEP guns pointed at us.

"Identify!" the guy in front yells.

"Uma Jemison G0C54D1235!"

He blinks on her and says, "Checks out." Then he turns to me. "Identify!"

"I . . . I . . . I . . . *Choooo!*" I sneeze. We're close enough that the droplets from my nose and mouth spray across on his face.

"Uck!" He wipes himself clean with his sleeve.

"Sorry!" I say. "I was put on the Shuttle against my will. I don't want trouble."

He reaches for his hood, calling, "Medevac!" but before he can get it over his head, he wavers and swoons backward, crashing into the guards behind him. The other three look on, confused, then one by one, they fall in a heap on the ground around him.

"What the—" I yell. "Is that because of me?" I ask, but my voice is lost beneath the blare of another siren.

"We have to get out of here." Uma yanks me away. We hop over a low wall onto a moving sidewalk, then hop the next wall onto the walkway going in the opposite direction. One more hop, and we're across the hall from the loading bays. Uma ducks into a narrow alcove, saying, "Darshan, open HabiTrail."

I follow and see a square of gray tile in the center of the floor retract to reveal a trapdoor.

"How did you—"

"Get in!"

"What is this?"

"Just go," she says, looking over her shoulder as the siren wails louder and the lights flash brighter in the hall beyond us.

I scurry down the ladder, the gun bouncing across my back, with Uma stepping on my fingers as she hurries after me.

"Four guards down!" someone yells.

"Close hatch!" Uma commands. I hear it lock in place above us.

We drop into a dimly lit hall and run. My legs feel better, less wobbly, but I don't make it very far before I'm doubled over, coughing and wheezing. "Wait. Stop," I pant, and drop to all fours. The gun lies on the floor beside me.

"It's okay." Uma stands over me, rubbing circles on my back. "We're safe for now. No one will think to look for us in here." She glances up. We hear footsteps overhead. Boots on the ground. Heavy thumps. I imagine more bodies falling. "At least for a while."

"Where are we?" I scan the blank white tube that goes on in two directions.

"The HabiTrails," she says. "They run all around the outside of the station, but no one ever uses them. Except me."

Up ahead I make out the shadow of an intersection where another tube branches left and right.

I peer up at her and say, "I'm scared."

"I know! Those guards . . . and the guns and—"

"It's not that!" I slowly straighten up. "I don't know what's wrong with me. I've never been this sick. Even when the Peruvian llama flu pandemic hit and millions of people died, Castor and I didn't get it. Do you think I'm the reason everyone is passing out?"

Uma thinks this over, eyebrows flexed, the side of her cheek between her teeth. "Could be. Or it could be me. Could be some bacteria carried up on the Shuttle. Could be a virus that mutated here first . . ."

A cloudy memory swims in my mind. A thin black snake about to strike. A woman holding my face too tight. *Tell them I'm on my way.* But I don't know who she was or what she wanted. I shake the dreamlike image from my mind and ask, "What if it is me? What if I give you this sickness and then you pass out like everybody else, and . . ." I can't say more because the thought of being alone on the Moon, away from Earth without Castor and Aurelia and Quasar and my mother, is too frightening to comprehend.

"If I haven't gotten it by now," says Uma, "I'm probably immune."

I calm down a little bit. "But what are we going to do? We can't stay in this tube forever. Eventually they're going to look in here."

"I know someone who will help us." Uma motions me forward. "Kepler's mom, Curie. She's one of the best immunologists on MUSC. She has her own lab. If anyone can figure out what's going on, she can."

"But will she protect us?" I grab the gun off the floor.

Uma bites her cheek again, then says, "I hope so."

◯◯

Since Curie didn't answer Uma's pings, there's only one thing left to do. I follow her through the unmarked maze of the HabiTrail. Like a Moon gopher tunneling underground, Uma knows her way without hesitation. She leads us to another ladder, then slowly pokes her head out of the hole above. I hold my breath, hoping nobody's up there with a shotgun, waiting for us to pop out. Uma looks down and whispers, "It's okay," then waves for me to climb up after her.

We emerge into a different alcove off a different hall, although it all looks the same to me. We peek around the corner into a corridor, this one lined with closed-door labs and curtained windows instead of loading bays. I expected MUSC to be a horrible, cold, sterile space—a cross between a surgeon's office and a prison, but it's not. It's beautiful and quiet here. The colors are muted and warm. Gray floors, white walls specked with blue and silver shimmering under soft lights. And there is a hush that I've heard only in nature. No chattering Yoobies, no constant product Streams, no nattering holos competing for attention. The only sound is me, wheezing and sniffling as we pad cautiously down the hall.

"Where is everyone?" I whisper as we pass doors marked EARTH MATERIALS PREPARATION LAB, COLD STORAGE, GEOLOGICAL SAMPLING, STATISTICAL BIOINFORMETRICS, PATHOGEN CENTER.

"Working," says Uma, as if the eerie silence is nothing unusual.

She pauses in front of a door labeled ADVANCED IMMUNOLOGY and requests permission to enter. When the door doesn't budge, she says, "Darshan, override security," and it immediately *shlush*es open.

"Whoa," I say. "How did you—"

"Castor," Uma says.

An ache fills my chest when I hear my brother's name. "If he were here . . ." My voice catches in my throat. This is the first time my brother and I have been more than a hundred miles apart in our lives, and I feel like something in me is missing. Like I'm an ExploroBot without a leg and Castor has half my mind, only he's down on Earth and I'm up here, our connection interrupted, and I don't know what to do without him except to follow Uma.

Inside the lab, a tall woman sits bent like a question mark over a microscope, with both hands on the table in front of her. Her soft brown hair spills forward like a curtain, hiding her profile.

"Curie?" Uma calls softly. "Curie, it's Uma. I need help." The woman doesn't budge.

I press my sleeve over my nose to keep from sneezing so I don't startle her.

Uma looks at me with trepidation, then inches closer, calling more loudly, "Curie? Curie? Can you hear me?" She doesn't answer, so Uma touches her shoulder and the woman tumbles to the side.

We jump and scream as the body topples, smacking the edge of the counter as it falls to the ground. We stand over her, staring at a thin trickle of blood flowing from a gash on her forehead.

"MediBot! MediBot!" Uma shouts.

A small yellow canister wheels out from under a counter. Uma points it toward Curie and commands, "Check vitals. Stop bleeding. Make sure she's okay! My gad, what's wrong with everyone?"

We stand back, arms wrapped around each other as the MediBot gets to work. Two tentacles shoot out. One scans her body, reading vital signs. "Temperature normal. Blood pressure normal. O_2 levels normal," it announces as the other arm locates the bleeding, then sprouts additional, smaller appendages to close and bandage the wound.

As I watch, I have another foggy memory, this time of a bot clamped on my chest, pushing something up my nose. Like a DopaHack but not. *Ironic*, someone said. *Using your stolen tricks against you?* I shake the image away, not sure if it was a dream or real.

"Bleeding stopped," the MediBot announces.

"We need help. We have to find someone!" Uma's voice escalates with alarm. "Darshan, ping my mother!"

She waits, staring at her Lenz for several seconds, then she stamps her foot. "She's not answering. She must be in the mines. Unless . . ." I see her shiver. Goose bumps crawl over her skin.

"What is it?" I hug her tighter.

"What if everyone on the surface is unconscious, too? What if we're the only ones and—"

Behind Uma, a holo screen shimmers. "Look!" I point. She whips around. "Hello!" She runs toward the holo, shouting, "Who's there? Hello!"

"Mom?"

Uma stops. "Kepler?"

A tall, lanky guy with big brown eyes and wavy blond hair laced with red shimmers in the center of the floor.

"Uma?" he says, and reaches out. "Oh, my gad! Is that really you? What are you doing back on MUSC? Why are you in my mom's lab?"

Uma runs to him as if she's going to throw her arms around him, but of course, he's not really there. "Something horrible is happening!"

"What? What happened? Did you get caught?" He grimaces.

"Everybody is . . . they're all . . ." She stops and tries to find a way to explain, but the words won't come.

I step forward and say, "Everyone is unconscious."

UMA JEMISON

MOON UTILITARIAN
SURVIVAL COLONY

TALITHA AND I move Curie to a small couch in the corner of the lab, where we prop up her head on a pillow and cover her with a silver blanket from the emergency supply cabinet. Then Talitha curls up in a spinning chair beside Curie's desk while I pace around the lab for ten minutes, explaining the whole story to Kepler, who's down at a TourEsa casino on the surface with Gemini and a bunch of other kids from Cohort 54.

"Wow, Oom, I thought my Sol was bad," he says, arms crossed, eyes darting back and forth as he considers everything I've told him. "But I only ran out of money playing the VirtuSlots, and you—"

"I know!" I drag a lab stool next to Talitha and perch on the edge of it with my feet tucked into the rung to hold me steady. "Although you've got to admit, it's not exactly a surprise that my Sol trip would be a disaster!"

"Hey!" Talitha sniffs. "What about me?"

"Except for meeting you, of course!" I reach out and take her hand.

"Of course," she says, and keeps her eyes locked on mine with the smallest glimmer of a smile that makes my stomach flutter.

"Whoa, wait a sec," says Kep. "Are you two . . ."

I glance at him and blush. Talitha brings my knuckles to her lips and brushes them with a kiss.

"You are?"

I nod.

"You get the award for best Sol trip souvenir ever," Kepler says. He and Talitha crack up.

"You guys! Come on," I whisper, and cut my eyes toward Curie. "We shouldn't be laughing. This is serious."

"Sorry," Talitha croaks as her laughter turns to coughing. "It's just the stress." She ducks her head to catch her breath, but I see her glance at Kepler, who gives her a half grin and a thumbs-up.

"I knew you two would like each other," I say, secretly pleased. "But we have to do something. Your mom is unconscious! I can't find mine! Every time Talitha sneezes, people pass out! The whole station might be compromised."

"First, you should swab her." Kepler points at Talitha. "Seems like she might be the carrier."

"Yeah, we thought the same thing." I rummage through Curie's cabinets. Since I have no idea what the pathogen might be, I take one of everything: cotton swabs, centrifuge tubes, several kinds of reagent solutions, and three different kinds of prepared agar dishes.

"But then what?" I ask. "It'll take hours to prep and culture the samples, then I'll have to prepare them for the microscope or put them in the sequencer to look for a DNA match, which will take more time."

"You have to tell Fornax," Kep says.

"No way!" I almost drop the supplies I'm carrying. "She'll kill me as soon as she sees me."

"She's not there," he says. "She went down on a Shuttle yesterday to Zhongguo to buy the rights to the last rare Earth mineral mine. It was all over the MUSC Stream."

"Problem solved!" I say sarcastically as I set up a dozen ten-milliliter tubes in a rack plus six sets of sterile agar dishes and a handful of long cotton swabs on the countertop. I grab the back of Talitha's chair and wheel her over. "This won't hurt, okay?" I put on my gloves, then as gently as I can, I insert the gauzy end of a sterile swab into each of Talitha's nostrils.

"Ouch!" She flinches. "My nose is so sore!"

"Probably all the sneezing and wiping." I remove the swabs, cut off the ends, and drop them into the tubes of sterile solution, carefully voice labeling each one as I go. I swab her nose again just in case whatever's in her prefers a different growth medium. I zigzag the new swabs over the different types of agar pads, add a reactant dye, and close and voice label the dishes.

"You could go to Fornax's work space," Kep suggests as I repeat the entire process on myself in case I'm the carrier. "Do an All-Call page to find out who else is awake up there."

"I don't know how to do that!" I whine as I load the tubes into a centrifuge to separate out DNA. I pop the agar dishes inside a low beam radio frequency oven to speed their cultivation time.

"Micra would know," Kep says.

"Micra? Are you kidding me?" I march back and forth, ranting, "You know she hates my guts. I can't—"

"She's with Fornax. Remember?" Kepler says. "She's the CEO's personal lapdog for the month."

"Yeah, but . . ." I stop and cross my arms. "Micra won't accept thotz from me."

"But she will from me," Kep says. "You and Talitha get to Fornax's work space. I'll contact Micra and tell her to find you there."

"But . . . but . . ." I throw my arms out to the side. "It's bad enough being picked up by drones, nearly drowned, and chased by armed guards while watching people pass out in front of me—now I have to talk to Micra!" My heart is in my throat.

"She can't be that bad," Talitha says.

"You don't know Micra," both Kep and I say together. Then we look at each other and snort.

"No laughing allowed," Talitha teases.

"Yeah, well, it's definitely not funny," I say, hands on my hips.

"But it's going to be okay." Talitha stands up and puts her arm around me. "I'll be there. Right beside you." She sneezes, then sniffs loudly and wipes her arm beneath her red, dripping nose.

"You poor thing!" I pull her into a hug. Even though she's pale and bleary-eyed, being next to Talitha calms me. I feel grounded when I hold her, like we're back in Calliope underneath the stars. "And you're right. If we're together, we can do anything."

"Blech!" says Kepler.

"What's wrong with you?" I ask.

"Too much emotion," he says.

"You got a problem with that?" Talitha teases.

"Nope, obviously you two are perfect for each other," Kep says with a wink.

Holding hands, Talitha and I take the MediBot and walk the main corridors between the labs and Dr. Fornax's work space.

"Hello! Hello!" I call out. "Can anybody hear me?" But no one answers. Every time we see a body slumped on the ground, doubled over a work space, or slouched on a bench, or find a heap of people collapsed outside a Travelator capsule bank, we stop and check their vitals. And each time, it's the same. Heartbeat strong, breathing fine, temperature normal, but no one is awake. We send the MediBot on without us to check for other injured people.

I use Darshan's override to get inside Fornax's work space, where I'm greeted by the same white couch and orange zinnia on the edge of the familiar desk. The place makes my stomach churn.

"I've never been in this office for a happy reason," I whisper to Talitha.

"Maybe you can reach your mom from here," she suggests.

"Good idea!" I squeeze her hand and walk around the desk then command Darshan to reveal Fornax's work screen. To my surprise, it materializes.

"Dang," says Talitha. "Is there anything we can't do up here?"

"Wake everybody up," I say as I search for the CEO's direct connection to my mother down in helium mines. "Darshan, ping Persis Sarachik, chief of DrillBot repair." Darshan pings and pings the portable holo screen mounted to my mother's DrillBot repair station beneath the ground down below. I hold my breath, waiting for her to answer. Afraid that she won't. But then I see her! The image from below the surface is grainy, but her voice is clear.

"This is Commander Jemison," she says while working on a downed DrillBot.

"Mom?" I squeak.

"Uma!" she shouts, and drops her tools. "Uma, is that you?" She abandons the DrillBot and leans close to her screen. "It is really you?"

"Hi, Mommy," I say, fighting back tears of relief. "I've been trying to reach you—"

"Oh, thank gad!" She presses one hand over her heart. "Ever since your communication cut out yesterday, I've been worried sick and—"

"I'm back at MUSC!"

She whoops and hollers and tosses her arms up in the air. "Then I'm coming home right now!"

"No!" I say. "You probably shouldn't. There's a—"

"Oh, no." She grabs the controls of her portable repair station and turns it around to head back up to the surface. "They can dock my pay or demote me, but nothing's stopping me from seeing you."

"Mom, wait!" I yell. But she disappears from my screen. "What happened?" Frantically, I tell Darshan to ping her again, but nothing will go through, then a holo of Micra takes over the screen.

"For gad's sake, Uma, what in the name of Mars . . ." she snarls.

"Who's that?" Talitha asks, rearing back.

"That's Micra," I mutter.

"How could you cause this much trouble?" Micra snaps.

"I didn't CAUSE anything!" I yell at her.

"You're mired so deep, you'll be lucky if you're that food service lady's assistant for your LWA!" Micra says.

"Hey!" I shout, and charge at her with my finger pointing. "Don't you bad-mouth Randazza Marmesh!"

"Stop it! Come on," Talitha says, holding me back from punching through Micra's holo. "We need to work together."

"Who's that?" Micra asks, nose in the air.

"My name is Talitha. I'm Uma's . . ." She stops and sniffles loudly, trying to hold in yet another sneeze.

"Girlfriend!" I say, with my shoulders back and my chin up.

Micra blinks back her surprise, then she huffs, "Only you, Uma, would bring an Earthling back from your Sol trip."

"Only she would be so lucky," Talitha says as she takes my hand.

To my surprise, for the first time ever, Micra has no comeback. She seems so much less threatening without Cassio and Alma at her side, or maybe she's not as scary because I have Talitha by mine. Whatever it is, at that moment I realize I don't have to fear Micra. She has no special power. She's just another Moon girl, like me.

"I need you to get Dr. Fornax," I command.

"Oh, gad." Micra cringes. "She is NOT going to like this."

⦿⦿

As with most things, Micra's completely right. Once I explain the situation to Dr. Fornax, she goes ballistic. Her holo, projected life-size in the center of the room, stomps around, calling me irresponsible, disloyal, and a disgrace, as if I've somehow caused all the problems on MUSC. With each condemnation, I shrink, wishing I would be sucked into a wormhole and spaghettized, until Talitha steps up and shouts, "Hey!"

Dr. Fornax's holo stops. She crosses her arms and looks Talitha up and down, then demands, "Who the hell are you, talking to me like that?"

"Who the hell am I?" says Talitha. "Who the hell are you, talking to Uma that way?"

"I'm the MUSC CEO," Fornax barks.

"And you're damn lucky we're here, or by the time you return, every single person in this survival colony will probably be dead! We're the only two up here who are awake. No matter who we are, you're going to have to work with us if you want to solve the problem, so you better be nice."

Talitha says all of this, then she doubles over, racked by a coughing fit. I rush to her side and help her to the white sofa.

Dr. Fornax huffs, but she stops haranguing me. "First, you need to get this Earthling into quarantine." She jabs a finger toward Talitha, who's wheezing and exhausted. "I'll put out an All Call on my Stream,

asking anyone conscious to identifty themselves. Next, we need to figure out what pathogen is taking everybody down."

"Hmph," Micra sniffs. "Funny how Uma always said a microbe
would be the thing that would bring the station down. You sure you didn't
plant it, Uma?"

My mouth drops open, and I can't speak.

"Stop it!" Dr. Fornax snaps at Micra. "Uma wouldn't do a thing
like that, and you know it."

Micra shrinks back and pouts with her arms crossed and a scowl
on her face.

"I already swabbed Talitha and myself," I say, my face still burning
from Micra's accusation. "I'm isolating the DNA in Curie's lab and also
growing cultures just in case we need more. Once I have the pathogens,
I'll run the code through our database to see what it could be, but the
results won't be ready for hours."

"Good work," Dr. Fornax says, and I feel myself blush at her compliment more than I wish I would. "Listen, Uma, although I still have
control of the station, everything I can do from here will be on a time
delay, so in case we need to move quickly, I'm giving you full security
clearance."

Talitha and I glance at each other. I don't mention that I already
have it through Castor's blanket override.

"And also—" Fornax says, but Darshan flashes a message on my
Lenz.

Call from Kepler.

Not now, I answer, and try to stay focused on the list of things
Dr. Fornax is telling me to do.

Answer! Kep thotz to me. *Urgent! Project!*

Fine! I thotz back, then I command, "Project Kepler," out loud. His holo beams out from my Lenz to the center of the floor across from Micra and Dr. Fornax.

"There's something happening on Earth that you should see," Kepler says. "Turn on RayNay DeShoppingCart's Stream."

"What in the—" Dr. Fornax starts to say, but Kepler interrupts her. "Now! Look!" he insists.

I command the screen behind her desk to blink on. We all wait, breath held, until I access D'Cart's Stream. Then we see the pointed nose of a white rocket thrust up from a spiraling dome.

"The Observatory!" Talitha cries.

Up and up the rocket rises, like a strange metallic flower, as the thunder of engines fills the air. The building shakes, cracks run down the white walls, fire erupts from the exploding doors and windows, sending a blast that scorches the dry grass and engulfs the trees as the rocket launches into the bright blue sky.

"No!" Talitha screams, and runs toward the holo as if she could stop it.

"And in this historic moment," D'Cart's voice narrates the scene as the rocket arcs away in a cloud of destruction. "The first RayNay DeShoppingCart spaceship, *Res Extensa*, leaves the Earth's atmosphere!"

"This has been playing on a loop all day," Kepler tells us. "At first I thought it was a joke, but, now, I don't know . . ."

Then D'Cart shows up on her Stream. She's fresh faced and smiling from the cockpit of the rocket. "Hey, you guys!" she squees. "I'm heading to the Moon, just like I told you I would someday, and I can't wait for you to join me—"

"Zaniah Nashira!" Dr. Fornax growls.

"Zaniah Nashira?" I yell. "I thought she was dead."

"Zaniah Nashira!" says Talitha, smacking her own forehead. "That's who it was."

"Who the hell is Zaniah Nashira?" Micra shouts.

Everyone talks at once—Kepler, Micra, Talitha, and me, trying to piece together what each of us knows into one coherent picture, until Fornax's voice, louder than all of us combined, shouts, "Initiate contact with *Res Extensa*."

D'Cart's Stream fades, and the screen behind the desk glimmers. We all stop chattering and stand in a silent circle as we wait. Dr. Fornax and Micra huddle together by the wall, Talitha and I stand by the couch, Kepler is across the room, and then in a pop of light, RayNay DeShoppingCart (or is it Zaniah Nashira?) appears.

"Who is this?" she demands. "Who's contacting me?"

The screen shot is a close-up of her face, so it's impossible to tell where she is. Is she really in a spaceship heading toward us, or could she be down on Earth playing some enormous prank?

"This is Valentine Fornax. CEO of the Moon Util—"

"Oh, it's you." D'Cart rolls her eyes. "I wondered how long it would take—"

I step forward. "Are you really Zaniah Nashira?"

"Yes," she says. "You're that Moonling girl."

"All these years . . ." I study her, confused. "I wondered where you were, what your life became after you left MUSC, if we were anything alike. And there you were, right in front of me the whole time, selling foot spas and germ wands on your silly Stream?" I shake my head, disappointed. "I really expected . . . more."

"Oh, I've done plenty!" D'Cart says with a scowl.

"You destroyed the Observatory!" Talitha shouts.

"Talitha?" D'Cart startles when she sees her. "You made it!"

Talitha fights back tears. "You killed Aurelia!"

"Oh, no," says D'Cart. "I wouldn't do that. I'm not a monster. Aurelia is fine. She's with me. Say hello to Talitha!"

The screen shot switches, and we see Aurelia's blinking blue-eyed faceplate. "Hello, Talitha," Aurelia says.

Talitha's knees buckle with relief. She balances herself against the arm of the sofa. "But how—"

"And look who else is here!" The screen switches again.

"Mundie!" Talitha gasps. He stares at us with dead eyes and dried blood crusted on his beat-up face.

"And I may have a few other surprises for you, but those can wait until I get there!" D'Cart says with a sickening smile.

"I've locked into the *Res Extensa*'s flight trajectory," Dr. Fornax announces. "Be warned, Zaniah, if you enter MUSC airspace, your ship will be obliterated."

"Oh, will it?" D'Cart snorts. "And how are you going to do that? MUSC has no real defenses, and we both know it. Especially with you, their *fearless leader*, down on Earth running after a fake mineral deal I set up."

Dr. Fornax flinches.

"And if my calculations are correct," D'Cart continues, "every MUSCie up there is in la-la land by now."

"You did this?" Fornax roars.

"Duh," says D'Cart. "I expected Talitha might be awake, but Uma Jemison? That's very interesting." She looks at me with a kind of sustained curiosity that makes my skin crawl, but then she shakes her head and shrugs. "Doesn't matter, though. It's not like one Moon girl can hold me off."

"Wanna bet?" Talitha says. She stands up and swings the PEP gun around her body to point it straight at D'Cart's holo.

"Talitha, no!" I whisper.

But D'Cart only laughs. "Really? One PEP gun? I'm so scared."

"You should be scared!" Dr. Fornax says. "You know the power of MUSC. You know what we are capable of. When I kicked you out the first time—"

"You didn't kick me out! I left!"

"No, I let you go!"

"Only after you took credit for the brain-to-brain interface technology I invented!"

"That BBI tech was developed under my tutelage, in my lab!" Fornax sneers. "I had every right—"

"And then you used it in the most hideous way—to make Exploro-Bots! It was meant to help the people of Earth!"

"It does help the people of Earth!" Fornax yells. "It gives soldiers and their families a second chance. The Wastelanders who fight your stupid Earth wars are expendable resources to you. Just another piece of trash to throw on the heap."

Talitha, Micra, Kepler, and I look back and forth from Fornax to D'Cart as they shout at each other.

"Without us, how else will the human species continue?" Dr. Fornax asks. "Once you idiots ruin everything on this hellhole of a planet, those of us on MUSC will keep the human race going. On the Moon. On Mars. And beyond. Without us—"

"Without you, everyone will be better off!" D'Cart shouts back. "When I take over MUSC—and make no mistake, I'm taking it over—I'll bring up my followers and do away with the horrors of the ExploroBot program, and your people, the ones who perpetrated these crimes against humanity, will be my technoslaves!"

"Oh, my gad." I turn to Talitha. We inch closer to Kepler's holo. "They're like children arguing over toys."

"Yeah, it's like they forget the rest of us are real people," Talitha says.

"Someone should tell them we're not chess pieces in their stupid game," Kepler adds.

I glance over at Micra. Even she rolls her eyes as Fornax and D'Cart continue their squabble over who will have universal dominion over extraplanetary colonization.

"I can't decide which one's worse," I admit.

"Dr. Fornax with her half-dead humans," says Talitha.

"Or D'Cart with her revenge fantasy and legions of yammering consumer-tech-enabled followers," Kepler adds.

The two of them keep arguing, getting louder and louder, until we're all startled by the door to Dr. Fornax's office *wheesh*ing open.

"Hello?" someone calls. "Is anybody there?"

MY HEART BUOYS in my chest when I hear Talitha's voice through my headset. When I catch a glimpse of her on the split screen in front of D'Cart, I can hardly breathe. She looks terrible. Ashy skin, cracked lips, red-rimmed eyes, and raw skin beneath her nose. D'Cart's virus has ravaged her, but at least she's still alive. I try to maneuver myself into D'Cart's tight-framed shot so Talitha can see me and know that I'm okay, too, but D'Cart's PEST buzzes just beyond her nose, so nothing behind her is visible to her viewers. I try yelling, but my voice only reverberates inside my helmet. Literally nobody can hear me scream.

So I'm stuck. Sitting helplessly watching and listening as two megalomaniacs argue over the fate of humanity. And what's new? Haven't the little people—the poor, the displaced, and the powerless—always been strapped in for the ride while the powerful jockey for control? My mother says there was a time when people stood up to authority and fought for what was right. They called themselves the Resistance. But I don't believe her. My mother makes stuff up.

"I should have never let you on MUSC in the first place," Fornax tells D'Cart. "Now we test for social attachment before we take scholarship kids so we don't end up with sociopaths like you!"

"You're the sociopath, controlling everybody's lives," D'Cart shoots back. "Dictating what they wear, when they eat, what they can watch and listen to, and deciding everybody's job for the rest of their lives!"

"So we can stay on task and get things done!" cries Fornax. "Not like you Earthlings with your constant distractions and endless consumption."

"Our desire for more is what makes us human!"

"More what?" Fornax bellows. "Earthlings have produced nothing of value in nearly a century."

"Value? You want to talk about value! I own an entire city and have millions of followers all over the world who worship me and my products!"

I tune them out and stare at the receding Earth. When I was a kid, I spent hours scavenging for equipment to build myself a rocket so Talitha and I could escape. I designed systems. Analyzed trajectories. Built prototypes and dreamed of bigger things. I scoured the MUSC Dump for something I could use as fuel.

When I met Aurelia, I imagined she would be with me and Talitha when we finally made it off the Earth. But not like this. Never like this. Listening to D'Cart and Fornax bicker is enough to make me want to deep-space myself so that I can join my father and the other discarded ExploroBots who litter the universe on their endless ride to nowhere.

"I don't have to listen to this!" D'Cart snarls once she's had enough of Dr. Fornax's vitriol. "You're done, Fornax. And soon MUSC will be mine." She cuts the connection. The screen in front of her goes blank and, with it, my only link to my sister.

"Can you believe that woman?" D'Cart fumes, as petulant as a child. "She's a thief and a liar and an egomaniac and—"

"Takes one to know one," I mutter.

"What did you say?" She clicks on my mic.

Slowly and carefully, I repeat, "Takes. One. To. Know. One."

D'Cart whips around in her seat so she can look me in the eye. "Your attitude better change if you want me to save your sister when we get to MUSC, young man. I can easily obliterate her along with everybody else up there."

"Not if she obliterates you first!" I shoot back.

"Yeah, with what?" D'Cart sniffs. "Her one puny pulsed energy projectile gun?" she says in a stupid, baby voice. "MUSCies are a bunch of pacifist wimps who thought Earthlings were too stupid to ever reach them. PEP guns don't kill, they just disable for a time. They're basically useless."

"It'll knock you on your ass," I say.

"Actually," she says with a smirk, "I have reflective tech woven into my space suit. Clever, huh? Whatever they sling at me will ricochet right back. I'm rubber, they're glue, bounces off me and sticks on you know who!" She cracks herself up.

My heart sinks. I know she's right. No matter how smart and capable Uma and Talitha are, they're no match for D'Cart. She's been planning her revenge for years and has every detail covered. And I'm no use either. Harnessed into this seat, surrounded by mutant-zombie Mundie on one side and Aurelia, who will only listen to the madwoman driving this ship, on the other, I have no way of stopping her. But I refuse to give D'Cart the satisfaction of knowing that, so I say, "Never underestimate the ingenuity of a Wastelander."

She holds my gaze for a moment, then without a word, she turns away.

"Aurelia," she says, "how long until we dock on MUSC?"

"Three hours, thirty-two minutes, and twenty-nine seconds," Aurelia answers.

"There's no way they can mount a defense in that time," D'Cart assures herself. "They can't stop me from docking, and once I'm on board, that station is mine."

TALITHA NEVA

MOON UTILITARIAN
SURVIVAL COLONY

"RANDAZZA!" UMA CRIES, and runs for an elderly Earth woman who stands in Dr. Fornax's office doorway. The woman catches Uma in a strong hug.

"Thank gad, it's you, starshine!" She kisses the top of Uma's head. "I thought I was the only grown person alive in this place. What in the name of Jupiter is going on?"

"Is anyone else awake?" Uma asks.

"Just the babies in the nurseries and the under fives," the Earthling says. "I've checked on all of them. The NanniBots are doing fine, but their human caretakers are all passed out cold like everybody else."

I sneeze loudly, breaking the quiet.

"Good gad, child, you're sick as a dog." Randazza steps toward me.

"Don't!" I cry, and jump away.

"We think she's infected with something," Uma says.

"Nonsense! You've just got a little Earth cold." Randazza presses her cool palm against my forehead. Her touch calms me for a moment. "You're burning up. All you need is a nice cup of tea and some rest."

Both Uma and I wait for Randazza to topple over, but nothing happens. She stays upright, blinking at us like we're crazy.

"Whatever's taking everybody down must be airborne," Uma says.

"Not possible," says Dr. Fornax. "We have the finest air filtration system ever built. Pathogens can't—"

"And it only affects people with an implant," I say. Everyone turns to stare at me.

"You're right," says Uma, as if something's dawning on her for the first time. "The only people who haven't been affected are me and now Randazza."

"Or the babies and the young ones," Randazza adds.

"Can't be," says Dr. Fornax, almost to herself. "What Earth pathogen could infiltrate our air system or cross the blood-brain barrier to disrupt the implants? You've only been up there for a few hours. Nothing moves that fast!"

"We'll know what it is for sure when the sequencing is done," says Uma.

"You don't have that long to wait," Dr. Fornax says. "The *Res Extensa* will dock in less than three hours. You need to secure the station. Now."

"Don't you have some kind of shield or automated blasters to protect you from invasion?" I ask.

"This isn't an old sci-fi movie!" Dr. Fornax says. "Up until ten minutes ago, we thought nobody from Earth could get to us. There hasn't been a rocket built down there in over a hundred years!"

"Could you use the ExploroBots?" Micra asks. "Line them up around the perimeter of the station as protection?"

"And what?" I ask, horrified. "Let the *Res Extensa* plow into them?"

"Yeah," says Micra like I'm stupid. "It'll slow her down and maybe deflect her from the docking arm to save everybody else on board the station."

"No!" Uma jumps up, hands out. "We can't put ExploroBots in harm's way."

"Now you sound just like that nut job Zaniah Nashira!" Dr. Fornax says. "Yammering on about the humanity of the ExploroBots. You know she's the one who—"

"I never liked the ExploroBot project!" Uma shouts. "The way you use those people is wrong."

"They're not people any longer," Dr. Fornax insists.

"Yes they are!" Uma and I both say at the same time.

Dr. Fornax draws in a deep breath as if she's trying to stay calm, then she says, "I'm not going to argue the finer points of utilitarian philosophy and ethical design with you. Right now, we have to stay focused on the problem at hand. I'm not convinced that using the ExploroBots would work."

Micra flinches as Fornax shoots down her idea.

"As I see it," Fornax continues, "the only way to keep Zaniah Nashira off MUSC is by stopping the *Res Extensa* from docking, and the only way to do that is to override the system and manually control the robotic landing arm. Which is exactly what you're going to do, Uma."

"Oh, no. I can't do that." Uma backs away.

"Gemini could do it," Kepler says. "He's the best one in our cohort at remote control."

"That's true," says Micra.

"But he's at TourEsa with you, isn't he?" Dr. Fornax asks.

Kepler nods, and Fornax shakes her head.

"By the time he takes a Moon rover back to the MUSC elevator on the surface, the *Res Extensa* will have docked."

"Could you patch him in from the surface to control the robotic landing arm?" Micra suggests.

"It's worth a try," says Dr. Fornax. "The loading arm is going to be tricky to override, though. We purposely designed it so that even if everyone on board is compromised, one of our ships can land. Just to be safe, I'm docking all ExploroBots out of the way and initiating station lockdown now."

"Lockdown?" Uma asks. "But my mom is on her way up from the surface."

"She'll have to wait," says Dr. Fornax. "Nobody comes or goes until the *Res Extensa* is safely out of our orbit. And that's an order I expect you to follow, Uma."

⊙⊙

While Kepler goes off to find Gemini and Randazza checks on the children, Uma takes me to her domicile to rest. I'm so exhausted that I can barely walk, and I'm wheezing worse than a Yoobie pug on a smoggy day.

Her place is tiny—just a common area with a few seats surrounding a constant family photo stream, a kitchen as stark and utilitarian as a lab, her mom's room with its bare-bones bed and dresser, and Uma's personal space, which is a little shrine to Earth.

"So this is where you grew up?" I take the PEP gun off my shoulder and lay it on her desk as I watch images of plants and animals rotate across her wall under a blue-sky ceiling with images of clouds. "Was that your dog?" I point to the pix of a pointy-eared brown pup.

"Yes, that's Mahati." Uma melts a bit. "Wasn't he adorable? You can see why I was so excited to meet Quasar."

"Oh, Quasar!" I slump down on the floor, too exhausted to climb up into her sleeping berth. "Do you think my pup is okay?" Now I wish I'd grabbed the little toy dog to hug.

"Yes," says Uma. She runs her hand over my clammy forehead and bristly hair. "Your mom is taking great care of him in Calliope. Castor's probably with them by now, too."

"I miss my family so much it hurts," I say, but I'm too tired to cry.

Uma grabs two pillows and a blanket off her bed and covers me up on the floor.

"Is that your mom?" I point to a pix of a woman scanning across her wall. She is tall and broad shouldered, with Uma's wide smile.

"Yes, her name is Persis," says Uma with a sad smile.

"She's pretty. Like you," I say as my head sinks into the pillow. "I'm sorry Fornax locked her out."

Tears quiver on the rims of Uma's eyes.

"Why don't you override the lockdown?" I suggest. "Let your mother in."

"If I can reach her before the *Res Extensa* gets here, I will," Uma says. "But, otherwise, Dr. Fornax is right. The station needs to be on lockdown until we know D'Cart is nowhere near us. I left my mom a message letting her know what's going on and I'll see her when this is over. But, gad, I just . . . I just want to . . . I don't know. Hug her! You know?"

"Of course you do; you're human," I say, then add, "After being up here, that saying takes on new meaning, doesn't it?"

Uma looks at me quizzically and presses her cool hands against my hot forehead. "Your fever is spiking again."

"Growing up here must have been really odd," I say, getting woozy with exhaustion. "Moonlings are . . ." I try to put my finger on it. "I don't know. It's like, I'm sure Kepler is a great guy and he seems to care about you a lot, but he didn't seem all that upset when you told him that his mom was unconscious." I close my eyes for a moment, then open them again, trying to focus on Uma's face above me.

She sits beside me and hugs her knees to her chest. "MUSCies don't show much emotion. They consider it weak to be vulnerable. And they aren't as close to their parents as Earthlings are. Everyone here is born ex utero. Sperm and eggs are matched in a lab to optimize natural selection and avoid inbreeding, then all the kids are raised communally in the nurseries while their parents work. And families don't necessarily stay together. Here, people just sort of love who they want when they want, which isn't a bad thing unless you lose the people you love most. Even if they live together as a family unit, they don't see each other all that often. Except for my family. We were different, until Dad died. So . . . I don't know. Maybe they don't get as attached to their families as we do."

As she says this, I get teary thinking about my mom. "I have to find a way to let my mom know . . ."

"We will!" Uma assures me. "I promise. As soon as this mess is over."

"I'm so sleepy." I snuggle down in the blanket, which smells wonderfully of Uma. "I can't keep my eyes open any longer."

"Just rest," says Uma. She leans down and kisses me on the forehead. "I'm going to check on the pathogen samples. I'll come back for you in a while."

"What if . . ." I try to say but my mouth won't work right. *No what ifs* echoes through my brain as I'm pulled down into the blackness of exhaustion.

UMA JEMISON

MOON UTILITARIAN SURVIVAL COLONY

I RUN INTO our domicile and dive down on my bedroom floor. Everything is going wrong!

"Talitha, wake up!" I shout, then shake her heavy body. "Wake up! Wake up! Please wake up." She rolls back and forth but stays limp beneath the blanket. "No, no, no." I grab her shoulders. "I should have never left you alone! Please don't be unconscious." I pull her up. Her arms flop; her head lolls to the side. "I need your help!" I look around my room for something to rouse her. "I can't do this alone!"

I hear those words leave my mouth with a pathetic little sob, and I stop. "Come on, Uma!" I chastise myself as I hold Talitha close. "Pull it together."

Gently, I lay Talitha back down on the floor, and I take a breath, resolving to be stronger. "Divide the problem into parts," I say aloud, as if I'm coaching myself. "That's how you do it in a lab. Then solve each part of the problem in order. Problem one . . ." I swallow hard and try to break down everything that's going wrong, but all I can do is cry, because the truth is, I have no idea what to do.

"How can I be such a loser?" I yell at myself.

"You're not a loser."

I look down and see Talitha peering up at me. I dive toward her again. "You're awake!"

"Oh, my . . ." she groans. "I passed out so hard!"

"Thank gad," I sputter. "For a minute, I thought . . ."

Her eyes flutter as she works to keep them open. "I could hear you calling me, but I just couldn't wake up!" She yawns long and loud, then draws in an enormous breath and lets go the loudest sneeze I've ever heard. Something silver flies from her nose and skitters across the floor.

We look at each other.

"What the hell?" she says.

I crawl over and pick it up. "It's a little disk."

"That is so creepy!" Talitha says.

"Yes, it's very disturbing." I shove it into my pocket. "But we don't have time to think about that."

"Why? What's going on? How long was I out?"

"A couple of hours." I take her hands and pull her to a sit. She looks better now. Her color is back, and her nose isn't running as much. Her skin is cool to the touch. "Can you stand up? Can you walk?"

"Yeah," she says, still shaking off her nap.

I help her up, making sure she's steady on her feet before I fill her in. "Kep found Gemini, but for some reason, they can't patch him in remotely or disable the robotic loading arm, and D'Cart is getting closer. She'll be here any minute and I haven't been able to reach my mother . . . and . . ."

Talitha shakes herself fully awake. "What are we going to do?"

"We have to get to the loading bay to stop the *Res Extensa* from landing!" I tug her out of my room. She stops in the common area, then runs back and grabs the PEP gun, which she throws in the rear of Randazza's delivery vehicle that's waiting in the hall.

"We tried," I tell Talitha as I drive like a maniac, squealing around corners and speeding through the corridors as fast as I can, avoiding the bodies dotted along the walls.

"Over and over. Micra and Fornax and Kepler and Gemini, everybody did everything they could to patch into the system and gain control of the robotic landing arm, but it just won't work. And nobody, not even Darshan with his blanket override, can disable it without shutting down the entire station and stopping rotation, which would wreak all kinds of havoc because gravity would be gone. Which means the *Res Extensa* is going to dock, and once it docks, the doors will open and D'Cart will come inside."

I take a corner too fast, and the delivery vehicle leans precariously onto two wheels. "Whoa! Whoa!" we both yell. Talitha grabs the steering wheel and rights us again.

"If she gets inside, we'll ambush her. Take her out!" Talitha says.

"She has Mundie and Aurelia under her control," I argue as I take a ramp up onto an AutoWalk and speed forward. "We're no match for them."

"So what are we going to do?" Talitha asks.

"They want us to use ExploroBots."

She gasps. "But Fornax said that wouldn't work."

"Without control of the landing arm, it's the only option we have left," I tell her as I exit the AutoWalk and careen around one more corner to the docking area.

"No," says Talitha, shrinking back. "You can't let them—"

"Not them." I screech to a stop in front of the red armored truck still flashing its lights over the bodies of the guards strewn across the corridor. "You. You have to do it."

"Me?" she pulls away.

"I saw how well you drove those AutoPods on Earth. How you caught the fish with one swipe of the net. You have excellent control and hand-eye coordination. And you didn't flinch when we landed and you looked out at the stars whizzing by. I get sick immediately, too dizzy to focus and concentrate if I look outside the station. I can do a lot of things, Talitha, but I cannot do this."

Talitha searches my face. "I can't either," she whispers.

"If you don't . . ." I start to say, but can't finish.

Then I hear my name. From inside the secondary loading bay, Dr. Fornax calls.

Talitha and I run inside, where Randazza and I have set up several holos. Dr. Fornax, Micra, Kepler, and Gemini are each projected in the tiny space, but Randazza is no longer there.

"Finally!" Micra says when we run inside. "I thought you'd never get back."

"Micra, shut up," Kepler says. "You're doing fine, Uma," he calls to me. "Talitha, you all right?"

"Who's that? An Earthling?" Gemini sneers. "Can she be trusted?"

"Both of you, shut it!" Kepler elbows Gemini away. His holo trips out of the frame. "Don't pay attention to them," he tells us. "You're going to do great."

A large holo against the back wall of the loading bay projects the progress of the *Res Extensa* from a stationary camera fixed to the nonrotating elevator shaft leading to our station. The ship is even closer than I thought. I take the mesh hood that will connect Talitha to the ExploroBots and shove it onto her head. "Does it fit? Can you see? Is the Lenz in the right place?"

"Yes, it's okay, but . . ." Her voice shakes as badly as her hands. "I don't know what I'm supposed to do."

"Okay." I take a deep breath, shutting out the noise of the others all talking at once and try to calm myself. "Look out the window. I can't do it with you or I'll get sick, but Gemini is watching on a screen from the surface, and he'll walk you through the process. I'll watch from the stationary camera image back here."

I keep my head turned away while Talitha steps up to the window behind me and gazes out.

"Look to your left," Gemini tells her. "Do you see the Shuttle docked beside you?"

"Yes," says Talitha. "Is that the one we came on?"

"That's right," says Gemini. "You're in the loading bay next to it. Just below where you're standing is the secondary robotic landing arm where the *Res Extensa* is going to dock. See it?"

"Yes," she says. "I see it."

From the holo projection on the back wall, I glimpse the arm, reaching out as if in slow motion, under water, unfurling from the station with the grace of a dancer about to catch her partner.

"Okay, get ready," Gemini says. "The *Res Extensa* is going to pass by."

Talitha gasps. "I see it. It's so close. There it goes!"

"Right," says Gemini. "Remember, you're spinning because you're on the station. The *Res Extensa* is orbiting you while spiraling down toward the landing arm. It'll make five passes, then on the sixth one, the loading arm will be in position to grab it. Now, look up. Do you see the row of ExploroBots tethered to the station?"

"Yes," she whispers. "I see them."

"You're connected to their CPUs through the mesh hood on your head. They're connected together so they'll move as one," he explains. "All you have to do is put enough of them in position so the *Res Extensa* plows into them and gets knocked off course just enough that the landing arm won't reach it."

"No," says Talitha. "The ExploroBots will be obliterated if I do that!"

"Yes, but the station and everyone on it will be saved," Dr. Fornax says impatiently.

"But you said yourself it might not work," Talitha says to Fornax. "That ship is going fast. It might just plow right through them without consequence. There has to be another way."

"If you're so smart, what is it, then?" says Micra impatiently.

"I don't know," says Talitha.

"But we better figure it out because here it comes again!" says Gemini. We all watch the small white capsule pass by, closer to the station than it was the last time.

"What if I position the ExploroBots to grab on to those black rectangular wings on the back of the ship and push it off course so the landing arm can't reach it?"

"The solar panels attached to the tank?" Fornax asks.

"Yes," says Talitha.

"That's a great idea!" I yell.

"It's too risky," Dr. Fornax says.

"Yeah, if you miss—" says Micra.

"But what if I get it?" Talitha asks. "What happens to the *Res Extensa* then?"

"Exactly what you said," Kepler replies. "It'll be knocked off course and won't be able to land."

"And then what?" Talitha asks.

"Most likely, eventually, it'll fall back to Earth and burn up on reentry," Dr. Fornax says with far too much satisfaction.

"With Aurelia inside," Talitha says sadly. She turns to me. "She's like my second mother . . ."

I sigh. "I know."

"She's AI," Dr. Fornax says. "She won't feel pain or fear."

"But ExploroBots might," Talitha insists. She turns back to the window. "What will happen to the ExploroBots if they push the ship off course?"

"Nothing if they let go in time," says Kepler. "As long as they let go, they should stay tethered to the station and be fine."

"Here it comes again!" Gemini says.

"You have to do this now! Move the ExploroBots into position!" Dr. Fornax barks. "Or everyone at MUSC, including the two of you, will die."

Talitha ignores Fornax. I press my back against Talitha's. Over my shoulder, I whisper into her ear, "You don't have to do this. It's okay."

"No," says Talitha. She reaches down and finds my hand beside her leg. We weave our fingers together. "I'll do it, but I'll do it my way. Gemini, tell me how to work the ExploroBot connection."

"All you have to do is think through step by step how you want them to move," Gemini tells her.

"Oh, is that *all*?" Talitha says.

"The more specific you can be, the better they'll respond," I say.

"How do I make them move when there's no gravity?"

A fleeting memory of floating with Kepler the night before I left drifts through my mind. "It's like swimming," I tell her. "Imagine kicking your legs and moving your arms as if you're in water."

Everyone is quiet again as Talitha connects her mind to the ExploroBots' bodies. With my back against hers, I can feel her stand tall and drain the tension from her muscles as her shoulders drop and her sternum lifts. She swallows hard, then takes a clean, even breath. After a few seconds, she says, "It's working! They're moving."

Kepler, Micra, and I erupt in a cheer, but Dr. Fornax shushes us.

"You have to think ahead and move to where the rocket is going to be on the next pass, not where it is now," says Gemini.

"Just like when you caught the fish," I say.

"I understand," says Talitha. I glance over my shoulder at her. She shifts her left shoulder and swoops a bit. "There we go," she says. "I'm getting it now."

"Here it comes again," says Gemini. "That's pass four. It's getting closer!"

I catch sight of the stars spinning outside the window and have to look away as my stomach lurches. My whole body tenses when I turn back to the holo and see the *Res Extensa* getting closer and closer as it circles the station. From the stationary camera following its path, I can see it clearly as it passes. It's a small conical ship with a large window taking up the front and six smaller, round windows dotting the perimeter of the crew module. Protruding from the tank in the back, two long solar panels, like rectangular black wings, rotate to position the ship in place for the robotic arm to capture it. As it looms nearer, I can make out the shapes of D'Cart and Aurelia through the front window.

"I see them," I gasp.

"Here it comes!" says Gemini. "This is pass five!"

"I'm close!" says Talitha. Everyone inhales. I watch on-screen as the ExploroBots, swimming in a row, align themselves above the tail, then reach out just when the ship glides past. Their silver fingers stretch forward.

"I missed!" Talitha cries, and the *Res Extensa* keeps going.

"Damn it!" Fornax snarls.

"It's okay," says Kepler. "You were really close."

"Pull them in a little bit," Gemini says. "And turn fifteen degrees to your left so you'll be in position on the last pass to reach out before the landing arm gets them. Then all you have to do is give the ship a push and let go."

"Okay," says Talitha. "I think I can do it."

"I know you can," I say.

I watch as on the far side of the station, a little door in the belly of the *Res Extensa* opens and an umbilical connection unit protrudes. The small ship spins ninety degrees to line up with the robotic arm still making its elegant trek across the black sky divide. As the ship slowly turns, the circular windows come into view and I see more people on board.

"There are others in there!" I exclaim. "Who does she have with her?" I step up closer to the holo and squint. "External camera one, zoom in," I command. The image tightens up, but remains blurry.

"Almost there," says Talitha. "I'm reaching out."

"Here it comes," says Gemini. "You're lined up."

I hear the others inhale. I hold my breath, waiting for her to connect, but then I see a flash of brown. A furry face. Small pointy ears. "Quasar?" I say aloud. "Zoom in! Zoom in!"

The *Res Extensa* creeps closer as the robotic landing arm strains forward. The ExploroBots reach out their arms. Then on the screen, just as the ship passes the camera and leaves my view, I see Castor's face in the window, plain as day.

"Stop!" I scream. "Stop!"

TALITHA NEVA

MOON UTILITARIAN
SURVIVAL COLONY

WHEN UMA YELLS, I jerk my head away from the window, breaking the connection with the ExploroBots in my control. On the large holo projection behind me, I see the fleeting image of my brother's face peering out the window of the approaching ship.

"Castor!" I shout, and run to stand with Uma.

"Quasar, too!" She points to the image of the ship as it disappears from view.

"What are you doing?" Dr. Fornax screams.

"You idiots!" Micra screeches.

"The loading arm almost had it!" Gemini yells.

"Go back! Go back!" Fornax cries. "This is the last chance."

"I can't fling them into space!" I yell. "That's my brother on there!"

"What if it's a trick?" Uma asks.

"You saw him!" I shout.

"What if it was a holo?" she says.

"What if! What if!" I yell, clutching at my head.

"Now!" Dr. Fornax yells. "Now!"

"I can't do it!" I say. "I won't!"

Uma grabs my hand. "Of course not," she says. "You're human. He's your brother."

We turn and face the window, side by side, staring at Castor, staring back at us. His eyes are wide with terror as the robotic landing arm connects to the belly of the *Res Extensa* and pulls it in to dock.

"You two are the most worthless—" Dr. Fornax starts to scream.

"Holos off!" Uma shouts, and the images of Fornax and the others blink away. "I've had enough of them," she snaps. "We'll do this our way. Where's the gun?" she asks as the ship locks into place.

I pat my body and look around the room. "I don't know!"

We look at each other, then we freeze when the loading bay door hisses open.

"What now?" I whisper.

"We have to buy some time," Uma says, clutching my hand tight. "Pretend to go along with her. Make her think we're on her side until we figure out what to do."

D'Cart is the first one through the door. She marches onto MUSC, head held high, surly grin on her face.

"Ah!" she says, taking a deep breath. "Home, sweet home. How I've missed this place." She looks at us and laughs. "Not!"

"Hello, Zaniah," Uma says, and steps forward with her hand extended. "It's so nice to finally meet you."

"Oh, is it?" she asks. "You called me silly and said I was a disappointment." She keeps her hands on her hips.

"That was just for show." Uma blushes and looks down. "I didn't want Dr. Fornax to know how I really feel. But I got rid of her." She peers up.

D'Cart narrows her eyes. "What do you mean, got rid of her?"

"Disconnected," Uma says with a shrug. "We don't need her any longer now that we have you."

Aurelia wheels through the door next. Without thinking, I run to her. "Aurelia! I'm so happy to see you."

"Hello, Talitha," she says, and lets me hug her. "I am happy to see you, too."

Next, Mundie marches out and stops. Uma and I both gasp and back up.

"Oh, don't worry about him," D'Cart says. "I've got him in my control. Just like I'm going to have everybody here soon enough."

"Do you have my brother?" I ask, peering through the doorway, fearing it was a trick like Uma thought or, worse, that he's in her control, too.

D'Cart sighs, annoyed. "He's with us. And your dog." She rolls her eyes. "That was Aurelia's brilliant idea."

"Thank you," says Aurelia.

"Castor? Quasar?" I call, my voice quivering with anticipation.

I hear a little yelp, then Quasar dashes through the door. He runs in circles, yapping and dancing on three legs. Uma and I both drop to our knees and catch him up in our arms. Then Castor walks through.

I stand up, not breathing. He looks at me, eyes moist, face twisting with emotion. "It's you!" I yell, and run for him.

Castor catches me in a tight hug.

"*Wolflo em.*" I whisper our twin language in his ear. *Follow me.* He looks at me quizzically, but I lift my eyebrows and repeat, "*Wolflo em.*"

I step away from Castor and say, "I'm so happy that you're here! Now that we're all together, we can help D'Cart take over."

He nods slowly, then turns to D'Cart. "How can I help you?"

"Well, well, well. That's better!" D'Cart says, glancing at my brother. "I see you decided to change your tune."

"Yeah. You were right. This place is great," Castor says, with a complete lack of emotion. "Now that I know Talitha's safe, I'll do whatever you want."

But D'Cart doesn't seem to notice that he's such a bad liar. "Good," she says, swanning around the loading bay, looking things over. "First, I need to go to Fornax's office to hack the MUSC cybermind. Shouldn't be too hard now that we're on board and through security. Then we can take over the MUSCie implants and get this show on the road."

"But wait!" Uma says, her eyes darting back and forth. "Do you want to speak to Fornax?"

"Why?" D'Cart's face twists like she ate something nasty.

"So she knows you made it on board. You can rub it in. Want me to call her up?" Uma asks.

"That's a great idea!" I say, trying to buy more time. "In fact, you should Stream it when you confront her!"

"Yeah!" says Castor. "Show all your followers how you stuck it to the MUSC CEO! That would be epic."

A little grin plays at the corners of D'Cart's mouth. "That would be nice," she says as she thinks it over. "Good for ratings. Can you call her up?"

"Definitely," says Uma. "Just give me a second."

"But keep her on mute," D'Cart says. "I don't want to hear her mouth."

"Fornax's holo will be over here," Uma says, pointing toward the back of the bay. "So you stand over there by the exit, facing her, to get the best shot for your Stream."

D'Cart moves, and Aurelia stays by her side.

"Wait, I don't want her in the shot," says D'Cart. "Aurelia, you go wait over there by Mundie in the back. I want everyone to know that I did this alone."

Dutifully, Aurelia wheels over to Mundie, who stands so still I think he might be dead on his feet. "What happened to his face?" I whisper to Castor.

He grins slyly and whispers, "Quasar and I kicked his ass for you."

"Should I launch my PEST now?" D'Cart asks. "How's my hair?"

"You look great," says Uma. "Get ready. Here goes!"

As soon as Uma reconnects to Dr. Fornax's muted holo, D'Cart launches her PEST and opens her mouth, but then a person rushes into the loading bay from the hallway with a PEP gun raised over her head.

D'Cart spins, eyes wide. "What the—" she says, just as the butt of the gun connects to the side of her head. She crashes to the floor.

"Mom!" Uma yells, and darts across the room. The woman tosses the gun to the ground and catches Uma in her arms. "How did you get here?" Uma asks.

"Randazza let me in," her mother says.

Behind her, Randazza peeks around the door frame. "Did you get her? Is she out?"

"Like a light," Uma's mom says.

"Good!" says Randazza. "I didn't survive fighting in the Water Wars on Earth and claw my way up here, then work this job for twenty years, slinging food for MUSCies, to have some little snot like Zaniah Nashira come back and take it all away. I'm going to retire soon. Be sitting pretty, too. Dr. Fornax might have her head up her ass half the time, but she provides nicely for people who are loyal."

"How'd you know not to shoot her?" Castor asks.

"Huh?" says Uma's mom.

"Her suit has reflective tech woven in. A blast from that gun would have turned on all of us," he explains.

"Oh," says Persis, blinking back surprise. "I didn't know how to shoot the gun, so I hit her instead."

"That girl always was a pain," Randazza says, standing over D'Cart's body. "I've known Zaniah since she was a child. Fornax brought her up here an orphan, just a tiny slip of a thing. She was mad as hell. I tried to take her under my wing. Nurture her, but she wanted nothing to do with anybody. She was always demanding and thought she knew best. Couldn't listen to nobody for nothing. That girl gave Earthlings a bad name on MUSC."

"What do we do with her?" I ask.

"Put her back on the ship!" Uma says, still holding tight to her mother, who won't let her go. "Before she wakes up."

Castor grabs D'Cart's arms, and I take her legs. Quasar chases after us, barking at the body. We pass Aurelia, who stands passively waiting for the next command, but I see Mundie lurch.

"Agh," he groans and blinks.

"That blow might have broken the connection between him and D'Cart," says Castor.

"Poor guy," I say, almost feeling sorry for him. "Once he wakes up, we'll have to explain what happened."

"Maybe he'll be a little nicer now that we saved him from a life as a technoslave," Castor says.

"I doubt it," I say as we harness D'Cart into the captain's seat of the *Res Extensa*.

I wipe my hands across the seat of my pants and follow Castor to the door, saying, "Good riddance," over my shoulder before we step into the loading bay with Quasar at our heels.

Ahead of me, Castor goes down sideways. Before I can react, a blow comes hard and fast and throws me back. I try to scream but the air is knocked out of me. When I look up, I see Mundie on top of me. This time, his eyes are alive with spite.

"You think you can get away from me!" He smacks me hard across the face with the back of his hand, then yanks me up by the front of the shirt.

"Talitha!" I hear Uma scream.

Mundie wraps one hand around my throat and presses me against the wall of the ship. "All those years, following you around like a damn dog, waiting for you to notice me."

Quasar runs, teeth bared, but Mundie kicks him away. He lands with a high-pitched yelp and rolls out into the loading bay. Aurelia darts across the doorway toward the dog.

Mundie squeezes tighter as I fight to kick and punch, but his arms are long, and I can't make contact with his body. Through the doorway, I see Uma swipe the PEP gun from the floor. The edges of my vision go gray and blurry. I gag and sputter, then I hear a *BOOM*. Electricity fills the air. As if in slow motion, I watch a silver wave of energy travel through the portal and envelop Mundie's body. He stiffens for a moment, then goes slack. The wave reaches me just as his fingers leave my throat. I watch him go down as the jolt of the electricity hits my body and I slump, too.

MOON UTILITARIAN
SURVIVAL COLONY

I STAND WITH the gun in my hands, my whole body shaking, but I can't move. I've never held a weapon. Never hurt anyone. And it doesn't feel good. "Did I get him? Did he go down? Where's Talitha?" I scream.

Aurelia cradles a quivering and whimpering Quasar while Castor shakes his head, still dizzy from Mundie's blow. He picks himself up off the floor and stumbles back into the *Res Extensa,* yelling, "I need help!"

Mom, Randazza, and I all cram into the cockpit where Mundie has fallen like a tree across Talitha's limp body.

"Help me get him off her," Castor says.

The three of them lift Mundie as I slide underneath to free Talitha. For the third time in one day, I hold her unconscious body next to mine. "Oh, Talitha! Oh, no. I'm so sorry," I cry over her. "I didn't mean to hurt you."

They dump Mundie's body into the seat next to D'Cart and harness him down.

"Let's go," says Randazza. "We've got to get out of here and lock that door behind us before they both wake up."

Castor helps me carry Talitha into the loading bay, then he takes

Quasar from Aurelia's arms and checks him over while I sit on the floor with Talitha on my lap.

My mom squats beside me. "This is her?" she asks quietly. "The Earth girl that you love?"

I nod, because I can't talk, because if I talk, I'll cry. And if I cry, I might not stop. I never thought I'd meet someone like Talitha. Someone who makes me feel as if I belong because she accepts me for who I am and she likes all the things that might seem strange to others. Once I did meet her, I assumed my time with her was fleeting. A mere moment on the Earth, then memories that I would carry back to the Moon in my heart. And so, to have her in my arms and know that I have hurt her is too much for me to bear.

"I can't lose her," I say.

"You won't," Mom assures me. "It was just a residual shockwave. Probably through his hand to her body. She'll wake up any minute and be fine."

"No, not that." I hold her tighter. "I mean, when all of this is over. When D'Cart is safely gone and the people all wake up and Dr. Fornax comes back . . ."

"What do you want to do?" Mom asks. "Go back to Earth with her?"

I see the pain in her eyes. Her memories of her time down there. Having to return and carve out a life from trash without my father at her side. It's too much to ask of her after everything she's given up for me. I soften my grip on Talitha, but I can't let her go. Not yet.

"How is she?" Castor asks. He leans close to her face. Their profiles are the same. Soft bristles of Mars-colored hair. Warm skin scattered with bright freckles like a starry night sky. The slope of their noses, the jut of their chins. But I could never mistake them for each other. All planets look the same from far away, but zoom in, and they are unique. Talitha has an essence that makes her who she is.

"*Latihat, kewa pu*," Castor whispers in their strange twin language.

We all stare down at her, waiting, and finally she sighs.

"Oh, thank gad!" I cry, then softly pat her cheeks, calling, "Hey, hey! Are you waking up? Are you okay?"

For the third time, she blinks up at me with eyes the color of evergreens, then she says, "Seriously? Again?"

I laugh softly, trying not to cry. "Last time," I tell her. "Promise."

She sits up. "What the hell happened to me this time?"

"Uma shot you," Castor says with a laugh, while he strokes Quasar's fur.

"Did not!" I help her to her feet.

"Actually, she saved you from that zombie mutant Mundie." Castor shudders.

"Where is he?" Talitha looks around the room, frightened.

Castor points to the window, outside of which the *Res Extensa* sits.

"We're going to have to do something with them soon," Randazza says.

"Uma." Mom jerks her head toward the holo we all forgot about. "Fornax is trying to tell us something."

From across the room, I see Dr. Fornax's holo, gesticulating wildly on mute.

"Do I have to unmute her?" I ask.

"Probably should," says Mom.

"Ugh," I say, then command the sound on again so Fornax comes across loud and clear.

"You have to get that ship out of there now!" she shouts. "Initiate system launch."

"Override!" I say, surprising even myself.

"What?" snarls Dr. Fornax. "What are you—"

At that moment, standing on the precipice of MUSC, with the stars whizzing by, one foot away from a ship that could take us back to Earth, everything becomes clear to me. "I have some demands," I tell her.

"You don't have time for demands," Fornax says.

"Then I'll make it quick!" I mute her again before she can respond.

Fornax throws her hands up in the air and irately shakes her head, but I stand my ground.

"If you want your station back, you need to listen to me."

Fornax bites her tongue and narrows her eyes as she stops shouting at me all the way from Earth.

"Before I'll launch the *Res Extensa,* I want three promises from you."

She crosses her arms tightly against her chest and scowls.

"First, you will grant asylum to Talitha and Castor and make them honorary MUSC citizens if they want to stay here."

Castor and Talitha look at each other, then at me, then at Fornax.

"They are good enough and smart enough to join us, and without them, we wouldn't have succeeded here," I say.

Dr. Fornax looks to the ceiling, but she nods in agreement. Castor and Talitha gasp, then hug with Quasar barking at their feet.

"Second, I want my LWA to include regular visits to the Earth."

Dr. Fornax wrinkles her nose and shakes her head as if I've asked for something disgusting.

"You need to find me a job that involves the Earth, or I won't be happy here."

"Do it," Mom tells Fornax.

Dr. Fornax grits her teeth, but she nods for the second time.

"And third"—I take a deep breath, because I know this one's a doozy—"you must end the ExploroBot program."

This one catches Fornax off guard. She stares at me for a moment, then her face softens. She's not angry like I thought she'd be, just confused. She points to her mouth, then clasps her hands together as if to say please.

"Unmute," I command.

"Uma," Dr. Fornax says calmly, "you don't understand. What we do with the ExploroBots is for the good of all humankind. Someday the Earth will not be livable and the rest of the universe will be our home, and without ExploroBots—"

"No matter what you try to convince yourself of, Dr. Fornax, the ExploroBots are people," I say. "For all the nonsense spouted by D'Cart or Zaniah or whatever her name is, she's right about one thing. Just because you replace their body parts doesn't mean you make them less of who they were."

"And," Castor joins in, "if you're going to use human beings as your technoslaves, you're no better than Zaniah is, because she planned to do the same thing to your people when she took over up here."

"Who are you?" a voice asks, then we see Micra creep into the holo frame from behind Fornax. This time it's a genuine question, not a condemnation.

Castor does a double take when he sees Micra. He stands up tall. "My name is Castor Neva." I see Micra studying him closely as he says, "I am an Earthling. You may think of me as just some guttersnipe from the Wastelands, but my father helped build this place."

"Oh," says Dr. Fornax. "Your father was an ExploroBot?"

"Our father," he says, and puts an arm around Talitha's shoulders. They are mirror images.

"My husband, too," says Randazza, with her chin held high. "I came here to be near him." My mother lays a hand on her back.

"Well, er, um . . . thank you all for your family members' services," Dr. Fornax mutters. "I hope the payment—"

"No," says Talitha. "It wasn't enough. It was never enough."

Dr. Fornax shuts her mouth for a moment, then she takes a deep breath and says, "I'm sorry for your losses. I truly am. But your loved ones would not have lived on the Earth. Their injuries were too great. And the work they did here has helped us create a world for the greater good. We're expanding. New colonies are being built to accommodate all of our people—"

"But what we have here benefits such a small group," I argue. "And the price is too high from a few individuals. You've built this place on the backs of people like their father and Randazza's husband, but you haven't truly compensated them by bettering their lives."

"It's not that easy to stop," Fornax insists. "I have more stations half built!"

"Look," I say. "I know that without the ExploroBots, we'll need to develop newer, better technology that will allow us to accomplish the things we want to accomplish. But isn't that what you educate the cohorts to do? We are ingenious, creative, and excellent problem solvers."

"I can't do it," Fornax says. "Your friends can stay, we can find you an LWA that involves a relationship to Earth on behalf of MUSC, but I won't compromise our future."

"Well then, I won't launch the *Res Extensa*," I say, stepping back. "And all of us, Castor, Talitha, my mother, Randazza, Aurelia, and the dog will board that MUSC Shuttle in the next loading bay and go back to Earth to take our chances down there. When D'Cart wakes up, she'll waltz back onto this station to take over MUSC and all its citizens, and you can come back up here to clean up your own mess."

I hold my breath and don't make a sound. I wait for my mother to protest. For Randazza Marmesh to say no way is she going back to Earth. But they don't. They stand firmly by my side.

"Your choice," I tell Fornax, who stands mute on her own. "But you're going to have to decide soon, because D'Cart and Mundie will be awake any minute."

"Okay, fine," Dr. Fornax says, completely exasperated. "But it'll take time, Uma. We're going to finish those other stations, then phase out the program properly."

"I'm okay with that," I say, and smile with relief. "We'll begin deportation now. Darshan, initiate robotic loading arm," I command.

"Initiating arm," Darshan concurs.

Slowly and gracefully, the loading arm pushes the *Res Extensa* away from the MUSC station. On board, through the front windows, we see D'Cart stir. Her eyes flutter open.

"She's awake!" I say.

"What'll happen to her?" Talitha moves closer to my side. I take her hand and hold it tight.

D'Cart sits up, startled and afraid. She looks out and sees all of us staring back at her. She bangs her fists on the window and screams, but we can't hear her. I watch her lips move as she punches something on the screen in front of her. Out of the corner of my eye, on the other side of the room, Aurelia's blue-lit eyes flash.

Castor sees it, too. "No!" he shouts.

Aurelia whips toward us, arms out, but Castor's quick. He scoops Quasar off the floor and jumps in front of us with the dog held out like a shield. "Aurelia, keep Quasar safe!" he shouts.

Aurelia stops in the center of the room, her eyes trained on the dog writhing in Castor's arms.

"What are you doing?" Talitha yells at her brother.

Out the window, I see the loading arm has fully extended and cocked back like an elbow.

"I programmed Aurelia to always keep Quasar safe," Castor explains, his voice shaking. "I think my command is overriding whatever D'Cart is asking her to do."

We all cast our eyes from the bot, still stalled in the center of the floor, to the window where the loading arm pauses, waiting for the station to reach its apogee for maximum orbital trajectory. Then the arm releases, flinging the *Res Extensa* with Zaniah Nashira, aka RayNay DeShoppingCart, headlong into space.

"Transmission lost," Aurelia says, and rolls backward away from us to reposition herself by the wall. "Awaiting reconnection," she announces.

Slowly, carefully, Talitha walks toward the bot. "Aurelia?" she says cautiously. "Are you going to hurt us?"

Aurelia turns her face plate up to look at Talitha. "I have no orders to do so now," she says, and we all sigh with relief.

Castor kisses the white star on Quasar's head, then sets him on the floor, but he keeps a wary eye on Aurelia.

"What will happen to the Yoobies and AlphaZonia once D'Cart is gone?" Mom asks from where she gazes out the window into the blackness.

"Most likely AlphaZonia will collapse beneath the weight of its own hubris, then something or someone will come along and take its place. It always does," Dr. Fornax says.

"Humans are as wily as bacteria," I say. "We continually reinvent ourselves to exist even in the most desperate circumstances."

"How right you are," says Dr. Fornax, turning to me. "And now it's time for you to wake our colony."

CASTOR NEVA

MOON UTILITARIAN
SURVIVAL COLONY

WHILE UMA AND Talitha head to Curie's immunology lab to check on the pathogen and find a way to wake the others, Persis takes me to an Intelligence lab so we can dismantle Aurelia. The episode in the landing dock spooked me, and I don't want to take any chances that D'Cart could connect to her again.

"Amazing," says Persis as we dismantle Aurelia's head and attach it to a diagnostic podium while her body stands useless beside the wall. "This is exciting for me. I've never gotten to work on a robot as intelligent as this one."

"Thank you, Persis," says Aurelia's head. "That is a nice compliment. I hope my complexity lives up to your expectations."

Persis laughs, delighted. "My DrillBots are smart, but they don't engage with me like this! I don't know how you do it."

Persis's comment is clearly rhetorical, but Aurelia is far too literal to get the nuance, so she answers honestly. "I'm designed to use observations from my experiences as feedback to update my behavior algorithms. I have noticed that speaking directly to humans by using their names and thanking them makes them feel more attached to me."

"Uh . . . yeah," says Persis as she finishes hooking up Aurelia to the processor. "I wish a few more MUSCies had the same social skills as you."

"I'm going to access your CPU now," I tell Aurelia gently.

"I understand," she says brightly. "You'll find my neural web is quite intricate and ever changing."

"Yeah, I know," I mutter as Aurelia's deep learning code is revealed to us on the holo screen. "D'Cart created this beautifully complex neural network in you, but she left out a moral code. Instead, you're programmed to follow her instructions without regard to how they affect others."

"Sounds like a few people I know," Persis jokes.

I take a deep breath, then dive in to unravel the impossibly long and tangled algorithms that make up the general intelligence central to Aurelia's mind.

After hours and hours, I've gotten no closer to successfully overriding D'Cart's ultimate control of Aurelia.

"I can't do this!" I throw my hands up in disgust, then collapse onto the work space facefirst.

"Are you frustrated, Castor?" Aurelia's head asks me from the podium.

"Yes," I grumble. "When I was younger, somehow I created a blanket override in you, but now I don't see how to do it. Maybe you're much more complex than you were back then, or maybe I got lucky before."

"Perhaps," says Aurelia. "But it is also true that you did not install a blanket override in me previously."

"Yes, I did!" I sit dumbfounded for a moment, then begin to question myself out loud. "Didn't I? After we'd been with you for a year? I hacked your code and installed an override so you would do what I wanted."

"Because Zaniah Nashira allowed it," Aurelia says.

"Of course!" I smack my forehead. "I feel so stupid."

"You are not stupid, Castor," says Aurelia. "You successfully wrote and installed the override algorithm in me, but I needed Zaniah's permission to run it."

"Wait," says Persis. "What about Quasar? Didn't you program Aurelia to always keep him safe?"

"I guess Zaniah allowed that, too, right?" I say, annoyed.

"No," says Aurelia. "She did not see it, or more accurately, she did not know to look for it. You hid it well, Castor, deep in the heart of my processor."

Persis smiles. "That's something at least!"

"Not really," I say. "Even if we could install code for keeping individuals or groups of people safe, it's exactly the kind of thing D'Cart will be looking for and undoing."

"If she survives and still has access," Persis says. Then she turns to Aurelia. "Do you believe Zaniah could have access to your CPU in the future?"

"Yes," Aurelia says simply.

Persis and I exchange looks.

"Well," says Persis after a few moments of pondering the implications. "As long as we keep her head and her body separated, she can't physically hurt anyone or damage the station if D'Cart tells her to."

"That's fine for now," I say. "But Aurelia's not whole until we put her back together."

"Then, the only thing I can think to do is to wipe her central processing unit and start again," Persis says. "Otherwise, if Zaniah survives, she could reestablish control from afar."

"I can't do that!" Tears sting my eyes, which catches me off guard.

Aurelia blinks at me. "Are you crying, Castor?"

"I don't know why," I mutter, swatting away the tears. "It's stupid. With everything that's happened—getting caught by D'Cart, thinking Talitha could be dead, watching the Observatory blow up while I abandoned my mother on Earth—this is what makes me cry?" My nose runs as my eyes continue to leak. "It's just that, if I replace your CPU, you'll no longer be you, Aurelia! And I already feel like I'm losing everything and everybody familiar to me. I don't want to lose you, too!"

"I don't know about that," Persis says, studying the code on the holo screen in front of us. "People's brains get rebooted in different ways. Strokes. Trauma. Amnesia. Dementia. Does that mean they're no longer who they were?"

"If you lose memory of who you are and all of your experiences, aren't you then a different person?" I ask.

"Maybe not," says Persis. "Maybe you regain yourself or at least make a new version of who you were when you are surrounded by the people who love you."

"I don't think it's like losing a limb," I say. "You can't just train a replacement brain. Isn't your mind fundamental to who you are?"

Persis shrugs. "It's a very old question that gets asked again and again in new ways each time we make a technological leap. What's the brain? What's the body? How are they different, and how are they connected? What makes us each uniquely ourselves? But maybe those are the wrong questions to ask in this situation."

"Then what should we be asking?" I say, exasperated.

Persis thinks this over, then she says, "Maybe the question is, what's best for Aurelia?"

"I know what best serves me," Aurelia's head says.

"What is it, Aurelia?" I ask. My heart speeds up, and my palms sweat. I hold my breath, waiting for the answer, hoping D'Cart isn't speaking through her.

"I was created to learn from my mistakes," Aurelia tells us. "That is fundamentally who I am and who I would like to continue to be."

"Even if that means we replace your brain and take away all your memories?" I ask.

"Humans worked so hard to overcome catastrophic forgetting when they created artificial intelligence," Aurelia explains. "But maybe forgetting what Zaniah taught me is the best way to save me."

"For someone with no moral code, you are the least selfish being I've ever encountered," Persis says.

"But there's so much important stuff in here!" I motion to the endless lines of code running across the screen. "We can't get rid of it all!"

"Maybe we can mine out the good stuff and save it," says Persis. "Just like I do down on the surface of the Moon."

"Really?" I ask, blinking back my disbelief.

"It's worth a try!" Persis says.

The lab door opens. Uma comes inside with Talitha and Quasar at her heels. A pang of jealousy ripples through my gut. Talitha and Quasar have always followed me.

"The pathogens are ready," Uma says, clearly excited. "Want to take a look with us? I'm going to scan and sequence them."

I perk up at the offer and jump to my feet, but then I hesitate and look back at Aurelia, watching me. "I should probably . . ."

"No, no, you go with Uma," Persis says. "I'll stay here with Aurelia. I'd love to look through her code some more. This is all so fascinating to me. The MUSCies never let me close to these labs. They think I'm just a lowly repair person with no capacity to understand how AI works, but they underestimate me."

"They underestimate all Earthlings," Uma says.

○○

In the immunology lab, Uma removes the glass tubes from the centrifuge and loads them into a device no bigger than a tabletop convection cooker.

"What's that thing do?" Talitha asks.

"This is called the GenExtSeq, which is short for genetic extractor and sequencer," Uma says. Her eyes light up, and she talks quickly as she explains. "First, these tiny automated pipettes will draw off the DNA that was released into the solution when we broke up the specimens in the centrifuge. Then it'll sequence the DNA and look for potential matches in our database."

"This is why I love immunology." Uma beams as she opens the radio frequency oven where the petri dishes have been cultivating. "You get to handle specimens, grow things, watch life unfold and collapse in front of you. It's the closest thing we have to gardening."

"Yeah," I say, ogling the centrifuges and vortex machines and thermocyclers and other things I can't name but would like to get my hands on. "I could stay in here for a week and never sleep."

"You'll fit right in up here," Uma says with a delighted laugh.

"Oh, I don't know about that," I say quietly.

"Isn't it interesting, Castor?" Talitha says from where she snuggles Quasar on the floor. "Since we've been here, you haven't tried to steal anything."

"Of course, I haven't," I say. "What would I do with this stuff?"

Talitha stares at up me. "Sell it on Earth, duh?"

"Dang, Talitha, you're a bigger thief than I am!" I say, but I know she's right. This is the first time in my life that I've walked into a place and haven't immediately thought about what I could dismantle, hack, or swipe for my own benefit. And I'm not sure why. Maybe it just hasn't occurred to me yet.

"Hmmm," says Uma as she lays out the dishes on the counter.

"Some of these did nothing, but look at this one!" She holds up a petri dish covered with a gorgeous swirl of blue and green striations with tiny bright dots of deep orange spiraling out from a white center. "That is from a swab of Talitha's nose. I added dyes so we could see the contrast better."

"Looks just like a galaxy," I say.

"What do you think it is?" Talitha stands up to join us at the counter.

"Some kind of virus and bacteria combination from the look of it," says Uma.

"I didn't know viruses and bacteria could be so beautiful!" Talitha says.

Uma lets go a tiny gasp of surprise. "That's exactly what I always say!" Then she and my sister gaze at one another with goo-goo eyes.

"Gross, you guys. Stop it," I say.

"Jealous?" Talitha asks.

"Hardly," I say, but that's not exactly true. Watching my sister and Uma cozied up together, heads cocked toward each other, grins on their faces, uncovers a hole inside of me. It's one thing to stay on MUSC to learn, but I don't think I could ever fall in love with a Moonling or feel truly welcome here.

"You'll get used to it," Talitha jokes.

"I'm not sure I want to stay," I admit.

"I thought you'd be excited," says Uma. She carries the galaxy dish to the largest machine in the room and sets it gently on a small loading platform.

"Looks like a vending machine," Talitha laughs.

"This is Tiny Titan!" Uma pats the machine fondly as the specimen is drawn inside and the little door closes tight. "It's the most powerful all-in-one sample preparation unit and 3-D holographic electron microscope ever built. We can see everything that's happening inside from this holo projection."

We crowd around to watch a small robotic arm remove the top of the petri dish, then the bottom of the dish with the material is moved into another chamber, like a pizza going into an oven.

"First, it'll stabilize and freeze the sample to preserve it." A burst of thick white spray covers the dish. "When that dries, the specimen will be encased in hard resin so it can be sliced." An arm comes down from above, plucks the frozen disk out of the dish, and moves it to another chamber, where it's suspended upright like a medallion. Next, a bright red beam of light scans the tiny frozen galaxy.

"Now watch this!" Uma says, inching closer to the projection. "This is my favorite part! First, the laser cuts the disk into cross sections." The scanning beam breaks into a row of lines that slide down through the disk like a bread slicer. "It'll do that over and over," Uma says. "Cutting it into smaller and smaller units until we have ultrathin sections, one tenth of a micron thick. It'll be too small to see, but in a few minutes, those ultrathin slices will be prepped onto slides and loaded under the electron beam for us to study."

"Whoa," I say, almost dizzy with excitement as I watch the process unfold in front of me.

"The electron microscope is what's truly amazing," Uma says. "It's as strong as the Zeiss telescope but instead of looking far away, we can see the universe right beneath our noses."

Talitha and I lock eyes at the mention of the Zeiss.

"We have to find Mom," she says to me.

"I know," I say. "I'm trying." I've replayed the scene of the Observatory's destruction over and over in my mind since I left the Earth, and I've pinged Talitha's old device at least a hundred times, but our mom has yet to answer. I'm too afraid to think about what that could mean. "We'll keep trying," I tell my sister, because what we need now is hope.

"And then what?" Talitha says. "You're just going to go back?"

I shrug.

"You obviously love this stuff," Talitha says, motioning to the Tiny Titan. "If you stay, you can finally go to school and use your brain for something more than thieving and have a better life and—"

"I was doing just fine down on Earth," I protest.

"Yeah, except when you got us caught and nearly killed by a lunatic who wanted to take over this entire survival colony," Talitha says.

"You should be grateful for that!" I tell my sister.

"Why?"

"That's how you met Uma," I say.

"True!" Talitha pecks Uma on the cheek.

"You two are so in love it's annoying," I say, and look back at the machine so I don't have to watch them fawn over each other.

"Our love is beautiful," Uma says.

"As beautiful as that?" I point to the projection of bright green spheres covered with orange and blue protrusions.

Talitha steps up closer to peer at the image. "Is that what was inside of me? In that silver disk up my nose?"

"Oh, my gad . . ." Uma zooms in on one of the critters, getting closer and closer until we're looking at only a single ball. "Bacteriophage!"

"Bacterio-what?" asks Talitha.

"Phage. Viruses that infect bacteria to reproduce inside them," I say, crowding in with Uma.

"How do you know that's what it is?" Talitha asks.

"By their shape." Uma points to the image. "The big green ball is one bacterium. A single cell. They're much larger than viruses. These little blue and orange protrusions are the phages." She zooms in on one bacteriophage for us to study. "See the funny multifaceted prism on the top? That's the head, or capsid. It's filled with nucleic acid or DNA that has the virus's instructions for replicating. The head sits on top of this stalk, or sheath, that's balanced by these tail fibers."

"Those things that look like spindly spider legs?" Talitha points and Uma nods.

"The phage inserts little tail pins, these things that look like spikes below the base plate at the bottom of the sheath. Then it burrows down, sending in the DNA from the capsid, through the sheath, into the bacterium, where it will reproduce." She zooms out again so we see the full image of the phage-covered bacterium.

"They look like lunar landing modules," says Talitha.

"No," says Uma, stepping back. "They look like MUSC."

I burst out laughing. "We're nothing more than a giant bacteriophage stuck to the Moon!"

Giddy and tired from all that's happened, the three of us giggle stupidly at the idea.

"You know what's more creepy?" I ask. They look at me. "There are billions of those things still in the air and more inside the brains of nearly everyone on this station."

That kills the mood. We all stare at the image.

"Let's see if the DNA sequence is done yet," Uma says. The three of us hurry back to the GenExtSeq and wait as the machine spits out lines of As, Gs, Cs, and Ts.

"What's it doing?" Talitha asks.

"Looking for known DNA matches so we can identify the phage," Uma explains. "Come on, come on," she coaxes as we watch the code roll by.

After a few more seconds, the screen displays the message: No known matches.

Uma shakes her head. "That can't be right. This database has everything. And I mean ev-er-y-thing! DNA from bacteria and viruses found everywhere from the Earth's upper atmosphere to the bottom of the ocean and inside volcanoes; fossilized samples from Mars and off meteorites that fell to Earth; viruses that have wreaked havoc for centuries like hantavirus and Marburg and rabies; every influenza variation, rhinovirus, rotavirus; swabs from tribes in the Amazon that died out hundreds of years ago; new mutations of Ebola and dengue and HIV running amok on Earth last week. I'm going to run it again."

We all wait with bated breath, but the same error message pops up.

"I don't understand," she says.

I step back, thinking over my conversations with D'Cart. "I do."

Uma and Talitha look at me.

"This phage doesn't come from nature. D'Cart must have engineered it," I tell them.

"Then . . ." Uma holds her head in her hands. "What are we going to do? I can't whip up an antidote for something we've never seen before."

We all stare at the screen. I think through the problem, one step at a time. "Wait," I say. "It's not the phage that matters, right?"

"Of course it does!" says Talitha. "It knocked everyone out."

"Right, but the first step is stopping the spread," I say. "And for that, we don't have to kill the phage . . ."

"You're right!" says Uma, popping up again. "We have to get rid of the host bacteria. Without the bacteria, the phage can't reproduce."

"Exactly!" I say.

"Huh?" says Talitha. "I don't get it."

"Think of it like this," says Uma. "If the phage is MUSC and the bacterium is the Moon, if you get rid of the Moon, you'll definitely get rid of MUSC."

"So . . . you're going to blow up the Moon?" Talitha asks.

"In the universe of these little critters, we are!" says Uma. "If . . ." She pauses to take another sample tube from the centrifuge and load it into the GenExtSeq. "We can figure out what the bacterium is."

"It's from here," I tell them.

"Can't be," Uma says.

Within seconds, we have a readout.

"Look at that!" I point at the screen. "ExB2435. It was formulated for the ExploroBot program. I found it in the MUSC Dumps."

"It's the goo?" Talitha asks.

I nod. "It's a carrier. You can piggyback other things on it. I used it to send in the harmaline for DopaHacks, and D'Cart used it to transport the phages across the blood-brain barrier."

"But if it was made by MUSC for the ExploroBots, why is everyone here so susceptible to it?" Talitha asks.

"It's a combination of *S. mitis* and *S. pneumoniae*, plus some other stuff I don't recognize," Uma says, reading from the screen. "*Streptococcus pneumoniae* would explain the runny nose, coughing, and wheezing you experienced. And MUSCies would be particularly susceptible to *Streptococcus mitis,* because they have a low white blood cell count. My guess is, since MUSC only intended to use it in the ExploroBot Creation Center on Earth and ExploroBots never share our air, they didn't think it could get to us."

"But somehow this organism has been altered to ramp up the reproduction rate," I point out. "Wouldn't it usually take a half hour or more for something like this to spread?"

"Yes," says Uma. "D'Cart did something so it can hop from person to person in less than ten seconds."

"And that's why everyone with a neural web implant who breathed it in passed out?" Talitha asks.

"And why we stayed awake," Uma says. "D'Cart didn't want to kill the MUSCies, just put their conscious minds on hold while their bodies kept running, spreading the infection, until she could get here and take control of their brains."

"Just like MUSC does to the soldiers when they become Exploro-Bots," Talitha says.

"Exactly," Uma says.

"So what do we do now?" Talitha asks.

"Fight phage with phage!" Uma says. She opens Curie's cold storage containment area and rummages among the vials. "We'll try some different pneumococcal phage lytic enzymes, like Cpl-1 or Dp-1, to see if they'll kill off the combo *S. mitis/S. pneumoniae* critter. If that works in the lab, we can grow enough antidote to spray through the ventilation system, which could stop the infection from spreading further."

"Then we have to deal with the damage done inside the brains of all the people who are now asleep," I say, talking as fast as Uma as I pull together my thoughts. "D'Cart's next step was to hack into the cybermind. She said we'd be able to overwrite the instructions on everybody's neural webs. So, in theory, we might be able to hack into the cybermind and install a patch that would fix the damage, then we could reboot the system so everyone comes back online."

"Would that work?" Talitha asks.

I shrug. "If it doesn't, it won't cause any harm. People will either wake up and be fine or they'll stay in this state and we'll have to try something different."

"While you're in there . . ." Uma says as she preps cultures with different combos of phage-fighting enzymes. "Can you reprogram some of their neural web code?"

"To do what?" I ask.

"Have compassion for Earthlings?" Uma says with a dark chuckle.

"Insert a hatred for the ExploroBot program? Make them all appreciate dogs?"

"Worth a try!" I joke.

The lab door opens, and we all jump, afraid we've been caught cracking jokes about reprogramming the brains of everyone on MUSC. But it's Persis, carrying Aurelia's head on the podium.

"Talitha? Castor?" Persis says. "I think that you should see this."

"Is everything okay?" Uma asks as the three of us move toward Curie's desk where Aurelia's head now sits.

"Aurelia, could you please project the image you showed me?" Persis asks.

"Yes, of course," says Aurelia. Her left eye dilates to black, and she projects a holo to the middle of the floor.

We are looking down on Earth. Immediately, I feel a twinge of longing for the blue sky and green trees and wish I could pull in a breath of fresh air. Beneath us, a person moves around the perimeter of a precarious cliff, where rubble lies strewn as if a giant hand has toppled a mountain. Radial arms of a blast pattern cover the scorched ground like rays from a black sun. Glittering stones, bits of twisted metal, sparkling shards of quartz, and splintered scraps of wood alternate along the striations in an intricate and beautiful pattern.

"Where is this?" Uma asks.

"Aurelia connected to a drone on Earth—" Persis begins to say, and then I recognize the place.

"It's the Observatory!" I nearly shout. "Or what's left of it now. That's the view from one of D'Cart's drones. It must have survived the blast."

"Is that Mom?" Talitha tucks herself in beside me.

"Zoom in, please," I ask Aurelia. She brings the drone close enough for us to clearly see our mother moving about with purpose, collecting pieces of the ruin like a little ant, then placing them deliberately in the design she's creating.

"Look how gorgeous it is!" Uma says.

"Only Mom could make art out of total destruction," I say, and feel my heart swell with pride.

"Mom! Mom, can you hear me?" Talitha shouts.

"We haven't been able to make contact with her yet," Persis says.

"Of course not. Look!" I step closer to the holo and point to Talitha's old device that lies on a rock ten feet from our mother. "I'm pinging her again!"

The device flashes.

"Aw, jeez, Mother! Pick it up!" Talitha yells at the image.

"She'll see it. Give her time," Persis says calmly.

"Wait! Look. She's heading that way," Uma says.

"Come on, Mom! Come on," I say, trying to shoo her over toward the rock where the tiny beacon beckons to her.

"Maybe I should send her a brain wave!" Talitha closes her eyes and presses her fingers against her temples.

"I can try to invade her dreams," I say. My sister and I snort. Persis shoots Uma a look.

"Their mom is—" Uma starts to say.

"A little wacky," I tell her.

"But in a good way," Uma adds.

"Oh, how I miss her!" Talitha cries.

Mom passes the device and picks up a large chunk of what was likely Observatory wall, now pockmarked and speckled by debris from the blast. She struggles to lift it, then, cradling it in both hands near her belly, she duckwalks back toward her sculpture and stops. She seems to ponder the flashing light on the rock, as if debating what it could mean.

We all jump and shout, "Pick up! Pick up!"

As if she heard us calling from the Moon, she tosses aside the chunk of wall and dives for the device.

We watch her struggle to get it on her head. On my HearEar, her voice, scratchy and distant, calls our names. "Castor? Talitha? Castor? Is that you? Talitha?"

I hold up my cuff to project her holo to the room, then I launch my PEST so we can all see one another.

"Mom! Mom!" Talitha jumps up and down and waves her arms.

Mom's knees buckle, and she falls to the ground in a heap. "I thought I'd lost you. I thought you were gone from me forever!" she sobs.

"We're here!" I tell her. "We're safe!"

"But, but, but . . ." She looks all around. "Where are you?"

"We're on the Moon!" Talitha says.

My mom looks up into the dark blue evening sky, where the first stars have begun to glimmer. "The Moon," she cries with such sadness that I know, right then, I can't stay here. My mother can't lose everyone she loves to this sterile rock in the sky. And she'll never be able to come here. She's too connected to the Earth.

"But I'm coming home," I tell her. Beside me Talitha flinches but can't seem to speak. "Somehow or another, I'll get back to you."

TIME STAMP

MOON
DAY 1, MONTH 7, MUSC YEAR 94

EARTH
JULY 17, 2XXX

MOON UTILITARIAN SURVIVAL COLONY

"HOLOGRAM OR REAL?" I whisper to Persis as Valentine Fornax struts onto the stage of the large MUSC auditorium to begin Cohort 54's Life's Work Assignment ceremony. Sitting between Uma's mom and Aurelia, Castor and I fit right in. Like everyone else, we wear blue and white MUSC tunics and sit quietly, waiting for the CEO to speak.

"Real," Persis whispers. "This is a big day on MUSC. Dr. Fornax always announces the LWAs in person."

I scan the rows of Cohort 54 members surrounding the central stage down below us. Uma is easy to spot among her peers. She's the only one with dark, springy curls and warm brown skin—the most beautiful one of all. The pale Third Gen Moonlings still look like maggots to me, although I suspect Castor finds them attractive, or one of them, at least.

I lean over to my brother. "Where's Micra?" I tease.

He cuts his eyes toward me and scowls. "I don't have a thing for her," he insists.

"Yes, you do," I prod. "Admit it."

He shakes his head, but I know I'm right. I've seen the way he seeks her out just to argue with her and how she lingers whenever he's around. It's enough to make me barf if it didn't make him so weirdly happy.

I glance past Castor to Aurelia, who blinks blue-lit eyes as she takes in the new experience. Burnell Chen-Ning sits on the other side of her. He was thrilled to get his hands on her and has taken a shine to Castor, who spends most of his days in Burnell's AI lab helping to re-write Aurelia's code.

Dr. Fornax clears her throat. She stands tall and proud, her shock of silver hair perfectly coifed into a swirled wave on top of her head. She's even more imposing in person than she was as a hologram, but I've come to greatly respect her. As soon as she landed on MUSC with Micra, she zipped herself into a special ventilation suit to be protected from the phage, then set to work, double and triple checking Uma's calculations for enzymatic counterphage spray that would stop the bacterial infection from spreading, then she helped refine the neural web patch code Castor wrote to reboot the MUSC cybermind. We all worked around the clock for seventy-two hours, Randazza feeding us and taking care of the youngest MUSCies while Persis, Uma, Castor, Micra, Dr. Fornax, and I applied the antidote, rebooted the system, then walked the halls and checked the rooms until we accounted for every single person. Miraculously, everyone survived.

Down below, I see Kepler elbow Uma. As usual, they are side by side. Her shoulders shimmy, and I can tell she's suppressing a laugh. I could almost be jealous of their friendship if Kepler weren't so nice. He came back from his Sol trip early to help out once it was safe. When he first saw Uma, he hugged her so tight, I thought that he might squish her.

Dr. Fornax shifts and clears her throat again. Every person in the auditorium waits silently for her to speak. The air is thick with expectation. This is the first big gathering since *the Incident*, which is what they call their near demise, in classic MUSC understatement. As if almost being taken over by a disgruntled former MUSCie were a minor thing. A blip in their history. A dot on the time line of their inevitable universal dominion. As much as I appreciate the calmness and logical nature of MUSC, their lack of emotional resonance makes me crazy half the time. I want to jump up and wave my arms and shout, *You all almost died!* But of course, I don't. I'm a guest here and grateful for it.

"Thank you for joining me for the fifty-fourth annual awarding of Life's Work Assignments to a cohort of MUSC progeny," Dr. Fornax finally says. "This year marks a particularly momentous time in our history, and it is with profound gratitude and deep humility that I stand before you to celebrate the newest members of our work community."

The crowd shifts and murmurs. I glance at Persis, who looks at me with eyebrows up. She leans over and whispers, "Gratitude and humility are not words I've ever heard her speak."

"We have been through a harrowing time," Dr. Fornax says. "And once again, science has seen us through. We have survived because there is no alternative. Survival is in our name. It is in our nature. It is in our very DNA."

I clutch the arms of my seat. Persis and Castor sit up taller on either side of me. Even Uma stiffens in her seat and looks back to find us. We lock eyes and wait for Fornax to acknowledge what our small group of Earthlings did to save the Colony.

But she doesn't.

Those few sentences are all she has to say about *the Incident*. Uma and I look at each other and shake our heads. Persis slumps beside me, and Castor bristles as Dr. Fornax moves on.

"Our ancestors came here nearly a century ago seeking solace from an increasingly chaotic, war-torn Earth," Fornax says. "A place where science and logic were being replaced by dogmatic adherence to a misrepresentation of the past. A place where humans fought for dwindling resources rather than delving into discovery and innovation. A place for the few with little left for the many. And I'm sad to say, little has changed down there, which is why our survival and continuation of the species are imperative for the future of humanity."

The crowd erupts into controlled applause, but I can't join in. The whole thing feels like a giant pat on the back for themselves with no regard for how close they came to losing it all.

"And with that," Dr. Fornax says, "I give you the Life Work Assignments for Cohort 54."

Annoyed and frustrated, I zone out as Fornax calls each cohort member in alphabetical order onto the stage to announce a work assignment while the crowd politely applauds. Instead, I daydream about the things I miss most on Earth—strawberries my mother grows, fluffy clouds that look like whales, squirrels spiraling up a tree, date palms swaying in a breeze, the smell of sage, mud between my toes, my mother's hugs most of all. I don't yet know when I'll experience any of those things again, but I'm determined to go back. Being cooped up on the station is taking a toll on me. Sometimes I stand at the windows, gazing out at the universe spinning beyond, and I think of jumping.

"Kepler Jackson," Dr. Fornax says, which pops me out of my reverie. I watch him lope onto the stage, his lanky limbs loose and lithe, with a goofy grin on his face. The applause feel warmer somehow when he's up there. Nobody could dislike Kepler. Fornax shakes his hand and announces, "Following in his mother's most capable footsteps, Kepler will join our immunology team to work specifically on foodborne bacterial outbreaks."

The polite applause dwindles as Kepler makes his way back to his seat next to Uma. I sit up tall, and Persis takes my hand. We wait, each trying not to squirm with excitement, or is it dread, to find out what Uma's LWA will be. Uma has fretted for two weeks about her assignment, and Fornax has kept a steely silence. Uma oscillates from being certain she'll end up a miner like her mom as punishment for leaving MUSC to thinking she'll get something reasonable, like an immunology placement with Kepler for coming back and helping to save the colony. I think she should get whatever she wants, but then again, I'm in love with her.

I watch Uma sit up taller, then hunch her shoulders with anticipation. My heart beats in my throat. Fornax opens her mouth and calls, "Fermi Kaku."

Persis and I look at each other and wait a beat for Dr. Fornax to correct herself. Persis squeezes my hand until it hurts, but Dr. Fornax doesn't backtrack as the girl on the other side of Uma marches onto the stage and receives her assignment.

"What the hell?" I whisper to Persis. "She skipped Uma!" I hiss.

Down below, Uma sits stunned. Then I see her slump and slump some more. Kepler reaches out and puts his hand on her knee to comfort her.

"This kind of things happens sometimes." Persis loosens her grip on my hand, and her face goes slack. "She gets overlooked, but eventually . . ."

"Eventually?" I whisper fiercely. "That's not good enough! I'm saying something!" I start to stand up, but both Persis and Castor grab my arms and yank me back down into my seat.

"Just wait," says Castor. "Maybe—"

"Maybe nothing," I snarl as the next member of the cohort is called forward. "This is bull—"

"Talitha, please," Persis begs. "If you make a scene, Uma will be mortified. I'm telling you, it'll be worse if you do. Just . . ." She looks at me, heartbroken once again but resolved to make the best of it as she always has, being an Earthling on MUSC. "Just let it go."

Let it go! I can't believe what I'm hearing or that we're all accepting this treatment without sticking up for Uma. Persis, Castor, Kepler, every one of the jerks on MUSC who owe their lives to her! We're all sitting idly by as each and every other member of her cohort marches across that stage.

Castor keeps his hand on my arm, anchoring me to the seat, but I vow to take Uma away from this place. First chance we get, we're out of here, I promise myself. Even if we have to hijack a damn Shuttle. Earth could be on fire or in the middle of a nuclear war, but if this is the way someone like Uma is treated up here, I'd rather live in a bunker down there. I plan my revenge and our escape through the rest of the assignment announcements, and I don't hear a thing because I'm so angry.

The only thing that brings me out of my internal rage is the silence that pervades the hall after the last person in Cohort 54, Tesla Volta, sits down. Then Fornax turns to face the crowd and takes an audible deep breath.

"I had to think long and hard about the last assignment that will be given today," she says.

Persis gulps beside me. Castor lets go of my arm but grabs my hand. Uma slides down so low, I can barely see her head above the back of her seat.

I lean over to Castor and whisper through gritted teeth, "I swear to the stars above, if she doesn't call Uma's name and give her something good, I will torch this goddamned place."

He leans over to me and says, "I'll light the match for you."

"At MUSC, we pride ourselves on our ingenuity, our creativity, our problem-solving skills, and our ability to turn good minds into great thinkers," Dr. Fornax says. "We do this through rigorous education and socialization from the moment each child comes to us. And for that we have been greatly rewarded. We have the best technology in the universe.

The best quality of life possible. And we're expanding. Three new stations are being built on the Moon even as we inch closer to fulfilling our quest for colonizing Mars. But . . ."

She stops. Swallows hard and takes another deep breath. "The truth is, it's not enough to be sophisticated thinkers. The real test of intelligence is how well we use our minds. Great thinkers don't always follow traditional paths. They question authority when necessary. Take risks, even if that might mean personal harm. And they look for answers in unexpected places. Our last recipient has distinguished herself as a maverick in our midst," Fornax says.

Persis sits up ramrod straight. Castor grips my fingers until they turn white.

"She is the most innovative, creative, loyal problem solver in her cohort, and we all owe her a debt of gratitude that we cannot possibly repay. Please join me in welcoming Uma Jemison to the stage."

Uma is slow to get to her feet, as if she can't quite believe her name has been called. Kepler practically drags her into the aisle, where she walks on shaking legs. Persis has gone slack beside me, but I can't hold it in any longer. As soon as Uma's foot hits the stage, I jump to my feet, waving my arms in the air and cheering out loud like I'm at a GladiatorBot Smackdown. Castor joins me on his feet. We hoot and holler our approval like the true guttersnipes we are, showing our Earthly colors, and we couldn't care less. Let the MUSCies sit politely. My brother and I are bringing down the roof on this place.

Persis joins us, then Randazza, then Kepler. Curie stands up and claps her hands above her head as she whistles between her teeth. Burnell Chen-Ning stands and cheers. Aurelia follows. Soon half the kids in Cohort 54 are on their feet. Then the parents start to rise. Until finally, every person in the auditorium is standing and cheering for Uma, who can't seem to believe what's happening.

Fornax motions for everyone to quiet down. The cheering stops, but everyone remains standing, some people still murmuring to the others around them, talking about how they woke up and discovered that this girl and her Earthling friends were the ones who saved them all.

"As I said," Dr. Fornax goes on, "I had to think long and hard about the right assignment for Uma." A genuine hush falls over the crowd. "She has many talents. She is a gifted immunologist, a top-notch problem solver, and at the top of her class in botany, but perhaps her most distinguishing characteristic is empathy. This is a trait she brings with her, not something we have instilled, because to be sure, MUSC could infuse more of her type of compassion into our curriculum, and we will."

The crowd mumbles uncertainly at this statement, but Fornax doesn't let that throw her off. She keeps going, plowing on with supreme confidence in what she's saying.

"Uma also brings a true love of Earth with her. She is the finest scholarship student we've had the honor to accept into our program, but more than that, she has shown me that there are many others like her on Earth. We pride ourselves in using resources well, but we've neglected one of the most fundamental resources in the universe."

She pauses as we consider what she means, then she says, "Humanity."

Dr. Fornax turns to face Uma. She towers over her but somehow looks small as she reaches out to lay a hand on Uma's shoulder.

"For your LWA, I am creating a new program called MESC—the first Moon to Earth Survival Colony and soldier rehabilitation center down below. This will be a sanctuary for any Earthling, regardless of background, who requires assistance following the devastation of war. There, you will continue the important work of applying brain-to-brain interface technology to retrain soldiers with catastrophic injuries so they can rejoin their families as productive members of society. And if we're lucky, and I know we will be, we will find individuals with good minds that we can foster into great thinkers like you."

Uma is so flabbergasted that she covers her mouth with both hands.

"And in order to facilitate that," Dr. Fornax says, "I have commissioned this." She points to the center of the stage, where a hologram of a small shuttle is projected. "This six-seat Shuttle will be at your disposal. You may travel to and from Earth as you wish to oversee the program."

Uma covers her eyes. Her shoulders shake. Castor and I wrap our arms around each other, both too stunned to speak. Beside me, Persis fights to keep her composure. Around us, the crowd erupts into wild applause. And most unbelievable of all, Dr. Fornax wipes away a single tear that has trailed down her cheek as she steps forward and pulls Uma into a deep, long hug. Over the cheering, we hear the final words Dr. Fornax says, "I'm proud of you, Uma Jemison. So incredibly proud of you!"

TIME STAMP

Moon
Day 1, Month 11, MUSC Year 94

Earth
November 6, 2XXX

"READY?" TALITHA ASKS, and squeezes my hand.

I sit beside her, strapped into the sleek new six-seater Shuttle Dr. Fornax commissioned for our team to commute to MESC—the new Moon to Earth Survival Colony. The past five months have been non-stop preparation for this moment. We assembled the team, oversaw reconstruction of the ExploroBot Creation Center, sent down equipment for our labs, and set up a system to identify Earthlings we can help, but still, I'm not sure I'm ready for this moment. There's so much left to do. So many loose ends. So many unknowns. So much what-iffing that goes on in my mind.

I look over my shoulder. Burnell Chen-Ning, the mentor I chose for this project, sits behind us with his son Gemini, who is also on the team. Burnell is the best AI engineer on MUSC and has a true love of Earth, so he was a no-brainer to join us. I can't deny that Gemini's understanding of BBI tech is the best in my cohort, and honestly, once I gave him a chance, Kep was right, Gemini is a decent guy. He still gets on my nerves, but he can be entertaining, and he's undeniably good at what he does, so he's with us, too.

In the third row, Aurelia sits beside Castor. They are coming down for this initial visit to help us set up the lab in the newly reconstructed facility and to visit Rhea.

"Yes, Mom," Castor says. He sees me looking at him and rolls his eyes. "We'll call you as soon as we land. I know, Mom. But we're going to be busy. We're coming there to set up the lab. Of course we'll make time for you. Yes, Quasar is fine. Remember, he survived the ride up here . . . Yes. He's right here beside me. Do you want to see him?"

Castor leans over so he can send Rhea an image of Quasar patiently panting from his specially constructed crate anchored to the floor. Almost everyone on MUSC is sad to see Quasar go. He's become the unofficial MUSC mascot, trotting freely around the facilities, greeting everyone he meets, and being spoiled rotten by Randazza, who cooks full meals for him every day.

"Don't you think having Quasar around brought out more empathy and compassion in the MUSCies?" I ask Talitha.

"Definitely," she says. "I've never seen them act so goofy as when he runs up. They totally drop their guards!"

"Maybe we should start an Earth-to-Moon dog rescue," I joke. "Our motto could be *Science might see us through, but having a dog by your side makes everything better.*"

"Fornax would *love* that. First soldiers, now dogs? She'd lose her mind." Talitha chuckles at the idea, then she says, "But even if she'd go for it, it wouldn't be fair to the dogs. I mean, I can barely take being cooped up in the station all the time. Imagine what poor Quasar feels. I can't wait for fresh air and warm sunshine and the smell of plants and clouds overhead and—"

"I know just how you feel," I assure her, and pat her hand. Life on MUSC is hardest on Talitha. She's a caged animal up here. Like Rhea, she is deeply connected to the Earth and has become increasingly unhappy without the natural rhythms of our ancestral planet.

I look past Talitha, out the window at the crowd gathering in the loading bay to see us off. My mom, Gemini's mother, Kepler, and Micra stand in a row.

"Do you think your mom will ever come down with us?" Talitha asks.

I shrug. "I hope she will, but I don't know. I've asked her a million times to join our team. I think she'd be great at developing tech-enabled prostheses for injured soldiers, but she always says, *No, when I left Earth the first time, it was forever.*"

"I can understand that," Talitha says. "Maybe it's too painful for her to go back without your father. And maybe she wants to stay close to the last place he was alive. Like for me, sometimes it's comforting to be up here, where I know my father died."

"I suppose so," I say, and glance out the window on the other side, hoping to catch a glimpse of the silver-wrapped bodies tethered to the field of the dead, but they aren't visible yet. Not until we take off and circle the dark side of the Moon. "Still," I say, "I hope someday she'll at least come down to meet your mom."

"They'd like each other," Talitha says.

"Maybe we can get your mom to come up here," I suggest.

Talitha looks at me and guffaws. "Can you imagine Rhea on the Moon? She'd cover the walls with weird murals made from recyclable materials until Dr. Fornax's head exploded."

I giggle at the idea of Fornax and Rhea meeting. Then I elbow Talitha and point at the loading bay window, where Micra has pressed her palm. Beside her, Kepler snickers. We both glance back and see Castor with his palm on the Shuttle window.

"I can't believe they're together," Talitha whispers.

"Yeah, I know. So weird. All this time, I thought she hated Earthlings. Turns out, it's only me she despises."

"She's just jealous of you," says Talitha.

"I highly doubt that."

Talitha turns to look at me. "No, it's true," she says with complete sincerity. "She told Castor that she had always been the star child until you showed up and pulled attention away from her. She was especially angry when you befriended Kepler and he liked you better than he liked her."

I shake my head. "Even if all of that is true, and I'm not sure it is, she still dislikes me for who I am, Earthling or not."

"Yep," says Talitha with a laugh. "She thinks we're both annoying."

"Aw, who cares what she thinks," I say, and look away. "She makes Castor happy. That's all that matters."

"He won't admit it," Talitha whispers to me as she watches her brother, still eye-locked with Micra. "But I think she's half the reason he's coming back up here when this trip is over."

"Really?" I say. "He loves his work in the lab with Burnell."

"Yeah, but he could easily do that down on Earth," says Talitha. "I thought my mom would be heartbroken by his decision, but she just said, 'As long as I know you are safe and doing what you love, I am behind you one hundred percent.'"

"That's sweet!" I say. "I love your mom."

"Yeah," says Talitha wistfully. "So do I. I can't wait to see her."

"Are you looking forward to starting the MESC Stream?" I ask. Talitha will be our communications coordinator, finding the best ways to get the word out about our facility via Stream to humans all over the world.

"Yeah," says Talitha. "I am excited. It'll be nice to use my Streaming abilities for something good for once."

"We'll never be able to take everyone who needs our help," I say, my stomach starting to tie up in knots.

"You're right," says Talitha. "We won't. But we'll start small and grow and do the greatest possible good we can."

I nod, assured by her confidence in our directive. Then we both sit quietly for a moment contemplating what it means to return to Earth.

"Do you ever get afraid that D'Cart will find us when we're there?" Talitha asks me quietly.

"I think about it sometimes," I admit. "But since nobody's heard a peep from her . . ." I trail off.

D'Cart's stream has been white fuzz since we flung her off MUSC, but the Yoobies barely seem to notice that she's gone. As long as they continue to receive their universal basic incomes, they'll Stream and party and create endless meaningless memes as trash piles in the streets around them.

"Then again, she disappeared once before," I point out. "If she landed safely on Earth, she could be anywhere, biding her time, reinventing herself . . ."

"Or she could be star dust by now," says Talitha. "There's no way of knowing, and we can't worry about her because we have important work to do."

"That's true," I say, and kiss her knuckles.

"Countdown to launch will begin in one minute," the cybervoice announces. A ripple of excitement and fear goes through my body. I squeeze Talitha's hand tighter.

In front of us, in a pop of light, Dr. Fornax's holo appears. "Greetings, MESC Team! This is a momentous day in our colony's history. Are you ready to go?"

"Yes!" everyone around me says, but truthfully I'm still not sure, and so I sit quietly, thinking back to the last time I boarded the Shuttle for Earth.

I was so confused and scared and uncertain then. I was running away, in search of a different version of myself—perhaps one that never left the Earth or lost her father. I wanted to feel like I belonged somewhere but couldn't imagine where that place would be.

The cybervoice begins the countdown. "Ten . . . nine . . ."

I never could have imagined that belonging wouldn't come from a physical space but from a place down deep inside of me. I had to accept myself before I could fit in anywhere.

"Eight . . . seven . . ."

This time, as I'm preparing to go, I know who I am (part Earthling, part MUSCie), whom I love (I feel Talitha's fingers woven into mine), and what I want to do with my life (help Earthlings while preparing humanity for our inevitable off-planet future).

"Uma?" Dr. Fornax's holo says. "Are you ready?"

"Six . . . five . . ."

Once my father counted down for me.

"Four . . . three . . ."

He stood waist deep in the water at the end of a pier and beckoned, *Jump, Uma, jump.*

I take a deep breath and sit up tall. "Yes," I say. "I'm ready."

"Two . . . one . . ."

The rockets rev as the loading arm releases and the cybervoice says, "Launch!"

ACKNOWLEDGMENTS

Writing a novel can feel like living on a planet of one, but publishing a book is a gargantuan effort involving many. And so ... to some of those many I offer an HER-CrB GW (that's Hercules-Corona Borealis Great Wall—the largest structure in the universe that shouldn't exist but does)–sized Thank You!

My editor, Liz Szabla, and her team at Feiwel & Friends for lovingly seeing this process through from beginning to end. Special thanks to Rich Deas and the art department for another gorgeous cover and book design.

My agent, Stephanie Kip Rostan, and all the fine folks at Levine Greenberg Rostan for a decade of excellent career guidance, interesting conversation, and hand-holding when I need it.

Theodore Muth, Associate Professor of Biology at Brooklyn College, for welcoming me into his lab and answering all my questions about microbiology with such enthusiasm and good humor.

Justin Skirry, Associate Professor of Philosophy at Nebraska Wesleyan University and author of *Descartes: A Guide for the Perplexed*, for taking the time for an email correspondence.

My dogs, Mahati (gone now but always in my heart) and Holtzmann (very much here and in the moment).

Emily Franklin, the other half of my brain, without whom none of this would be nearly as fun.

My children, always and forever.

And Dan, the one and only intergalactic lovebot of my universe.

Thank you for reading this Feiwel and Friends book.
The friends who made **SUPERMOON** possible are:

———————

JEAN FEIWEL, PUBLISHER

LIZ SZABLA, ASSOCIATE PUBLISHER

RICH DEAS, SENIOR CREATIVE DIRECTOR

HOLLY WEST, EDITOR

ANNA ROBERTO, EDITOR

CHRISTINE BARCELLONA, EDITOR

KAT BRZOZOWSKI, EDITOR

ALEXEI ESIKOFF, SENIOR MANAGING EDITOR

KIM WAYMER, SENIOR PRODUCTION MANAGER

ANNA POON, ASSISTANT EDITOR

EMILY SETTLE, ADMINISTRATIVE ASSISTANT

STARR BAER, SENIOR PRODUCTION EDITOR

———————

Follow us on Facebook or visit us online at mackids.com.
Our books are friends for life.